ISBN 13# 9780977202546

THE MAN FISHER

A Novel

by
Richard Landerman

This is a work of fiction. Some of the names, characters, places, and incidents are either the product of the author's imagination or are used fictitiously.

Sortis Publishing

This book is for Milton L. Weilenmann, Missionary, Teacher, Civic Leader, Businessman, Friend

ACKNOWLEDGEMENTS

A work like this is not possible without the help and support of many people. First, I would like to thank my wife, Janet. Being married to someone who wants to write and won't quit until he gets the monkey off his back has to be a frustrating experience for the non-writing spouse; but we weathered it yet again without a divorce. I am grateful for her suggestions, ideas, and insights as I wrote; and for her meticulously-edited final drafts. I am also grateful to Kristen Grimshaw who was so helpful in editing the initial drafts; and working out the many mistakes – syntax, subject/verb agreement, punctuation, etc. – all those little details I tend to skip over in my rush to get my ideas down on paper.

Thanks to many unnamed people who helpfully provided material for some of the characters in the book. Thanks also to several friends: Tom Williams, Ev Peck and Clyde Larsen, for their critical comments and suggested changes and additions to help parts of the story move along. A special comment of appreciation is needed for my good friend Denise Crane for her authentic cover art. I know she did a lot of research into the Tlingit culture before she even started the first charcoal concept drawings. Thanks to my son, Mark Landerman, for the author's photo (it was a memorable day fishing with him and two grandsons on the South Fork).

A large amount of thanks and appreciation must go to my publisher, Mike Webb, and for his faith in me as a fledgling writer. I hope I don't disappoint. At every stage of the writing and publishing process he has been easy to work with and supportive of my ideas. Through this experience he has become a supporter and a friend. He's high on my list of guys whom I want to fly fish for salmon with in Alaska.

And finally, my everlasting gratitude to Milt Weilenmann, a lifelong friend, mentor, and role model for whom this book is dedicated. He inspired a lot of us of my generation to be our best, to dream of accomplishing lofty goals, and doing good for others. Unfortunately, he died before he could read the final version. He has passed on now, but I hope someday he will be able to know how many lives he touched in a positive way.

PROLOGUE

The clock was winding down. Northern Arizona had the ball safely in the hands of their short, stocky freshman point guard. Montana State set up a zone defense minus one man who shadowed the NA guard. Tad Wessman continued to dribble around the perimeter, hounded by Montana State's best guard, who towered over him by eight inches. Wessman did not notice the MSU player guarding him; he was testing the defense for weaknesses and his eyes were moving back and forth between the time clock and his own seven-foot center filling the lane, also guarded closely.

In the stands Teddy Buckley and a couple of his mates from the MSU Rugby squad were swigging beer from longneck bottles, flirting with the coeds on the row in front of them, hoping to pick them up after the game. These guys really didn't care much about the score or the outcome down on the court; they were interested in a different score.

The game was close; MSU, the home team, had a one-point lead, and the clock was steadily ticking down to just under ten seconds left in the game. The Northern Arizona Lumberjacks were setting up for one last shot.

Wessman faked a move to his left, taking his man out. He made a quick move to the right, cut toward the basket dribbling twice, pulled up and with barely one second on the clock drained a twenty-foot jump shot, swish, nothing but net. The buzzer blared. Game over. Regular season over.

The crowd of thirty-nine hundred partisan fans in the field house fell silent. The Lumberjack bench stormed the court and lifted Wessman on their shoulders. NA had won the game *and* the conference championship. Montana State Bobcats were knocked out of the running for any post-season bid that year.

"How the hell did he do that…?" one of Teddy's buddies wondered.

"Do what?" Teddy asked. He had missed the dramatic finish.

"Make that jump shot."

"Did you see how high that little guy can jump?" another of his team mates exclaimed. Teddy just grinned and turned his attention back to the girls in front of him.

Teddy left the field house with a foxy brunette, a sophomore from Great Falls. Her daddy was a big cattle rancher and had many choice private fly-fishing waters on his vast holdings that spread from the rolling plains clear up into the forested mountains. Teddy was as much interested in the fly-fishing, the pheasant, chukar and Hungarian partridge and sharptail grouse hunting in the man's wheat fields, and the ducks and geese along the river bottoms as he was in the cute daughter.

It was snowing heavily as Teddy left the field house with the sophomore named Bridget. She buried her face deeper in the coyote-fur lined hood of her wool stadium coat and snuggled against Teddy. He was much taller than she and his ears were sunburned on top; his nose was a little crooked from so many injuries inflicted in Rugby scrums, but that only enhanced his rugged good looks.

Coach got his Lumberjacks out of the locker room and back on the team bus as quickly as he could. No hanging around for a sock hop in the field house. Under the best of conditions it was almost a twenty-hour drive back to Flagstaff. The snow was sticking and the driver was worried about the first stretch down the canyon from Bozeman along the Gallatin River through Big Sky to West Yellowstone. Then they had to go over the hump to Ashton, through Rexburg, Sugar City, Rigby and Idaho Falls; down I-15 through Salt Lake City and south to Nephi, where they would exit the new super highway. The rest of the trip would be on the old narrow, slower, winding two-lane U.S. 89 down through southern Utah, through Kanab, south and east, rimming north of the Grand Canyon and crossing the Colorado River, south again and finally arriving in Flagstaff sometime tomorrow evening. If they were lucky. The driver was glad he had a good nap during the game. He was also glad coach was licensed to spell him off at the wheel.

"Heard you were the hero, Tad," the driver said as Tad Wessman boarded.

"It took a lot of help. Everyone stepped up tonight – couldn't do it without them," Tad generously replied.

That was early March of 1969.

PART I

SOMETHING DIFFERENT

Teddy sat on the bank of the Madison River and watched. It was the last week of September, 1969. The trees above the river were golden and flame orange, the air was cool. The sky had that autumn-washed blue color that always surprised him with its clarity and pureness. His client, a man in his early fifties, was showing his daughter how to correct her back cast. Teddy was an expert fly fisher and a darn good teacher when it came to fly-casting basics. But for now, Teddy just sat and watched.

While he observed the lesson, he smoked a Camel, his second of the morning. His personal policy was to always ask the client if it was okay before he lit up. The client usually approved, especially if he or she was also a smoker, but if the client disapproved, then no smoking. This guy hadn't objected when Teddy took out the pack of smokes, so he took that for an okay. Teddy sat downwind a short distance away. The man was doing all right and it felt good to just sit and relax in the morning sun, savoring the tobacco, the bite of that first drag .

"I'm trying, Daddy, really I am," the daughter said.

"I know you are, Marley. Just try again like I showed you, only slower. Let the line load up." She gave him a blank look. "It means, oh, I don't know how to explain it any better." The man turned to Teddy.

"Need some help?" Teddy asked.

"I can't explain what it means… you know, *load up*."

Teddy took a last drag, crimped the glowing end and ground the butt between his fingers over the stream; he paused to watch the tobacco crumbs floated away in the current. He dusted off the seat of his jeans, and walked over to them. He hadn't really wanted this engagement; he had planned to do some last minute shopping and fix some things on his truck before his departure for the winter season in Patagonia (with a couple of detours to fish the Provo with a pal, then the San Juan and maybe the Animas and Cimarron in southern Colorado and northern New Mexico).

He had signed on for another tour in southern Argentina and Chile, guiding wealthy fly-fishing clients for his employer, a world-famous fly shop and guide service based in Jackson Hole. But when he saw that one of this pair of clients was an unattached single girl, his interest grew and he took the one-day job. The guy might be a big tipper; there was no such thing as too much cash in your pocket, Teddy had been taught by his family.

Teddy faced Marley and smiled reassuringly. She smiled back and shifted to her other foot. In spite of the bulky chest waders and fly-fishing vest, all brand new Orvis stuff purchased that very morning from the fly shop, it did not escape Teddy that she was very pretty. "Do you mind? Here's the best way to show you. It's a *feeling* thing, you know…?" He stepped behind Marley and put his strong, sunburned arms loosely around her. "Hope you're comfortable; it's easier to teach you this way."

"It's okay," she quickly responded. He smelled slightly of tobacco, not really too unpleasant, she thought. She also liked his after shave: spicy - plain, straight- forward; nothing trendy or heavy like a lot of guys were wearing these days. She especially liked his strong, sunburned arms encircling her. They both looked at her father for his approval. He nodded to go ahead with the class.

"Okay," Teddy said, "I'm going to hold your casting hand and help you feel the line load up in the rod. It will come at the end of your back cast. You'll feel it. Then you start the forward cast. Got it?" Marley's blond pony tail bobbed up and down under her new fly-shop logo ball cap. Then Teddy got a slight trace of her scent: woodsy, spicy, with a hint of citrus, he noted. Clean. Fresh. "Don't fight what I do; just relax and let me do the work at first." He gripped the hand that held the rod, felt the tenseness in her arm relax. Her hand was strong but her skin soft.

Teddy helped Marley through the hardest part of learning the delicate art of fly casting: the back cast. Within a few minutes Marley had the feel of it. Reluctantly, for both of them, he stepped away from her. "Now try it on your own. Remember to wait for the *feel* of the line loading," he gently reminded.

Marley false cast several times, letting out line, then made the final back cast. She got it and a big grin spread over her freckled face. "I felt it!" she squealed. Her father grinned at Teddy and nodded his thanks.

"Ready to start sticking some trout?" Teddy asked.

During their lunch break, Teddy sat on the bank with Marley's father by a small campfire, while Marley continued to fish. "She's so much like her mother," her father said. "Once she commits, there's no stopping her. Thanks for showing her how to do it. I'm afraid I've created a monster."

"I can think of many things worse than being addicted to fly-fishing," Teddy said as he offered his client some hot coffee. "You like it black or with sugar, cream?"

"Neither, actually. Thanks, but I don't use coffee."

"Tea? I can whip up some hot tea."

"We don't use that either."

"We?" Teddy nodded toward Marley who was approaching them now.

"Wow! That was great! I'm starved - what's to eat?" She flopped down next to Teddy. The whiff of her scent again moved something inside him. He didn't know why, but it reminded him of seeing new lambs and calves every fall when he arrived in Patagonia to start the winter fishing season. Everything was upside down there. He was feeling kind of upside down close to Marley right now.

"I was telling Mr. Buckley we don't use coffee, Marley." Teddy figured there must be a reason but he didn't ask.

As if reading his thoughts, Marley piped in "We're Mormons, you know, Mr. Buckley."

"No, I didn't know, and please, call me Teddy."

"Well, we are." And that was that.

During the afternoon float, the dad, Mr. Durrant, hooked himself in the thumb while releasing a feisty rainbow that suddenly slipped out of his grip. "Flip! Will you look at that!" He held up his thumb with a large purple leech pattern streamer fly deeply imbedded.

"Gross!" Marley turned pale and quickly averted her eyes.

Teddy had expected Mr. Durrant to break out with a stream of four-letter words. Any other client would be swearing a streak by now. "Good thing these're barbless hooks, right Teddy?" Teddy swallowed and nodded (he'd forgotten to crimp down the barb) as he helped pop out the hook with a looping length of heavy leader material. Good thing, for sure, he thought as he swabbed the puncture wound with Merthiolate.

They approached the boat take-out ramp and Teddy asked, "Did you have a good time, Marley?"

"The most fun ever outside of M Men and Gleaners!" she laughed. Teddy wanted to ask her if he could see her again, but his courage failed him. He just grinned back and nodded. "What the heck's M Men and Gleaners?" he wondered.

After he secured his drift boat on the trailer, Teddy approached Mr. Durrant. "The question is, sir, did you have a good time?"

"Sure did, young man. Maybe we can do this again next year?"

"You bet. Just ask for Teddy Buckley. I'll be here. And…," he added, "let me know in advance what you'll be drinking so I can stock up."

"Oh, you mean the coffee thing? Don't worry about it. I apologize if Marley got a little zealous about us being Mormons. She's planning on leaving for a mission soon. To Honduras. I guess she's kind of practicing her pitch. This was our last time together before she leaves; you know, daddy and daughter thing?"

Teddy was really blown away by this latest revelation about Marley, this vision of loveliness, alone in Honduras? Sure, she'd proved how tough she was, but far away from home in a third world country? What's a mission? How long will she be there? Doesn't use coffee or tea? Young Adults? No swearing? And what's a Mormon, anyway? A million questions.

Mr. Durrant approached Teddy and handed him a generous tip. "Tithing," Mr. Durrant said, grinning.

"Huh?" Teddy responded. Mr. Durrant chuckled and patted Teddy's shoulder. "Are all dads alike, sort of weird?" Teddy wondered. Would his own kids someday think of him as weird, too? He hoped he'd be different.

Marley insisted on sitting next to Teddy in the front seat of his old Ford pickup. Its happy, cluttered dustiness, with trout flies stuck all over the dash board and visors, its dirty windshield with the spider web cracks had never bothered Teddy. Until now. Now he was wishing it was cleaner so he could make a better impression. Mr. Durrant took the window seat, tipped his felt fedora over his eyes and quickly fell asleep. Teddy and Marley were more or less alone now for the two-hour ride back. During the shuttle back to Jackson Hole, Teddy got up enough courage to ask a few of the questions swirling around in his head. Marley was smart, enthusiastic, and seemed very sure, telling him about her family, her schooling and hobbies. She shared with him her tastes in music and books, and she shared her religious beliefs. In the fall, night comes early in Jackson Hole. It was past dark as they pulled up in front of the Durrants' motel. Teddy could barely see her face in the weak light from a street lamp. Marley turned toward Teddy and said with plainness and courage: "I know that all the things I've been telling you are true. Joseph Smith did actually see the Father and His son, Jesus Christ." Then she quickly kissed his cheek, slid across the seat and out of his life. He didn't sleep much that night. Too many thoughts, remembering her scent.

CHAPTER TWO

TEMPLE SQUARE

As a practical matter, there are really only two seasons in the life of a fly-fishing guide: the short summer months from the end of May until the end of September spent in choice fly-fishing spots like Jackson Hole, Utah's Green River, Alaska, the Montana spring creeks and other destinations. Then you have the winter months in the Bahamas, Belize, New Zealand, or Patagonia. The in-between months, spring and late fall, were the "shoulder" months when a guide like Teddy was free for awhile to do some fishing on his own, provided he had the money.

Teddy mopped up the last of the giant breakfast burrito, slurped down his coffee, left a generous tip for Barb, his favorite waitress, and paid his bill. Outside the café he paused to take in one last look at downtown Jackson Hole, if you could call it a downtown. Except for a stray black lab out for its morning stroll, the square with its famous elk and deer horn arches was empty. The early morning air was tinged with frost. He heard a bull elk bugling out in the game preserve. A few more days and it would be October. He felt the excitement of getting on the road. His drift boat was stored for the winter; he had gathered his last paycheck for the season, plus some advance travel money to get him to the Patagonia. He had almost two weeks of freedom before he had to report for work. Teddy felt like a kid the day school gets out for the summer.

His plans, if you could call them plans, were to stop off in Utah for a couple days to fish the Provo with one of his guide buddies, Zack Zundel, then hit some waters in northern New Mexico, the San Juan, and so on. Maybe stop off at Lee's Ferry for big rainbows below Glen Canyon Dam on the Colorado. Then double back through Las Vegas and play a couple hundred on the blackjack table. Pick up I-15 and cruise on down to Los Angeles, store the truck and hire a taxi over to LAX to catch the long flight to Buenos Aires.

Like Teddy, Zack was a totally committed fly-fisherman and eagerly looked forward to the precious few days off to do some fishing for himself. That was one of the drawbacks about guiding: the thing you loved most became your daily bread.

Fog hung low across the recently harvested hay meadows south of town. Flat Creek flowed dark and inviting through the meadows. Through the mists Teddy could barely make out the meandering lines of hawthorns and copper birches that lined the creek. Teddy hunched down in his jacket and tried to tune his radio to some rock music. He was leaving Jackson for a season, and that included its ever-present country music. Soon it would be the South American version, gaucho music.

About a mile before he reached Hoback Junction he came around a curve, almost running into a small herd of elk, probably a family. There was one big bull, a six-pointer, three large cows, and several large calves. They hardly gave him any notice. As he entered Hoback, Teddy checked his gas gauge. He hadn't gassed up in Jackson, but he thought he had enough to get him to Afton, where gas would be a few cents a gallon cheaper. There was a strong scent of skunk in the frosty air. Some family dog probably got in a skunk fight during the night; the dog and its owners were the sure losers.

Thirty minutes later Teddy came out of the morning shadows of Snake River Canyon and was met by brilliant sunlight as he approached Alpine Junction. Out of habit, he almost turned right, toward Palisades Dam and the South Fork put in, instead of left, toward Afton, Cokeville, Bear Lake, Evanston, and Salt Lake City.

"Teddy Bear!"

"Zee!"

It was nearly two o'clock when Teddy pulled into the parking lot of the Wagon Wheel Café in Heber City, Utah, where he was to meet Zack for a quick lunch before they hit the section of the Provo River below the town of Francis. It had been only a couple of days since they parted in Jackson, but they bear hugged like they hadn't seen each other in years.

"Coffee?" the waitress asked Teddy. She filled his cup. "How 'bout you, hon?", she asked Zack. He put his hand over the cup, turned it over.

"No coffee?" Teddy asked.

"Naw, it gives me an upset stomach. Besides, you know what coffee does, and we're gonna be on the river with no outhouses anywhere," Zack said. Teddy eyed him suspiciously and shrugged. Okay, whatever.

"What are we using today, Zee?"

"I hear some guys are still getting action on hopper patterns in mid day. Plus there's a few caddis coming off in the afternoon, and then maybe some PMDs or BWOs towards dark. The caddis are small, maybe size sixteen, and really dark, almost black. If none of that works, there's always nymphs."

"Sounds good to me; I got plenty of flies, all sizes. Otherwise we can tie up a few streamside. Let's eat." Their hamburgers and fries arrived and they tucked in

Fly fishing can be either a communal activity, or it can be a solitary experience. By habit, top fly fishing guides like Zack and Teddy sort of fall into a system of trading off on every other hole, run, or riffle. That way, each got a shot at the good water without the messiness of arguments or hard feelings. If the other guy caught bigger fish or more of them, okay. You just patted him on the back and congratulated him. Next time it might be your turn for honors. That's how they fished through the warm afternoon into early evening. Teddy wasn't really counting; they were both sticking a lot of trout, mostly browns, but Teddy had brought two nice rainbows to the net, as well as a couple of pretty brook trout, a Provo River Grand Slam. He was having a lot of fun, soaking up some freedom before jumping back into the guiding business again.

But as he occasionally watched Zack fishing, he noticed his friend didn't seem to be into it - he wasn't sharp, missing many strikes. He looked like a man with a heavy load on his mind, just going through the motions. Just about dusk, they came together. Teddy pulled on a sweatshirt against the advancing chill. "What are ya thinking, Zee, fish until dark, or go someplace and eat?"

"I just saw a big guy slurping away up there under that overhanging tree." Zack pointed to a bend just a little way upstream that washed under a cut bank, with a good sized copper birch hanging its golden branches down over the water. This would be a challenge, but Teddy was up to it if Zack was deferring.

"Think I should give it a try?"

"Go ahead, Teddy Bear. It's tricky, but you're the guy that can do it."

"What's he feeding on?"

"I'd say a Blue Winged Olive, about size eighteen." Teddy nipped off the caddis he'd been using, and deftly tied on his own Pale Morning Dun, not the BWO Zee had recommended. He grinned at Zee, stripped out some line and made a couple of false casts as he approached the target. He sized up the situation, figuring out the best approach. The best angle would be from above.

He moved slowly, scrunching down, slipping heron-like into the stream, wading only a few steps out to get more clearance for his back cast. He knelt down, water rushing up around his chest, almost to the top of his waders. He sat there motionless for a full two minutes before he began his cast. He would have only one shot at this big guy - this one cast had to count. Darkness was fast closing in; it would be hard to see the take if it did eat his fly.

Teddy glanced at Zack, who gave him a thumbs up. Teddy planned to make a steeple cast with a mid-cast mend to the left so the fly would have the longest possible drift before the current dragged it under. At this moment he was glad he had a bamboo rod, an 8.5 foot Granger Aristocrat; one with a soft, slow action, perfect for flicking dry flies with the least effort. He was also glad there was no wind to fight.

Teddy made his move, felt the line load up, and with a slight flick, the fly moved forward. The line collapsed in a serpentine pile several feet above the trout's lair. The little PMD artificial daintily settled on the water and sped forward a few inches on the bending current. Teddy and Zack saw the splash simultaneously; out of habit Zack whooped. "Fish on. Oh, yeah!" Teddy yelled.

The brown was large, big enough to leave a wake as it turned and plunged downward with the tiny fly. From instinct, or many hours of experience, whatever it was, Teddy hesitated just a fraction of a second before he applied a slight upward pressure with his casting wrist. And the fight was on.

The trout ran for deeper, swifter water, heading downstream. The Provo is smallish, as rivers go, so Teddy did not have a lot of fighting room. He gave the trout all the slack he dared, wanting to keep him on the reel as much as possible. The Granger did much of his work, absorbing the stress throughout the length of its golden shaft. The fish was no match for the strong current and the supple bamboo. After ten minutes the fish began to tire. Teddy reeled, steadily earning line. He looked up and realized the trout had him downstream a hundred yards. He reeled gently a few more times and the fish rolled onto its side; Teddy worked the fish into Zack's waiting net.

They took a minute to admire his size (twenty inches long, easily four, maybe five pounds); his large, dark spots and brilliant fall coloring. He was a male and soon would be ready to spawn. Teddy wished he had a good camera to record his catch. Maybe he should invest in a good camera instead of buying yet another rod or reel. They gave the fish back to the river and started the short hike through the cottonwood bottoms back to Teddy's truck. The woods had the pleasant odor of crushed leaves, dying underfoot.

Driving the short distance to Zack's parents' home in Park City, Teddy asked, "So what's bothering you?"

Zack's nodding head shot up. "I'm working over a decision I need to make." Then a silence followed, lasting about a mile.

"You thinking of getting married?" Teddy knew that Zack had a girlfriend from high school who lived in the town of Midway he was really sweet on.

"No. Nothing that easy. Naw, well, you're gonna laugh…"

"No I won't laugh. Looks like something serious that's got you really worked up."

"Well, you knew I was a Mormon…?"

"No, I didn't know that. Say, what's with everyone being a Mormon, anyway?"

"Not everyone. I'm just talking about me right now. Well, you probably didn't know I was Mormon because I never really *acted* like one around you. You know, sort of hanging out with the guys and going along with what everybody else was doing at the time…?"

"Yeah, I guess… so?"

"Well, Mormons aren't supposed to do that kind of stuff."

"Stuff…?"

"You know, drinking beer, and other… stuff."

"Yeah, I know. I just learned you're not supposed to drink coffee, either, right?"

Zack shifted uncomfortably. "Guilty as charged."

"So what's this all about? What's the decision? You gonna go straight now? Shape up and quit the beer and coffee. That it?

"More than that. My bishop called me into his office Sunday, and I'm trying to decide if I'll go on a mission."

"You too?"

"You know some other Mormon guy going out?"

"Not a guy - a girl. She and her dad were my last clients just yesterday, before I left Jackson. She's a Mormon. She's going on a mission. To Honduras. What a waste."

"What do you mean, a waste?"

"Man, she was some babe. She told me all about that James Smith stuff, you know, seeing God and all. Honduras. What a waste."

"Maybe from your perspective. But if you really believed, were committed, you'd see it different."

"Is that your problem, you don't know if you're committed to the idea?"

"Man, two years is a long time, away from your family, your girlfriend, fly fishing, guiding on the river."

"Two years?"

"Yeah, and no dating, plus I get to pay for it all out of my own pocket."

"You Mormons *are* crazy. I think you need to be committed, all right… to an institution!"

"Tell you what, where you staying? Never mind, cancel it and stay with us. My folks have plenty of room. Then tomorrow I'm going to take you to Temple Square and maybe you'll understand better."

"I have a better idea. I think I'll drop you off and go buy a six pack! By the way, I thought only Catholics and chess boards had bishops."

———————————

CHAPTER THREE

ON THE WRONG ROAD

Teddy squinted into the setting sun. Instead of driving south to the San Juan River in northern New Mexico, his original destination, he was now driving west across the Bonneville Salt Flats about thirty miles east of Wendover. There was a cloud cover when he left Salt Lake City, but now that was gone. It was getting warmer; he rolled down both windows for some breeze. Out of habit he pulled his dark glasses down from their perch above the brim of his ball cap, adjusted them and settled in his seat.

A lot had happened to Teddy in the last forty-eight hours. Some big changes were happening in his life, and he was glad for the solitude of the open road to sort everything out. He fiddled with the radio but found only static or country music. He wasn't in the mood for country, so he switched it off. An eighteen-wheeler belching diesel fumes overtook him.

At Zack's insistence Teddy had cancelled his reservation at Scotty's Motel on North Temple in Salt Lake. He was glad he did. The Zundels were gracious in opening their home to Teddy. Mr. Zundel was a high school history and economics teacher, and he coached JV baseball for extra income. He was friendly and plain. But inside him Teddy sensed there was a major-league intellectual. He explained to Teddy that he'd always wanted to be a college professor, but being Mormons, they opted for a large family (Zack was the oldest of seven). He gave up the quest for the doctorate and settled for getting his master's degree. Mr. Zundel was also something called a counselor in a bishopric. Teddy didn't have a clue, but he smiled and nodded at this revelation, like he really knew and was in on the scoop.

Zack was a lot like his father, Teddy noticed. Teddy wondered who he was more like, his own mom or his dad. Mrs. Zundel stayed at home as a full-time mother. She was also something called a Relief Society president. Teddy nodded knowingly at that information, too. They all knelt for family prayer around the large dinner table. Zack was asked to give grace. Teddy averted his eyes, knowing this was an awkward moment for his friend. Zack's prayer was short and to the point: glad we could all be together, bless the food, we thank thee for family, bless our loved ones, bless Teddy as he travels, amen. Teddy reminded himself that his family had never prayed. Nor could he remember the last time he had knelt by his bed reciting the memorized child's prayer, now I lay me down…

Another eighteen-wheeler blew past Teddy; he checked his speedometer, fifty, so he sped up a little. "What's the point?" he thought, so he relaxed and slowed back down to the hypnotizing rate he'd held for over an hour. The sun had dropped below some mountains to the west. It was fast growing dark, and Teddy saw the lights of Wendover ahead. The lights made him wonder if there were any homes with families like the Zundels in Wendover. Were there families kneeling together around their kitchen table for evening prayers, followed by a delicious home-cooked meal? Family chatter, the day's activities discussed? What was his own family doing at this moment? Dining out at some posh restaurant? Dad fretting over the Pirates? Both parents attending some black tie social or charity function, hating every minute of it?

As Teddy approached the first Wendover exit, he was gripped with an overwhelming desire to call his mother again, just to reach out, to connect with home. He pulled into a Husky gas station and used the pay phone. "Mom? It's me again. Nothing, really, I just wanted to let you know I was okay. What? Hard to hear you with trucks pulling in and out of here. Yeah, I'm on the road. Headed to San Francisco, Treasure Island. I don't know if I'll get any time after processing in. Maybe I'll get to come home for a few days before I ship out to wherever… Mom, I don't have a clue where the Marines will send me. Most likely Vietnam. That's where the Marines are fighting right now. What? Damn, 'scuse me, darn trucks! You're going to pray for me? No, I'm not laughing. That would be really nice, Mom. Yeah, I'd like it very much to have you pray for me. I gotta go. Call you later. I love you. 'Bye."

The second night at the Zundels, Zack and Teddy took the tour of Temple Square (as Teddy had promised Zack he would - interesting, nice landscaping). Before turning in for bed, Teddy called home for the first time in over a year. Even though it was late at night in Pittsburgh, Teddy really felt a need to hear his own mother's voice. He wasn't prepared for the news.

"Teddy? Thank God you called!"

"What? What is it, Mom?"

"I have a letter here from the Department of Defense. What? Of course I didn't open it, it's addressed to you! What? You want me to open it? Teddy, I called the trout store in Jackson Hole. They didn't know where you were, said you'd left several days ago and nobody knew where you were going. Really, Teddy, you should let people know where you are. I taught you better than that."

"Okay, Mom, it's all right. You found me. So go ahead and open the letter…"

Teddy majored in political science at Montana State University in Bozeman. His family was wealthy enough that he could have gone to any Ivy League school had he chosen. His grades were average, but money would have secured him a place in the freshman class at Harvard had he wanted it. But several summers out West as a boy had gotten him addicted to fly fishing, and he chose MSU because it was in the heart of the best fly fishing in the world. Poly Sci was a gentleman's major; it would allow Teddy to fly fish and play rugby. He could deal with his future later. Law school? Business school, a banker like the rest of his family for several generations back? He'd figure it out later…or maybe not. Maybe he'd just be a river guide.

Teddy wasn't dumb, but a couple of times he almost flunked out because he spent too much time fly fishing and not enough studying. One summer back home, on a dare, he and a high school friend decided to join the Marine Reserve Officers Corps, much to the deep embarrassment of both families. Teddy was thereafter committed to attending weekly "drills" plus two weeks of active duty each summer. He also had a two-year commitment for active service sometime in the future. For Teddy, the future was somewhere way out there over the horizon. Somehow, with fly fishing and guiding, he just forgot about the active duty part.

As part of the graduation ceremonies at MSU, Teddy had been awarded his gold second lieutenant's bars. After graduation, he tossed the bars in a duffle crammed with other stuff he would store or give to the Goodwill. Then he headed to Jackson Hole for the summer guiding season and forgot about being a Marine officer. Until last night.

Teddy stood in the kitchen of the Zundel home in Park City, Utah. Listening through their pink princess wall phone he heard his mother rip open the letter. She began to read with a trembling voice. "Okay, Teddy, are you ready for this? I don't know if I can do this. (Sobbing) Dear God, give me strength. Okay, here goes. It says: To Second Lieutenant Edward Mellon Buckley, USMCR. Greetings. You are hereby ordered to report to MCRTC Treasure Island not later than 1200 hours, 1 October 1969, where you will be processed into active service in the United States Marine Corps. There you will receive appropriate indoctrination courses and further orders as to your final duty station…," she read. Her voice dropped off and Teddy could hear his mother softly crying in her kitchen that she seldom cooked in, back in Pittsburgh.

Now, in the falling darkness of Wendover, Nevada – or was it Utah? - thinking back on that phone call the night before, Teddy said another silent prayer as he pulled back onto Interstate 80, again heading west toward Treasure Island, in San Francisco Bay. "God," he thought, "it must be awful to be a mother and send your son off to war."

He had about seventeen more hours to report for active duty. He still had his fly- fishing gear, his rods, reels, fly boxes, and waders with him. He smiled at the thought of trying to find any trout streams in the Vietnam jungles.

CHAPTER FOUR

F.I.G.M.O.

Somewhere around two-thirty in the morning, Teddy pulled off the Interstate just west of Donner Summit in the Sierras for a quick nap. He thought he remembered going over Donner Summit. He also thought he remembered the sign saying something about California state highway 20 – Grass Valley, Marysville. But in spite of countless cups of strong, black coffee (bought in Elko, Battle Mountain, Winnemucca - every town across northern Nevada), by now he was so rummy from lack of sleep, he wasn't even sure of his own name.

He drove back under the Interstate, turning in to a CalTrans lot that stored heaps of salt and gravel for winter highway maintenance. He pulled his pickup between two big, orange dump trucks to block out the glare of a mercury-vapor light high up on a pole. It was near freezing, but he was asleep before the engine block stopped making its pinging and popping noises.

The shrill gabble of fighting mountain blue jays woke him up. He was stiff and cold; a panic gripped him as he looked at his watch: eight o'clock! His truck roared to life; he sprayed gravel all over the two big orange trucks as he spun out of the CalTrans lot and back onto the Interstate. He only had four hours to make Treasure Island, or he'd be AWOL. Wrong way to start off with Uncle Sam. And worse, he'd be hitting Sacramento at the height of morning rush hour. Now he regretted his loafing along at fifty all the way. How could he be so stupid?

As he roared recklessly down the western slope of the Sierras, he was the one passing the big eighteen wheelers this time. His coffee-filled bladder nagged him. He ignored it. He could no longer ignore it and finally had to stop. He pulled off the next exit, doubled back under the underpass and got some relief. As he was zipping, he checked his watch again (habit), then realized he was now on Pacific Time - an extra hour gained. More relief.

Teddy's two weeks of processing for active duty in the Marines went by in a blur. The Marines have a thing about keeping their men fit. Up at four-thirty. Five mile jog to get the blood flowing. Chow (Navy cooks, darn good, surprisingly). Close Order Drill. Inspections. Meetings with Navy Yeomen to process endless amounts of paperwork. Visits to sick bay for medical exams and shots: jabbed all over for Plague, Yellow Fever, etc. He felt like a human pincushion. Navy Hospital Corpsman: "You never know, sir, you may get orders to 'Nam. We give everyone the same series because, well, you never know…."

Teddy thought that being a river guide had made him physically fit. Yeah, somewhat. At least he was fitter to some degree than a bunch of college guys who had spent their summer lying around the pool at their country clubs or on the beaches. "Flabby! You're all a bunch of dough bellies!" their drill sergeant had yelled, with a few choice expletives thrown in.

Every night after polishing his shoes and all the brass on his new uniforms, Teddy fell into a deep sleep as soon as his head hit the pillow. The first weekend when he was dressing in civvies for a trip into San Francisco, he was surprised at how much weight he had already lost. His clothes felt looser. He looked like he was playing dress-up in a bigger brother's clothes. It felt good to be physically fit.

He spent his first Saturday morning in Alameda, finding a place to store his truck and fishing stuff. He could send for the fly rods and other gear once he got settled in a new duty station. That is, if there was any trout fishing to be had, which he doubted would be his luck. He would bring the truck back for storage just before he shipped out to wherever...

He took the Bay Bridge over to San Francisco - it was crowded and slow going. Being a fisherman, and out of curiosity, he went to Fisherman's Wharf for lunch. He treated himself to fresh crab and sourdough bread, eaten slowly as he leaned over the wharf railing and tossed crumbs to seagulls. It was washed down with a cold draft beer. Now he knew firsthand what all the hype was about. The crab, bread and beer tasted delicious. The crisp salty air was also delicious.

Teddy drove around for awhile, not really knowing where he was headed, not caring. He parked in the underground lot at Union Square on Post Street. When he came up to ground level, there was a marching band dressed in powder blue and gold uniforms, filling the square, playing a college fight song. He asked someone on the fringe of the crowd what was going on.

"It's game weekend at Stanford, man."

"So who's this band, these guys playing here?"

"It's UCLA's marching band. It's a big tradition; they always play here just before the game at Stanford."

"Cool."

"You from Southern Cal, UCLA?" the man's girlfriend asked Teddy.

"No. Why?"

"You're really tan. You look like a surfer. And your ears, they're burned bad. You look like you got some serious melanoma."

"No. I'm a river guide." Blank stare. "In the summer I guide fly fishermen in Jackson Hole. Wyoming. It's my job. I was on my way to Patagonia to do the same thing for the winter months. But instead, I got ordered to active duty with the Marines. I'm at Treasure Island for processing right now."

The young man, dressed in baggy pants, sandals, Mexican fisherman's knit poncho, beard and long hair tied back in a pony tail, eyed Teddy's new sidewall crew cut. "You going to 'Nam? You're going there to napalm innocent kids and civilians!" He had a nasty edge to his voice.

Teddy held his ground. "I don't know where I'm being sent. And even if I did know, I couldn't tell you for reasons of national security."

"What a load of crap!" blurted out the girl. She was thin, had long, blonde hair, and was dressed in a tie-dyed cotton skirt; her wrists, arms, and throat were draped with hand-made silver and turquoise jewelry. Maybe they make it for their living, Teddy thought.

Teddy was surprised at their strong reactions. "Tell you what," he said, in an attempt to make peace. "I'll bet deep down inside, we have the same political convictions. I majored in poly sci at Montana State, by the way. Let's go get a beer and talk it over. You must know some good places around here?"

"Uh, it's okay. Peace, man." The young man made a vee with two fingers.

"Peace," the girl said, making the same sign.

"Peace," Teddy said, as the uniformed Bruins began playing a marching band arrangement of Paul Simon's "Bridge Over Troubled Water."

The second week was mostly spent in a classroom without windows. Teddy learned that his job designation for the next two years would be with the military police. He was taught principles and techniques of military police, especially riot control. The military instructors repeatedly made references to recent riots on the nearby campus of Cal Berkeley, illustrated with many graphic black and white photos. Teddy thought it strange no reference was made to other college campuses, where the military was also involved in keeping peace.

A young Navy Lieutenant, Sandy Torgersen, from Minnesota, instructed them in the Uniform Code of Military Justice (the "UCMJ"). Torgersen earned his law degree from Minnesota, and was now attached to the Judge Advocate General Corps. He was a Navy lawyer, trained in military law and justice. "Knowing the UCMJ will become vital in the work you gentlemen are about to begin. When you make arrests of military personnel, you must know which article of UCMJ applies. If a Marine or Navy guy is injured or killed on your watch, you will need to know, according to UCMJ, whether it was 'in the line of duty' or not. The answer to just about any question that will arise on your watch can be referenced in UCMJ. It's your Bible. Read it; know it. At the end of this course you will be tested. Be prepared." For the first time in many years, Teddy burned midnight oil studying. After lights out, he studied with a flashlight, a blanket over his head.

During the afternoons of Week Two, Teddy and his classmates were taught the rudiments of hand-to-hand combat. They learned how to disarm and neutralize an aggressor, with or without a weapon. Having played Rugby helped. Some. Teddy wasn't prepared for the foul play inflicted by their instructors.

The Instructors. Torturers would be more precise. There were four of them, straight from the Spanish Inquisition, each with a different "expertise." But they all held one thing in common: they were Marine sergeants who hated Reserve officers with a passion. They had all seen some form of combat; they all had rows of multi-colored campaign ribbons - "fruit salad" in military terminology - hanging from their blouses (*"blouses*, gentlemen, not shirts!"). And they were all sadists. Teddy had at least three sneaky kicks to the groin to prove it. He managed to deflect a groin kick from Instructor Number Four. Barely. He got a nasty grin and an order to watch himself always: "Never trust your enemy, son. Never let down, never turn your back. Ever." It was funny how they all called him "son" even though they couldn't be more than a few years older. Whatever.

The week passed quickly; his bruises and inoculated arms healed, and Teddy found himself at Travis Air Force Base north of San Francisco, headed somewhere. He still didn't know where he was going. His orders were sealed. He could open his fat brown envelope only after the captain of their MAC - "Military Air Command"- flight gave them the okay over the plane's intercom.

The Boeing 707 lifted off at 1649 hours in a light, drizzling rain. Teddy had a window seat. The fields below were a bright green. Strange for this time of year, he thought. As if reading his thoughts, a black Navy chief petty officer seated next to Teddy said, "Looks a lot like 'Nam. Those fields down there are rice. Just like 'Nam. You'll see, yessir, just like 'Nam."

"You already been there, I guess?"

"Yessir, two tours already. I volunteered for a third."

"Why?" Teddy blurted out without thinking. It was an unspoken military rule he'd quickly learned: never ask another guy personal questions until you become shipmates. He apologized.

"It's okay, sir. Marriage problems. I was gone for a year, came back home to find she had somebody else to keep her from being lonely, if you get my drift. So what was there left for me? No home, no wife. A third tour sounded okay, 'specially since I'm not close to any real action to worry about. The combat pay's good…"

They were interrupted by the captain's voice on the com: "Gentlemen, you may now open your orders." It was also the signal it was okay to light up. There was a frenzy of smokes being lit.

Funny, but Teddy had really cut down on his own smoking habit the last two weeks. Somehow, smoking and five-mile jogging didn't work together. The heavy smokers were all bent over puking by the first mile. Teddy thought he'd probably just quit. The aircraft's cabin quickly filled up with a thick bank of smoke. Teddy felt a little sick from it. Then there was a frenzy of paper ripping. Then a babble of groans, laughter, and voices muttering "F.I.G.M.O."

"FIGMO? What's FIGMO?" Teddy asked the grizzled Navy Chief.

"You don't know FIGMO?" Teddy shook his head. "Shoot, son. That stands for 'F***! I got my orders!'"

"I see."

"Where you goin' to? Ain't you gonna open yours?"

"Yeah, I guess so." Teddy ripped open the envelope. He quickly read down the first page, not understanding any of the abbreviations, the military jabber, the coded language. The Navy Chief leaned over, pointed his finger at the line that mattered: "You lucky dog. You goin' to Guam!"

Teddy didn't know whether to be relieved or worried. On the one hand, he kind of liked the idea of combat, even with its known mortality risks. On the other hand, curiosity about Guam caught his imagination.

Where's Guam? What's Guam? Do you call the natives there Guamese? Or what?

"Guam." He said it out loud. It sounded like some kind of skin disease.

CHAPTER FIVE

WHERE AMERICA'S DAY BEGINS

Teddy stepped down the big jet's ladder and set foot on the tarmac at Andersen Air Force Base, Guam. It was four o'clock in the morning; it felt like a sauna. His clothes quickly stuck to his body and his cramped legs were wobbly. He took off the wool tunic that had warmed him on the long, freezing flight over the Pacific. He shouldered his duffle and looked around; too dark, not much to see beyond the few floodlights near the passenger terminal. Above the entrance was a sign "WELCOME TO GUAM, WHERE AMERICA'S DAY BEGINS." He thought about that for a moment but was too tired to figure it out. After claiming his other pieces of luggage, and waiting an hour, Teddy caught a dark blue military shuttle bus to his temporary barracks: Naval Communication Station, Guam, Marianas Islands. He would later move in to permanent housing, but for now it was the Bachelor Officers' Quarters, the BOQ, as it was known in military jargon.

The bone-jarring ride from Andersen AFB to NCS wound on a two-lane paved road through a jungle, or "boonies," as it was known in this part of the world. A convoy of big trucks passed them. They were heavily loaded with bombs – five hundred pounders - headed for Anderson AFB.

"Welcome to the war," Teddy thought. The bus pulled off the highway, taking a sharp right at a Y, and pulled up at the guard shack. A Marine corporal, looking sharp at this early morning hour, complete with sparkling white gloves, stopped the bus and climbed aboard. He came down the aisle, checking everyone's identification. He looked at Teddy's, snapped a salute, "Thank you, sir." Teddy saluted back. "You're welcome, corporal." The corporal, whose ID badge said LCpl Ramirez, smiled and moved on down the aisle.

He was dropped at the Admin Office, where he was to sign in. Teddy signed in at the office marked "Watch." A sleepy Navy yeoman third class rose to a leaning attention and gave him a sloppy salute. "Morning, sir. Help you?"

"Second Lieutenant Buckley reporting for duty, sailor."

"Yessir, sign here. I'll get someone to show you the way to the BOQ."

Teddy signed the log book. A new day on Guam was dawning. Through the louvered window, Teddy could now make out a very pink sky back in the direction of Anderson. He saw low, puffy clouds, and palm trees waving in a breeze. Everything was now tinged with the pink and orange of the rising sun. The breeze blowing in through the open window, however, brought the putrid smell of a dead animal. "Phew. What's that stink? Does the air always smell like that around here?"

"No, sir. Oh that? That's a sea turtle one of the guys killed a couple days ago. The shell's right outside the door. Wanna see it?" Teddy shook his head. All he wanted was sleep.

Teddy was rudely awakened by someone smacking the soles of his shoes with a night stick, alternating with pounding his metal bed frame. "On your feet, soldier!"

Teddy opened one eye to see the offender. "Huh…?" He saw a short, skinny man, at least sixty years old, waving the night stick in a menacing manner. Because the man was dressed in tropical tans, Teddy wasn't sure if he was Navy or Marine. Right now it didn't much matter; the guy was exercising some semblance of authority, and Teddy could sort that out later. He rolled off the cot and stood on his feet. This guy was really short; Teddy towered over him.

"I'm putting you on report for violating a standing order, soldier."

"Excuse me, but who are you, and what order did I supposedly violate?"

"You speak to me when I say you can speak, is that clear?"

"Uh, I think maybe you're some kind of officer, I'm not sure. I'm also an officer and I believe that merits some kind of introduction?"

"I'm Chief Warrant Officer Baxter. I'm the Admin Officer here, third in command. I'm also the officer of the day and that means I have to inspect the barracks. That includes the BOQ where you happen to be at this moment. Just because you're an officer doesn't give you the privilege of sleeping on top of the covers in your uniform, especially with your shoes on. I'm putting you on report. Give me your name, rank, and serial number!" Teddy had already learned during his short time in the military that it doesn't pay to argue with anyone with officer's rank, especially one with a clipboard. It could all be sorted out later on higher appeal. He complied, giving Baxter the information he was seeking, all the while wondering who this crank was and how, when, and where was Teddy going to have to interface with him.

Baxter filled out a form and handed Teddy the pink copy. Baxter retained the original (white), the blue, yellow, and green. That's the military: everything in multiple copies - never throw anything away. Teddy noticed Baxter's handwriting looked very neat. Feminine, but neat. "Thanks," Teddy said, as he took his pink copy.

"That's 'thank you, sir'. And I'll expect a salute, soldier." Teddy saluted and gave him the expected reply. Baxter huffed out. "What the hell was that?" Teddy wondered.

CHAPTER SIX

NCS

Teddy showered, shaved, and got dressed in his one clean uniform: tropical tans with short-sleeved blouse, no necktie. He had nearly slept through the morning chow. Now he was ravenously hungry. He stepped outside into a blinding sun and roaring heat. It felt like he was in the boiler room of Hell. Nearby was a huge diesel engine roaring and belching blue smoke. It seemed to be some kind of power- generating plant.

He wandered toward a group of buildings where several Navy personnel were entering, removing their white caps as they went in. That must be the chow hall, he guessed correctly. He entered, and out of habit, fell in at the end of the line. Several Navy men in blue dungarees stared at him. The man in front turned and spoke. "You must be new here, sir. Officers go to the head of the line."

Teddy felt a blush creeping up his neck. "How new do I look, he wondered?" All these guys were so tanned or sunburned. His skin was already turning a pasty white from two weeks in the fog and gray skies of Treasure Island. And just a few weeks ago he had been on the river, in the sun, rowing a drift boat, guiding high-paying clients. What a change. Teddy got his chow and looked round for a place to sit down. The helpful

Navy man pointed to a table in the far corner. The only officer Teddy could see was Baxter, who looked like he was bowing his head in prayer. Nothing unusual about that; lots of military guys openly prayed over their food. Was Baxter a Christian, he wondered? A Muslim? A Jew? Wouldn't it be a kick if he was one of those Mormons, too. Teddy sat down across from Baxter and began eating.

Baxter surprised Teddy. He offered his small hand across the table and said, "I'm Chief Warrant Officer Lloyd Baxter, Admin Officer. We met earlier this morning. Welcome to Guam. Hafa D'ai."

Teddy closed his open mouth, swallowed, then remembered his manners. "I… I'm Second Lieutenant Teddy Buckley. I'm sort of new here. I just had a long flight and I guess I just fell asleep on the bunk…." Teddy couldn't tell what Baxter was thinking: this man had learned long ago the fine art of keeping his face expressionless. They ate in silence for several minutes. Baxter broke the silence.

"You're probably wondering what an old guy like me is doing here." Teddy shrugged. Two could play this game. "I put in thirty years and retired. I had a good job with an insurance company in Seattle. When Vietnam came along, I wanted to volunteer. At first, the Navy wouldn't take me back. That is, with my old rank. But I know a few well-placed people in Washington, and in the Pentagon…." Baxter winked knowingly. "So I pulled in a couple favors people owed me, and here I am."

"Interesting. And what did Mrs. Baxter think of your volunteering?" Damn, I broke the privacy rule again, Teddy berated himself.

"Oh, she's okay with it. She's used to me being gone for long tours of duty."

Yeah, I'll bet she's okay, Teddy thought. If you treated her like you treated me, she's probably relieved that you signed up. Has the house to herself now, her cats, and her African violets. Teddy's thoughts reverted to his own grandparents in their old age. They split up around age eighty-eight when Granddad accused Grandma of having an affair. Teddy chuckled, caught himself, as Baxter gave him a hard stare.

"Was there something funny in what I just said?"

"I'm sorry; my body clock still hasn't caught up to real time. Guess I'm kinda punchy right now. What was it you just said?"

"I said, 'technically, even though you're just a second lieutenant, you outrank me, but that since I was Officer of the Day, I outranked you when I put you on report.'"

"Oh, that stuff. You don't really think you're gonna make that petty crap stick?" Teddy regretted that comment as soon as it left his lips.

Baxter wasn't finished with his meal, but he swept up his tray, stood at full attention, and said, "Just you watch me make it stick, soldier! I'll see you at the Captain's staff meeting at 1430 hours!" He gave a sharp military about face, and marched out of the chow hall.

Baxter reminded Teddy of many fly-fishing clients who seemed to suffer from the same syndrome. They weren't there for the love of fly fishing. They were there for other reasons. They were trying hard, too hard, to prove something. Pushy. Bragging. Constantly belittling others. Running down people of other races, religions, gender. Keeping score (number of fish caught, size, you name it). Wanting to get even. Loud and rude in restaurants, at hotel desks or airport lobbies. Throwing their money or titles around. Probably the kind that got shoved into the girls' rest room by the bigger guys when they were freshman in high school. Never got over it.

He called it The Little Man syndrome. Or maybe somebody else named it that. Whatever. It really applied to Baxter. There's something truly weird about a man in his sixties, retired, somewhat of a success, willing to leave Mrs. Baxter, hearth and home, to get back in the military. Must have been the rush of power he has over other people. Something he had in the Navy but lacked on the outside. If he joined up, he'd have it back again, the power. That was it! The power.

Teddy reckoned he was going to be spending a lot of his time covering his backside against Baxter. The guy was sneaky, not to be trusted. After all, he pulled strings to get back on active duty. As far away as Washington. In the Pentagon. Who knows what dirt he had on senior officers? Or maybe even a congressman or senator or two? The President? Naw…? You think? Possible. Anything's possible in these crazy times.

"And I'm not a soldier, mister. I'm a Marine!" he shouted at Baxter's retreating back.

After getting directions from a helpful Filipino steward, Teddy walked toward the Admin offices where he'd meet the Captain and the other staff officers in a few minutes. As he walked, Teddy remembered something odd about Baxter: he wasn't drinking coffee. Is he a Mormon, too? Teddy wondered again. Nope, couldn't be… And yet, maybe so… That would be too weird.

CHAPTER SEVEN

THE WORLD ACCORDING TO PENNINGTON

As Teddy figured they would be, the flaky charges Baxter wrote up against him were quietly dropped, but not without the help of his new and very able yeoman, Chris Pennington, Navy Yeoman First Class. Deep down, Teddy knew he had only won the battle, not the war. He sensed Baxter would work hard for his revenge.

Chris Pennington. Here was a peach of a guy, in Teddy's estimation. He was tall, lean, studious, quiet, efficient, discreet, resourceful, all the things a young, green Marine Reserve officer lacked, but desperately needed as he took his first command. Pennington came from the Seattle area; he was from an apparently prosperous lawyer's family who lived in the east side of Seattle, in the ritzy community of Bellevue. The town's name didn't register with Teddy.

Like many others of his generation, Chris had joined the Navy Reserve while still in college to avoid the draft while he completed his degree in English at University of Washington. So he was educated, and in literature, too. That boded well for Teddy, who sorely lacked skills in writing. Not that it mattered a lot how good (well?) you spelled in the military. But there were tons of paperwork, reports to be filled out, filed, retrieved, referred to sometime in the future, maybe. Teddy knew he could rely on Pennington to do this thankless task, freeing him up to command.

Teddy's first command was a company of thirty Marines, all assigned to guard duty at NCS. They also had a rotating assignment to assist the Marine MP's on the Island. Every fourth week Teddy's company would be required to provide ten men for MP duty at one of the other Navy stations. In between, they manned the guard shack at the only entrance to the NCS, provided nightly patrols of the entire base within a barbed wire periphery of several miles in area; plus they guarded the "Bunker," as it was known.

The Bunker was the heart and soul of NCS Guam. It was a large concrete building without windows placed in the center of a large radio antenna field. The entry into this area, known simply as "the Field," was also protected by a guard shack, where two armed Marines kept sentry. To enter, personnel had to show both military ID and their Top Secret security badges. The antenna field contained three hundred sixty antennae, each approximately two hundred feet high. Each antenna represented one point on the compass, thus three hundred sixty degrees would be listening to electronic transmissions from around the globe at all times. This constant flow of information was fed into the Bunker where top secret work took place at all hours.

Besides one utility entrance, the Bunker had only one single doorway entering the building. Each entrance was heavily guarded, twenty-four hours a day, seven days a week, by two armed Marines wearing flak jackets standing guard, not sitting.

Outside, the Bunker was typical military design. It was approximately eighty by eighty feet, two stories high. The only identification on the exterior was a small black and white sign with an assigned building number.

Inside, the Bunker actually had five floors: two above ground, and three below. The two top floors housed administrative and technical personnel. They either did yeoman (secretarial-type) paperwork, or they worked on maintaining the many pieces of expensive state-of- the-art electronic equipment housed in the Bunker.

The remaining three floors below ground level housed numerous large computers, plus the three hundred or so Navy men trained in using the computers, or radiomen who listened to the electronic intelligence being fed them by the antennae outside. They were not simply radiomen, though. Each one had spent over a year, over two thousand hours, in some secret military school, learning language skills. There were guys trained in Chinese (both Mandarin and Cantonese), Korean, Russian, Japanese, Arabic, Spanish, French, and Portuguese. There were also a few elite sailors who spoke, read, and translated several African tongues. Everyone knew the communists were actively infiltrating Africa, and our government needed to know…

Teddy learned that he had missed two (well, three, if you include Chappaquiddick) very exciting world events by just a couple of months. While he was stroking a drift boat on the South Fork in Idaho, a man was walking on the moon. The boys in the Bunker were monitoring the radio signals being sent to earth, first-hand.

They also told him about the USS Pueblo incident off North Korea. The North Koreans had captured one of our Navy ships, the USS Pueblo, that just happened to be loaded with electronic gear with super snooping capabilities. It would be a major disaster if a ship like this fell into enemy hands. There was too much at stake. The North Koreans claimed the Pueblo had strayed inside their territorial waters; maybe it did, maybe it didn't. But it was cruising too darn close to the line for comfort. Its capture created not just an international incident, but a diplomatic crisis. The North Koreans were telling the world that since the ship was inside their waters, they had a right to board and capture. They maintained they did not have to turn the vessel or its crew back over to American military authorities.

That's what the Koreans were saying publicly. But what was being said privately was known very clearly by the boys in the Bunker. What they heard was something more along these lines:

Russians to Chinese: "These idiot Koreans are *your* clients. What's going on here? You want Americans to start World War Three? Better check it out. Fast!"

Chinese to Russians: "We not know anything except what Koreans tell us. Maybe they lying, maybe not. We not know for sure. We check it out, get back to you."

Chinese to Koreans: "You stupid pigs! Why you do dumb (expletive) thing like that! You better fix fast or no more rice shipments! Give that ship back to Americans. You dig?"

Chinese to Russians: "Everything OK now. All fix up."

Russians to Americans: "So sorry, but we know nothing of how or why it happened. Our people will find out and get back to you. By the way, comrade, maybe we can trade a few political prisoners in exchange for information and getting your sailors freed up…?"

And so on. Teddy was sorry he missed watching the language specialists in action. Apparently they had a fun time. This was all related to Teddy by Pennington, since the boys in the Bunker all had Top Secret security clearances and were forbidden to talk about it outside the Bunker walls.

He and Chris talked about the Pueblo over beers in the NCO club after work one evening (Teddy could visit the Non-Commissioned Officers club, but Pennington, since he was enlisted, couldn't visit the Officers Club without an invitation from an officer – it's not democratic, but it's the military way of doing things). Teddy figured, since they now had a pretty good working relationship, he could also ask Pennington about Baxter. But first, he had to know about this strange-tasting beer. Pennington explained that due to the humidity in this part of the world, all beer and soda drinks were treated with formaldehyde, to preserve it.

"You mean I'm going to turn into a laboratory frog?" Teddy joked.

"No, sir, that only happens to us Navy guys. You know, Navy 'Frogmen?'"

After two more glasses of the awful-tasting brew, Teddy finally asked Chris about Baxter.

"Baxter…? He's a mystery inside an enigma inside a puzzle," Chris laughed. "He's a very complex guy. Not your normal thing to do, is it? I mean joining the military at his age? My dad is nearing retirement, and he'd never do it. Thought Baxter was crazy when I wrote home and told them. Told me to watch that guy, that's what he said. He thinks maybe what Baxter says is true. That he managed to get back in because he had some dirt on someone high up in the Pentagon. My dad's pretty active in the Democratic Party. He thinks Baxter had something on Slade Gorton."

Teddy looked blank. "Who is Slade Gorton? Sounds like a comic book character."

"He's the ranking senator from Washington."

"Oh…"

"I dunno, why do you think?"

Teddy took a deep sip and thought. He had to be careful here. Should he mention the Little Man syndrome theory? Should he be tactful? Pennington interrupted his thoughts. "Wanna know what I think? I think it's because of his size. Look at all the short guys you meet in life, what are they like?"

Teddy shrugged, "I dunno, I don't know many circus troupes."

Chris laughed, showing well-kept teeth. Lawyer's kids had some real advantages in life, he thought. "I mean, look around you. How many guys in here are as tall as you or me?" Teddy looked around.

"Can't tell; they're all sitting down. Except that one guy over there playing pinball and he's Filipino. They're all short, so he doesn't count."

"Now there's a generalization for you. Another?"

"Sure." They called for fresh beers.

"Now listen," Chris lowered his voice and got serious. "I see the records of the guys coming in to report for duty. I type up the charges for Captain's Mast and courts martial. I see with my own eyes the official reports that go into their permanent military jackets, their records. They always show how tall these guys are. Plus, another thing they all have in common. They're always getting into trouble." Teddy thought about that. "Bet you another beer you can't guess their average height."

"You're on." Teddy thought for a minute then guessed. "Five nine."

"Wrong. Five six!"

"Big difference."

"I think it does make a difference. See, the guys getting in trouble, and the guys who sign up as cops or military, same difference, they tend to be that much shorter. I believe they would kill for just that three more inches. Somehow it really does matter. You see them, almost every one, when they dress in civvies to go hit the beach? Cowboy boots!"

"That's your point? They tend to be short?"

"The point is, *sir*, they seem to try harder proving their manhood. They walk around with this big chip on their shoulder all the time and miss out on the sweetness of life."

"Define sweetness for me."

They toasted to "Sweetness" being at least six feet tall.

CHAPTER EIGHT

WHAT DO YOU KNOW ABOUT THE MORMONS?

Teddy's first staff meeting with the Captain (or the "Old Man," as a Navy commander – land based or on a ship - is affectionately called by his men) went off okay. Teddy was asked to introduce himself, tell something about his background. He learned that some of the other officers were reservists like he was, pressed into active duty because of the national emergency, the conflict in Vietnam. He got several verbal pats on the back when he related his recent employment: rowing fly-fishing boats with rich clients down scenic rivers. "He should be in the Mekong," someone offered. They all laughed at this ironic joke.

Besides the Captain, Navy Captain Scott Jeffers, there were his Executive Officer ("XO") Jack Ford; Baxter, the Admin officer; Lieutenant (j.g.) Terry Duncan from Oklahoma, the legal officer; and Warrant Officer Bill Monahan, the Supply Officer, who also did double duty with construction and maintenance on the base.

The last to be introduced to Teddy was Navy Ensign Clark Tanner, from Utah. Tanner was the new base Security Officer, a code name for officer in charge of making sure all personnel kept their required security clearances current. He also kept certain secret codes - known only to him and the Captain - for various procedures and manpower movements and deployment should an actual enemy attack occur. Everyone understood Tanner's to be a position of high trust.

Tanner was recently married; his new bride, Cynthia, would arrive sometime later when base housing was available for them. In the meantime, Tanner was housed in the BOQ. Within a few days of his arrival, Teddy was moved in with Clark, to make room for a dozen Petty Officers who arrived for new duty assignments. The old enlisted barracks were full to capacity and overflowing with new personnel arriving daily. Teddy and Tanner had enjoyed a week of each having a room to themselves, a luxury in the military, where cramped sleeping arrangements are the norm and solitude the exception. Teddy soon learned that the base had approximately 400 military personnel (including Teddy's platoon of Marines), and almost 100 civilian employees, mostly Guamanians.

One evening after work, Teddy was relaxing on his bunk in shorts and a tee shirt. Clark was down the hall in the shower. There was a knock on the door. "Enter," Teddy said. A young Navy man in dungarees came in, handed Teddy a packet of mail.

"These finally caught up to you, sir."

"Thanks." Teddy sorted through the mail, spotted a letter from Zack. He ripped it open and read quickly down the page.

Clark entered the room, drying his hair. "Hey, Clark, check this out. I got a buddy from Utah, Park City. He's a Mormon. Says he's going on a mission for his church to Honduras. You're from Utah. Are you a Mormon, too?"

"Yes, I am. You say he's from Park City?"

"Yep."

"Actually, I grew up there, too. What's his name?"

"Zundel. Zack Zundel. You know him?"

"I sure do. I went to Park City High School. Had his dad for a teacher, in History. I even played baseball for brother… I mean, Mr. Zundel. He's the greatest. He was almost like a dad to me. Zack was something like a seventh grader when I graduated high school. Glad to hear he straightened up, got worthy to serve a mission."

"I don't get it, this mission thing. What is it anyway, that it's such a big deal with you Mormons?"

"It will take me a long time to explain. How much time you got?"

Teddy shrugged. "Looks like I'm gonna be here on this rock for two stinkin' years. But I hope it won't take you that long. How about the shortened version?"

"You mean like the small plates?"

"Huh?"

"Sorry. An insider Mormon joke."

Clark began dressing, and Teddy was amazed at what he saw. For the first time, he noticed that Clark was putting on some kind of long underwear! First of all, in the heat and humidity of Guam, everyone seemed to be dressing down, shedding clothes if possible. Second, the underwear was unusual because of its length - it sure wasn't official military issue. Clark noticed Teddy staring. "Special issue. They're called temple garments and they have special religious meaning to me."

Teddy nodded. He'd have to build up the courage to ask him about the temple garment thing. Just like he would eventually screw up his courage to ask Clark what he thought about Baxter. But in the meantime, he'd stick to something less dangerous, like the subject at hand: Mormons and missions. "So tell me about this mission thing. Why do Mormons go on missions, as you call it? And, by the way, I know a girl who's going on a mission to the same place, Honduras. Can't understand that one."

"First of all, how much *do* you know about the Mormons…?"

Three hours later, Teddy was yawning so much he finally had to turn in and get some sleep. He would find it hard to sleep though - there were a lot of questions still rolling around in his head.

Clark started out with the same story Marley Durrant had related: about this young man named Joseph Smith (Teddy had gotten it wrong – he thought it was *James* Smith) who prayed in a grove of woods on his father's farm in New York a long time ago, and came out saying he saw God and Jesus Christ. That was hard to believe. Teddy heard of people having dreams and claiming to see visions, but seeing God and Christ? No way! He kept this opinion to himself. But now he'd heard the same story twice, and it sounded the same both times.

Apparently, young adult Mormons, especially boys, when they get to be about 19, to show their devotion to their faith, go somewhere for up to two years, sometimes longer. They go out to teach the gospel, but it sounded to Teddy like there was a big effort to convert, especially when they started out telling this Joseph Smith tale. These guys didn't get paid anything for doing this; they mostly paid their own way. He gave them some credit for this; it was admirable, he thought. At least it showed commitment to their beliefs.

One really weird thing: no dating. For two years. They didn't ask to be sent to any cool places; they just accepted their call to wherever the Lord sent them. They left their family, girlfriends, car, jobs, school, everything else behind, and went off for two years. Then they tried to pick up again where they left off. Too bad; two years behind everyone else in the race of life, thought Teddy.

That left a big question in Teddy's mind: what about sex?

"We believe in being chaste when we enter into the marriage covenant. Preferably in the temple. Both husband and wife are taught from the time we're small to refrain from premarital sex. So, no, missionaries don't date, don't have sex on their missions. And to be worthy to go on a mission, no sex before the mission, either."

Did that have something to do with those long garment things? Did Mormon women wear them, too? Teddy wondered if Zack had qualified on this premarital sex thing. He was thinking about Tanner's reference to Zack cleaning up his act to be worthy to go on a mission. "Well, probably none of my business," Teddy thought.

Teddy learned there were even two missionaries now here on Guam. They'd just arrived a couple of weeks earlier. They were sent by their mission president in Hawaii ("his finest") to "open up Guam" to missionary work. Would Teddy like to meet them? No. Thanks, but no. But secretly he would like to just get a look at them, see if there was anything strange about them, which he believed there must be to do what they do.

"Did you go on a mission?" Teddy yawned for the third time.

"Yes, yes I did. I served in the Dallas, Texas, Spanish-speaking mission."

"So you know Spanish?"

"Si, si."

"What's Spanish for lights out?"

But before they turned out the lights, Teddy read Zack's letter one more time. He thought he felt something of Zack's enthusiasm, his eagerness to get going on this mission. Teddy's two final waking thoughts before he fell asleep were if Honduras is anything like Guam, that excitement will melt in the first hour. Zack had left a forwarding address for his mission headquarters in Honduras just in case Teddy wanted to write (he did).

Teddy also wondered if he could write to Marley Durrant care of the same address.

———————

CHAPTER NINE

WHERE'S THE FLY FISHING ON GUAM?

For over a month Teddy managed to steer clear of Baxter. Teddy's duty schedule required him to be on call 24 hours a day. At first he hung out some at the Officers' Club, thinking he could possibly meet an interesting woman. That proved to be frustrating. There weren't very many female officers on Guam. He did meet one woman, the wife of another junior officer, a Naval Air Corps AWACS pilot who was gone a lot on hurricane-scouting flights. She seemed quite bored and lonely. But she was cute. And very sexy. Too sexy. Teddy avoided her - he was not looking for trouble.

Then he hung out occasionally at the NCO club with Chris Pennington. That also proved frustrating. Teddy had little in common with the "lifers" who virtually lived there. Their common nexus: either single (divorced — the family thing, a common casualty of the military lifestyle), or else they were waiting for base housing to open up so they could bring wife and kids over from stateside.

To fill his time productively, Chris spent many of his off-duty evenings running the base library, a job that was natural for him. Out of sheer boredom Teddy stopped in one evening and visited awhile. He asked Chris to recommend a list of good books he could read. "What kind of reading do you like?"

"I dunno. Light stuff… Novels, action, Westerns, historical things. I read some Hemingway for English classes in college. I like Jim Harrison, stuff like that." Chris made up a list and handed it to Teddy the next day at the office. Teddy was surprised to find some books of the Bible, along with Shakespeare, included. He hadn't expected this. "Psalms? Songs of Solomon? Ecclesiastes? Proverbs? This is religious stuff!"

"It's considered *literature* by most scholars."

"If you say so."

Pennington was emphatic that it should be the King James version. Teddy borrowed a new copy from the chaplain, then he beat a hasty retreat before the padre could start asking any questions.

Very early in his first month of duty Teddy was introduced to another military term: *cumshaw*. Nobody knew its origin, but everybody knew its meaning: the ability to find stuff and get it. Buy, trade, barter, blackmail, whatever- the object was to get hard-to-find goods or services. Teddy also met the island's acknowledged Cumshaw King, Don Leonard, known to most everyone as "The Lizard."

The Lizard was a Navy Chief Boatswain's Mate (pronounced *BOW-sun*), a senior grade petty officer. What he actually did at NCS Guam was anyone's guess. He was sometimes spotted driving a faded blue Navy pickup truck around the base. More often, he would be somewhere else on the island, away from NCS, in Navy dungarees. Most all the time Leonard's appearance was anything but military: dirty uniforms; scuffed, unpolished shoes; longish hair; his white uniform cap spotted with black, greasy fingerprints, and so on. The truck was always piled with non-military junk inside and out. This bothered Teddy, who liked things neat and tidy.

Teddy also wondered how Leonard got access to every military base on the Island, even the bases requiring a security clearance. Boatswain's Mates traditionally worked on ships or other water craft, kind of the Navy version of a handyman, an all-purpose fix-it guy - skills not really much needed at a communications station. Was he like Baxter? Did Leonard also have something on somebody in a high position? Or was he really a very useful handyman, a fix-it guy?

For his part, the Lizard felt it was his duty to pay a social call on this new Marine lieutenant just to make sure Teddy knew that Leonard's services, on or off duty, were available. If Teddy should ever need anything, be sure and come to the Lizard first. (For a price - nudge, wink, laugh. "Just kidding, sir!" Or was he?)

Teddy was curious about what Leonard actually did. "You need boonie housing that's on the approved list? I got it. Need something hard to find at Navex (the Navy Exchange, or military version of a department store)? Got it. Need your car repaired fast? Bingo! Got boys on call to do that, too." Leonard moved uncomfortably close, lowered his voice. Teddy recoiled at the guy's bad, boozy breath. The Lizard stuck a thumb in his own hairy chest; no mandatory white tee shirt. "Women? Leonard makes the intros, get it?" (Another nudge and wink. Teddy cringed again at the reek of his BO.) So he openly admits to being a pimp, too?

Leonard had married a Guamanian woman, who methodically produced a large batch of kids for Leonard to support. Don had put in for, and officially gotten, many successive tours on island. He was, therefore, almost a native, and very well-connected locally. Must be a lot of payoffs, Teddy mused.

Teddy's instincts said this guy spelled trouble, Big Trouble. It was inevitable. He just *smelled* of trouble. (Okay, so he also just plain smelled; he was fat and sweat a lot.) He was too slick for Teddy's comfort; he would bear watching. Closely. Teddy wasn't sure either if Leonard's activities fell within whatever his job description was. So Teddy would keep an eye on this guy all the same. One obvious question came up right away: the Navy pickup and the gas it used: all Navy business, all the time? Probably not. The Lizard lived off-base in boonie housing, close to the larger naval base down island. Whatever. Teddy had more pressing business now.

Teddy's next in command, his platoon's senior enlisted man, was a grizzle- haired senior master sergeant, named Guy Brooks. Brooks hated his Christian name. Teddy knew he was going to like Brooks when he read his name on the duty roster, even before the two met. The fisherman in Teddy made an immediate connection to the name. Brooks was close to one year away from retirement (thirty-five years, including a lot of combat). He was average height and build, with piercing gray eyes to match his short cropped hair. The first day, after they introduced themselves, Brooks spoke. "Permission to speak, sir."

"Speak, sergeant."

"Sir, may I make a suggestion? Actually, it's a request."

"Sure. Ask away."

"Sir, I've worked under a lot of officers in my career, sir. And in my experience, the best arrangement is if you let me run things. Sort of."

"Sort of? Meaning?"

"Well, you're the C.O., sir. But you're new, you're Reserve, and these guys and me, well, we'll be around a long time after you collect your medals and go back home to your country club and sports car. Sir."

Teddy gathered his thoughts for a minute before responding, Brooks standing at precise attention the while. His situation reminded Teddy of his days guiding on the river. Technically, the client was the boss, because he had the money – the "golden rule," as guides called it. But as a practical matter, Teddy was in charge there: he knew the river, its hidden dangers, the many secrets and tricks required to tame it. He also knew the water, the fish, the climate, bug hatches, and so on. He had the store of knowledge and experience to bring the client safely back home. Experience there trumped rank, position, age, even money. "Okay," Teddy said, "provided...."

"Sir?"

"Provided, that sometimes, for reasons entirely my own, I might have to step into a situation. In the meantime, I won't get in your way, and you won't get in mine."

"Good. Then we have a deal, sir?"

"I didn't say there was any deal, just our private working arrangement. We'll see how it goes, understood?"

"Sir, yes sir."

"Brooks, let's keep the lines of communication open. We're both on call for the base and for each other twenty-four seven. Okay?"

"Yes sir." Brooks grinned, and they shook on it like gentlemen do.

Teddy really missed his fly fishing. He needed to go fishing – any kind of fishing would do, so he talked it over with Clark, and they decided to get their names on the fishing excursion boat list. Leonard got wind of their plans and offered to get them on a private fishing boat. "No waiting list and a sure catch guaranteed." Teddy knew from experience there was only one way a sure catch was guaranteed. And he wanted no part of this scheme.

The good thing about the Navy excursion boat and crew was that the craft and crew were certified sea-worthy. A spot on board could be had for just a few bucks, all day, including lunch and an ice chest full of cold drinks. And since Clark's a Mormon, there's more beer for me, Teddy reasoned. He kidded Clark about it; Clark took it in good humor.

The day finally came, and the two fishermen reported to the boat basin, U.S. Naval Station Guam. Teddy noticed their fishing boat was tied up across the water from a pair of nuclear submarines. He hadn't even known there were nuclear subs on Guam. Their boat was clean and sparkling: gray with dark blue and white trim. All exposed wood and metal had been polished until it shone. The twin diesel engines thrummed smoothly at idle, no missing cylinders. This was a first-class operation. It appealed to Teddy's newfound sense of neatness, orderliness. This was, for the military, classy.

They had awakened on a weekday long before dawn, the only time spot they could get on this popular fishing craft. Clark suggested they pray before they left their room. Teddy nervously eyed Clark. "I'll do it," Clark volunteered. At least he didn't insist they kneel. This was a strange experience for Teddy. Clark prayed that the elements would be tempered in their favor, that they would enjoy safety and smooth sailing (funny, since it wasn't a sailboat) and that the skill of captain and crew would be manifest.

Teddy mumbled his "amen", and quipped, "You forgot to ask for lots of big fish." As they drove their requisitioned van to the boat basin, Teddy said "I wonder if any of my fly-fishing clients ever prayed for me."

"Maybe that's why you had such a safe record as a guide."

"Maybe."

Fat clouds hung low over the ocean as they pulled out; the water was smooth and glassy, reflecting the oranges and pinks of the coming sunrise. "Not good," said Teddy.

"Why?" Clark asked.

"Fish like cloudy weather, just makes it better fishing. Dunno why."

His prediction proved accurate. It wasn't a successful fishing trip.

Clark hooked and played a large barracuda to the boat. As one of the crew was readying the gaff hook, the other boy yelled something in Guamanian, and pointed.

"What's he saying?" Teddy yelled.

"He sayin'…" He never got to finish. The barracuda was savagely attacked by an even bigger fish – a wahoo - which tore the barracuda in half just behind its gills. That was it. Just like that, as fast as you could snap your fingers Clark's prize was gone. They hauled in the barracuda, or what was left of it, the mouth still opening and closing, its eyes staring dully, never knowing what just happened.

Cruising back to the NavSta boat basin, Teddy asked one of the boys if he knew of any fishing spots on the island where he could use a smaller, sporting rod and reel.

"Talofofo. That's the best place."

The other boy nodded his agreement. "Best place."

That's all the information Teddy could get out of them. They tipped the captain and his crew of two boys generously. It wasn't their fault the day wasn't successful. Having been a guide, Teddy knew very well the part fickle luck played in fishing success.

"We had a good time. Thanks."

"Sorry you guys didn't get more action."

"It's okay," Clark said. "That was plenty exciting for me."

"Yeah, me too," Teddy said.

"Maybe next time?"

After the thanking and tipping ritual, Teddy turned around to look. The two subs were gone.

"They come and they go," the captain said.

Clark and Teddy needed some personal items, so they stopped to check out the Naval Station's exchange, which was much larger than the one at NCS. Inside, Teddy was naturally drawn to the section marked "Sporting Goods." He was sure they would not have anything resembling a fly rod. He was happily surprised to find they had a fairly large rack of them. "Lots of guys buy them just before they go back stateside," the clerk explained. Whatever. This was the closest Teddy had been to heaven in weeks. The rods were mostly made of fiberglass, not bamboo, but were good quality, brand names he recognized. He found a rod close to what he wanted: a Fenwick brand, nine feet in length, a six weight. Not perfect, but it just might work for what he had in mind. He matched it up with a basic Martin, single-action reel, a Cortland fly line, and some spools of different weights of mono to build his leaders. The clerk showed him some locally made saltwater flies; he bought a dozen. They were tied on double-ought hooks by a local fisherman. "Talofofo? Sure, I've heard that it's pretty good," the clerk said. "Try the channel as the tide is either going out or coming in. Cast across and let it sink; then bring it back in with jerky movements."

To Teddy, that sounded a lot like fishing big streamer flies in the fall for spawning South Fork browns. His eyes misted over.

CHAPTER TEN

SISTER TANNER

A week before Thanksgiving, Teddy learned why Mr. Zundel was such a major figure in Clark Tanner's life. Clark's dad died before he was twelve years old ("just before I was supposed to be ordained a deacon"). After the funeral, Clark, his mother and younger sister moved from California back to live with the grandparents who operated a small dairy farm just outside Park City, Utah. Their closest neighbors were the Zundels.

So it came to be that Clark grew up very much a part of the Zundel family, who let him spend as much time in their home as he wanted. Mrs. Zundel gave Clark's sister free piano lessons. Mr. Zundel, a Mormon bishop at the time, ordained Clark a deacon in something called the Aaronic Priesthood. Teddy thought it peculiar a boy could be ordained to be a priest. "Not a priest – a deacon," Clark corrected.

Clark's parents had married as high school sweethearts right after graduation. They moved to Sacramento right after the wedding, hauling all the unopened wedding gifts crammed into their little VW Beetle. They spent a couple of days around Lake Tahoe for their honeymoon, "where apparently I was made," Clark stated matter-of-factly. "I was born in

Sacramento exactly nine months to the day they were married." After his dad died his mom never remarried.

Clark's grandparents on his father's side lived in Southern Utah. Both died of cancer after long illnesses. This was when Clark was about fifteen; he was well-acquainted with death. His mother's parents were a good deal older than Clark, hard-working farm folk whose lives revolved around a rigid routine: up at four o'clock for milking and chores, breakfast and more chores. "Dinner" was a light mid-day meal followed by a nap for Grandpa on the parlor floor. Grandma joined him, lying on the divan, watching her beloved "soaps."

Then came the afternoon milking followed by "supper," their evening meal. They would watch some television or listen to KSL radio for the weather report, then go to bed early.

"Did it ever change, ever vary? Did they ever take a vacation?" Teddy asked.

"Not to my knowledge. If Grandpa got sick, Grandma took over and did the milking and other chores."

Teddy learned that the grandparents were Mormons, too, but they were something called *inactive*. "That danged dairy farm had them so tied down they could never leave it, couldn't even go to church, or so they claimed," Clark said.

"Why not hire somebody to come in and help out?"

"Why spend money? They had me and my mom and sis. We all worked for our room and board. That was the trade."

"They never paid you?" Teddy asked.

"Nope. I always resented Granddad being such a tightwad until it came time for my mission, and then he really came through. He told me he had really wanted to go on a mission himself when he was young, but because of the Great Depression he never got to go. There wasn't any money left for such luxuries as church missions. 'Sonny,' he said to me, 'I'm going to send my money on a mission with you. Now take good care of my money. Don't spend it on foolishness like a lot of those missionary boys do.'"

"And did you? Take care of his money?"

"Darn right," Clark said. "I came home with quite a bit still in my account. I offered it back to him, but he refused. Told me to use it toward college or marriage, whatever I wanted to use it for."

Teddy was truly touched by the old gentleman's kind heart. He never told Clark about the trust account in his name at the family's bank back home, set up by his great-grandfather, one of the bank's founders. It must be worth several millions in principal by now, not counting the annual dividends and interest from wise and prudent holdings that were reinvested, quietly compounding with ever-increasing dividends and interest. The trust would come into Teddy's hands when he turned age twenty-five, only a couple more years. Funny thing, Teddy never thought much about that trust. It was just there, sometime out in the future, growing fatter every hour, every day. Until it was time for Teddy to take over his own fortune and manage his own investments, the bank's professional money managers (the "suits") were the trustees.

In the meantime, he'd leave the interest and compounding stuff to them. That's why they wore boring dark suits, white shirts and dark ties to work every day, to toil in their little cubicles over boring reports and boring spread sheets.

Teddy accompanied Clark to Andersen AFB the day Mrs. Cynthia Tanner regally swept off the MAC flight and down the steps, landing on Guam like a conquering empress. Her face was flushed, her eyes pinched; she shielded them against the burning sun. Clark was as nervous as a high school junior picking up his first prom date. He offered Cynthia the traditional island greeting gift, a lei made of fresh Plumeria blossoms. Cynthia did not approve of public displays of affection, but just this once she turned her face to allow Clark a chaste peck on her cheek. Cynthia turned and offered her hand to Teddy. "You must be Mr. Buckley."

"Please, it's just Teddy."

"Teddy, then. Clark's told me so much about you. I'm Cynthia Tanner, but you *must* call me Cindy." So Cindy it was. In the background several Filipino civilians were unloading the luggage from the plane's deep belly. Teddy helped gather her many suitcases while Clark brought the car - his ancient Volvo wagon - around for loading. Cindy looked around, "So this is Guam?"

The base housing list moved so slowly that Clark had given up hope that a vacancy would ever open up for him. So he finally gave in to Leonard's pressure and the Lizard "cumshawed" a boonie house for

Clark and Cindy. It wasn't much, just a three-room shack without air conditioning in Tamuning, a small village in the jungle. It came complete with a host of stray barking dogs, an army of chickens, curious children, and hundreds of roosters that started crowing hours before dawn. "You get used to the crowing real soon," Leonard promised.

"How much did you have to spiff (code for bribe) the Lizard to find this shack for you?" Teddy quizzed Clark.

Clark gulped, blushed, and confessed, "Actually, I didn't pay him anything, at least not directly. He never takes money, he says. But I suspect there's a kickback in there for him… somewhere."

The Tanners, at Teddy's request, dropped him off at NCS. "Nice to finally meet you, Cindy."

"You, too, Mr. Buckley."

"Please. It's Teddy." She smiled and waved a regal good bye. As he watched the old Volvo disappear out the main gate of NCS, Teddy felt a sudden emptiness. Clark had become his best friend over the last two months. It would be Thanksgiving in a few days and he now had the room in the BOQ all to himself. It felt strange to be alone in the center of this ever-crowded military environment.

Shoot, he said out loud, he'd even miss Clark's strange underwear. And his habit of reading his Book of Mormon (scriptures, he claimed, which Joseph Smith, their prophet, translated with the help of God). He also admitted to himself, he was even going to miss Clark kneeling by his bunk in prayer each night. Teddy laughed as he remembered the times he had tucked Clark into bed after he fell asleep on his knees.

On the short ride from Andersen to NCS, Clark informed Cindy he had invited Teddy over for Thanksgiving dinner "plus maybe a couple single enlisted guys from the branch. Maybe even the missionaries, if that's okay with you."

Cindy had turned around in her seat and said to Teddy, "He's such a softy for stray dogs and cats."

CHAPTER ELEVEN

FLY FISHING TALOFOFO

Thanksgiving Dinner with the Tanners was set for three o'clock in the afternoon, a strange hour, Teddy thought. He didn't think they would get a turkey for the feast. The Navy Commissary at NavSta had been out of frozen birds for over two weeks. As if by magic, the Lizard came through again. Teddy wondered what jacked-up price Clark had to pay. He also wondered how many frozen birds Leonard had managed to buy up in advance, thereby creating an artificial shortage. If, say, the Lizard had managed to buy up five dozen or so birds, how many members of family, and their friends, would it take to skate around the one-bird-per-customer limit the commissary had set? And where would Leonard manage to keep them all hidden, properly frozen until his desperate, last-minute customers showed up, cash in hand? Just like scalping hot concert tickets. Perfect example of a pure market monopoly, Teddy mused.

Teddy's central plan for the day revolved around trying out his new Fenwick fly rod at Talofofo. He wasn't sure what he was fishing for, or what he'd do if he caught anything, but he was game to try. The solunar tables indicated a strong tide running out starting around eleven o'clock in the morning. He figured if he left NCS at ten he could get there in plenty of time, have some fly fishing action, lie on the beach awhile with a cold beer, and still get back to the Tanner's shack in time for Thanksgiving dinner. Looking back, he should have aborted the plan before he started - everything went goofy on him from the start.

The requisitioned pickup wouldn't start. The one enlisted sailor on duty in the motor pool allowed him to trade for another vehicle, a van. It took a precious half hour to fill out all the necessary paperwork and transfer his gear. The young Seaman was the lowest swab in the motor pool pecking order; he was also the newest guy. "Good luck," he said, handing Teddy the keys. Good luck? What the heck does that mean? Teddy asked himself. He should have listened to his gut, telling him this was a portent of things to come. On the other hand, how was that lowly Seaman to know the van was almost out of gas or that its fuel gauge was faulty?

Teddy had never been to Talofofo yet; he was simply trying to follow a handwritten map and directions he'd gotten from a fellow officer who had been there many times. "It's easy to get to Talofofo. Just get on the cross-island highway, head east, and pretty soon the road bends south, pretty much following the coastline…" This would be the windward side of the island, so named because the prevailing winds blew constantly from the east, thus making the seas and the coastline rougher on that side. But he was assured that, although there weren't any nice beaches over there, it's so darn beautiful, that's compensation enough.

The van ran out of gas about two miles short of the village of Talofofo. "Great," he thought, "I can sit here and enjoy the lovely compensatory scenery, or I can get out and walk." He opted to walk and try to find some gas. He was pulling out his new fly rod and gear bag when a boonie truck approached. He flagged it down. Full of teenaged Guamanian boys, it slowed and stopped. There were six of them and only one of him, not good odds if they tried any rough stuff. Even with his military police training he knew he was outmanned. Teddy's men frequently told true stories of American military personnel getting beaten up or worse by gangs of native thugs, usually teenaged boys.

It was too late now for Teddy to back out. He climbed aboard their ancient pickup, one leg inside, the other hanging over the tailgate. He held on tightly to his rod. One of the younger guys pointed at the rod and spoke. "You gonna fish?" Teddy nodded. "That's a weird lookin' pole, man." Teddy nodded again.

They reached the village, pulled over, and he climbed off. "Know anyone who can sell me some gas?"

"You're lookin' at it, man!" They drove away laughing.

Teddy stood in the hot gravel between the highway and the entrance to a run- down boonie shack. Above the door was a weather-beaten sign that said "Gas-Beer-Pop." He saw no gas pump, nothing indicating it was a gas station. The sun beat down, a steady warm wind blew in from the Pacific, bending the row of palm trees behind the gas station. A small girl sat on a rough patch of grass beside the door playing with a mangy pup.

The front door opened and a round, squat woman came out hefting a mesh bag filled with groceries. The little girl reluctantly left the puppy and followed her mother up the road, their rubber flip flops slapping out a rhythm: the little girl's quick steps beat out two for every one of her mother's. Music poured out of the open door, The Beatles again, singing "Hey Jude." So it was a grocery store, too?

Teddy went inside, not bothering to knock; the puppy followed. There was a greasy counter plus a few stocked shelves. The bags of basmati rice and gallon jugs of soy sauce looked suspiciously like those sold at the Navy Commissary. The few times he'd been in the commissary he observed a lot of grocery carts overloaded with rice, soy sauce, frozen chickens and pork ribs, all being pushed by Guamanian families. Those Guamanians lucky enough to land a civil service job with the military also got commissary privileges, supposedly only for themselves and immediate household members. Teddy soon learned that "household" was a very elastic term on Guam, intended to be stretched as far as possible. Everyone on Guam was a cousin.

His eyes adjusted to the dim light. Along the back wall was an ancient refrigerator clanking noisily. He guessed there was cold soda inside, maybe beer, if he was lucky. There was beer, two brands. Teddy chose two quart bottles of San Miguel, made in the Philippines, which seemed to be the favorite in this part of the world. It was much preferred over the Japanese brands, and for good reason. The Japanese had occupied the island for several years during World War II, making life extremely miserable for the natives. Guamanians were truly happy when the Americans liberated the island. They now held an island-wide day of remembrance every July to commemorate the event. The non-Japanese beer wasn't very cold but would have to do for now.

As Teddy started for the front counter there was a huge commotion coming from the back room, someone shouting in Chamorro, flip flops slapping the floor, running in his direction. Something furry was streaking along the bare concrete floor at him. He looked down and in the semi-darkness, his eyes still not fully adjusted to the dim light, he thought he saw a large cat racing toward him. A teenaged girl was running after the animal in hot pursuit.

She was slashing furiously at the thing with a mop stick missing the rag mop part, screaming "Mong Mong! Mong Mong!" Teddy thought that was Chamorro for "cat." He was wrong. The furry thing scampered over his sandaled feet, trailing a long, scaly tail. That was no cat – it was a huge rat! This thought clearly dawned on his consciousness precisely as the girl came down hard with the metal end of the mop, directly across the arch of Teddy's exposed right foot. She missed the rat, but the large gash she made in Teddy's foot started gushing blood. Teddy dropped the bottles of beer which shattered on contact with the concrete floor. What a mess.

It took awhile to stop the bleeding. Teddy was concerned about getting back to sick bay to have a Navy medic put in stitches, as it was obvious from the gaping wound it was going to require some. He helped with the cleanup, even paying for the spilled beers.

The sour-faced owner sold him five gallons of gas ($1.00 a gallon!) poured out from a big tank around back (Stolen from the Navy? Supplied by the Lizard?). Teddy was forced to leave a healthy deposit for the Army surplus gas can. He'd have to return it to get his $20 deposit back. The girl who injured his foot drove him back to the stalled van in the family car, a shiny new Ford Mustang. Grocery business must be good in Talofofo. He thanked her and tipped her a dollar.

"I'll bring the can back in awhile."

"I can take it for you. I can wait."

"Uh, I need to get my $20 deposit back."

"Oh, yeah, I forgot."

The tide was fast ebbing out of the estuary when Teddy finally got there, parked the van, strung up his new fly-rod and tied on a fly. The fly wasn't much to look at: a local job made of badly-dyed rooster feathers, but it would have to make do for now. He hobbled over to a likely spot and started casting into the wind. It had been over two months since he last cast a fly that fall day on the Provo with Zack. It seemed like a lifetime and a galaxy removed from where he stood now. The warm, steady wind dried the sweat he had worked up pouring the gas into the van. It felt good.

Teddy walked across a narrow spit of black volcanic sand, exactly the opposite of the white coral stuff on the beaches the other side of the island. He correctly guessed that was why the only luxury hotels were built on the white sandy beaches and not here. He stepped into the surf, waded out until the cool water was nearly up to his armpits, and laid out a cast. He stripped the line back in, thought he felt a bump, but nothing. His second cast was even better than the first, more line laid out, almost sixty-five feet, he thought. This time he counted to ten to let the fly sink deeper into the surf. Then he began the retrieve, strip, strip, strip, pause. Then he stripped in more line and felt a hard strike.

His rod bowed, line ran off the reel quickly and soon he was into the nylon backing. Teddy tightened down the tension on the reel to slow the fish. He played his fish for fifteen minutes, cranking in line each time the fish ran and tired more. Finally, he brought it to his hand, a dark blue and silver, bullet-shaped thing weighing about six or even seven pounds, he guessed. Teddy held it up by the tail, avoiding its many sharp little teeth. A small crowd of native boys, all brown as prunes, had gathered to watch. They clapped and cheered when he held up his prize. "What is it?" he called to them.

"A *skippy*!" one boy called back.

"A *what*?" Teddy asked, as he waded back to the small beach. He laid the flopping fish on the sand, wishing he had a camera to record the catch. "It looks like a bluefish to me."

"No, it's a skippy," the boy insisted. It looked a lot like the many blues that Teddy had caught off Martha's Vineyard when his family summered there: same bullet shape, torpedo head, sharp teeth, silver belly and dark blue back - an aggressive, quick, strong, bulldog fighter. He had read somewhere about skipjacks, the Pacific cousin to the Atlantic bluefish. Both were definitely smaller members of the tuna family.

"You want it, or shall I throw it back?"

"Yeah, man, we'll take it! They cook up real good if you use a lot of soy sauce." Teddy handed them the catch and they ran down the beach toward their home, laughing.

It was almost five o'clock when a tired, dirty, injured Teddy walked out of the NCS medical clinic, with twenty stitches in his foot, to return the evil van to the motor pool compound. He was not surprised that nobody was there to take the keys back from him or fill out reports. "Screw it," he said aloud.

Ten minutes later under the hot steady stream of the BOQ shower, Teddy wondered how the Tanners and their artists' colony of homesick Mormons were enjoying their expensive turkey feast.

"I never did like cold turkey anyway!" he shouted into the jet of hot water.

CHAPTER TWELVE

MEANWHILE, BACK AT THE LTC

The group of missionaries, eleven of them in all, agreed to meet each morning for "family" prayer before classes started. Zack, or Elder Zundel, as he was now called, began to emerge as a natural leader, even if his Spanish wasn't coming along as fast as the others. He attributed his ability in getting others to do things to his several summers guiding on the rivers in Wyoming, Idaho, and Montana. One stunning blond, Sister Marley Durrant, caught his eye the first day they arrived at the Language Training Center in Utah. Zack was thrilled to know she had also been called to labor in Honduras. She had straight white teeth, strong blond hair, and a perfect figure. Her face and arms were evenly tanned, obviously not from a bottle. Tennis? Swimming?

The Honduran missionary group spent a lot of time in each other's company. They attended Spanish classes together all day. They prayed together. They ate their meals together. At lunch the second Sunday Zack arranged to sit across the table from Sister Durrant. After silently blessing his own meal, Zack got up the courage to speak directly to her on a personal level for the very first time. "So, Sister, where do you come from and what did you do before your mission call?"

"I was born in Provo when my folks were attending BYU. But I was raised in the Bay Area, you know, Northern California. After high school I attended Cal Berkley on a music history scholarship. I guess that's about it. Now, how about you, Elder?"

Zack swallowed and felt a warm flush creep under his white collar and knotted necktie. He pulled to loosen it.

"By the way, before you launch into yourself, I really like your tie. It's kind of bold for a missionary, though, don't you think?"

"Wild, you mean," piped in another elder. Zack was slightly rankled. This was his setup and he didn't want anyone else moving into his territory. But he had to admit it was a bold tie: a bright shade of mauve with forest green stripes.

"Well," he began, "I'm pretty much the opposite. I was born and raised a country boy in Park City, Utah. I don't have any real talents, unless you count rowing a drift boat and tying fly fishing knots."

Marley Durrant's eyes widened. "Oh, really? Where, did you learn to do that?"

"I was a river guide for three summers out of Jackson Hole, Wyoming."

"Yes, yes, I know where that is. I went fishing with Daddy just a couple weeks before I reported here. We, I, was in Jackson Hole. I love that place, so clean, so… so untouched, don't you think?"

Zack agreed. The table chatter changed subjects several times, but Sister Durrant didn't join in; she had a far away look in her eyes, like she was back in Jackson Hole, remembering something. Or someone. They finished eating and headed down the hallways to their separate dorm rooms for an afternoon of self-study. Sister Durrant caught up with Zack and laid her hand softly on his arm. Electricity shot through his body, every nerve was now on full alert.

"Elder Zundel, I met a young man in Jackson Hole. He was my, our fishing guide. I don't suppose… Well, I thought you maybe would know him? His name was Teddy something, but I forgot his last name. Fairly tall and good looking…?" She blushed slightly.

"That would be Teddy Buckley. My roommate and best friend at Jackson! You know him?"

"I don't really know him, but we shared something."

"Shared something?"

"Yes. He's not a member of the church. I'm sure you knew that already." (Zack knew that all right.) "I bore my testimony to him. I hope I didn't scare him off the gospel."

Zack laughed. "I don't think anything scares Teddy Buckley!"

C H A P T E R   T H I R T E E N

WHAT MARRIED WOMEN
ARE GOOD AT

Teddy suffered no real setbacks in his relationship with Clark Tanner. Clark understood pretty well that things beyond our control can mess up the best of plans and good intentions, no matter how well thought-out in advance. Teddy expressed hope his failure to show for Thanksgiving wouldn't damage his new relationship with Cindy. Clark didn't think any harm was done there. He was wrong.

"Clark, where's your friend Teddy? Isn't he kind of late?"

"Clark, the food's getting cold. Don't you think we should go ahead and start eating?"

"Clark, surely Mr. Buckley would call his regrets if he isn't coming?" (This last remark with a frosty edge, even though the Tanners had no telephone service in their boonie shack.)

Cindy Tanner gave the incident a lot of thought in the days following. She concluded that since Teddy was a bachelor, he naturally felt he could come and go as it pleased him. It did not occur to her that since he was commander of a company of MPs he could have had an emergency. Her natural instinct was to conclude that Teddy was not feeling the natural tug of hearth and home, or the affections of… a wife. That's what he lacked: commitment to the institution of marriage. She could certainly fix that.

So Cindy went to work, but she grossly underestimated her quarry. Teddy was not obtuse, nor was he lacking in experience with women. He'd had his share of flings and romances in high school and college, and even a few flings with the coeds who flocked to Jackson for summer work. But the romances always seemed to run out of steam. To him it was curious how these affairs of the heart died a month or so into his summer job. He was really just too busy to even check his mail. When he did, he was too tired to answer letters.

Cindy Tanner soon realized that there were not very many available suitable single women on Guam (translated: Mormon girls). That was the first problem.

The second and greater problem was Teddy himself. He was not a member of the Church. LDS girls are indoctrinated from a very tender age to believe in, and aspire to, the *ideal* marriage. The ideal LDS marriage has the girl getting engaged to a worthy (translated: returned missionary) young man and the marriage is sealed in the temple. Period. No exceptions. Cindy reasoned that leading one of the two available single LDS girls on the island to the altar with Teddy would be far less daunting than getting Teddy into the waters of baptism.

Like many married couples, Clark and Cindy engaged in "pillow talk." That is, once in bed for the night, after prayers and just before falling off to sleep, they talked about serious things: topics that required some focus, without the normal daily distractions like television, and so forth. Cindy's strategy was to get Clark enlisted and committed to the *cause*. Her strategy was to work on Clark's natural missionary zeal. Cindy only had to plant the seed and make the suggestion. "Teddy would make a wonderful member of the Church, wouldn't he?"

Or, "Clark, I can just see Teddy as an elder's quorum president. Can you see that happening someday, in your mind's eye…?" Yes, that was it; that definitely sounded more natural. Cindy would then be free from the missionary effort to do what women do best: match-making. Bring boy and girl together and give them the *nudge*.

The *nudge* is the final push over love's precipice.

Sometimes you have a reluctant girl. She sees too many flaws or faults in the guy. However, there's still that voice in her head reminding her about her biological clock ticking away relentlessly.

On the other hand, the guy may be the problem. Sometimes, not often, but sometimes, the guy needs to be reminded he has hormones. The matchmaker helps that out with a little bit of "packaging." You suggest to the girl that maybe she should lose a little weight. Maybe some strategic padding here and there is necessary to make up for Nature's deficiencies. (No, that's not cheating, just enhancing the basic material.) Maybe she needs some new makeup, a new hairdo, a new fragrance, perhaps.

Men, be on notice: you don't stand a ghost of a chance. It's like the story of the Three Little Pigs and the Big, Bad Wolf. Two brothers were dumb and trusting. They got devoured early in the story. But the third Little Pig. Ah, now. He was smart, resourceful, not easily beguiled. And most of all, he got up earlier than the Big Bad Wolf. He went to bed long after the wolf had fallen asleep in front of the Late Show. In other words, he worked harder than the wolf.

Moral: you may think you're the Big, Bad Wolf, but if you're not like the Third Little Pig, you're gonna get cooked.

As with every plan, it's the little things that can lose the battle; it's the small nuances of weather, terrain, non-combatants getting in the line of fire. There will always be variables over which you have no control.

In the case of Cindy's plans for Teddy – from their pillow in the dark, with crickets loudly chirping outside their open window – Clark sensed where this was all headed.

Clark gently reminded Cindy that Teddy had his own agency. "I know that."

"He's entitled to exercise that agency where accepting the gospel is concerned. Maybe," Clark speculated, "maybe Teddy's one of those souls who may not accept it in this life. Maybe he'll accept it in the Millennium."

Cindy hated it when he used doctrine on her to win an argument. No matter. She'd press ahead on her mission. Clark would just have to come through with his part (that is, if he knew what was good for him)

CHAPTER FOURTEEN

A SHOT IN THE DARK

While Clark and Cindy were having their pillow talk, Teddy was taking care of a grisly task: someone had died that very night on NCS grounds, a hunting death.

Hunting on the base was legal and allowed in certain areas, provided you had a valid Government of Guam hunting license. And provided you filled out the required military paperwork in advance: what part of the base, date and hours, with whom, what weapons and ammunition being used (make of firearm, caliber, serial number, etc.), and so on.

On this particular day Don Leonard had arranged a hunting party for himself and two friends. They were going after wild pigs. There were many herds of the beasts on NCS; many large boars had been killed in the past. Don hoped to supply a good-sized pig as the main course for a fiesta in honor of one of his Guamanian wife's relatives. A fiesta in Guam is a celebration, a picnic, a barbeque, to honor special days such as birthdays, first communion, marriages, and the like. It was a great honor for a "Statesider" to be invited inside the family circle to a fiesta.

The preferred main course for a fiesta was a whole roast pig. Don was confident they could bag a pig, but it took some planning and luck. One hunter was needed to drive the pig out of the boonies into the open ground, where Don Leonard would be waiting in his camouflaged stand with a twelve-gauge shotgun loaded with buck shot. The third man, also with a loaded shotgun, was there to back up the first shooter just in case.

Leonard's party checked in with the Officer of the Day and signed the required Navy paperwork. But the yeoman on duty forgot two things: he forgot to ask for and check for valid Guam hunting licenses. And he failed to note on the paperwork that Don was also carrying a Navy-issue Browning .45 automatic pistol strapped to his hip. The Lizard, being too cheap to buy the required Guam hunting license, created a diversion so the yeoman would overlook the technicality (and the Browning .45 automatic). All these facts later became part of Teddy's Line of Duty report.

Leonard's party signed in the log and left the watch deck around 1630 hours, riding in the Navy pickup that was perpetually signed out in his name. Driving within the base speed limit, it would take them nearly a half hour to reach Area 3-B, the most remote part of the base, but also known to harbor one especially large and mean boar hog. He was a smart one. He had eluded many other good hunters for several years now.

When Teddy arrived at the MP offices, through a window he could see the Lizard sitting alone, hunched over. He looked shrunken somewhat, smaller than his claimed three hundred pounds (official records had him weighing much more; he could have been discharged for being grossly overweight). Teddy took a deep breath and entered with Chris Pennington. Leonard made no pretense at observing military order, he didn't bother to stand or salute. Teddy let this discourtesy slide. He sat down across the table from Leonard. Pennington sat on the end between the two men and set up a tape recorder. When he was ready he nodded to Teddy.

"Tell me how it happened, Leonard, in your own words." Pennington clicked on the tape recorder and flipped open his steno pad to keep notes. Teddy officially opened his investigation. "Let the record show that the following is the voluntary verbal account of the shooting incident reported at NCS Guam, 1 December 1969, at approximately 2145 hours. I am First Lieutenant Edward Buckley, USMC Reserve, with Navy Yeoman First Class Pennington assisting. The following testimony is given by – state your full name, military rank, and so on, Leonard."

"I'm Donald Leon Leonard', Boatswain's Mate First Class, USN."

"Do you freely give this statement; you're not acting under any threats, promises or physical or mental stress?"

"Yeah, sure, I mean yes sir, I do."

"Good. And do you understand you have the right to counsel. And that you have the right to remain silent. That anything you say today may be used against you in a military or civil court proceeding later?" (Teddy read this from a newly-printed card labeled *Miranda Warning.*)

"Hey, wait a minute. That sounds like I done something criminal. I never. It was an accident pure and simple!"

"Nobody is accusing you of anything at this point. The new Navy UCMJ Regs require me to read you this warning. Do you want to proceed?"

Leonard thought for a moment. "Yeah, I guess so."

"Either you do or you don't. Which is it?"

"Yeah, let's get it over with."

"So, tell us what happened."

The facts seemed simple: The Lizard took his brother-in-law, Paul Lujan, a Guamanian civil servant employed at the Naval Station, and Paul's best friend, a man named "Dicky" (Ricardo) Cruz. Dicky owned an auto repair shop in Tamuning Village; he was reputed to be a lease hound for the Lizard. Dicky's part in their various enterprises mainly was to sniff out boonie housing whenever it became available, sign a master lease on the place, and then military personnel would then sign sub-leases with Dicky. Teddy learned that Dicky and Leonard had over fifty leases presently under their control. On the day of the hunt Paul Lujan was second shooter, backing up Leonard. Dicky was the beater. His job was to make a wide circle out through the dense jungle growth and try to drive the beasts back toward Leonard and Paul Lujan, who were concealed and waiting in a blind in some scrub brush. The two shooters waited on the far edge of a clearing across from a known trail used by wild pigs; the trail emptied into the small clearing.

The clearing was about thirty yards across; it held a small watering hole, an old bomb crater from WWII where the pigs habitually came at dusk to drink and wallow in the cool mud. Paul and Don waited in the heat and humidity swatting clouds of aggressive mosquitoes. No pigs, no Dicky, no sound of anything moving. Just the constant whining of hungry mosquitoes.

Paul became worried. What if the pigs had ambushed and injured or even killed Dicky? Pigs were capable of that. They discussed the situation. Paul insisted he should go out, circle back around the way they had come and try to find Dicky's trail, just to be sure he was okay. If he found Dicky and he was all right, Paul would fire one single shot into the air. If Dicky was hurt or in trouble, or Paul thought Dicky was lost, Paul would fire two shots. That meant Leonard should come toward the sound, fast.

Paul was gone maybe twenty minutes when Leonard heard two quick shots from Paul's twelve gauge shotgun. The Lizard got up from the blind and started to cross the clearing when he heard a noise in the brush just ahead. It had to be a pig; it was almost dark and he wasn't sure, but he fired two quick shots from his own twelve gauge in "that general direction just in case it was the big guy comin' at me. Right after the second shot I heard a scream. To me it sounded like an injured pig screaming. Then no more noise. I wanted to make sure the animal was dead before I went into the brush to see if I killed it."

"Was it dark now?

"Yeah, pretty much dark now."

"Go on…"

Leonard continued. He described how he had pulled the Navy-issue Browning .45 from his holster, at the ready. He moved carefully into the brush about ten more yards along the pig trail. He heard another noise, a crashing in the brush coming toward him, sounds of running, pounding on the trail, heavy grunting and breathing. He and Paul Lujan happened on Dicky's prone, bleeding body at the same time. "I puked my guts out right there on the spot, man. I mean, Jeez Criminy, I had just killed one of my best friends. I mean, Lord have mercy!"

"How could you know if he was dead or not?"

"He was just lyin' there face down with blood all over him and all over the bushes around him and he wasn't movin' or breathin', just still."

"I thought you said it was almost dark."

"I shined my flashlight on him. He wasn't breathin', Lieutenant." Leonard's eyes were moist with tears. Real or fake?

"Then what?"

"I left Paul with Dicky and I drove on the double in as far as the Comm

Bunker in the antenna field (highly classified communications building). I ran up to one of your Marine MPs and told him what happened. He was the one must've called you, sir."

"Just curious, what size load were you using in your twelve gauge?"

"Number one buckshot."

Lieutenant Buckley looked at Pennington to see if he had any questions or anything else to add. Pennington shook his head no. Leonard sat there head bowed, wallowing in his self pity. Suddenly Teddy felt a wave of revulsion for this pathetic slob wash over him. Teddy sucked in a breath and straightened up. "Okay, we want to keep you here overnight in the brig..."

"Hey...!" Leonard interrupted.

"...for observation and... for your own safety."

"I ain't never been in the brig before!" Leonard lied. Teddy knew from his service jacket that Leonard had indeed spent many times in lockup: drunk and disorderly, insubordination, fighting, suspected petty theft of government property, using government mail service for his own private use, you name it. He had been busted several times from Chief down to Second Class. "You think I'm gonna go and blow my own brains out just 'cause I'm depressed or somethin'?

"No, in your case we're more concerned about possible recriminations." Leonard looked blank. "I'll use simpler words: *reprisals, revenge.* By the dead man's relatives or friends. It's happened more than once with military personnel on this island."

"Sir, no disrespect, but that ain't never gonna happen to me. I'm like family to all of them. I've been here and lived among them for years. Hell, my wife's a Guamanian, as you know. I'm almost as Guamanian as anyone else on this island. I've helped every damn one of them in one way or another; ask any one of them!"

I will, thought Teddy. I will.

"Okay, Don, I'll release you on your OR. You can return home but until further order, you will be confined to your living quarters, understood?" Leonard nodded a quick yes. "And we'll also ask for that Navy-issue sidearm and the keys to the pickup." Leonard slowly handed over the keys and the Browning .45 to Pennington who made out a receipt. "Fine. Petty Officer Pennington, could you arrange a ride home for Leonard?"

After they left, Teddy's next task was to supervise the MPs and medics in recovering Dicky's pellet-riddled corpse. Dicky's family had already been notified of his death and were demanding the body be turned over to them. This was a ticklish situation; Teddy tried to explain that until he had completed his "in the line of duty" report to the Old Man, the body stayed in his custody.

How long?" He'd try to be done in two or three days; the situation was complicated due to tomorrow being Friday, then the weekend and all…

"Man, this isn't right," Dicky's brother shouted over the wailing of Dicky's widow. "That sunnuvabitch Don shoulda been the one got shot!" the brother yelled over his shoulder at Teddy as he left.

Teddy had a feeling he should post a couple of his MPs in a jeep parked right outside the Lizard's house. Just in case…

Under bright lights in the base medical clinic, naked and laid out on a metal gurney, Dicky's body looked like it had been used as a target for rifle practice. Dicky was running toward Don when he took both loads at about thirty foot range in his upper arms, torso, neck and face. Dicky never stood a chance. His pasty white skin was no longer the deep dusky brown of an island native. His now-pale skin contrasted sharply with the dark purple puncture wounds, with ugly black and blue bruises surrounding each pellet hole.

"Over forty-five pellet holes so far," the examining doctor told Teddy.

CHAPTER FIFTEEN

BOONIE BEES

With Pennington's help Teddy worked almost around the clock through the weekend to try and wrap up his Line of Duty report. He tried to stick to the facts and only the facts. Whenever he began to stray with speculative comments, Chris brought him back to the facts. There were several things that bothered Teddy about the case beside the obvious, such as Leonard's lack of a valid Guam hunting license and his carrying a Navy-issue sidearm while pig hunting. True, Don had obtained the necessary permit to hunt on the specified area of the base. Obvious also was his use of a military vehicle. Most of those factors pointed to an accident in the line of duty.

Early Monday morning Teddy submitted a preliminary draft of his report to the legal officer. Teddy concluded that, in spite of his misgivings, the bulk of the facts in the case pointed to Leonard having been in the line of duty when the accident happened. That legalism didn't matter to the man's family: Dicky was still dead. Line of Duty only mattered to the Department of the Navy.

Teddy and Jack Ford, the XO, had fallen into a routine of having coffee together on Monday mornings. Teddy filtered a copy of his report through

Jack prior to the Monday afternoon staff meeting with the Old Man. Teddy appreciated these briefings with Jack; many times already the XO had saved an inexperienced Teddy from some embarrassing incidents by being the sounding board and guiding Teddy through the office politics. Most notable was keeping CWO Baxter, the Admin Officer, Teddy's nemesis, at arm's length.

Teddy wondered why Jack had taken such a personal interest in him. "I like you, Buckley. And you never know what the future brings, do you? I mean, take this unfortunate accident right in our own back yard, as it were. One minute this Dicky fellow is running down a path in the woods, full of life. Then bang! Mowed down. In his prime. And now what's his poor widow to do, and all those children? A big family, all young kids. Pity."

Jack took a sip of his coffee and continued, as if answering a question. "No, I don't know if I'm going to stay in this Man's Navy much longer. I put in for a sea billet, command of my own ship, but I got turned down. Pentagon politics; apparently I made a few enemies at Annapolis years ago and they never forgot it. On the other hand, it never hurts to have some powerful contacts on the outside, does it? What I'm driving at, dear boy, is that I hope we can keep in touch after… I started to say after the war, but that sounds too bloody sentimental doesn't it?"

Teddy marveled that Jack continued to use the prep school jargon of his youth and a year at Oxford after so many years working closely around hardened, foul-mouthed Navy men and Marines. Jack suddenly changed the subject back to the Leonard case, but to Teddy, it was clear what Jack had been driving at, the let's-keep-in-touch part. "So, Buckley, what do you think will happen to Leonard now?"

"I don't have a lot of experience in these kinds of matters, so I couldn't say. You mean as far as any possible charges by the Guam authorities?"

"No, that won't happen. Navy has jurisdiction since it happened on base. I'm asking your recommendation of what we should do to him – this Leonard fellow? He's kind of a blot on all our personal records now…"

Teddy was beginning to see a light. It could either be a fast-moving train coming at him, crushing him if he got in its way. Or he could play ball and jump on board the train and ride along in comfort. One thing he was not sure of: what would the Old Man and the XO do with the Lizard now? He'd heard tales of men getting shipped out to obscure and highly undesirable postings literally in the middle of the night. He would not be surprised to see Leonard dealt with that way. Teddy tried to find a small portion of Christian pity in his heart for the man; it wasn't easy.

Another thing Teddy was sure of: Jack had apparently done some research on Teddy Buckley, had discovered his family's business connections, the rumored banking fortune back home in Pittsburgh. Was that the reason for the talk about keeping in touch? All his life Teddy got an uneasy feeling in his gut when people began to get too close, to try to use him for his contacts or his rumored wealth. The ironic thing was Teddy was wealthy on paper only. His wealth was all tied up in a 25-year trust. He would not have access to the trust moneys until his 25th birthday, August 25, 1972. Until then, he had to live and make do on his monthly officer's salary.

In times past whenever the fortune hunters got too close for his comfort, Teddy could escape, slip off with his drift boat and head down river. Or hike up one of his secret little Alpine streams with his light fly rod, chasing happy little brookies or native cutthroat trout. But here he was trapped. His brain ached. He felt he needed a powerful antidote to the stress, the creeping depression and loneliness that were circling him, steadily, slowly closing in. Alcohol was not the answer, not this time; too many responsibilities. Fly fishing Talofofo-style wasn't the answer either for what he was seeking.

Call it inspiration, call it desperation. He thought of Clark. He went back to his office and picked up the phone. "Clark? I need someone to talk to."

It was late afternoon when the staff meeting dispersed for breakout sessions. Clark made some excuse to need Teddy's advice on something. They slipped into a private booth in the O-Club. "A ginger ale with lime," Clark ordered.

"I'll have the same," Teddy said, surprised at himself.

Clark had gotten his undergrad degree in psychology at Brigham Young University. It was either that, or his two years as a missionary for his church. But Clark was a good listener. He asked a few questions on point. When Teddy was more or less finished, Clark took a fresh cocktail napkin and his pen and said, "I'm writing out a prescription for you."

"Good one, but may I point out you're not a doctor."

"Maybe not the traditional kind. But you might say I'm sort of a doctor for your spirit right now." He wrote, then shoved the napkin across to Teddy.

It said "Go out and find somebody who needs you."

"That's it? What the hel... I mean heck is that supposed to mean? I don't get you sometimes, man!"

Then Clark related a story he'd read about a wealthy man who felt constantly ill. The doctors didn't know what was wrong with him and no treatments seemed to help. He couldn't snap out of his constant miserable feelings. So he went to see a new doctor. The new doctor examined the businessman. Then he wrote out a prescription: go out and find someone who needs you. This man was a huge success in business; he thought the doctor was a quack. He left in a huff. In the elevator going down, he pulled the prescription out of his pocket, ready to throw it in the trash. Then he thought for a minute. He'd paid top dollar for that doctor's advice; maybe he should give it a try. So he went out on the street in New York City to try and find someone who needed him.

His route back to his office took him through Grand Central Station. There he saw a young woman sitting in a corner, weeping, looking quite miserable. He stopped and asked her what the matter was. She was too embarrassed to answer, but he kept quietly asking if he could help. He finally got her story. The young woman was from out of town; she was supposed to meet her mother, but alone, confused, she didn't know what to do. She had been waiting for her mother in Grand Central for two days, no mother. It turned out she was in the wrong train station. Her worried mother had been waiting all this time for her in Penn Station!

The businessman went out, bought the girl some flowers and something to eat. Then he arranged for his personal limousine to drive her across town where the two women were reunited. He called his doctor and said, "You know, doc, that formula really works. I feel much better already!"

"So you're saying I'm self-centered?" Teddy asked.

"No more so than anyone else."

"What, then?"

"This may sound corny, but have you ever experienced giving of yourself, in the Christian sense?"

"Oh, the mission thing again?"

"Sort of, kind of… the same principle, but on a scale that fits your time and place. Do what you can for others here and now."

"I'll think about it."

"I have an idea," Clark said. "I'm involved in a little community service project that could include you. What are you doing Saturday? I'll pick you up at 7:30 A.M. Wear some old work clothes. Do you have a pair of work gloves?"

Clark drove them past a shiny new church situated on a hill near the Naval Air Station. It was solidly built of cinder block, painted a sparkling white with ochre and olive green trim. The grounds all around were newly landscaped and clear of trash. "That's our new ward building."

"Pretty nice looking."

They drove on to the village of Agat. A few minutes later they pulled up in front of a World War II surplus Quonset hut, set back from the road. The lot it sat on and the gravel path leading up to the front door were overgrown with wild grass and weeds taller than Teddy. There was a hand-painted sign beside the door with some writing that looked to Teddy like Chinese characters. They stopped in front, next to three other vehicles. A party of Statesiders in work grubbies piled out of the other cars, gardening tools in hand - rakes, hoes, shovels. "What's this?" Teddy asked.

"The prescription for your case of the blues," Clark grinned.

Teddy followed Clark up to the entry door. He read the small subtitle in English written on the sign below the large lead type of Chinese characters: KOREAN BAPTIST CHURCH – AGAT TOWN GUAM. In spite of, or perhaps because of the conflict in Vietnam, Guam was experiencing an explosion of new construction: new apartments, homes, hotels, offices, roads, schools. A second invasion of Guam was underway –American-style development. There would soon follow strip malls with fast-food places and movie theaters. The sleepy little island was being transformed into another American suburb.

The construction companies were rushing to get the jobs done. They hired many contract laborers from the Philippines and Korea. The workers slaved around the clock, sometimes working double shifts, glad for the work, grateful for the extra money to send home to help their impoverished families. The work left no time for play, and, for the faithful, little time for church. There was no time for these workers to volunteer for cleanup projects around their humble little church. In stepped the Mormon work party.

Clark introduced Teddy to the other guys. He was surprised to see CWO Baxter in the group. Teddy learned Clark was something called their Elder's Quorum president. He was learning that Mormons were an organized bunch. Clark gathered the men around and assigned someone to say a prayer. The prayer was short and asked the Lord to bless them with strength to perform their service to this little congregation of their brothers and sisters (that was a new concept to Teddy). The prayer also asked for safety from harm or accident (that was useful, Teddy thought).

Clark checked to see if one of the brethren assigned had gotten the required burn permit from the village. Burn permit? "We need to burn down the weeds first," Clark explained. "That gets rid of the rats, any snakes that might possibly be living here… and the boonie bees."

Teddy had heard of boonie bees – much like their cousin the wasp. But boonie bees could sting you multiple times and still live to sting again. They had a nasty sting that raised huge welts. Their poison could make even a large, strong man sick for awhile.

A crowd of curious neighbors began gathering. A few brought their own tools and offered to help out. Later, after the smoke and ash had been sprayed with a garden hose and settled down, the party set to work. In two hours they had the place clean, if not exactly sparkling, inside and out. Teddy got stung by a boonie bee twice on the back of his neck. A neighbor lady offered a home remedy to put on the sting: some aloe juice from a live plant in her garden. In a few minutes he was feeling better, if not totally healed.

It was nearly noon when the Mormon elders, neighbors, and a few of the Korean parishioners who'd shown up with their pastor all sat down to rest. They were sweaty, sooty, stung and tired. Several cars pulled up and out came Cindy Tanner and several Mormon women carrying picnic lunch. Everyone was invited to join in the feast. The Korean pastor was invited to say grace on the food after it was spread. They ate and talked and laughed among themselves. New friendships were made.

Teddy was amazed at the transformation: not only did the cleanup enhance the building and the neighborhood, he could detect a palpable spirit in the air, but he wasn't quite sure what it was. Christmas was coming soon - maybe that was it.

Clark sat down on the curb next to Teddy. "Well…?"

"You know, I just realized it's almost Christmas." Teddy grinned.

As the work party was breaking up, Cindy found Teddy and pulled him by his elbow. "Come with me; there's someone I want you to meet." Teddy sensed a set-up. Cindy led him to a group of ladies who were cleaning up the last of the picnic. Cindy had singled out Mary Emma Penrod as a possible match for Teddy. Emma, as she was known to the Mormon congregation, was a contract teacher for Gov Guam, partway through her teaching contract. She wasn't a knockout beauty - Cindy admitted there was room for some *slight* improvements on Emma. But since she was one of the two eligible single Mormon girls, in Cindy's opinion, Emma would have to do. "Teddy Buckley, this is Emma Penrod."

When Teddy got back to the BOQ, he found a note from Pennington waiting for him. It read: LEONARD WAS SHIPPED OUT LAST NIGHT TO PATROL BOAT IN MEKONG. HOUSE TORCHED TO GROUND. NOBODY HURT.

CHAPTER SIXTEEN

CHRISTMAS CHEER

After he cleaned up and changed into comfortable civvies Teddy checked out a pickup from motor pool and drove down island to the Navy Exchange and Commissary. He had some personal things he needed, including some Christmas cards. This would be the first time he could ever remember sending cards. He also wanted to get a few things to bring to the Tanners' Christmas dinner party. While Cindy was introducing him to Emma, she had skillfully invited both of them to the Tanner home for Christmas dinner. After the Thanksgiving fiasco he couldn't say no.

Teddy was now good friends with the guy who managed the sporting goods department at Navex. Teddy had been thinking for some time about a trip to Japan in April for some much-needed R&R. He had heard a few rumors about possible trout fishing in Japan. His reading lately only fueled the rumors and he was determined to check it out for himself.

Bernie, the sporting goods manager, confirmed to Teddy that indeed there *was* trout fishing in Japan, good trout fishing in some places. One big problem: most good streams were private waters, owned outright, or leased out for years in advance by the numerous Japanese fly-fishing clubs. You had to be a member or a close relative or really good friend or business client of a member. But there was one possibility. Bernie had heard it was possible to pay a rod fee or to rent a beat for a day or two through a recognized local guide. He said he'd check it out and report back if he learned anything interesting. Teddy thanked him then began looking at the latest shipment of new rods.

"Here's one I think is just right for you, from what you've told me about your fishing style and Japanese streams" Bernie said. He handed Teddy a nice little fiber glass rod. Teddy flexed the little rod. It was seven and a half feet in length, a five-weight two-piece, made by the South Bend Company. It was very flexible with a slow action best suited for casting dry flies with small tippets, he judged. Its action felt similar to one of his favorite bamboo rods back home: his H.L. Leonard Catskill Model 39H. He missed his bamboo rods. He put the rod down and asked Bernie to accept a deposit to hold it for him for a few weeks. "No problem, sir."

Teddy walked across the broad parking lot to the Commissary. He was amazed to find a heap of fresh-cut Christmas trees in front. He bent down and breathed in the sweet spicy scent of Douglas fir. Several families were busy picking out their perfect tree. He showed his military ID card, took a basket and started pushing it randomly around the store; he had no idea what he was looking for.

The big military grocery store was designed more like a self-serve, no-frills warehouse. Teddy wondered if American grocery stores would ever adopt this format as a way to increase their profit margins. Inside he savored the air-conditioned atmosphere. The semi-dark, cool cavernous store was packed. Many shoppers were simply pushing carts around, not really buying - a few moments respite from the scalding heat and humidity outside. Probably a good half of the shoppers were islanders, civil servants with one of the coveted perks: a commissary card - status and privilege. When they shopped the commissary the entire family shopped: dad, mom, grandmas down to the youngest kid, pushing three, maybe four carts. By the time they reached the checkout lanes, the shopping carts would be piled high with bags of Japanese sticky rice (the preferred kind), gallon jugs of Kikkoman soy sauce, frozen whole chickens, and a recent invention: disposable diapers, institutional-sized bales of them!

At other times Teddy was bothered by this, such as when he remembered all the similar commodities piled on the shelves of the little country store in Talofofo. He remembered "Mong mong!" and he laughed. Hey, it's Christmas. Cut them some slack.

What the heck. He piled his cart with the same items to give as Christmas gifts to the married guys in his platoon with young families and small incomes. Hey, it's Christmas.

Christmas Eve Teddy stopped by the Tanners to leave a gift and wish them a happy Christmas. He spotted a red Datsun coupe parked behind the Tanners' old Volvo wagon. As he stepped out of the motor pool van he was met by a strong wind whipping up a fury. Typhoon coming? Cindy met him at the door, very chirpy. "Come in, we've been expecting you." Teddy followed her inside and soon met the owner of the red Datsun coupe. "Teddy, you remember Mary Emma Penrod?"

Mary Emma, as she liked to be called, was a nice enough girl, pleasant, soft (translated: slightly plump), with kind, smiling eyes. She seemed perfectly at ease meeting Teddy again; she was experienced at meeting people, he guessed. Teddy assumed she was single; this was another set-up by Cindy, no doubt about it. After they were seated and Cindy supplied Teddy a cup of Christmas punch – Mormon style, no alcohol - Mary Emma started the conversation. "So, I understand you're in the Marines?" Cindy had briefed her. How thoroughly, he wondered.

"That's true, ma'am."

"Oh, it's 'ma'am'?"

Teddy laughed at his faux pas. "What am I supposed to call you?"

"My students all call me 'teacher'."

Teddy wasn't surprised - she fit his image of the single, spinster-ish teacher. "What do you teach?"

"I teach typing and office skills at Dededo Junior High. I came here under a two-year contract with Gov Guam." (Anyone who'd been on the island for any time shortened the title.)

"How long have you been on the island? Do you like it – teaching?"

"Yes, I love it. I'm halfway through my second year."

"Will you re-up?" (Teddy reverted to the military slang for *re-enlist*.)

"I don't know. It depends…" her voice trailed off.

This is a sad girl, he thought. He changed the subject. "Where do you come from – in the States?"

"Utah."

"I should have guessed," he laughed, as he shot a look at Cindy. He was trying to convey *I hate being set up.* Cindy maintained an innocent smile.

"Cindy tells me you're from Pittsburgh," Mary Emma said.

"Originally…my family still lives there, all of them, mom, dad, brother, married sister, grandparents, uncles, aunts, cousins. Have done for generations. Me, I've mostly been out West since right after high school." Why was he giving so much personal information to this stranger? These Mormons had good social skills; they seem to instinctively know how to put a stranger at ease.

"What do… I mean, what *did* you do? Before the Marines?"

Teddy had a strong feeling she already knew his CV, thanks to Cindy, and possibly Clark, too. He played along; what could be the harm? He wasn't really leading the girl on, was he? Outside the wind was intensifying in force and strength. It moaned through the cracks around the window sills. "I mostly guided. You know, a river guide?" She looked blank. "Fly fishing. I was out of Jackson Hole in the summer. In the winter it was Patagonia for the same thing, only everything was turned upside down, you know, the seasons."

"I *love* the Patagonia! I was there for part of my mission!"

Oh, no. He groaned inside. Not another female missionary. Did they go on missions if they didn't get an offer of marriage? Or did they really feel a commitment? He had come to terms somewhat with Z's fervor and commitment. He knew his friend well enough to know Zack would not fake a thing as serious as a mission for two whole years. How could you go through all the stuff that was asked of you and keep a head fake going for that long?

Suddenly the power went off. Nobody panicked, everyone was used to power outages on Guam, an every-day occurrence somewhere on the island. "I'll get the candles," Clark volunteered.

They stopped speaking momentarily, conversation interrupted as they adjusted their eyes to the darkness. Above the howling wind there were suddenly several loud thumping sounds on the tin roof of the Tanners' hut. "What's that?" Teddy's voice came out of the darkness.

"Avocados falling from our tree." Cindy's voice.

"They sound like really big ones."

"They're about the size of cocoanuts - one of them makes almost an entire meal. I have discovered so many new avocado recipes. You really should take some home."

"Where would I keep them?" Teddy asked.

An aura of light shimmered down the hallway toward them. Clark, his arm extended, looking like some specter from a grade-B horror film, carried a tall candle. It gave off a lot of light, Teddy noticed.

"Maybe now you can see the gift I brought." Teddy wanted to escape; the soft light could give a single girl ideas. Chris Pennington helped Teddy pick out a nice book of art for the Tanner's coffee table — or whatever substitute name Mormons give a coffee table.

"How sweet!" Cindy gushed. "Isn't that just sweet of him to give this thoughtful gift to us, Mary Emma?"

"It's perfectly beautiful," she agreed.

Cindy pushed aside a big, black leather-bound Bible (he naturally assumed it was a Bible) to make room for his new offering.

"I hate to run," Teddy said, "but I'm sort of on duty tonight. Big drinking night and all that, so…" He saw the surprised looks on their faces. "Oh, no, I didn't mean for me, I'm on duty and my MPs will have their hands full all night long…" They all looked relieved.

"No, you can't leave until you have some of my special Christmas cake," Cindy insisted..

"It really is good cake," Clark offered. "In fact, it's her special best." Cindy blew Clark a kiss.

This is getting too gooey, Teddy thought. "I hope you all don't think me rude if I eat it on the road."

"Well, okay," she pouted. She had this pout thing down really well, Teddy noted.

Teddy escaped with a large slice of her special cake on a paper plate, wrapped in a napkin; it felt very heavy for just one slice of cake. Good thing it was dark so he couldn't see what he was eating. He had two aging spinster aunts who competed every Christmas to see who could make the best mince tarts, or fruit cake, or whatever. He always had to graciously choke down their spicy offerings. Every year as the aunts aged and their taste buds degenerated, the spice content got heavier.

To please Cindy, Teddy took a tentative bite. The cake seemed to be full of nuts and raisins and some other fruit he couldn't identify. It was laced heavily with ground cloves and other spices. He quickly determined what the fruit was: the cake was packed with those candied citrus fruity chunks that Teddy didn't like. "Oh, great… fruitcake!" He got a couple of blocks away and chucked it out the window. Maybe some boonie critter would eat it.

Sometime after midnight one of his men woke him. "Sir? Sir, sorry, sir, but we need you in the office. Soon as you can, sir." He groped for his pants and shirt, still not awake.

When he got there, two of his Marines with MP armbands were applying first aid to three of his other men. The three were pretty banged up with cuts, bruises, swollen lumps on their faces, bloody knuckles. He didn't need to ask what happened. They were in a fight and either alcohol or a girl, or both, had been involved. "Want to tell me about it?" The bloodied ones averted their eyes. One of the MPs spoke up.

"Sir, well it was like this, sir. They was attacked by a gang of civilians – islanders plus some Statesiders. They had to use physical force to defend their selfs. It's all in our official report right here, sir." He handed the report to Teddy.

Teddy scanned it then howled with laughter. "Is this true, private?" He pointed to the one with the bandage-swathed head.

"Damn straight, sir." The private didn't look Teddy in the eye but stared at the floor.

"*Eighteen* civilians against just you three? Amazing. How did you have time to count them, I mean defending yourselves and all…?"

One of the other combatants piped in. "Well, we had some help from a few Squids, sir." (*Squid* being Marine slang for sailors.)

"Unh huh… a 'few' you say? How many's a few? And why didn't you put that in your report, corporal?"

The MP shrugged and looked away. "Didn't think it mattered if the Squids got credit or not."

Teddy stepped squarely in front of the corporal. "Let me see your hands, corporal." The man showed the palms. "I mean the backs of them."

"Your permission, sir, I'd rather not."

"The backs of your hands, corporal. That's a direct order." The MP reluctantly showed Teddy his palms again. "Other side. I want to see your knuckles." Then to the other MP, "You show 'em, too." All four hands were skinned and bleeding. Teddy chuckled. "So you guys got in a fight at the Surf Club in town. *All* of you were involved. Plus some civilians. Plus some sailors. Plus MPs, who are supposed to be *keeping* the peace."

"And some Air Force guys too!" the third injured Marine chimed in. The others tried to shut him up. Too late.

Teddy looked at his slippers and pondered for a full minute before speaking. He struggled to look grave and official. "All right, this better be the last time anything like this happens, hear? Get cleaned up. And Ramirez…?"

"Sir…?" The head bandaged one responded.

"Get yourself to sick bay right now and get that bite on your ear looked at. I hope the guy… or was it a girl…?"

The others howled with laughter. "It was a girl, sir!" someone confessed.

"Shut up!" Ramirez shouted, which only made them all laugh harder.

"Well I hope *she* didn't have rabies… or some other horrible disease," Teddy snickered.

The men snapped to attention as Teddy left. He stopped outside the door and left it open a crack to eavesdrop. When the teasing of Ramirez and the laughter subsided, Teddy heard someone say "For an officer, he's one cool son of a…." He closed the door and smiled to himself.

A fresh Christmas dawn was breaking over Guam. Red light streaked through the clouds to the east. As Teddy walked back to his room in the BOQ he heard "Hey Jude" blaring from the enlisted barracks across the quad. Merry Christmas, he thought.

CHAPTER SEVENTEEN

DEATH BY ANTIBIOTIC

Other than a few more bloodied noses and skinned knuckles, the 1970 New Year dawned without further incident. Teddy's parents back home were well, judging from his mother's annual *A Christmas Message from the Buckleys.* He was embarrassed by his mother's references to "Teddy valiantly serving his country in the cause of peace." No question her sentiments were well-meant. He had some doubts about her praises; he didn't feel they were deserved. He was a long way away from any fighting, any danger. He thought about Dicky Cruz's unfortunate death. Heck, a guy could get killed just as easily by his best friend in a freak hunting accident as by a Viet Cong sniper.

As for the war itself, he kept his personal views private; he did not have the luxury of expressing opinions, except in confidence with Clark or Chris. However, his doubts about the war in Vietnam were fed and nourished constantly by what he heard and observed around him every day. Daily, truckloads of bombs - two-hundred-pounders, five-hundred-pounders - rolled steadily past NCS on the back road bound for the B-52s at Andersen Air Force Base, and, ultimately, Vietnam.

About every other day the massive B-52 bombers took off from

Andersen, flew their long-range missions to targets somewhere in the jungles of 'Nam, then returned twenty-four hours later. You could feel the ground quake for miles around when the bombers took off - the ground literally shook under your feet and dishes rattled. The first time he felt it, Teddy thought he was in an earthquake. Clark said the noise was so loud that as far away as the Mormon chapel near Naval Air Station, people preaching sermons or saying prayers had to stop until the noise subsided.

And it didn't help much when he and Chris Pennington had discussions about the war. "A freakin' waste of money, not to mention the lives lost or ruined on both sides," Chris said vehemently. (He actually used much stronger language.) That was always Chris's bottom line.

Somehow Teddy had missed the protest movement in his college career; Montana State was not exactly a hotbed of revolutionaries. Oh, there were a few mild demonstrations at MSU, very low-key, which nobody really took notice of. Teddy was too occupied chasing girls, playing Rugby or hockey, or off somewhere fly fishing. Then it was cram, cram, cram for midterms or finals.

An incident in early January involving a newly-arrived Navy enlisted man brought the war to the forefront of Teddy's consciousness. The young Seaman, Brian Dodge (unfortunate last name, Teddy mused), had been ordered to stand trial in a Summary Court Martial. Seaman Dodge, as was his right under the UCMJ, requested that Teddy, an officer, defend him. Teddy dug into the facts of the case in his usual thorough fashion.

Dodge could have been written up on report under a "non-judicial" section of the UCMJ. In other words, his case could have been handled at the weekly tribunal called "Captain's Mast," which was not a trial, nor even a court-martial. Petty, lesser offenses like fighting, disobeying a senior person, drunken and disorderly, etc. were the usual matters brought to Captain's Mast on Monday mornings. But the senior command at NCS wanted to make an example out of Dodge, so they decided on a Summary Court Martial. That would send a message to the troops that things were tightening up around here.

Dodge was officially charged for violating a section of the UCMJ for "causing self-inflicted bodily harm in order to avoid duty." Dodge had swallowed an entire bottle of sixty-one erythromycin tablets in a pathetic suicide attempt.

"Why'd you do it, Dodge?" Teddy started out in his interview, getting right to the heart of the matter.

"I wanted to kill myself."

"Why did you want to do that?"

"I hate being in the Navy; I hate everything about it."

"Does that include me?"

"No, sir. Sorry."

"Why'd you join?" (Teddy already knew what the answer would be; it was fairly telling about the times they were living in.)

"I didn't have any options. I was in graduate school almost finished with my doctorate. My lottery number came up and my draft board had no sympathy for what they called draft-dodging college boys. I got a draft notice; I didn't want to die in some stinking jungle. I hate this war."

"You said that. Why didn't you move to Canada? Lots of guys like you are doing that." Dodge didn't answer. "Or, you could have registered as a CO." A shrug. This guy was a hard case. Teddy knew what fate awaited men like Dodge.

"This Summary Court Martial will convene," Jack Ford, the Executive Officer and number two in command barked. "Seaman Dodge, you have been charged under a section of the Uniform Code of Military Justice with willfully inflicting bodily harm upon yourself in order to avoid duty. The record will show that upon Seaman Dodge's request, First Lieutenant Edward Buckley, US Marine Corps, is representing the defendant. Seaman Dodge, do you wish to make any statements for the record before we proceed by way of excuse or mitigation of the charges?"

"Seaman Dodge, please stand to address the court," Pennington directed.

Dodge stood. "No, sir."

"Then the court will enter into the record that Seaman Dodge has entered a plea of not guilty. Is that correct, Dodge?"

"Yes, sir."

"Yeoman Pennington, who is acting as clerk of these proceedings will now read the charges in the report." Pennington read the lengthy report where Dodge was charged with the violation. It also set forth all of the details as reported and signed by the duty officer that particular night in question. When he concluded, Pennington told Dodge "You may be seated."

Jack now spoke to Teddy, "Mr. Buckley, do you wish to question any of the facts in the incident report that was just read into the record of these proceedings?" Teddy declined. "Then you may now put on your evidence."

Teddy did his duty; he did his best to put on a good defense and give Dodge a shot at a lesser charge. Teddy called the senior medical officer at NCS as his first and only witness. He was sworn in and Teddy began. "Doctor Levine, I show you what has been marked as Defendant's Exhibit One. Could you identify this?" Pennington handed Dr. Levine a clear plastic bag marked "Def Ex One," containing a brown plastic pill vial.

"Yes. This is an empty prescription bottle for ninety capsules of the drug erythromycin. The patient's name on the prescription is Seaman Brian Dodge."

Teddy continued, "Did you or someone under your command prescribe the drug erythromycin to Seaman Dodge?"

"Yes."

Teddy tendered the exhibit and it was accepted into evidence. Teddy continued.

"What is the drug erythromycin?"

"It's a mild-level antibiotic. It is frequently used as a common substitute for people with allergies to penicillin."

"What does it do if taken in large doses, the physical effects on the body?"

Doctor Levine laughed. "In layman's terms, you'll get a bad case of the runs."

"Could you put that in medical terms, doctor?"

"Yes. In medical terms, it could cause diarrhea."

"And that's all? Can it cause death?"

Doctor Levine laughed again. "Death...? No... Maybe a bad headache."

"That's the worst of any injury to the human body?"

"Yes."

"What's the normal prescribed dosage of this drug?"

"It depends on the nature of the patient's illness. For Dodge, I think he was suffering from strep throat, if memory serves. The dosage on this bottle says one capsule three times daily."

"In your expert medical opinion, did Seaman Brian Dodge physically harm himself in any way, did he inflict any harm to his own body, when he ingested sixty-one capsules of the drug erythromycin all at the same time, and did that act thereby make him incapable of performing his military duties?"

"No."

"No further questions. We rest, sir," he said to Jack.

The court martial was held before a single officer as judge: Jack Ford. Seaman Dodge's fate was now entirely in Jack's hands at this point. "This court is in recess while I consider the matter," Jack said.

Jack Ford deliberated barely three minutes, just long enough to smoke half of a Lucky Strike cigarette. He jammed the butt in the ashtray and returned exhaling a blue cloud. Jack got right to it. "Seaman Brian Dodge, you are hereby found guilty as charged. As punishment you are fined one month's pay. You are hereby demoted one pay grade to Seaman Apprentice. You are confined to the base for one month. And you will serve forty hours of extra duty. Is that clear? Any questions or statements you'd care to make?"

Dodge didn't wince; his expression was blank as he stared straight ahead, past Ford. Teddy had warned Dodge to just keep his mouth shut, act humble and penitent, just take his medicine, no pun intended. But Dodge could not resist one last shot at the Establishment. "Yes, Commander Ford. How do I appeal?"

Jack went red. "This court is adjourned!"

"Attention on deck!" Chris barked, as Jack stormed out.

Within an hour, Dodge filed his own hand-written appeal. He was summarily shipped out during the following night to a Navy submarine tender in the Gulf of Tonkin.

CHAPTER EIGHTEEN

DREAMING OF FLY FISHING MT. FUJI

The same night Dodge was shipped out, Teddy woke up at two-thirty with severe pains in his lower back. He had a powerful thirst and a wave of nausea swept over him. He needed to get to the bathroom - and fast- before he puked all over his bed and himself. He swung his legs over the edge of the bed and stood. That's the last he remembered before everything went black and he fell to the linoleum-tiled floor in a heap. He awoke a day and a half later in the hospital on the hill by COMNAVMAR with catheters stuck in both arms. He rang for a nurse; a Navy corpsman rushed into his room.

"Sir…?"

"What am I doing here? I don't remember…"

"You blacked out. Someone found you face down in a pool of vomit, unconscious. We ran some tests and they found you had some serious kidney stones. You've had surgery to remove them, they were that large - and serious, sir."

"Just how serious is… *serious*?"

"They were truly life-threatening, sir. I'd say that's serious enough for emergency surgery."

"Other than when I was born, and had the end of my you-know-whats-it cut off, this is the first time I've had any surgery. Funny…"

"Sir?"

"I don't feel a thing."

"Right now you're heavily sedated with pain killers."

"Legal drugs, huh? How long do I get to keep this high going?" Teddy laughed hysterically at his own drug-induced joke.

"Not sure, sir, maybe up to a week, maybe more. Depends…"

"How long have I been out?"

"About forty-eight hours."

Teddy lay back on the cool sheets and waves of darkness and heavy sleep engulfed him again. A little later that evening Brooks, his company sergeant, his second in command, came in to brief Teddy and assure him things were running smoothly. Teddy was awake, barely. He had refused his dinner; looking at the institutional food gave him nausea again. "The men, they're pulling for you, sir. We all hope you get back to work real soon."

"Yeah, I'll bet they want me back real soon. While the cat's away and all that."

"No bull, sir."

"Well thanks. Tell them all thanks."

The Navy doctors wanted Teddy up and moving around as soon as it was medically prudent. They didn't need to worry, as he was very eager to find some activity between the morphine-induced periods of blackness. Convalescence turned Teddy's familiar schedule, his routine, upside down. He slept all day and was awake all night, it seemed. He walked the deserted, dimly-lit halls, slowly increasing his speed until he almost felt normalcy returning to his legs and feet. The wound and stitches in his back were driving him crazy with itching. He wished they could do something about that. His room was around the corner from the ICU ward. Around the corner the other direction, through double doors, was the maternity ward and nursery. He could hear the muffled cries of the newborn babies.

The first night on his feet he could only walk as far as the night nurse's desk that divided the wards, then it was back to his room, rest awhile, then repeat.

During the second night of his walking therapy, when he reached the nurse's desk, he was close enough to the ICU ward he thought he could hear men moaning, even screaming. Maybe he imagined it, he wasn't really sure. A lot of really weird stuff was going through his head now, both while he was asleep and awake.

Teddy took the turn to the right this time, on through the double doors, to the maternity ward. He was curious; he wanted to see the newborn babies. A young couple was straining to see through the large glass windows. Curious, Teddy shuffled as close as he dared, hanging back a discreet distance. He could hear them talking. The conversation was strange. He thought he overheard them say things like:

Man: "She has a large nose. And she's awfully red."

Woman: "Her nose is no bigger than normal. And her color is normal for newborn babies."

Man: "Are you sure we're ready for this?"

Woman: "Emotionally I'm prepared; I'm just not ready to bring her home yet. This happened so fast; she wasn't due for three more weeks, remember? You need to go to the BX tomorrow and get things, disposables, blankets, formula and bottles, lots of things." She looked up at him with tear-filled eyes, unable to speak. He nodded. They embraced and walked back toward her room hugging each other close.

An orderly passing by saw Teddy. "Those folks are Navy. They just had a brand-new baby girl. Ain't she precious?"

The third night while walking, Teddy was now certain he heard someone screaming, but this time it was a different pitch, a different voice, higher. Teddy stopped and asked the night nurse, a young Seaman/Hospital Corpsman, if he was imagining, or did he just hear someone scream out. Was that somebody who was seriously injured?

"Yes, sir, you're right. They come in here almost every day from 'Nam. Those guys in there…" he inclined his head toward the ICU. "They're all pretty well shot up bad."

"How bad? I mean, will they live, any of them, or is it hopeless?"

"Some will. We hope all. We do our best to try and help 'em. But, you never know. There's two MediVac flights a week going stateside. The ones that make it in here for the first twenty-four hours or so, we rotate out on the MediVac."

"The ones who don't? Make it…?"

"Body bags. They go home on a different flight."

Teddy let that sink in. "Okay if I have a look? I'm not being morbid or anything. I just… all of a sudden I *feel* something and I really need to know…"

"I think I know what you mean, sir. Sure, it's okay. I'll show you, but don't touch anything. And here, put on this mask."

The rooms in ICU were darkened. For Teddy it was the most surreal thing he had ever experienced. There were two patients in the first room. Both were hooked up to IVs and monitoring machines. Humming or blipping sounds came steadily from the machines. But the machines could not drown out the low moans coming from the men. And hovering over everything was the smell of burned or rotting flesh.

One patient, an unconscious Marine, lay under a white sheet, his torso clearly outlined in relief and visible in the low light. The outline ended right below where his waist should have been. Then… his body just ended. There was nothing below - he was legless. Teddy, who never cried, found hot tears flowing down his cheeks. Here he was, he realized, standing on two perfectly good, strong legs. He was free to move about, at will, under his own power. And this poor guy, if he lived…well, he'd never be the same man. Never mind the enormous obstacles of coping with the loss of limbs: what about the trauma, the scars on his soul and the irreparable harm to his psyche?

Suddenly, Teddy felt an overwhelming sense of anger and guilt. Guilt because he had taken his ROTC training in college so lightly. Back then, it was just a lark, a great big joke. Something to kid about. Guilt, that by now wearing his country's uniform, he somehow shared in the responsibility for this young man's tragedy.

Guilt, because unlike some other students, he had never spoken up in one particular poly sci class when his professor had pronounced the war in Vietnam as illegal, wrong by every tenet of international law.

Guilt, because Teddy had looked the other way at all the mild demonstrations at MSU, somewhat embarrassed by this public display of emotion, commitment to a cause.

Guilt, because when he was happily floating the Snake or Madison with a rich fly-fishing client, he was sucking up for a fat tip; never once giving the war a thought, never thinking about the other young men his age bleeding and dying in the jungles..

Guilt, because he had never taken a public position on a war that deep in his heart he *knew* was immoral, was wrong. Dear God in heaven, he asked, what are we doing to these boys?

"Is he going to make it?"

"From all of his life signs it looks like he'll die sometime later tonight. His body is going through the classic steps of shutting down, of dying. Sorry, sir."

"Yeah, me, too. So sorry." Teddy stood humbly at the foot of the unknown dying Marine and silently wept.

Teddy's own recovery was set back when his incision developed infection. His Navy doctor apologized, as if it was personally his fault. "Hard as we try, this damn climate causes more post-operative infections than other places I know. We'll keep you here on antibiotics and watch you for a few days more."

"Can you prescribe me some erythromycin?" Teddy inquired.

"What...? Why that? It won't do much good for your particular brand of infection. Are you allergic to penicillin?"

"No. Sorry, it was just a private joke." That must have sounded pretty weird, Teddy thought, as the doctor continued his rounds.

Teddy's sleep patterns began to return to semi-normal. But he was having some interesting dreams. When he was awake he thought about the dreams. He began to think deeply. He thought about his home and the family he grew up with. How had that influenced his life to the point that he had become quite single-minded about his great passion: fly-fishing? Did other people consider him shallow or selfish because of his obsession with fly-fishing?

He then thought about Marley Durrant and her close relationship to her father. What went on in that home while she was growing up to make her that way and to make her close to a parent she liked to be with, that she so obviously loved?

Did he really love his own parents, compared to the way she loved hers? He had to admit that he had never been close to his parents and his two siblings. He chalked that up to all the time spent at prep schools, away from the influences of home. And then there were all the summers growing up when he was sent out West alone.

Teddy had never wanted for any of the physical comforts of life. He had been provided anything he ever wanted, within reason. He was given lavish gifts for Christmas and birthdays, whether he wanted them or not. He ate well, never went without food; the cook saw to that. He never walked or rode a bus or a bike like other boys; he was driven everywhere by a hired driver in a big, expensive car. Until he finally escaped to Jackson, where the uniform was jeans and fishing shirts, he had never bought his own clothes. They just somehow appeared, neatly laid out on his bed by the maid, fresh from their boxes proudly bearing the logo of Brooks Brothers Boys Department, Madison Avenue, New York City. He still remembered the Navy blazers, tweed sports coats and flannel slacks; the button down shirts and striped repp ties; the serious Navy pin-striped suit and cordovan wing tip brogues. All were exact miniature versions of his father's and grandfather's wardrobes.

He never had to ask for money; from the time he could remember he had a weekly allowance with no accountability as to how he spent it. Each year on his birthday the allowance was increased to meet his growing needs and wants as a fledgling consumer.

He personally was never required to give donations to the poor or to charitable organizations. That detail was all handled in a businesslike, serious manner in early January each year by the family's *suits*, the small army of accountants, lawyers and trust officers from the bank. In fact, he realized, he wouldn't know how to even begin to give charitable alms. Charity was on his mind as he remembered Clark saying something about how he and Cindy gave ten percent of everything he made to their church. Teddy's reaction to that was ten percent is a pretty big chunk from anyone's wallet. How did Clark manage, and, the bigger question, *why* does he do it?

Clark said it was not a question of money; it all had to do with faith. Teddy didn't get that one, but still he thought about it.

He began to think about the kind of family he wanted to have - that is, if he ever got married. She would have to be pretty at least - not necessarily a beauty, but pretty, pleasant to look at. He tried to imagine Marley Durrant with gray hair and a few wrinkles. She still looked pretty in his mind.

Teddy began to form feelings about children, something he had never once thought about. How many is the right size of family? He was afraid his thinking had been strongly influenced by the many fly-fishing and guiding friends he had. As a bunch, you had to admit they were not very stable. In fact, most of them were downright self-centered and flaky; without some drastic attitude changes, they were definitely not family material.

A sense of sadness almost bordering on what he thought might be depression began to envelop Teddy. He determined he'd better think about other things, like fly fishing. All these deep thoughts he was having started to worry him. He was not a serious guy but just the opposite. He considered himself as a pretty well-adjusted, happy person, optimistic about the future.

Still, he knew he was almost in his mid-twenties and after his military hitch, then what? He had to start making some plans for the future, however sketchy they may be at this point. He was beginning to question if he wanted to be a fly-fishing guide the rest of his life. Why not own a fly-fishing shop in some place like Jackson, or Ennis or Twin Bridges, Montana or even in the Teton Valley of Idaho just over the pass from Jackson? He had always liked the little town of Victor, Idaho. Land was really cheap on the Idaho side of the Tetons, away from Jackson Hole. He could pick up a small spread with a stream running through it, a feeder creek that finally emptied into the Teton River. In his mind he could really see the place. It cheered him up somewhat. He'd just have to be patient and see what happened in a year or so and fill in the details then.

One thing for sure: he was not going to be a lawyer, accountant, or a banker, professions his parents had expressed hope he would enter some day. He refused to be tied down to a desk, wearing a suit and tie. That would drive him crazy in less than a month. He doubted he had the temperament for law school or an MBA program leading to the banking profession. Besides, he had guided too many of those professional dudes. All they seemed to talk about was the price of their rod or reel, the name brands, how much money they made, where they lived, or what kind of cars they drove and how many were parked in their garages. The vast majority of them couldn't cast a fly worth a tinker's damn. The worst seemed to be the accountants: keeping score: How many fish caught? How big?

Teddy always had to look the other way and avoid the eyes of his fellow guides when these sports got back to the lodge and lied - flat-out *lied* - to their buddies about the number or size of fish caught, how long they played the fish before netting him. Yadda yadda yadda. The worst shame he felt as a true sportsman was when Teddy had to become a pimp - yes, literally a pimp - and catch at least *one* good-sized trout for the client to hold up for the grinning photo, just to prove to everyone back home or at the office that he was an honest-to-goodness- fly-fisherman.

No. No accounting, law practice or banking for Teddy, thank you very much. His last thought before falling back to sleep was: I'll turn twenty-five in a few short years; I inherit my trust fund – that must be a couple million by now at least. Then I can ask Marley Durrant to marry me, we'll buy a small ranch in the Teton Valley, raise chickens and milk cows, plant a big garden; I can open up a fly-fishing shop in Victor, and together we'll have lots of kids. We can live off the interest from the trust and never have to touch the principal.

"Jeez! I'm starting to sound like my dad. Live off the interest! Never have to touch the principal!" He was just as surprised by his thoughts of marrying Marley Durrant. More surprising was the idea of *lots* of kids!

The night nurse poked his head in. "You all right, sir?"

"Fine," Teddy said sheepishly.

"I thought you were in pain, or something. Do you need anything?"

"No, I'm okay. Thanks."

To help kill time, Teddy began to keep a journal. He was surprised that he didn't have much to say at first. Then he wrote down his thoughts about marriage, family, the dream spread in Victor, decisions to be made about money, that sort of thing. He also recorded some of his more memorable dreams. He doodled in the margins with pictures of rivers, drift boats, fly rods, trout flies, even trout.

Clark visited Teddy every day, and every day he brought something baked by Cindy: cookies, brownies, banana bread (not bad). In spite of the alluring goodies Teddy didn't have much appetite; he lost weight. "Doctors know what caused your stones?"

"They said I'm not drinking enough water; seems a familiar story because the water's so lousy here. That, plus too much salt, plus calcium buildup. I have to quit adding milk to my coffee," he joked.

"Seriously, I really need to get out of here and back to work. I'm going stir crazy here and I'm darn tired of being poked with a needle every time I turn around. Not too good to lie around, too much time to think. I think constantly about fly-fishing and how much I miss it. I wander the halls at night when I can't sleep. I saw some of the 'Nam casualties in there." He gestured toward the ICU. "After seeing those poor mashed-up grunts, I'll never feel sorry for myself again. Ever." Tears began welling up in Teddy's eyes. Clark turned away to allow Teddy to compose himself. "Sorry. I never cry."

"Post-operative depression, maybe?"

"Maybe. Did I tell you I been having a lot of weird dreams?"

"Must be the pain killers."

"Maybe. But here, read this." He handed his journal to Clark; the pages were turned back to the place he indicated. It read:

"I was fishing. There's this most beautiful stream I've ever seen anywhere. I can't describe it. Clear, pure water. So clear I could see trout swimming and count the pebbles on the stream bottom below. And I felt so much at peace. And I felt really clean. I looked up and saw a huge mountain close by. It had snow on the peaks. I swear it was Mt. Fuji - in Japan. It was towering over me but I felt a force coming from it. I felt so alive, so full of energy, like I was full of an electrical shock."

"What do you make of it?" Teddy asked.

"I don't know; I'll think about it. You know I majored in psychology? We learned that dreams can have many meanings; you should never take them literally or read too much into them."

"I'm glad I wrote it down. It was a cool dream."

"Mt. Fuji…Hmm. Are there trout streams in Japan?"

"That's what I hear and I aim to prove it for myself. I'm taking some R&R when I'm better. I'm going fly-fishing in Japan, Clark."

CHAPTER NINETEEN

MORE PILLOW TALK

"How's Teddy doing?" Cindy asked.

"When I visited him tonight I noticed something different about him. Actually a couple of things."

"Yes…?"

"Well, first off, he seems - what's the word? *Softened.* He's so macho, so independent, the tough Marine-outdoors-woodsy-type. He seems to have changed. I don't know if it's the surgery or what. Just changed."

"What's the other thing?"

"As I was leaving, I noticed he'd been reading the Bible."

"Are you sure?"

"It was opened and face down on his lamp table."

"Clark?"

"Yes?" he murmured sleepily.

"Mary Emma is engaged."

"Really? Who to?"

"To *whom,* Clark, to *whom?*"

"Okay, *whomst* is the lucky guy?"

"Chip Beck."

"Good for them. You didn't have anything to do with this, did you?"

"Maybe…"

"I'm thinking of inviting Teddy to that Servicemen's Conference in Japan next month," Clark mumbled as he fell asleep.

CHAPTER TWENTY

SAKURA

Teddy put in for two weeks of R&R effective immediately. Jack turned him down flat. The note Jack scribbled in the margin of Teddy's leave request said "see me." He met with Jack at first opportunity and learned that the Department of Defense was quietly starting to reduce the troop level in Vietnam; in fact, it had already started the process. "Does that mean we're withdrawing?" Teddy asked. Jack gave a noncommittal shrug that could mean anything, your guess.

"For us at NCS it means we're going to be short-handed on personnel for awhile, especially officers, until the CO and I figure this out. We're already short three officers. Our legal officer has been transferred to COMNAVMAR (Commandant Naval Forces Marianas), effective yesterday. And our admin officer, Lloyd Baxter, and your good friend, Clark, are also being sent up to COMNAVMAR as part of this consolidation. The Old Man has pretty much shoved this into my lap to deal with. He's busy sending out his resumes to various defense contractors back home. You remember he retires in a few months?" He paused to light up a Lucky. He inhaled deeply and blew out a cloud of blue smoke; in no time it saturated the small office. All the time Teddy had been hospitalized he had not smoked once. Yesterday, when he was discharged from hospital he thought it would be great to take up the habit again, but suddenly the smoke in Jack's claustrophobic cubicle was making him a little ill. "Can you wait a month or so until I have this personnel thing worked out?"

"Sure. No problem."

Using a piece of red yarn as a "fly" and a hula hoop as his target, Teddy eased his frustration by casting his new fly rod out on the lawn behind the BOQ every chance he got, just to keep his casting skills sharp. He researched as much information as he could gather about trout fishing places in Japan. He never touched a cigarette again.

Orders for leave finally came through for Teddy. He was granted two weeks in Japan starting the first part of April. He booked a seat on the *Yokota Flyer,* a vintage C-130 cargo transport that had been converted to haul as many passengers as possible. It was so named because every morning at 0700 hours it loaded up and flew out of Andersen. The Yokota Flyer was actually a fleet of several transport planes. One would fly a northerly route above the Pacific, passing over several islands en route: Saipan, Iwo Jima, Okinawa, finally landing some five or so hours later (weather and headwinds willing) at Yokota, a US Air Force base on the outskirts of Tokyo. Every afternoon, the Flyer would re-fuel and return to Guam loaded with tired military vacationers. There was no charge to military personnel and their dependents with orders, which included official leave papers.

A few weeks earlier Clark had extended an invitation for Teddy to join them for an LDS servicemen's conference at a resort center near Mt. Fuji. Teddy politely declined. Teddy's vacation plans centered totally around sampling the rumored great fly fishing in Japan. His plans did not include a conference with a bunch of Mormons. He wasn't even sure what a conference was, but it sounded to him like a lot of hymn singing, preaching and praying.

The church had arranged to invite all the Mormon servicemen on duty in the Far East: Vietnam, Korea, Japan, Guam, and the Philippines. Clark explained that mission presidents and their wives would attend, plus several general authorities (whatever that was). Most notable, Clark said, would be the visit of Elder Junior Hartmann, an acknowledged character, but a powerful and spiritual speaker, together with his wife, Colleen.

Pennington drove Teddy to Andersen early on the morning of departure. Teddy was traveling light: just an overnight bag with a couple of changes of fishing clothes and his new fly rod and reel. "See you in two weeks," Chris said as they parted.

"Sure. Thanks for the ride."

"Take lots of pictures for me." Teddy turned and walked into the passenger departure lounge. Through the large glass windows he could see Air Force and civilian personnel loading bags into the belly of the Yokota Flyer. He checked in and received his boarding pass. Behind him he heard a familiar voice.

"Teddy Buckley! What are doing here?" It was Cindy Tanner. He turned and faced her, Clark close at her side.

"Didn't Clark tell you? I'm off to Japan for two weeks of R&R, some quiet time fly fishing in Japan. I assume you're going off to that church conference in Japan, too?"

Their conversation was interrupted by a commotion; a crowd of passengers was off-loading from a bus, pouring through the front doors. It was the rest of the Mormon gang, the same ones he'd been introduced to that day they cleaned up the Korean Baptist Church grounds. Leading the pack, acting as self-appointed tour director, was CWO Lloyd Baxter. A Mormon? Impossible, Teddy thought. He hadn't ever acted much like a Christian towards Teddy. But he did turn up at the Korean church cleanup work party, Teddy remembered. Oh, well. At least he only had to endure the flight up to Yokota with Baxter aboard. Maybe he'd be lucky enough to be seated far away from the man and his mousey little wife.

Teddy spotted Mary Emma Penrod off to the side of the happy, boisterous crowd of Mormons. He waved to her and she returned his wave, beaming her gratitude for being recognized, relieved that Teddy showed no signs of jealousy. At least she seems like a Christian, he thought. She was clinging tightly to her new fiancé, a nice-looking Navy enlisted guy. They were holding hands, obviously much in love. Teddy wondered about the sleeping arrangements at a Mormon deal like this. Clark had long ago filled Teddy in on the Mormon taboo against pre-marital sex.

Overall, the Mormon group seemed very happy to be with each other, like they really liked being together, doing things together. Teddy had noticed that before at the clean-up party.

The weather was sunny and calm as they took off to the north from Andersen. Soon, however, the air became choppy and turbulent. The flight was rough and noisy; they bucked head winds all the way. The seating was crude and uncomfortable, hammock-style webbed slings suspended from the walls or hard benches with short backs for the center seats. A young mother wore herself out dealing with a sick, crying one-year-old baby. The bouncing bothered Teddy's still-tender incision scars. There wasn't much to see out his porthole except flat, gray oceans below.

A couple of hours into the flight the boredom was broken briefly when they passed over Iwo Jima at twenty thousand feet. It looked fairly forlorn and barren, despite the red rocks and patches of dark green jungle. Teddy found it hard to understand why Japan and America had fought so viciously over this rock, losing so many lives in the process. One of his uncles, also a Marine officer, was killed in the first American assault wave down there. Teddy tried to remember the uncle so he could at least offer a silent prayer of respectful remembrance. His feelings were false; he couldn't even feel a kinship for a fellow Marine, he was going on what others in the family had told him about the uncle he never knew.

Teddy turned his thoughts to the two weeks ahead. His plan was to spend at least a day or two in Tokyo, rest up from the flight, relax, maybe take in a Gray Line tour and see some sights. Late the second day he would meet up with his fly-fishing guide, who would take him by train to some trout waters a few hours north of Tokyo.

Teddy said goodbye to Clark, Cindy, and the other Mormons at Yokota and took the train into Tokyo. He towered above the Japanese passengers crowded into the commuter train. I probably look really goofy carrying this fly rod case, he thought. He checked into the Otani Prince Hotel and went to his room. He threw back the curtains and took in the vast spread of Tokyo through the omnipresent pall of smog. In the courtyard below was a formal Japanese garden, exquisitely laid out, the perfection of which could only be appreciated from his aspect above. Plums and cherries and flowering crab apples were in full bloom below. The gardens were edged with moss-covered, ancient volcanic rocks, interspersed by ferns and other plants he didn't recognize. He felt an instant kinship with the Japanese love of nature.

Teddy stretched out on his bed, luxurious by Japanese standards, kicked off his shoes and was soon asleep. He dreamed the Mt. Fuji dream again, but this time he was submerged in the stream, the water was cool but not cold to him; it flowed over and around him, flowed through and cleansed him. He looked up through the depths and saw trout finning lazily above him. He slowly floated up to join them. It seemed like they smiled at him; they moved aside to make room for him. He slept until early the next morning, waking with a powerful thirst. The Navy doctors advised him to drink as much bottled water as he could; he didn't want a repeat of those kidney stones. His appetite had also returned. It was about time, too; his clothes were falling off of him.

Breakfast was unique. This was a first time he had to choose between a Western-style breakfast (eggs and bacon), or Japanese style (boiled rice, salad, fresh fruit and cold, smoked fish). Might as well try it once, he decided. The fresh greens were a delight after all the refrigerated foods he forced himself to eat on Guam. He followed the lead of his fellow guests and doused the salad with rice-wine vinegar and soy sauce; he found it delicious, the last bite as savory as the first burst of flavor.

The tour bus was loaded with a polyglot of nationalities: Americans, Brits, French, Spaniards, Turks, Germans, Chinese from Hong Kong, and one Australian. Most of them had come to Japan for the World Expo in Osaka. Several had already been to Osaka, where the main attraction had been the moon rocks and space capsule exhibit in the United States pavilion. Teddy thought he could miss that trip.

In spite of the charm of Tokyo - the Meiji Shrine, the Imperial Palace, the famous Tokyo Tower, lunch at a classy restaurant in the Ginza - Teddy was restless. He began to wonder why he had even booked the two days in Tokyo. He really didn't care for crowds; he longed to be out on a trout stream, casting. He was getting eager to meet up with his guide.

That afternoon after the tour he took out his fly rod for the fourth or fifth time, attached the reel and strung up the line. There was a small park across the busy street from his hotel. Would he look weird if he joined all the Tai Chi practitioners and practiced his fly casting on the grass? He didn't care. An hour of lawn casting took his mind off the other matter that was beginning to bother him: no telephone contact from his Japanese fly-fishing guide. By now he should have heard from Matsui Kawai, his guide. He got help dialing Mr. Kawai's phone number from the hotel staff.

No answer. An hour later, and still no answer. He left instructions with the concierge to dial Kawai every fifteen minutes and went to his room to cool off from the smoggy grime and humidity of the day.

Teddy showered and changed into clean clothes, repacked his one bag and headed downstairs to wait in the ornate lobby. The concierge continued to dial up Kawai's number, this time every five minutes. Teddy waited impatiently; he was starting to feel like he'd been taken. His frustrated thoughts were interrupted with, "May I help you?" An impeccably dressed Japanese gentleman in a dark business suit was bending over him. He appeared to be in his sixties (but with Japanese men it was hard to tell); he had beautiful flowing white hair. His English was perfect, he sounded American.

"Pardon?"

"You look like you need help. I'm offering to help you."

Teddy stood. "Oh. Well, I was supposed to have a guy meet me here two hours ago, almost three, now. He's taking me fly fishing some place up north. I've called his number dozens of times but no answer. I paid in advance, too…"

"I saw that tube and thought it was either a map case or a fly rod. You don't look like an architect or an engineer, so I figured you must be a fly fisherman. We don't see too many fly fishers in downtown Tokyo."

"You fly fish?" Teddy asked.

"Yes I do, whenever I can."

"Your English is sure good. You almost sound American."

The gentleman laughed, his eyes crinkled. "Let me introduce myself. I am Jerry Hatamiya, from Denver."

"From Denver? Pleasure. I'm Teddy Buckley, from Guam. Well, actually from Jackson Hole, Wyoming." They shook hands formally.

"Yes, I know Jackson Hole very well. Been there many times."

"What are you doing here?" Teddy inquired.

"I was born in Japan but raised in the states. I work for an American company; I manage their Far East operations out of Tokyo." Mr. Hatamiya gestured for them to be seated.

"So where do you fly fish? Around here, anyway…?"

"Oh, there are many good places here, if you are lucky. Back home, in Colorado…? The South Platte, the Arkansas River, the Frying Pan, Big

Thompson, St. Vrain, La Poudre, you name it, I've fished it."

"Wow! I was a guide in Jackson. Now I'm doing a hitch in the Marines, in Guam. Here for some R&R. Looks like I'm screwed on the fly fishing, though…"

"Maybe not. Have you checked out of your room yet?"

"Yeah."

"I have an idea. I think I can arrange some trout fishing for you. Don't worry about a room for a few hours. I'll arrange a room for you to wait in while I finish up a business meeting. I'll meet you back here in a couple hours."

"You're kidding."

"No, not in the least. I know some very exclusive places to fish. I could use a break myself. Are we on?"

"Sure, you bet! But you don't have to do this, you know."

"Mister Buckley, I know I don't have to. I *want* to. It's a matter of Japanese hospitality to a stranger. Please, you'll be my guest?"

"Sure. Gee, that's swell. Thanks so much! I'll be ready and waiting."

"Good. Until later, then."

They shook hands.

CHAPTER TWENTY-ONE

WHY GOD INVENTED BAMBOO

The soft knock on the door woke Teddy. He must have been suffering from mild jet lag, or maybe he still tired easily after his recent surgery. At any rate, he woke confused, trying to remember where he was and why. A very polite bell hop spoke to Teddy, "Mr. Hatamiya requests your boot size, sir." He waited patiently for Teddy to figure this out.

As in waders? How did Hatamiya know he didn't bring any waders? The plan had been for that shyster Kawai to provide them. The Plan — booger The Plan! He'd make sure that NavEx Guam blacklisted the slippery, no-show Mr. Kawai forever. The bell hop waited. "I'm a size eleven medium. Here…" Teddy grabbed a pen and pad of paper from the beside table and wrote it out for him. "There." He handed it to the boy with a dollar tip.

Teddy was awake now. To kill time until Hatamiya called he flipped through the English version of "What to Do in Tokyo." His phone rang. The front desk was asking if he cared for a private massage in his room. He declined but asked for a couple of beers.

"What brand, sir?"

"I don't know. You choose for me.

"The hotel recommends Sapporo, if that is satisfactory?" Teddy agreed that would be fine. In five minutes the beers arrived, still cold and sweating, wrapped in a white towel bearing the hotel logo. He never asked the Navy doctors if beer was on his new diet; he guessed a couple wouldn't hurt much. He tipped the waiting boy and opened one.

He snuggled down in a fat lounge chair and took another gulp of the frosty brew. I could get used to this life, he thought: fat, fluffy pillows; a great bed, fresh-smelling linens. And the bathroom: my gosh, bigger than my room in the BOQ. Nice personal bottles of shampoo and hand lotion. Teddy never paid much attention to soap. But this brand, Shiseido, or however you said it, with its smell of crushed ferns, had an essence that reminded him of a summer night in the woods. This was how his parents traveled all the time - nothing but the best. He considered how just one night in a place like this could buy a new pair of waders or a top quality fly rod. He was musing on this, stroking the fat towels, when the phone rang again. "Mr. Hatamiya wishes to inform you that his private car and driver will meet you in front. Ten minutes, please."

Twenty minutes later Teddy was settled in the plush back seat of a new Lincoln Continental, Mr. Hatamiya's personal limo. Mr. Hatamiya, still dressed in his well-tailored business suit, sat opposite him, talking in Japanese on his mobile radio-phone. The driver wore a smart uniform complete with peaked cap. He was Korean and his name was Ki; he deftly drove the large American car in and out of the congested Tokyo evening rush-hour traffic. "Hai, hai. Moshi moshi," Hatamiya continued to conduct business. Teddy enjoyed the flaming orange-red ball of sun as it settled slowly over the Tokyo Tower to the west through the layer of haze as they swept by on a new super highway. On the tour Teddy had learned the Tokyo Tower was a replica of the more famous Eiffel Tower in Paris. Teddy caught a few English words from Hatamiya's conversations but had no idea what was being said. He tried hard not to eavesdrop.

Mr. Hatamiya finally completed his business. "There," he said, as he holstered the phone in the side pocket of his seat, "all done. Everything's arranged for us. I have access to an old inn out in the country. It's about one hundred-fifty kilometers from here, in the direction of Mt. Fuji. You'll like it, I'm sure. It's an ancient fortress, built on a strategic mountainside, now converted into an exclusive retreat for businessmen and their guests.

We'll have the place all to ourselves for as long as you like." He then said something through the divider window to Ki. Japanese, Korean? Teddy didn't know. "I asked him to please slow down a little. He loves to drive fast. He figures since we're bigger than everyone else on the road, they'll move over." He laughed. His laugh was light and free, almost childlike. "I took the liberty of getting you everything you'll need. It will be waiting in your room."

"You didn't need to bother; that's a lot of trouble, just for a stranger."

"I don't think of you as a stranger, you're a fellow fly fisherman."

"Thanks."

"I've been fishing with a lot of guides over the years, all around the world. You're all pretty much alike, almost like a brotherhood. I spotted that quality in you when we first met today." He looked directly at Teddy, his dark eyes piercing. Teddy had a feeling that Hatamiya could read his soul. But he smiled with his eyes at the same time; it was unnerving until he smiled. Yes, Teddy thought, it's like I've known you before, too.

It was after dark when they turned off the winding mountain road onto an even smaller trail that led upward through dense, dark pine and bamboo stands. The big car's tires crunched on the graveled road as they lumbered up and up through the forest. "This is a national forest," Mr. Hatamiya said. Teddy nodded. He was feeling tired. The road leveled out, narrowed; a small rabbit-like animal scrambled across the road, quickly disappearing into the underbrush that now raked the car's sides. In a few minutes the gravel path turned sharply. The headlights illuminated a clearing, and across the clearing stood an old stone fortress, gray and solid. A newer stone portico had been added to the original structure, and huge lighted torches burned on each side of the stone pillars. As they got out of the limo, a gusty wind whipped the torches, causing the flames to pop and sizzle. Teddy smelled pungent pine smoke, or was it incense? The smoke swirled around in the gale and he inhaled deeply, savoring the fragrance.

Servants poured out of the large edifice; they needed no orders but went quickly to work - Luggage and gear disappeared into the inn. The two guests followed while Ki stayed with his prized limo.

Inside the cavernous entry Mr. Hatamiya turned and faced Teddy, formally bowed, welcoming his guest. "Why don't we freshen up and meet down here for dinner in a half hour? There's a button in your room you can press if you need anything." Mr. Hatamiya said something in Japanese to an older man, who hovered nearby. The man responded and Hatamiya interpreted for Teddy: "I asked him the menu for dinner. He says fresh trout. I hope you like trout." He smiled.

"I haven't had any for so long I hope I remember what it tastes like!"

"Good. That's settled. See you later."

Teddy was led to his room by the old Japanese gentleman. He had slightly stooped shoulders and his head was closely shaved, but he wore a salt-and-pepper beard. Teddy liked him immediately. Pointing to himself, the old man said, "Me Sam, you Joe."

"Okay, Sam, I'm Joe."

"Okey-dokey, Joe." Teddy doubted his real name was Sam, but that was okey-dokey. This arrangement was less complicated. Teddy's room was built entirely of stone, a subdivision of the huge castle. Everything was made of stone: the floors, the halls, the walls, the ceilings. Teddy had read in some history book that stone was cool against the heat of summer while being warm in winter. He doubted the writer had any real-life experience with stone buildings. Central heating consisted of a massive fireplace so large that Teddy could have walked inside without bumping his head. A huge pinewood fire was roaring at full blast, shadows and fingers of light chased each other across the floor and up the walls. Oriental rugs covered most of the floor and ancient, woven silk tapestries hung on three of the four walls.

He suspected his bed would be a futon and he was right. Across the room opposite his bed was a private hot bath, sunken into the floor. He took off his shoes, as was the custom, and put on guest slippers. The floor felt surprisingly warm. The original fortress had been built above natural hot springs. The hot water had been cleverly engineered to flow under the floors from room to room throughout the entire building. A single wall provided aspect to the outside through a large shuttered window. Under the window was a solid oak table, an antique from some former dynasty. Then Teddy spotted them: set out on a red silk cloth were the loveliest bamboo fly rods he had ever seen, four of them in different lengths, all perfectly matched. They were displayed in ascending order from shortest to longest. He guessed the shortest to be about six and a half feet long, a three-weight. The longest was, he estimated, nine feet, a six or seven-weight.

Except for the slight differences in color shading, the maker had ingeniously figured out how to match the bamboo shafts perfectly. Was the slight shading in color planned? He thought it was. The shortest rod was a light blond, like the color of wheat stalks in late summer. As the rods progressed in length, the colors darkened until the longest was a deep amber-honey tone. The maker obviously knew some technique for this: heat flaming, or maybe a chemical treatment. Whatever it was, the effect was beautiful, marvelous. The silk windings worked the opposite. The longest rod was wound with white silks that when dipped in the lacquer finish turned them translucent. The next shortest rod was wound with light gold silks. The silks on the very shortest of the four rods were a deep, old-gold tone.

But the most beautiful and surprising bit of artistry was the lettering on the shafts of the butt sections, just in front of the winding checks. As you'd expect, the lettering was Japanese kanji. But instead of traditional India ink, the lettering was delicately inlaid mother of pearl. He was staggered by the sheer beauty as he stroked his fingers over the silky smooth finish.

That's a nice touch, he thought, decorating a fishing lodge like this. Or was it intended for him to fish with these beauties? They belong in some fly-fishing museum. I don't know how I could fish with them; I'd be too nervous. What if I broke one?

At dinner Mr. Hatamiya asked, "So how did you like that set of fly rods? Nice, eh?"

"Words can't describe."

"They're part of my personal collection. You struck me as a bamboo man, so I'm going to let you try them."

"I couldn't. They're too nice."

"I insist, and that's final. Surely you know that bamboo is much tougher than it looks."

"Sure. But I'd feel bad if I broke one of yours."

"Don't worry, I don't think you will."

"They're custom made, aren't they?"

"Yes, an old friend of mine builds them. He only turns out ten or twelve a year. They're back-ordered for about five years, so stand in line."

"I thought there was an embargo on Tonkin bamboo."

"There is, for Americans. But this isn't Tonkin bamboo; it's pure

Japanese bamboo, a very rare kind that only grows in a small, remote mountain area up north. They only harvest enough each year to build perhaps a hundred rods if they're lucky. Only a few master rod builders have the privilege, get the government patents, to pick out and harvest just enough culms for their own personal clients."

"How do you get to be a client?"

"You have to be introduced. After that he checks out your background, your references."

"Must cost a fortune, one of these rods?" Teddy regretted his faux pas.

Mr. Hatamiya said it was time to eat. "Do you mind?" He bowed his head and began offering a blessing on their meal. Teddy was surprised at this. When Mr. Hatamiya was done he looked up at Teddy's surprised expression. "You're surprised I'm a Christian? Not all of us are Buddhists, you know."

"Uh, yeah, okay with me, I guess."

"Eat up, big day fishing tomorrow."

Before bed, Teddy jointed up each one of the rods and false-cast with them. His trained hand quickly settled on the one he would use: a seven and a half foot, five-weight. It was built the old way with three sections. It feels a lot like my Leonard, he thought.

Teddy woke early next morning, refreshed. He was unnerved when old Sam shimmered into his room just as Teddy was settling into the steaming bath. Sam kept a discreet distance, busying himself laying out Teddy's clothes, making a cup of strong scalding, green tea.

After a traditional Japanese breakfast, under the portico they met Sam and a younger man standing ready beside a neat, topless Toyota Land-Cruiser. This would take them, their gear, and lunch down to the stream to fish. Bumping down to the river, Mr. Hatamiya explained that the estate included about fifteen kilometers of private, blue-ribbon trout water. Teddy was relieved to know that even though the estate had an ongoing fish propagation program for browns, technically they wouldn't be fishing for "planted" trout. Therefore, the fish would be smart and difficult to catch, he hoped. The rules of the estate required all fishermen to use barbless hooks and release the trout unharmed as quickly as possible.

The estate employed a fisheries biologist, who carefully supervised the hired help in stream grooming and culling out any injured, old or diseased fish. This day Teddy and Mr. Hatamiya would be fishing for native speckled, or rainbow, trout as well as propagated browns. He assured Teddy of a good time. The river - more like a large stream - flowed between two mountains at the base of a fairly deep gorge. A great deal of thought and planning had gone into engineering the stream's flow to keep the natural stream bed. The man-made design also created some fantastic trout habitat lacking in the original course. Every year spring snow-melt run-off scrubbed most riffles down to bedrock and moved boulders into unlikely places. Crews working for the estate used to toil long into the summer to repair winter damage. Runoff was rarely a problem now.

Habitat along the stream banks was designed to allow for the growth of native flora (with occasional pruning). The banks were planted with natural grasses, the varieties that would attract and make good cover for bugs. The stream bed itself was mostly native freestone: granite or lava in its origin, with scattered gravel or sandy spots where the flow slowed. Great care was taken to prune back low-hanging overhead tree branches, clearing the way for unobstructed back-casts.

Tradition at the estate required Mr. Hatamiya to formally invite Teddy to choose the first spot he wanted to fish, since he was the honored guest. Teddy pointed out a fishy spot. "What flies do you recommend today?" he asked Mr. Hatamiya, politely. The normal role of guide and client was now reversed for Teddy.

Mr. Hatamiya took a moment to look at the sky and squinted at the stream. He pronounced, "Soft hackle flies fished wet with a dead drift downstream work very well in this stretch. I have some for you." He opened an old fleece-lined, leather fly wallet. "These were tied by an old friend who fishes out of West Yellowstone a lot, Sylvester Nemes. Do you know him?"

"I know of him. We never met."

"Well, here, try these. Have you fished soft-hackle flies before?"

"I have a few times. This one looks like a pheasant tail. And this looks a lot like a Pale Morning Dun, very delicate." Teddy held up the fly for inspection. It was expertly tied and very pretty. "I like the soft hackles; they probably look like insect legs to a trout."

"Exactly," Hatamiya said. "Well, good luck. See you in a while."

When Teddy had tied the tiny fly to his size 6-X tippet and was ready, he made a cast across and slightly upstream. He allowed the fly to drift close to the opposite bank, letting out line until he reckoned he had about thirty feet out. He could feel the soft tug of the current as the line gently hooked around until the fly was straight below him. He counted to ten and made a gentle lift. He felt a soft strike and saw the trout's nose breach the surface. He stuck the fish and the fight was on. It felt strong and gave an energetic fight. He did not expect it to be a large trout in such a small stream.

Even though he was over a half-year out of practice Teddy played the trout skillfully, letting the pretty rod do the work, absorbing the shock of the stretched out tippet. The fish, a rainbow, soon turned on its side and the fight was over. It was a pretty fifteen-inch fish, dark olive back, silver sides with bright crimson gill covers, a bright red stripe down its sides and black spots peppering it all over. He handled it gently, slipping the barbless hook out of its lower jaw.

Teddy heard someone clapping behind him. He turned to see a grinning Sam bobbing his head up and down in glee. He seemed to be happier than the one fishing. "Numba one!" Sam shouted, holding up both thumbs. "You numba one, Joe!" Teddy gently gripped the trout near its tail, slowly moving it back and forth, sluicing cold stream water through its gills to restore oxygen and released it. The fish remained suspended in the clear water, still for a few seconds. It finned a couple times and with a strong thrust of its tail, was gone.

"Well done!" Mr. Hatamiya shouted from upstream.

"Thanks. The rod really worked nicely! It's a sweetheart."

Teddy and Hatamiya leap-frogged up the stream taking turns at every other good spot, catching and releasing many nice trout. They were all healthy, strong stubborn fighters - a good mixture of rainbows and browns. Teddy caught several rainbows, natives, evident from their parr markings. It was a great morning of fishing.

At around one o'clock, Sam and his young helper materialized out of the forest, lugging two heavy wicker hampers loaded with a picnic. "Lunch," announced Hatamiya.

The boys spread a blanket out on the ground, laid out lunch: salad, sushi, cold fried trout, drinks and sweet rice cakes for dessert. Teddy was ravenously hungry from all the exertion in the cool mountain air. Again, as Teddy expected, Mr. Hatamiya bowed his head, then looked up at Teddy. "Uh oh, here it comes," he thought.

"Would you offer thanks for us?"

How can I refuse? Teddy thought. "Umm… I really don't pray much. But here goes. Uh, Lord, thanks for this nice gentleman who has been a friend. And thanks for this nice place and for the good fishing we've had. And, uh, thanks for this nice food. Amen."

"Amen. That was a very nice prayer - simple – I like that."

They ate in silence, Sam and the boy standing a respectful distance away. Mr. Hatamiya spoke. "When we finish fishing this afternoon, I can offer you two options. I can have Ki drive you back to Tokyo, or wherever you want to go. Or…I can invite you along with me to a conference I need to attend, near Mt. Fuji." He gestured in the distance. "It's church-related. But I would be very honored if you could come as my guest."

"Can I think it over while we fish?"

"Of course, and I anticipate there may be a hatch today, some early dry-fly action… maybe."

And there was indeed a hatch by mid-afternoon: the bugs were small and dark, resembling Blue Winged Olive mayflies. Again, Mr. Hatamiya provided the flies; Teddy became totally absorbed in the fishing, happy that everything came together at the same time: stream conditions, tackle, the hatch, the right fly pattern, the weather. The rare perfect day fly fishing, and with nobody to guide. He could indulge himself to the fullest. He had never been happier. The rise was scattered at the first; then, as the afternoon wore on, they began catching more fish, mostly browns now, fat and golden as melted butter, with pretty spots of orange ringed with pale blue. He nearly forgot the invitation to attend Mr. Hatamiya's conference.

Teddy's decision was easy: he was indebted to this generous stranger who had taken him in and shown him such lavish hospitality. Never before had he been treated with such kindness. "I'll go with you but I don't have any clothes as nice as yours."

"Don't worry; a lot of the people there will be in military uniform. This is a conference for Mormon servicemen stationed all over the Far East. You'll fit right in."

Teddy turned around in his seat, watching the big building, the ancient stone fortress fade behind them. The stay had been too brief; he wished he could stay longer to fish, to sleep, to eat, to heal. Mr. Hatamiya tapped on the glass partition; Ki pulled the big Lincoln to the side of the narrow gravel road. Hatamiya stepped out, motioning for Teddy to follow. "From this aspect you see Mt. Fuji behind the inn. This is a very lucky day, for today you can clearly see the top, the ancient volcanic crater. It is very rare to view the top; it is almost always clouded over." Teddy had seen numerous snow-capped mountains in the Rockies, but the sight of the ancient Oriental Mecca nearly took his breath away.

"Thank you again for this, the view, the stay, the food, the trout fishing, everything. You have been truly kind; how can I ever hope to repay…?"

Mr. Hatamiya raised his hand to silence Teddy. "Perhaps someday you will; you can be my host and show me the kind of trout fishing Jackson Hole is famous for."

"You bet, anytime!"

CHAPTER TWENTY-TWO

AN ELDER NAMED "JUNIOR"

As they drove to the resort center where the conference was scheduled, Mr. Hatamiya buried himself in reading from what appeared to Teddy a well-worn, leather-bound Bible, or something similar. Hatamiya occasionally scribbled something on a yellow pad. It dawned on Teddy that this just might be the same church conference the Tanners and the other Guam Mormons were attending. Mr. Hatamiya smiled up at Teddy. "Why are you going to this conference?" Teddy asked.

"I have been asked to speak, to give a talk."

"I'm guessing you must be a pretty important man."

Hatamiya laughed. "Not really; I could be replaced in my business by any number of younger people, smarter than me."

"No, I meant in your *church.*"

"Oh, that. There are but a very few of us, Mormons, in Japan, relative to the large population of Buddhists, Shinto, and other religions. Yes, I hold a very responsible position in my company. But that's not the reason I have a leadership position in the church here."

"Well, what is the reason, then?"

"What faith were you raised in, what church?"

"I… my parents took me to the Episcopal Church, if that's what you mean. Why?"

"Did they teach you anything about priesthood authority, about callings to serve, and how those callings come?"

"No."

"We believe that a man is called of God to serve in these priesthood positions. You don't ask for a particular position, and likewise you don't refuse when you are asked to serve."

"Interesting."

Teddy stuck close to Mr. Hatamiya, who seemed to be at ease and relaxed among all the servicemen and women filing into the great hall. He was surprised to see so many still dressed in military uniforms - Army, Navy, and Air Force; he saw many Marines still in combat fatigues. What could motivate these guys to travel so far for just a church meeting? They could be having a good time in the many R&R destinations scattered all over the big cities in the Orient.

"Teddy!" He turned to see Clark, Cindy, and several of the Guam Mormons winding through the milling crowd toward him. "What are *you* doing here, of all people? A look of amazement spread over Clark's face.

Clark was all spiffed up in a navy blue flannel blazer, white button-down shirt and striped collegiate tie. All the Guam Mormons were decked out in suits or nice jackets; all wore white shirts and neat ties, even CWO Lloyd Baxter. Teddy suddenly felt under-dressed in his fishing clothes, clean as they were, having been laundered the night before by his new Major Domo, Sam.

As Clark and Cindy came to Teddy, he turned to introduce Mr. Hatamiya. "It's a long story. I'll fill you in on the flight home. First, meet a new friend of mine, Mr. Hatamiya…"

They shook hands all around. "Nice to meet you, Brother Hatamiya," Clark said. "I know you from your picture and article in the *Ensign*; it's great to finally meet."

Brother? Teddy wasn't quite used to this brother and sister stuff. And what's this about him being an ensign? Is he a Navy guy, too? He was confused. They entered the conference center; more than three thousand people were taking their seats. Mr.-Brother Hatamiya took his leave of them. "Teddy, I have to take my place now on the stand; time to do my part. I will find you after the meeting, okay?" Brother Hatamiya made his way down the aisle, pausing now and then to shake a hand, pat a shoulder, return an embrace. He finally joined a group of twenty or so men on the platform, all dressed in suits, white shirts and somber neckties. They were also joined by an equal number of women, all nicely dressed.

Suddenly, everyone in the hall rose to their feet, eyes centered on the stage. In walked a distinguished elderly gentleman, warmly shaking hands with the suited group. He was closely followed by a younger man, in his late forties or early fifties, and a nicely-dressed woman at his side. His wife, Teddy rightly guessed. They all sat, the audience sat, and the meeting began. One of the suited men came forward, stood at the lectern and spoke into the microphone: "Brothers and sisters… welcome to this conference for LDS servicemen and women from all around the Far East. We are aware that many of you have only just arrived from the battlefields in Vietnam…" His voice choked with emotion. The crowd was eerily silent. He continued, "From battlefields of conflict. We commend you for your faithfulness in attending. I promise you will be blessed for it.

"This conference is presided over by Elder Brockbank, Assistant to the Quorum of the Twelve Apostles…" The reference to *apostles* caught Teddy's attention.

Clark leaned over and whispered into Teddy's ear, "He was my mission president in Scotland." Teddy nodded silently; Clark beamed.

The speaker continued, "Accompanying Brother Brockbank is Elder Junior Hartmann, also an Assistant to the Twelve. We welcome also his lovely wife, Sister Hartmann. Sister Brockbank was unable to accompany her husband. We will remember her in our faith and prayers. We'll begin this meeting by the choir and congregation singing the hymn 'High On a Mountain Top.' After the singing, President J. Patrick Merkley, of the Hong Kong Mission, will offer the invocation."

Clark shared his printed program with Teddy, pointing to the words of the hymn on the back. Teddy grinned and shrugged; he never was much of a singer. But the theme of the song – mountain tops – appealed to Teddy. He could at least read and try to understand the words.

The meeting was scheduled for two hours. Teddy remembered why he didn't like church: as a boy he sat through many long, boring sermons on the hard wooden pews of Pittsburgh's main Episcopal Church. He hoped he could stay awake; his mind drifted back to the previous day's fly fishing, playing the many casts to rising fish, the strikes, the fight, the fish in the net. He longed to be on the stream again.

Teddy appreciated the chance to stand up and stretch at the hour-break. Clark sang the rest hymn lustily, if terribly off key. The audience hunkered down for the home stretch. The next speaker was Brother Hatamiya. Teddy sat up and listened attentively to a fine talk on the subject of Taking Christ's Yoke Upon Us.

He was followed by Elder Brockbank, who also caught Teddy's interest with a fish story. He told of a time in Scotland when he was a mission president. A non-member friend (by that, Teddy took it to mean "not Mormon"), invited Elder Brockbank fly fishing for salmon on the River Tay. He went on to make the point that "we can all be fishers of men, just like the Savior commanded his apostles of old." Clark had used a phrase a few times in the past, "The Gospel net drags in all kinds of fish." Its meaning now became more clear to Teddy.

Then something happened. In days and months to come Teddy would replay Elder Hartmann's talk in his mind over and over again, trying to recall exactly what and how he felt when that man spoke. It went something like this; at least this is what Teddy remembered:

Elder Hartmann: "I think I'm the only general authority named Junior. That's my given name. Kinda funny when the prophet calls your office and asks to speak to Elder Junior (laughter). I feel right at home among so many of you servicemen and women. I spent over twenty years in the Navy myself.

"I was raised a Baptist, right smack dab in the middle of the Bible Belt in Missouri. If you think Mormons have long meetings, you should've been raised as a Baptist (laughter). And the Mormons don't hold the record for the most church meetings you can go to in a week. No, sir. The Baptists got you all beat. There's a lot of sinnin' in this world to preach about, from Sunday clear through to Saturday.

"I want to tell you how I became a Mormon and why. Maybe some of you've heard I'm a convert to the Mormon Church. I said I was in the Navy. I was a captain of a ship. Out of San Diego. While I was on the shakedown cruise with my newly-commissioned vessel, my cute little wife got a knock on the door one day. Standin' on the door step were two young men. Mormon missionaries. They said they had a message for her and they were sent from the Lord Jesus Christ to deliver that message to her personally.

"Now my wife is very religious, I think more than I am. While I was young, out fooling around, she was in Bible study classes five days a week plus Sundays; she was raised Baptist, too, only she belonged to an even stricter congregation than mine was.

"In her church you just could not dance — no dancing, period. In mine, it was okay, once a month, provided the lights were on and you didn't hug. In my church they had deacons that went around separating the couples that were dancing too close together. They'd stick a Bible between the couples to make sure they were far enough apart. (Laughter).

"Anyway, she did the unthinkable: she let those guys into my house. While I was gone! (More laughter.) Well, when I got home from my two-month cruise, supper was all laid out on the table. I thought: This is romantic (laughter). Then I noticed there were *four* plates set out. 'Honey,' I said. 'We having company?' Then she told me she'd met these two nice young men and had invited them to dinner. Now that didn't set too good with me! (Laughter.)

"Then two handsome, *single* young men showed up. She introduced them as 'elders.' I was confused. The only elders I ever knew were old, bald-headed, sour-faced guys that showed up at our once-a-month dances to keep us teenagers apart with their fat Bibles (laughter).

"We pretty much ate in silence, I can tell you. After dinner we sat down and they brought out this flannel board with these little pictures and started talking about Jesus and his apostles and how the ancient church had lost the authority to preach and baptize. I got out my Bible to prove them wrong. I didn't want to hear this Mormon message. I already had religion, didn't I? That was good enough, wasn't it? I wasn't what you'd exactly call a golden contact, with all my questions and challenges. I'm ashamed now to have to admit I was mean to them; I was downright ugly to them. My grandma used to say, 'Junior, beauty is skin deep. But *ugly* goes clean through to the bone!' I was bone-ugly to those two humble Mormon missionaries. I found fault with their grammar (me, an Ozarkie from Missouri!); in my mind I'd criticize the way they dressed. I even criticized the way they read scriptures!

"But then something awesome happened; something wonderful happened to me because of two young men and their message. The short one, the quiet cowboy from Wyoming, stood up to me. He bore his testimony to me. He bore his testimony with such feeling, such conviction, and such a powerful spirit, a spirit I had never truly felt before. Now I've been in many a revival meeting when I was young. Oh, yeah, I had felt the spirit. But never until that memorable night did I really feel the *SPIRIT*. I knew I had to have more of that spirit, that message. I wanted more of what they were selling. I wanted them back.

"And that's how I became a Mormon, and it's all true.

Teddy looked around; many tears were being shed. Many brave men in battle fatigues were weeping without shame.

That same evening, Teddy was not sure what he wanted to do. Should he catch a bus back to Tokyo, take the Yokota Flyer home a few days early? The Mormon conference was going to last two more days; he wasn't sure if he should hang around, or would it appear rude if he left? Clark invited him to at least stay, have dinner, spend the night. Teddy could decide in the morning. Clark located a spare bed in the single mens' dorm rooms. The resort had a traditional Japanese bath; Teddy very much wanted to bathe and relax. As he walked out of the locker room, towel wrapped around his waist, Elder Hartmann bumped into him. "I'm sorry," he said. Teddy had a sudden impulse: he turned and grasped Elder Hartmann by the arm, turning him so they could be eye-to-eye. Teddy realized they were the same height. "Sir, can I ask you a question that's been bothering me?"

"Feel free… anything."

"Are *you* an apostle?"

Without hesitating, the man of God replied, "No, I'm not. But I'll tell you what I *am*. I am a special witness of the Lord Jesus Christ. It's my calling to go throughout the world and bear witness of him, any time, any place. Even in a Japanese bath!"

Something in his eyes, his voice, his earnestness, his entire being, spoke to Teddy's spirit. It said to Teddy: "This man has what you've been searching for. This man has the truth."

CHAPTER TWENTY-THREE

LETTERS FROM HOME

When Teddy got back to his BOQ room on Guam, there was a packet of mail waiting for him: catalogs from Orvis and L.L. Bean, a letter from his mother and a letter from Zack. The return address was from somewhere in Honduras. He opened it, curious. "Dude, thanks for the Christmas card. My folks sent it on to me and it finally arrived in time for Easter! Sounds like we're both in the same kind of place – hot, humid, lots of lizards and bugs. And lots of little brown-skinned people (ha-ha!). Just joking. I enjoy this work, I can't explain why. You just have to actually do it to know why. But I love it and I really love the people here. They are so gentle and kind. They share everything they have with us, which isn't very much. It's a lot different from guiding rich sports on the Madison River, that's for sure!" Then something caught Teddy's attention: "Oh, there's a lady missionary here who knows you, Marley Durrant. She asked for your address. Hope you don't mind, but I gave it to her. You lucky dog!" Teddy didn't bother to read the last paragraph. He scrabbled through the pile of mail until he found the pale blue envelope with the decidedly feminine handwriting. He turned it over a few times before opening it. It, too, had a Honduras post mark.

It began: "Dear Mr. Buckley (or may I call you 'Teddy' like Elder Zundel does?) As I write this it's my P-Day, or preparation day. That's the day we do our laundry, shop groceries, and 'recreate' (play games like soccer or baseball or basketball). We're also allowed to write letters home. So I decided to write to you. I understand you're on the island of Guam. I wonder what it's like. Do you still do any fly fishing? (I wish, Teddy thought.) I'll never forget our day together on the Madison River, where you helped me with my back cast. I still think of you and imagine you wondering whatever came over that silly girl from California, with her wild tales about a boy prophet and gold plates? Well… she's on a mission, still telling the same story and helping people change their lives for the better. My testimony, if anything, is even stronger now. I sometimes find myself wishing you could ever somehow believe the same as I do. Well, I still have lots to do today and my P-Day time is almost gone. Don't feel like you have to write back -that is, unless you'd really like to. It would be nice to hear from you, what you're doing, and all about Guam.

Warm wishes,

Your Friend, Marley Durrant

P.S. Are you very close to the fighting in Viet Nam? I hope that if you are, you'll stay safe. I'll remember you in my prayers that you'll be stay safe, okay?"

Teddy sat down at his desk, picked up a fresh sheet of writing paper, and began:

"Dear Sister Durrant, Marley, Thank you for your letter; it came at a good time for me, I needed the boost it gave my spirits. Yes, I still remember that day on the Madison. I also remember the courage it took for you to tell me about a boy who said he saw God and translated some gold plates an angel gave him. What a story, eh? I think of you often. But that's not all of what I need to say to you. I need to tell you about something that happened to me recently. It's a good thing that happened, a break-through, you might say. I was in Japan recently, attending a conference for LDS servicemen (someday I'll tell you how I ended up there.) At any rate, here's what happened to me….

PART TWO

CHAPTER ONE

BACK IN CIVVIES

Back on Treasure Island again, it took Teddy less than a week to muster out of the Marines. Getting a discharge was almost as complicated as enlisting: more piles of paperwork to fill out, psychological tests, pay request forms, security clearance de-briefings, pressure to re-enlist, physical exams - more needles in the arm.

Teddy: "Why?

Navy Corpsman: "Navy Regs, sir."

Jab. "Ow!"

His final day of active duty finally came. Teddy stood in line at the Pay Master's window, signed a chit, and gathered up a big fistful of cash for his last pay period plus a bunch of unused leave time. He tucked the bulging wallet into his hip pocket as he walked out of the building into the warm early-October sun. The sky was blue; a soft breeze scented with fresh salt and kelp was blowing in off the Bay. Dozens of white sails used favorable winds to tack back and forth across the chop bound for Sausalito.

Teddy inhaled deeply. What now?

The first day Teddy arrived at Treasure Island, after the tedious MAC flight from Guam to Travis A.F.B. via Hawaii, he had called to the storage yard, alerting them to charge or replace the battery and check the air pressure in the tires on his old pickup. Free of his contract with the Marines, he took a taxi over to Oakland, retrieved his truck and a few boxes of personal belongings, including his prized bamboo fly rods, from the storage company. He checked to make sure there had been no rodent damage to his rods; there was none, although something had chewed off the handle of his old leather briefcase, probably for the salt. He settled up the final bill and asked if he could use a rest room to change clothes.

A half hour later, in faded jeans, soft canvas fishing shirt; worn, gum-soled desert boots, topped off with a corduroy sport-travel jacket, he felt like the old Teddy again. He folded his military uniform with proper respect and stowed it away in his bags. After a couple of tries, the old truck fired up and thrummed like old times, a good sign. Teddy negotiated the heavy lunch-time traffic through Oakland and the spaghetti-bowl interchanges, took the freeway east through Berkeley, turned south on the 680 belt route at Walnut Creek, and cruised toward his destination: Danville.

Teddy lumped along at fifty-five miles an hour, normal speed on Guam, and the posted speed limit here. He was passed on both sides by cars and delivery trucks flashing by at more than twenty miles an hour faster then he was going. Life moved much slower on Guam; he had liked that island pace very much. Perhaps he'd drive this speed all the way across the country until he reached Pittsburgh. For sure, he planned to stop and fly fish along the way. There was no hurry to get home. He realized that the word "home" as it applied to him, was somewhat tenuous. Where was his home now really?

Other than a couple of wrong turns, Teddy at last found the address he was seeking. After talking his way past the guard shack at the gated entrance, he pulled up in front of the palatial neo-colonial home nestled comfortably in a classy compound, adjacent to the Round Hill Golf and Country Club. He pulled the worn envelope out of his shirt pocket and checked the address again to make sure. He took a quick look at himself in the rear-view mirror, grabbed a big gulp of air, and slid out of his ratty old pickup. Marley had no idea he was coming to see her. Zack had sent Teddy her home address several weeks ago. He hoped she would be home. He rang the bell and waited, nervously, feeling like he was picking up his first prom date. A Hispanic maid in a crisply starched uniform opened the door and waited. "Is Marley… is Miss Durrant home? I'm a friend of hers."

"Momentito." She disappeared into the huge tiled entry way and down a long hall, while Teddy's pulse increased and his chest tightened.

After two agonizing minutes, Marley appeared. She took his breath away. It took her a few seconds to recognize Teddy. She extended her hand, "Teddy Buckley, what a surprise! How nice to see you again! What are you doing here? Would you like to come in for a few minutes?"

That "few minutes" bit didn't sound too good, but he *had* come with no advance warning. He'd take whatever he could get. "Sure. Hope I'm not interrupting anything." Marley placed her cool hand at his elbow and guided him down the hall toward a tastefully-decorated sitting room. She had changed her scent; this one was new but fit her even more perfectly. Heck, she could go without fragrance; it wouldn't matter to Teddy.

Halfway to the room, Marley stopped and faced him. "I didn't recognize you at first. You've changed a lot. What is it?"

Teddy rubbed his hand over his crew cut and laughed. "Well, last time you saw me, I probably had dreads."

Searching, she fixed her eyes on his. "No, it's definitely something else. You have a different look. Maybe it's your countenance... Well, no matter. Come in and let me introduce you to everyone," she said gaily. They walked into the sitting room where a small gathering had taken place. "Mom, Daddy, this is Teddy Buckley. Dad, you remember him from our fishing trip to Jackson Hole?"

Mr. Durrant stood, clamping Teddy's hand in both of his and vigorously shook. "Yes, Mr. Buckley, Teddy, it's nice to see you again. How's the fishing?"

Teddy returned the handshake, answering, "I haven't been doing much fishing the last two years, sir. Actually, I just finished up a two-year tour of duty with the Marine Corps Reserve. I just got back from Guam."

"Guam… I had an uncle served there in World War Two. Hot place. And humid, I'll bet."

"Yes, sir, very humid at times. But you get used to it."

It was then that Teddy noticed for the first time another person in the room. A young man, with dark, serious eyes, dressed in a Navy blazer, gray flannel slacks, white shirt and smart club tie (a white shirt and tie, and it's not Sunday?) stood up and extended his hand. He was a little younger than Teddy, barely an inch taller than Marley. She moved to the young man's side, put her arm inside his, drew him close. "Teddy, I'd like you to meet my fiancée, Scott Matthews." Teddy noticed her engagement ring for the first time; it was obscenely outsized! "We were in the same mission at the same time. Scott came to ask Daddy for my hand. Isn't that just so old-fashioned and romantic? Scott, meet a family friend, Teddy Buckley." Scott blushed with embarrassment.

Teddy's heart sank. The sunny feelings suddenly drained away; confusion set in. All his life, Teddy had been trained for awkward social moments. As a gentleman of fine breeding, he was required to put a good face on situations just like this one. He came visiting as a hopeful suitor; now he was a family friend. Teddy sucked up his personal disappointment, shook hands all around and congratulated Scott and Marley profusely. "I'm so happy for both of you. I wish both of you all the happiness in the world." Those were the socially acceptable words that were taught and rehearsed many times past. Now they were just that: only words - hollow, insincere, dead of any meaning.

Because right at this moment, in his heart he knew, and honestly had to admit, he was insanely jealous of the young Mr. Scott Matthews. If only he, Teddy, had been here a month sooner, he could have won Marley's heart. If only he had put in for an early release from active duty, *he* would now be asking Mr. Durrant for her hand in that quaint, old-fashioned way. He could have gotten an early out – an early discharge; DOD was rapidly cutting back on personnel, preparing for the inevitable withdrawal from 'Nam. But he chose to stick it out for the full two years of his enlistment contract. That was the honorable thing to do, he felt then. Now he wasn't so sure he could tell what was right and what was wrong. He guessed that this Scott guy, rich kid, somehow wangled an active duty deferment from his draft board so he could serve a Mormon mission. This unhappy turn of events was confusing his own thoughts about a possible mission for himself.

"Thank you so much!" Marley hugged Teddy and kissed him on the cheek. Was he imagining, or did she linger, clinging to him a couple of seconds longer than the occasion required? He hoped. Or was this new small thread of hope imaginary?

"Well, I think I'd better be going. I'm sorry if I crashed your party."

"If we had a little more notice, we could arrange to have you for dinner…How about sometime later this week…?" Marley offered.

"Thanks, that's very kind, but I need to hit the road. I'm headed back to Pittsburgh to see my folks, my parents. I haven't seen them in awhile. My mom, well, Mrs. Durrant, you're a mother, so you understand these things…?" Her nervous smile was pinched.

Teddy waved good-bye and made a move toward the front door; Marley joined him. When they were alone, she whispered "I'm so sorry if this was embarrassing for you, which I'm sure it was."

"My fault for stepping into it." He smiled down at her. Her eyes pleaded with him for understanding.

CHAPTER TWO

THERAPY

Teddy drove north up the 680 belt loop as if in a trance. He didn't notice San Francisco Bay sparkling in the late afternoon or the sun slowly dropping to the west as he drove over the old high suspension toll bridge at Martinez. Water, any water, had a strong attraction for Teddy, but not this afternoon. He didn't see the remarkable picture of two mighty rivers joining forces just to the east of the bridge: the San Joaquin, coming from the south, and the Sacramento, coming down from the north, meeting a few miles east of there. Together, their brownish fresh waters merged into the salty green tides, pushing eastward against the incessant flow. He never noticed.

He did not remember merging onto I-80 north at Cordelia Junction. He was not mindful of the caravan of heavy diesel truck rigs and passenger cars that pushed inexorably north and east through the towns of Fairfield and Vacaville, past The Nut Tree, then through Davis and Sacramento, rising through the foothills of the Sierras through Auburn, cresting the mighty Sierras over Donner Summit, then dropping sharply down to Reno and other points east.

He turned off on a state highway at the college town of Davis and

133

drove north, passing trucks loaded to overflowing with Roma tomatoes, until he reached the dusty farming town of Woodland, where he stopped for a Pepsi and filled his gas tank at a Seven-Eleven. It was nearly dark. He didn't really taste the Pepsi; it was just something to drink. In the old days it would have been a cold beer.

The evening air was heavy with the fragrance of ripe tomatoes, billions of them, being processed into tomato paste, sauce, and other products at the massive cannery he passed on the outskirts of town. Behind him the sun, a huge orange fireball, was starting to sink behind the Coast range. The setting sun cast a thin golden lining upon the tallest snow-dusted peaks of the Sierras, just visible to the east. He didn't notice. Migrating mourning doves flew across the purpling sky in flocks, heading to their night roosts, bellies nearly splitting, full of kernels gleaned from the golden stubble of newly-harvested grain fields that lined the roads for miles. Teddy didn't see them, didn't hear the whistling sound their wings made in flight, didn't hear them calling plaintively to each other.

Teddy Buckley was not mindful of anything except his dull, aching heart until he reached the small farming town of Knights Landing, where he had to slow down for the tricky S-curve approach to the narrow drawbridge over the Sacramento River.

He was numb and bone-tired when he fell into his motel bed in Yuba City. He lacked the strength even to cross over the Feather River to find a motel in Marysville, Yuba City's sister town that shared the river, shared a common bridge. He skipped supper. He fell asleep still in his clothes watching mindless television; he neglected to brush his teeth or say his prayers. Teddy awoke sometime around three-thirty; the flickering blue screen casting weird shadows through the room. He stumbled out of bed, snapped off the TV and fell back to sleep, but not before he felt again the sting of rejection. It smacked him harder than he dared admit.

Teddy played with his breakfast in the motel's greasy restaurant. "Somethin' wrong with your food, hon?" the waitress asked. Tips had been slow this week and she did not need another grouchy customer.

"Nope, just not very hungry." He gave her a doleful look.

"Girl problems, huh." Teddy nodded. "Sure you don't want any coffee? It ain't all *that* bad."

"No thanks, bothers my stomach." Teddy lied, using Z's old excuse; he placed his hand over the empty mug. "But I could use some help, if you don't mind."

"Sure, hon. One thing Blanche is good at is advice for the lovelorn."

"I don't need that, thanks. I just need to find my way to the highway east to the Yuba River."

"Where you goin' to?" Teddy shrugged and said he just wanted to find a place to cast a line for some steelhead or maybe some trout. "Well, you're right on the very street to get you there as we speak. You just want to go straight that a-way, over the bridge and over the river to the Marysville side. Turn left at the third stop light after the bridge and then you turn left. Then just follow the signs that say Browns Valley and Grass Valley – the turnoff is probably about two or three blocks north from there. It's that way, the bridge." She pointed.

Teddy paid his check and left. He gathered up his bag, still unopened from the night before, checked out of the motel, and drove slowly over the bridge that spanned the Feather River. He turned left at the third light as Blanche had instructed, then drove north down a street canopied by tall London plane trees that arched over the street, their tops touching, blocking out the morning sun. The street bordered a pretty little man-made lake. He quickly reached the junction and turned east.

The fly fishing Teddy envisioned would bring him some peace at last, proved to be elusive. Oh, he had some moments of fun. Like the brace of fat, silvery rainbows he took on the Yuba. Then, on the recommendation of a local fly fisherman named Tony that he met on the Yuba, he caught a ten-pound hen steelhead next day on the Feather River, just a few miles north of a small crossroads named Robinson's Corner, about ten miles south of the town of Oroville. She took the small, dark fly Tony had given him - Tony had promised it was the best pattern on that river. He was right. She fought hard, jumping at least three times. He admired her perfect coloring, her black pepper-like spotting; she was chrome-bright, with pretty pink on her sides and rosy gill covers. He took a couple of pictures before he released her back into the water, apologizing for interrupting her upriver odyssey.

Teddy continued on up the Feather River canyon on highway 70, past the town of Quincy, then turning east. When he got to the railroad town of Portola at the headwaters of the Feather, he felt a sudden, anxious need to talk to Zack. Teddy gassed up his truck in Portola, shocked at the high gasoline prices. He stocked up on junk food: Diet Pepsis, Snickers bars, several bags of Cheetos.

Teddy stopped for a few minutes beyond the outskirts of Portola to admire Grizzly Creek, where it meandered through a culvert under the highway on its short drop to the Feather. A pod of nice browns was lazily rising to a Blue Winged Olive midge hatch in the pool just above the highway. Teddy marked the spot on his map, promising to return someday. He started up the truck and hunkered down for the long, all-night drive he would make to Park City. In the late afternoon sun, he noted the great meadows passing on his right, where the Feather River bubbled up out of sagebrush as a mere spring, the headwaters.

CHAPTER THREE

THE RABBI

Teddy arrived in front of the Zundels' modest home in Park City in the early pre-dawn. The outside air was chill; frost began to form on the inside of his windshield. The smell of an early snowfall was in the air this early October morning in 1971. No lights were yet on in the house; he hesitated waking them. Zack knew he was coming, but Teddy was not expected for another two days. He slouched down in the seat, pulled a down parka tighter around his shoulders, threw an old wool tartan blanket around his legs and closed his eyes. Right after he passed through Elko around midnight, the caffeine buzz from the six-pack of Diet Pepsi had worn off. He fought sleep all across northern Nevada and the Salt Flats, stopping every hour to run around the truck in the cold air, slapping himself awake.

Teddy woke to banging on his side window. "Hey, wake up! Teddy, it's me!" Teddy was blinded from looking directly into the rising sun. Then he made out the shadowed profile of someone looming in his face. A second later his brain kicked in and he recognized Zack's voice. He threw off the improvised bedding and stiffly crawled out of his truck. Zack clamped Teddy in a bear hug that cut off his oxygen. Teddy returned the hug with an enthusiasm and feeling that had never been there before.

"How you doin'? Man, you gotta lot of stuff to tell me about! But come in the house before you freeze, you nut! Spending all night outside, you're crazy! Mom's got breakfast ready, I can smell it." Savory smells of eggs, bacon, and maple syrup were indeed wafting out of the house. Teddy was ravenously hungry for the first time in many days. The first time he had really eaten since he had stopped almost a week ago in Danville…

After breakfast, Teddy took Zack for a ride in the truck. "We need to talk. I need a rabbi." That was their secret code word for serious talks, healthy doses of manly advice.

"Haven't heard that term for a long time."

"I know," Teddy admitted. "It didn't work out too good. I mean, with Marley, Sister Durrant. I blew it. I made such a jerk out of myself."

"Go ahead. I'm listening," Zack said.

They drove the ancient truck east on U.S. 40, past Heber City, as far as Roosevelt, where they stopped and bought greasy hamburgers and French fries, then turned and headed back to Park City. Teddy talked, Zack listened. They pulled in front of the Zundel home, Teddy killed the motor. He turned to face Zack. "What do you think I should do now?"

A mission had matured Zack. He left as an immature boy and returned as a wise young man. Teddy sensed the maturity in his friend, the maturity that wasn't there before. The old Zack would happily go along with whatever the rest of their gang, mostly footloose fishing guides, wanted to do. Now Teddy was seeking advice from the new Zack. After a long silence, Zack spoke: "What do *you* want to do? What do you think you should do?"

"That's just the problem. I thought I was at last ready to settle down, start a home, a family. You know… get married?"

"But she wasn't the right one?"

"That's also part of the problem. I really thought I knew she was the right one for me. I can't shake that feeling, no matter how hard I try to forget her now."

"Have you considered going on a mission now… I was going to say, now that you're *free,* so to speak?"

"I thought about it all night driving over here. I thought about it a lot.

And…"

"And…?"

"I think I'd make a lousy missionary."

"I'm surprised you'd think that. Why do you say that?"

"For one thing, I'm too old."

Zack snorted. "Listen, I had a companion who was older than you by at least five years. He was a convert, just like you. A whatchacallit scholar at some classy college in Maine. Left a doctoral program to go on a mission. No, I don't buy that age thing. What else?"

"My heart isn't in it now. Her turning me down just took all the fight out of me."

"Listen to you. You sound like you're on your deathbed, nothing left to live for. I know what the spirit can do for a guy, how it can compensate for any weakness. I had another companion who was so homesick he left me one day to walk fifty miles to the nearest bus depot. He was going home, he said, because he wasn't cut out to be a missionary. As if you're pre-destined for that calling or something. Mission president sat him down and challenged him, gave him a blessing to help him. Promised him that if he'd fast and pray, he'd catch the spirit of missionary work."

"And…?"

"He turned out to be the best missionary I ever saw. He finally just caught on fire; baptized hundreds! He was an assistant to the president before he went home." They sat in silence while Zack let this sink in. He continued: "I'm not going to tell you what you should do. Only the spirit can do that for you. But you got to think about it, make up your mind. Then pray and *ask*. The promise is right there in D&C section nine, man. Read it, will you?" And like the good missionary he had been, Zack got a commitment: Then will you earnestly pray about it?"

Teddy promised.

CHAPTER FOUR

CALM

A few miles east of Sidney, Nebraska, on I-80, Teddy's old Ford pickup truck finally gave out. It first started making funny noises between Evanston and Fort Bridger, growing more constant since he'd breached Lincoln Pass east of Laramie and started downhill to Cheyenne. He now regretted not stopping in Scotts Bluff to have it checked. Storm clouds had been gathering, the sky thickening with the threat of snow ever since he left Rock Springs. Teddy stuffed his rods into the duffel and braved the elements. A few stray flakes blew into his faced as he shouldered his load and left the truck steaming and hissing like some yellow prehistoric beast with massive rust spots, dripping mysterious burnt fluids. He hitchhiked into Sidney, arranged with a local garage to tow the old heap into town, and bunked down in a cheap motel for the night. He didn't get much sleep with the prairie wind constantly howling around the building and whistling through the seams in the window frames. It reminded him of a couple near-typhoons on Guam.

Sometime in the early morning hours, Teddy found himself on his knees beside his bed. He couldn't sleep anyway, so why not make good use of the time alone? He needed help, *big medicine*, Zack's irreverent name for the Holy Ghost. After a big country breakfast in a truck stop café, Teddy signed over title to the old pickup in lieu of towing fees to the garage owner and hopped a Greyhound into Omaha, where he booked the next available flight to home to Pittsburgh.

Somewhere around thirty-five thousand feet, as they cruised over Lake Michigan, just north of Chicago, Teddy had an epiphany: He silently prayed during this flight, not for safety, but searching for direction, for answers. It came to him suddenly and quietly: a palpable *peace and calm*, just like when he first gained his testimony. To pass time waiting for his flight in Omaha, he had read and re-read section nine of the D&C, just as Zack had counseled, verses seven through nine, regarding the process of personal revelation. In the week or so since he had said good-bye to Marley, he had filled the solitary road hours thinking about his life, his future, and what would be the most worth for him to do. And now, most of all, what did the *Lord* want Teddy Buckley to do?

During that long drive, if he could have written and driven at the same time, he would have easily filled a notebook with his thoughts and feelings. It all boiled down to this: Marriage or Mission? The only person he *thought* he had feelings for, the only one he had even considered for marriage, was now taken. The thought of starting a new search for someone else who could step in as his eternal companion, was daunting, to state the obvious. Zack had promised Teddy if he served a mission for the Lord now, he'd have time later and the Lord would somehow lead him to the right person in due time. Zack was right: Teddy was still young, compared to a lot of other people.

The words *you must ask me if it be right* resonated in his mind and heart, over and over, until he was almost tired of hearing it repeated. *I did ask you last night, Lord, when I spent those hours on that hard linoleum floor in a crappy motel in that hellhole Sidney Nebraska after my crappy old truck broke down. Remember our conversation? Remember, I told you the feelings of my heart. I told you what I had decided. I need an answer. Soon would be good for me… please?*

The jet passenger plane had been bumping through dense cloud formations since taking off from Omaha and reaching altitude. Just north of Chicago, thirty-five thousand feet above Lake Michigan, the clouds parted and glorious sun shone through.

Teddy's heart leapt with gladness as he felt for the second time the definite swelling in his bosom followed by an enveloping peace. How would he tell his folks he had decided to serve a mission? And at the ripe old age of twenty-four? He'd let the Lord figure out that detail for him. The big problem Teddy faced now was trying to figure out which bishop he needed to go to for help filling out the paperwork? Zack would know; he'd ask Zack when he had a chance to get to a phone and call with his news. He would be sure to thank Zack for his help and advice. He also felt he had to clear the air on one other small matter.

Teddy asked the flight attendant for a piece of writing paper.

Dear Marley,

I am so sorry and embarrassed to barge right in like I did last week. It was rude and thoughtless. I truly hope you're happy with Scott. He's a lucky man. You're probably wondering why I showed up like I did, unannounced. You wrote me some letters over a year ago, from your mission field. Remember? Those few letters affected me like no other letters I ever got. I don't know why. I wondered often what would prompt you to write to me, a virtual stranger, like you did. Now I know how you could do that: you have a testimony and you felt strongly the need to share it with me again, without any fear.

But back to the reason I dropped in on you: I guess being alone on Guam all that time and reading stuff into your letters, gave me what you might call romantic ideas about you. You'll never know the big plans I had for you, for us. When I stopped by to see you the other day, I actually planned to ask if we could date and maybe see what our relationship could develop into. I was willing to stick around the Bay Area and see you for as long as it took to find out. I had no idea you were spoken for (and you never told me in your letters, either).

Well, now I'm spoken for. You will find this hard to believe, but believe it - I have decided to serve a mission. When I find out where I'm going, and after I get a settled mailing address, is it all right if I write to you? As a friend, of course. Now that you are to be married, I could expect nothing more than your friendship, and I would always value it greatly.

All the best,
Teddy Buckley

Teddy hardly recognized Pittsburgh. Have I been gone that long, or is it just growing fast? His mother was happy to see him after more than three years. His father shook hands formally, stepped back and appraised the son that was now a man. "You've changed. You're different."

"I'm older than when you last saw me," Teddy laughed.

"I fixed you some supper," his mother said. "How long do you plan to stay? What will you do now with the rest of your life?"

"He can take his rightful place at the bank," his father said. Teddy smiled a non-committal smile.

Zack helped Teddy locate the bishop of his home ward. The bishop gave Teddy an inspiring interview and helped Teddy fill out the paperwork application to serve a full-time mission for the Church. They both agreed that a farewell in his new ward was not what Teddy wanted; he would be happy to just get on a plane and fly to Salt Lake City when the time came.

Teddy spent a quiet Christmas at home for the first time in three years. After he and his parents exchanged a few modest gifts, Teddy sat on the sofa holding his mother's hand, an intimacy he had not shared with her since he was a small boy. For the first time in many years he felt the warm feelings of home and family. He ate his aunt's home-made fruitcake for the first time ever. He told her he actually liked it, and he almost did.

Teddy's hands trembled slightly as he looked at the white business envelope from Salt Lake City with Office of the First Presidency as the return address. His mother cried when he told them he was going to serve a two-year mission for his new-found religion. "I'm not crying because you'll be gone again. Well… yes I am. Are you sure you have to leave so soon? You've only been home a few weeks."

"I have to report to the Missionary Training Center the first week in January, Mom."

"That's only two weeks!" She cried again, tried to wipe her tears, then said, "But I'm also very happy that you seem to have found something of value in your life. I have prayed that you would some day give up your vagabond life fishing or whatever it is you were doing out West, find a wife, settle down, have a family. Maybe this is the first step." Teddy wrapped his big arms around her and nestled her moist face in his chest.

His father scratched his head and wondered why Teddy had to go do this two-year thing. And you say you have to pay your own way? They don't pay you any salary to do this? I guess I just don't understand a religion like that. Well, good luck anyway. Alaska and Canada, eh?"

CHAPTER FIVE

SITKA

A chirpy voice crackled over the loudspeaker in the small air terminal in Juneau. "Alaska Air/Ellis Airlines Flight number 33 to Sitka is now ready for boarding. Please have your tickets ready. Have a nice flight."   Outside the small terminal, low gray clouds, pregnant with the threat of heavy rain, scudded past.

Teddy approached the faded Navy blue Grumman Goose aircraft hunkered on the tarmac under lead-gray skies. He queued behind a group of six Japanese businessmen, all in dark suits. Teddy was also dressed in a dark suit, white shirt and yellow paisley tie; his old tan Burberry was wrapped tightly against the icy wind that cut across the airport from the Gastineau Channel.

A hard gust of wind blew his pearl-gray felt fedora off his head; he grabbed but missed. It rolled and bounced across the runway and into a distant stand of dark spruce. He didn't care; he really didn't like the thing. When he was getting everything assembled to leave, his mother found out a hat was part of his recommended missionary clothing. She promptly ordered one up from Brooks Brothers; Teddy put up a mild protest about the hat, but she was his mother and it made her happy for him to wear it.

"Your father and grandfather have always worn hats to the bank. You're not completely dressed without a hat. That's how gentlemen of good breeding dress." The only hat he ever preferred wearing was a faded gold-and-blue MSU Bobcats ball cap on the river, preferably while guiding or fly-fishing.

But that was then. Now he was here. In Alaska for the first time, in mid-January, 1972. In a previous life, oh, how he had yearned for the chance to guide and fly fish in Alaska. Late at nights, he had talked to other guides in Jackson about their guiding or fishing experiences in Alaska. He listened jealously as they spun tales of ten-pound silver salmon, *chromers*, fresh in the rivers, right out of the cold Pacific waters. He drooled over stories of casting to fish with just about any artificial fly pattern you wanted to tie on. They hit anything. Not because they were hungry, it seemed. Spawning salmon are fiercely territorial - they hit the flies in front of their faces out of anger. But when you hooked up, oh, mama! Hang on and watch the acrobatics. Accounts of silvers leaping out of the water six, seven or more times in a row, trying to shake the hook, were told enough times that he truly believed it.

Maybe Elder Teddy Buckley would get a chance at some fly fishing in Sitka, his newly-assigned area of missionary service. He could send for a couple of his rods, reels, and fly boxes once he got settled.

The fading yellow logo on the side of the plane said it was owned by Alaska/Ellis Airlines, whoever that was. He swung his duffel bag into the belly hold, gripped the metal ladder, bounced up and took his seat at the back, near a window on the left side. The other side of the aisle was taken up by a group of Japanese businessmen, all in dark suits, white shirts, and somber neckties – they almost looked like mission presidents. As the engines coughed, sputtered, caught and roared into life, belching blue fumes into the cabin, Teddy buckled his safety belt. The co-pilot stuck his head back in the cabin and tried to shout a brief safety demonstration over the roar as the plane bumped off the apron and taxied onto the runway.

Shortly they were airborne, climbing over the Gastineau Channel, leaving the capital city of Juneau, Alaska, behind. Their route would take them in an almost southerly direction, over water most of the time. Estimated arrival in Sitka would be an hour and a half, just around dusk. The sky was getting fatter with dark clouds; they were soon completely enveloped in the gray soup. Frequently they would dart through patches of fading sunlight, but most of the journey they were bouncing around in the clouds. Halfway into the trip the plane banked sharply to the right, throwing the Japanese on that side into the windows. One man, who until then had managed to maintain his dignity, started barfing into the sanitary bag; he would continue this for the rest of the flight.

The pilot was taking the plane on a zig-zag course through some massive mountain peaks crested with ice-blue glaciers. Teddy guessed the age of the ice at a million years at least, maybe more. They were so close, almost touching the wing tips. Teddy swore he saw a family of mountain goats.

Suddenly they dropped down below the cloud bank, the engines throttled back, and they banked around one hundred eighty degrees to the north. For a few seconds Teddy's stomach was in his throat and he almost grabbed for the bag. The plane skimmed in low, barely twenty feet above the water and dropping fast. To his right, Teddy could make out a town flashing past, lights winking through the gathering dusk.

The pontoons skimmed the waves and bounced a couple of times. The plane slowed its speed, settled down into the water, and the pilot gunned the engines into reverse with full flaps. They floated and bobbed for a minute longer. Just outside Teddy's round, water-tight window, a pair of strange sea birds swam alongside the plane, seemingly fearless. He recognized them as the birds with the oversized, delta-shaped beaks - colorful puffins. Since the water level was halfway up his window, Teddy could see their little orange webbed feet paddling furiously below the water surface while their bumblebee-shaped bodies bobbed above the surface like fat little feather-covered corks.

With a sudden roar of engines and a lurch, the plane bounced up a rough concrete ramp, sea water spilling and blowing behind. The plane reached the level top of the ramp and spun around until it was facing the water. Then the pilot cut the engines and the roar died out. The sick Japanese businessman retched into a fresh bag one last time. He looked drained of life. His friends helped him down the metal ladder.

Teddy got out, stretched, and looked around. A stiff breeze was blowing from the northwest, fat drops of spattering rain being driven ahead of the front. He was glad they won the race with the storm. In the growing dark Teddy could make out many small, rocky islands across the narrow channel, thick with Sitka spruce trees. The sea was whipping up a chop; spray was blowing off the crest of the waves. This will be home for the next six months or so, he thought. The tide was running out; he breathed deeply of the mixed odors of sea water and kelp, their combined fragrances mingled with fragrant wood smoke blowing from someone's wood stove in a cabin nearby. It smelled pungent, like cedar. To the south, the lights of the town were now blazing, lighting up the low cloud cover.

Teddy waited for President Carling, the president of the small dependent LDS branch to meet him. Teddy shouldered his leather travel bag, picked up his battered green canvas duffel bag, the stenciled letters USMC faded from years of sun, weather and travel. He walked inside the metal Quonset hut that served as the Sitka air terminal and settled down to wait for President Carling. His senior companion, Elder Wessman, should have arrived already.

Teddy alternated between waiting outside the terminal wrapped in his Burberry and sitting inside by the glowing pot-bellied stove. President Carling should have picked him up an hour ago. A telephone rang. The lone airline employee answered. "Is your name Elder?" He extended the receiver to Teddy.

"Elder? This is Frank Carling. Look, there's been a screw-up at work and I had to stay to take care of some patients. I can't pick you up for a couple more hours. Maybe somebody there could give you a ride to the water taxi. I'll have someone meet you there to take you to my house." The line went dead.

Teddy asked the airline employee (cum mechanic and ticket agent) if there was anyone who could give him a lift into town. "Sure, kid. I'm closing this place down in a little while. Just got some paperwork to finish." Shortly they were in the guy's old pickup truck rattling over the pitted gravel road to town. The truck reminded Teddy of the beast that gave out near Sidney, Nebraska just a few months ago. The rain was now falling with a purpose. The single ancient wiper blade was too worn to be useful. "You're a Mormon, ain't ya?"

Teddy was surprised. "Sure. How'd you know?"

"I'm from Utah, too. Used to work at Hill Field in Ogden. Married a Mormon girl. Well she ain't a girl no more. Tried to convert me. Didn't do no good, but she tried." He spat a stream of tobacco juice out his window.

The window was stuck open and wouldn't roll up; rain blew in but the driver paid no attention. He reached his rough greasy hand across to Teddy. "Phil Tedrow. Most folks know me by 'Sparky.' I used to be an electrician. You can call me Sparky; I prefer that. Just don't put that 'brother' stuff on me. Deal?"

"Teddy Buckley. I mean Elder. It's a deal."

"What you doin' here? No… I think I know already. You come to preach, haven't you? My wife Betty will be happy." They made a sharp right turn inside town, pulled onto a slab of asphalt that jutted out over the water and stopped. "Here we are, water taxi. Frank lives over there on Japonski Island – locals call it Mt. Edgecumbe 'cause of the Indian high school there, the Braves, their mascot. Fits, don't it? You take the water taxi from here. It's the fourth house down from the docks. She don't like it here, my wife. Rains too much and no Mormons. Guess you'll change all that now, the Mormon part. Nobody but God can do anything about this damn rain. Good luck, son."

Teddy got out with his baggage. Phil Tedrow – Sparky - waved as he pulled away. The rain now came down in sheets; strong gusts had it blowing in circles sometimes. Teddy ducked under a lean-to and waited. Through the curtain of rain and gloom he could hear the pop-pop-pop of a small craft motor approaching.

The lone boatman pulled expertly alongside the quay, threw a painter, jumped off and tied up the small ferry craft. Several people got off. The captain motioned Teddy to get on board. A family had hustled to make the taxi and they clambered aboard with Teddy, a man, woman and a child. He couldn't tell the child's sex; he/she was buried inside an adult's yellow rain slicker. Teddy wished he could trade coats with the child; he was soaked through and so were his two bags. He shoved the bags inside the cabin, hoping the skipper wouldn't mind.

Seating was two wooden benches facing each other from the sides of the craft behind the cabin; above them a pitiful canvas awning flapped in the storm. The rain came at them horizontally now. At least the skipper would be dry in his snug cabin. The channel they had to traverse was a quarter mile across, Teddy reckoned. They cast off and headed into the chop, tossing on four-foot swells. Teddy turned his back to the gale and clutched his soaked trench coat tight around his throat.

Teddy's soggy shoes squished as he walked as rapidly as possible up the gravel road parallel to the channel that separated Sitka from Mt. Edgecumbe, lugging his soggy bags. He wished he had his fedora now; even a ball cap would help. He thought of pulling out his MSU ball cap but figured it was no use – he was soaked through now. The several houses set back and above the channel all looked the same: two-level duplexes painted government gray. There was one lone street light at the end of the housing row. Behind the row of houses the forest rose like a black wall. He couldn't make out any house numbers, but he didn't have an address anyhow. Fourth house up from the docks, Sparky said.

He bounded the stairs leading up to the two doors on the fourth house. Which door to knock on? He chose the one on the left and knocked loudly. His ears were greeted with the happy shrieks of children. A young mother opened the door a crack; the two children tried to squeeze past her – a girl aged about four and a boy half the girl's age, he guessed. The young mother was obviously quite pregnant, pretty far gone. She wore an apron over a flower print frock; her round face was ringed by dark brown curls. She wore thick, dark-rimmed glasses; she constantly pushed them off her nose.

She smiled and extended her hand. "Hi, Elder, I'm Maggie Carling. We've been expecting you. Come in - you're soaked. Sorry about Frank. He should get here any time now. This is Amy and her brother David. Can I get you something to eat? You must be starved. Oh listen to me chatter. What's your name?"

"I'm Elder Buckley, Teddy Buckley. I'm from Pittsburgh, I'm a recent convert and I've been out on my mission almost a month now. Could I please have a room to change out of these wet clothes?"

"Right through there, first room on your right. You'll get used to the rain after awhile. Everyone does; eventually you just don't notice it anymore. No, David, you can't go in there with Elder Buckley!"

While Maggie warmed his supper Teddy sat in the living room. The two children, Amy and David, alternated between staring at him and having fits of the giggles. Savory food smells came from the kitchen; Teddy heard Maggie humming some sort of children's tune. "We're having some red snapper that Frank and his friend caught. Hope you like it fried with grilled onions and fried spuds."

"Sister, I'm so hungry I could eat my shoes. Are you from Idaho?"

"Yes - how could you tell?"

"Spuds."

"Oh, that always gives it away." She went back to humming.

I know I've heard this tune somewhere, Teddy thought. "What's that song you're humming?"

"It's called 'I am a Child of God' – a Primary song. Do you know it?"

"Not really. I've heard it, but I never went to Primary."

Her humming was suddenly drowned out by the sounds of clumping feet on the porch. "Daddy!" the children shrieked, racing to the front door. Frank Carling loomed in the door frame, children joyously crawling over him. He was a big man with big hands and feet to match his frame. The next thing Teddy noticed were the man's soft, pale blue eyes – earnest and open. Frank shook his raincoat over the two kids, who screamed and laughed; he hung it on the peg next to Teddy's. Frank came over, offered his hand, his eyes smiling all the while, never leaving Teddy's gaze. "Hi, I'm Frank. Mind if we visit while we eat?"

They ate, talked, and listened to each other for an hour until Teddy was so dog-tired he could no longer focus. Teddy learned that the Carlings' house had been built in WWII as officer's housing. Back then, the Navy had an air base on Mt. Edgecumbe that employed over 30,000 military personnel and 7,000 civilians. (That explained the big hangar Teddy passed on his way to their house.)

Their small branch was part of the Juneau Branch, Juneau District of the Alaskan-Canadian Mission. There were about a dozen members in Sitka that Frank knew of: Frank, Maggie, and their children; there was Frank's one counselor, Larry London, a math/science teacher at the Indian high school on Mt. Edgecombe, married with four kids. Then there was dear, faithful Sister Betty Tedrow, plus a couple of sailors attached to a U.S. Coast Guard cutter stationed out of Sitka who came when they were in port. Frank guessed there may be many others. "Alaska is a strange place," he said. "A lot of people come here to get away from something. The rule is: don't ask about their past. You may get a nasty surprise."

"If there are other Mormons here, we'll find them," Teddy said.

Church meetings were held for now in the Carlings' home. Sacrament meeting and Sunday school were combined into one meeting; Priesthood meeting and Relief Society were held right after. There were no youth, so no MIA. All the meetings were held in the Carlings' living room. Music was supplied by hymns on vinyl LP records; they could really use an electronic keyboard, Frank mentioned.

After their Sunday meetings, the members of their small branch usually hung around and shared a potluck lunch, a "Munch-and-Mingle," as Maggie gaily called it from her kitchen. Teddy was coming around to the notion that Mormons actually *liked* each other. Simply visiting, feeling each other's spirit, was enough to keep them happy for the week ahead. He had noticed that when he was just a new convert on Guam.

"Your companion, Elder Wessman, was supposed to arrive tomorrow morning. But his flight out of Kodiak's been delayed again, I hear. They've been socked in by weather for a week. You'll get used to that; mail's almost always several days late. More spuds and gravy?" Frank Carling was obviously also from Idaho.

Teddy fell asleep that night on his knees praying. He woke up later and rolled into Amy's little bed. The kids had been moved to the living room sofa. Teddy and Elder Wessman would bunk in the kids' room until they could find their own digs.

CHAPTER SIX

DIGS OF THEIR OWN

Teddy wasn't fully prepared for Elder Tad Wessman. He wasn't sure what he expected; this was his first companion, the first real one since the MTC in Salt Lake and traveling to Vancouver with his group of other greenies. Teddy and Frank Carling waited outside Ellis/Alaska Air's Quonset hut as the PBY's engines died and the ladder was dropped to the ground. Wessman was nothing at all like the image Teddy had conjured in his mind.

A short bundle bounded off the plane from Kodiak and down the ladder. Elder Wessman crackled with energy, all five feet seven inches of him. Teddy extended his hand in the missionary crushing grip he had recently learned from Elders Nate Hill and Duane Madsen, the president's two assistants in Vancouver. Wessman grabbed Teddy, all six-feet three-inches, one hundred ninety pounds, and lifted him off the ground in his own crushing bear hug. Wessman was strong! An athlete…a wrestler?

"Elder Buckley! At last we meet. Your reputation is all over the mission. We're gonna do great together!" He dropped Teddy back to earth, spun and shook hands with Frank Carling. Teddy couldn't place Wessman's accent. West Texas? He noticed that when Wessman smiled his whole compact body seemed to radiate enthusiasm. His eyes more than sparkled, lighting up his entire face: from the crinkled corners to his apple-red cheeks, his face glowed with happiness. This guy is no phony, Teddy thought.

That night Elder Wessman offered their prayer at bedtime. Teddy did not fall asleep; he wanted to catch every word from this man's sincere, devout heart. Wessman slept in David's bed – it fit his compact body almost perfectly. Teddy's feet hung over the end of Amy's bed while his head banged the headboard. Teddy fell asleep turning over the words in Elder Wessman's prayer in his mind. "…and please bless Carla…" Carla…? Sister…? Recent convert? Girl friend? He'd wait to find out when Wessman naturally wanted to tell him about it. Mustn't get nosy.

Sunday morning – early. Elder Wessman bounced out of bed when their alarm went off at quarter to six. (The mission rules only required a 6 a.m.wakeup.) He fell to his knees next to Teddy's bed and slapped Teddy on the butt. Didn't this guy ever do anything slowly, calmly? "Roll out, Elder! No time off from gospel study today! Your turn to pray, I believe."

Teddy was suddenly self-conscious in front of his new senior companion. Not only did he barely know the first two of six discussions, he didn't think his praying skills were in the same league as Wessman's. On his knees, "Elder…? He hesitated.

"Yeah, Elder?"

"I'm still sort of new to all this stuff. Maybe you don't know, but I've been a convert barely a year. You know, kind of like culture shock…?"

Wessman laughed. "Hey, I know all about that. I'm a convert myself. I really know what you mean. But, Elder, the more you practice, the better you get. Just like football, or anything else. What is it you like to do for recreation?" (He said it *ree*-creation.)

"Uh… I like to fly fish."

"Fly fish? What's that?"

"Maybe on our P-day I can show you." Teddy took a deep breath and launched into a tentative prayer. Why did this praying in public thing still bother him so much, he wondered.

Frank Carling called on both elders to speak, or at least to simply bear their testimonies if they preferred. Teddy bore what he felt was a sincere testimony. In his Journal that night he wrote: *First Sunday in Sitka. Really nice members, friendly. They promised to share the gospel with their friends and give us referrals for teaching appointments. Bore my testimony in Sac. Mtg. Still getting used to doing this. Wessman bore his and I really felt the spirit when he did. He cries really easily. What's wrong with me? Will I ever get the hang of it? I learned this about Wessman – he's also a convert, but been in the church since his teens. He was a preemie, that's why his mother named him "Tad". He wrestled and played football at North Ariz. State College - I knew he was an athlete. And get this: he's engaged to his high school sweetheart! P-day tomorrow and we're going to look for a place. The Carlings are really nice, but we need to let their kids have their room back – and we need our own space.*

On Monday the two elders accepted Sister Carlson's invitation to use her washer for their laundry. They took turns ironing in the living room. It felt good to be wearing blue jeans, sneakers and a sweat shirt. Teddy noticed that Wessman's clothing was quite worn and threadbare. *That figures: he has less than four months to go and this should be his last area.* After laundry, ironing and letter writing, Wessman suggested they go out and look for a place. There were two real estate offices in town that doubled as rental agencies. They stopped at the first one on the main street of town just past the old Russian Orthodox church. It was squeezed between two saloons just opening for the day's business. Patrons, regulars, were already lined up outside, impatient.

"You boys new in town, aren't ye? I heard tell there was some young Mormon missionaries in town. You must be them."

Wessman wasted no time. "What do you know about the Mormons?" The realtor said he had some Mormon friends when he was growing up in California, but they never discussed the Mormon religion.

"Well, would you like to know more then?" Teddy joined in, getting the spirit of this missionary thing.

"I dunno; let me think about it some. Now let's see..." He flipped through a very thin stack of file cards. "Nope. No. Nope. That one's rented. Housing shortage here. Wish I had a bunch of money. Boy, I'd sure build me some apartments. Eight-plex, at least." He put the file cards down. "Sorry, but you boys're out of luck. No use trying the other realtor down the street, if that's what you're thinkin'. He's got the same listings as I do. It's a small market. I'll call you just as soon as somethin' comes up. You boys got a phone number?"

They walked dejectedly toward the docks and the water taxi. Suddenly, Wessman put out his hand to stop Teddy. "Let's pray," he said.

"What? Here…?" Teddy said.

Wessman didn't answer, but bowed his head and offered a prayer right there on the street, in broad daylight, oblivious to staring eyes. It was a short prayer, direct: "Lord, we need a place of our own and we really need it today. Please make it available to us. As your servants in need, we'd be most grateful. Amen." He stood for a full minute after he finished his prayer, head bowed. "Let's go back and see that realtor guy."

"But you heard him. You saw his file cards. No places. Besides, I think he's a shyster."

Wessman was already on his way back to the rental agent, jaw firmly set. "Well, we don't have a lot of options, Elder. The spirit just told me we should go back, and that's what we're doing. C'mon."

The realtor came out of his office, hurrying toward them. "Hey, boys, glad I caught you. I just thought of something. It ain't much, but maybe you don't care. I can show you now if you're interested."

They were interested. An hour later they signed a lease agreement. Teddy was suffering sticker shock; $200 a month for a two-room cabin a hundred yards back in dense woods. And they had to buy heating oil in order to have hot water to cook and bathe. And they had to pay for their own electricity. And it had no indoor toilet, only an outhouse. And they had to pump their water by hand outside to fill their storage tank for drinking and bathing later. And the roof leaked, they would learn later. And they learned it was owned by the realtor. Two hundred bucks split two ways was a hundred each. That was almost all their monthly budget shot just on a place to sleep! Wessman didn't blink. "Didn't anybody tell you Alaska was expensive? You don't look poor to me, pardon my saying so."

"Well, yeah, sort of. Elder Hill in the mission home in Vancouver said something about us sticking to a budget up here… And by the way, I'm not poor but I'm not rich either."

"That's not the rumor I heard going around."

"What did you hear?"

"Never mind, just forget I said anything?"

"No, I want to know so maybe I can set your mind straight on this. What did *they* say?"

"Someone told me your dad owned a copper mine in New Mexico - something like that."

"Look, I don't know where they got that idea, but it's false. My dad is a …. Never mind what he does, it doesn't really matter. My family is not paying for my mission. I have my own money; I saved most of my Marine pay for a year after I joined the church, thinking I would use it for either a mission or…" he didn't finish.

"Or what? Marriage?" Teddy blushed and nodded. "So you got a girl waiting back home?"

"No."

"You already got the *Dear Teddy?*"

"I talked to her and she encouraged me to go on a mission." Teddy felt bad for lying to his companion; he needed to get off this subject. Talking about marriage did no good for his spirits. But it was *mostly* true, he reasoned, we did talk about marriage… sort of. And I guess she did encourage me to serve a mission… sort of. At least Marley's example was encouragement to him, he believed.

Wessman was right: they were out of options; but, they reasoned, they would be out working most of the time - the cabin was mostly a place to sleep, bathe and change clothes, so it would make do. They could put up with a few inconveniences.

Teddy told Wessman of the time when, for several summers, he and his buddy Zack had shared a tent in the woods (on national forest land, where technically they had been squatters) because of the chronic housing shortage for summer help in Jackson as well as West Yellowstone. Many of these mostly college students could only find housing forty miles away in Star Valley, or in Afton. They car pooled to Jackson and back every day. The elders' immediate situation also reminded Teddy of the housing shortage on Guam. He wondered if he should consider building and owning apartment houses after his mission.

Good or bad, they now had a place of their own. The best part was that Wessman made a side deal with the realtor: he agreed to a first discussion in exchange for their renting his cabin.

CHAPTER SEVEN

A FRIENDLY GAME OF ROUNDBALL

They could see the Coast Guard ship tied up to the dock on the Mt. Edgecumbe side of the channel before they boarded the water taxi. Teddy's trained eye figured this cutter to be about the size of a Navy destroyer escort, maybe a little smaller. But for the Coast Guard and National colors fluttering proudly from the superstructure, it could have been easily mistaken for a Navy vessel. This was the first time in port for the ship and its crew in several weeks and the first time the elders had seen it. The Coast Guard crew had been out patrolling the dangerous, frigid waters of Alaska's Inside Passage, responding to distress calls and lost craft signals, a frequent happening this time of year - all part of their job.

On leaving the water taxi, as they were returning to the Carlings' house, their walking route took them right past an old, hulking WWII seaplane hangar. They could hear shouting and the squeaking of sneakers on hardwood coming from inside the hangar; above all, they could make out the familiar sound of a basketball bouncing on a court.

Wessman got a big grin on his face. "Elder, what time does your watch say?"

Teddy checked. "It's only two o'clock. Why?"

Wessman opened a side door; they looked in and saw a group of sailors in blue dungaree bell bottoms playing a very competitive game of basketball. Wessman pushed inside, almost running toward the game in progress. "We got time to play a quick game before P-day is over. Let's see if we can get in this game!" he shouted over his shoulder to Teddy. "You coming or what?"

The two elders watched on the sidelines for a few minutes, Wessman quivering, as eager as a pointer pup. The two teams were divided into Shirts and Skins. Wessman pointed out one player on the Skins team: "That guy is real clever at cheating. Watch when the guy he's guarding goes up for a shot."

"How do you know so much about basketball?" Teddy asked.

"I played in high school and college," Wessman grinned

They watched several more minutes until the Skins won at twenty-one points. The teams took a bathroom and drink break. Wessman casually strolled over to one of the Shirts. "Hey, you guys mind if we join in? We could use a little *ree*-creation."

"Sure, no problem, elders," the sailor grinned.

"How'd you know...?" Wessman's mouth was open in surprise.

The sailor stuck out his hand. "Hi, I'm Barry Bluth, from Salt Lake City. I served a mission just a couple years ago. Welcome to Sitka. And you're...?" nodding to Teddy.

"I'm Elder Buckley, Teddy Buckley, from Pittsburgh I guess you'd say. Pleased."

"And I'm Tad Wessman," Tad introduced himself.

The teams were gathering back on the court. Someone yelled "Hey Bluth! Who's yer friends?"

Barry didn't hesitate. "You guys all know I'm a Mormon, right?"

A chorus answered "Yeah, we know!"

"These two fellows are missionaries from my church here in Sitka. Okay if they play with us? Just watch your language, okay?"

"We want the tall guy," one of the Shirts said, pointing to Teddy.

"Well Elder Wessman, guess you're a Skin," Barry said.

Without hesitation Wessman began peeling off his shirt. What about your garments? Teddy thought. Wessman rolled the tops of his garments down, tucked them inside the waistband of his jeans. "Throw me the ball, let me take a few warm up shots," Wessman asked. He took the ball and shot several times from various angles around the top of the key, missing only one shot. Then he took a couple of quick layups. Teddy was amazed at his vertical leaping ability.

Wessman made himself de facto captain; he lost no time in rallying his new team mates. They huddled and discussed strategy. The one Teddy had identified as a cheater looked up from the circle of bowed heads, eyed Teddy and pointed at him, then at his own chest. Oh, great, Teddy thought, I get to guard the Cheater. The Cheater was nearly the same height as Teddy but probably fifteen pounds lighter; muscle definition in his biceps, forearms and chest told Teddy this guy kept in top shape.

Shirts lost the last game so they took the ball out first. Teddy was nearly the tallest on his team, so he naturally took a position as forward. Skins were fast in setting up their defense; Shirts had to pass the ball around the perimeter several times before Teddy could work free from the Cheater. He took the ball, faked a pass, spun and went up for a ten-foot jumper, easy stuff for Teddy.

As Teddy made his spin, Cheater reacted quickly, and cat-like moved into him. As Teddy went up for the shot Teddy got a quick whiff of strong tobacco odor on his defender. Cheater raised one hand high to screen; with his free hand he deftly hooked Teddy's waistband. As Teddy rose in the air he was jerked slightly off balance and fell back against the Cheater. The shot went sailing over the basket and out of bounds. Air ball.

They fell to the hardwood floor in a heap, Teddy crashing backwards on the Cheater. As they untangled themselves and got up, the Cheater came at Teddy with fists raised, in a boxer's crouch. He was breathing heavily, his face purple with rage. "You mother (expletive)! I'm gonna kill you, mother (expletive)!"

Teddy backed away with his hands raised in a peaceful gesture. The teams backed away into a loose circle giving the combatants room. Someone shouted "Fight!" Someone else shouted, "Shut up, man!" Nobody wanted officers involved in the incident; nobody wanted to be in the uncomfortable position of having to rat out his shipmates. "You pulled me down on that shot," Teddy said with an even voice.

"You're a liar! You're full of (expletive)! You banged me on purpose! C'mon and fight, gang banger!" He was slowly circling closer to Teddy, breathing heavily. Teddy wondered when this guy would make his first move. He was obviously a boxer or at least a darn good street fighter. Either way, he was dangerous and Teddy had to get out of this somehow.

"Look, I don't want to fight you. I don't know what your problem is, but let's just play ball. That's all we wanted, just a friendly little game of roundball."

"C'mon," the Cheater invited Teddy to come at him.

"I said I don't want to fight," Teddy spoke softly, lowering his voice. He fought to keep calm. "What will fighting prove? That one of us is tougher? Let's just get back to the game, all right?" He looked to Wessman for support. Why didn't his companion step in and help calm things down?

"You're just a chicken (expletive)!"

"I've been called worse by tougher guys," Teddy responded. How dumb of me, he thought. Wrong thing to say - I know better. Think, Buddy. Try to remember what you learned at MP School about crowd control…remember your hand-to-hand combat. Then Teddy had a flash of inspiration. "Look, fella, I don't know what your agenda is, but mine doesn't include fighting. But if we have to fight, I like to at least know something about my opponent, like maybe his name? I'm Teddy Buckley. What's yours?" Taking a risk of being sandbagged with a left hook, Teddy stepped closer, stuck out his open hand.

Cheater was a little surprised; he didn't smack Teddy but dropped his guard slightly, took one step back. Still keeping his guard up some, he said "I'm Michael Glass, Mike. We're wasting time. Let's get it on!" He was back in fighting stance.

Teddy stepped back to get out of Mike's reach and sized him up. The man was about six feet tall, maybe one hundred eighty pounds. Teddy figured he had a couple inches reach on the guy. But Mike was in excellent physical shape: arm, back and stomach muscles defined like thickly-braided ropes – no, more like steel cables! Teddy bought a few more valuable seconds. "Mike, let's you and me make a deal."

"Deal? What kind of deal?" Mike cautiously asked. He relaxed somewhat.

"If you insist on fighting, let's do it like gentlemen, in a ring with gloves. Three rounds. College rules. What say?" Teddy could see Wessman shaking his head in disbelief. "If I win, you have to listen to our message.

We teach six discussions about our church. If you win, you name the payment from me. Deal?"

Mike dropped his fists, scratched his head, thick with dark, curly hair. "This sounds like some kind of trick. How do I know you're not some kinda national champ or somethin'?"

"And how do *I* know you're not some kind of champ yourself?"

Mike just grinned slyly. Someone on the circle's edge blurted out, "He's All- Coast Guard light heavy runner-up!"

"Shut up!" Mike whirled and glared at the snitch.

"That true?" Teddy asked.

Mike just stood there with a nasty grin, his already swarthy face darkening with malice. Teddy glanced at Wessman; he just kept shaking his head. "Shake on it," Mike stuck out his hand. They shook on the deal. "Sucker," Mike taunted under his breath, as they moved toward the boxing arena. The crowd moved back, making way for the fighters

"Let's get it on then," Teddy said, ignoring the taunt. "Where's the ring? Who's got some gloves?"

The boxing ring was in a smaller, partitioned-off area of the hangar. The room was about thirty-feet square. On one end were wrestling mats; in the center was the canvas-matted ring. Several pairs of well-used boxing gloves hung from a wall. The smell of sweat permeated the room. Teddy silently prayed as they all moved into the boxing arena. Wessman moved close to Teddy and whispered "I can see the headlines: *Mormon Missionary Gets Killed In Fight.*"

"Thanks for the confidence," Teddy whispered back. "Do me a favor - just send up a quick prayer that this gorilla only maims me. You'll have to ship my broken body home. I'll just live the rest of my life on disability pay." Wessman shook his head again and grinned.

"I'll be in your corner, buddy. By the way..." Wessman whispered again, "I boxed in college, so I know a few things."

"Why don't you fight him then?" Wessman laughed as he hefted two pairs of gloves, held them up for Teddy to choose. "Any sport you *didn't* play?"

"Girl's Badminton," Wessman grinned. "Now listen to me, do what I say and just *maybe* you can keep from getting killed." Wessman advised and Teddy listened while Tad helped him lace on the gloves. "First, you gotta strip down to your skin. That way he can't grab your shirt and throw any close punches. Got it?" Teddy nodded.

"That's it, strip off my shirt…? Anything else?"

"Yeah, he's a smoker – means he'll get winded really quick. Just keep dancing and stay out of his reach. Third round move in and put it to him, work on his ribs, his body. That'll also affect his breathing. Then pray."

"Anything else?"

"Nope… good luck."

"Thanks a lot… coach…"

The two warriors met in the center of the ring. Teddy spoke first: "What are the rules? We need to know the rules first. Who's going to referee?"

"We don't need no freakin' rules and no freakin' referee, neither" Mike sneered.

"Okay, then. No referee. But somebody needs to keep time. Three rounds of three minutes each. Agreed?" Mike nodded. They touched gloves. In the brief instant of the ceremonial glove-touching, Teddy got a flash, an idea. Later, he would insist to Wessman that it was *inspiration*. "Then let's get it on!" Before Mike could react or get his guard up, Teddy came up fast with a left hook that smashed into Mike's nose. Blood gushed as Mike staggered back. Teddy quickly followed with a combination of hard jabs to his left eye. Then he quickly hammered Mike with the palm of his hand on his ear with a loud smack. The crowd groaned.

"You (expletive)! You said college rules!" Mike screamed in a high-pitched whine. He was spitting saliva and blood and his left eye was fast swelling shut. His ear was bright red and swelling dangerously fast; it looked like a misshapen purple eggplant. Mike's shipmates laughed at his screaming tirade, which only served to make him all the more mean and dangerous. He was badly wounded but not out yet. Blood was freely streaming into both eyes; he wiped hopelessly at his face as he charged Teddy, swinging blindly. Teddy ducked under Mike's wild punches and caught him in the ribs with a hammer- blow right as he came past. Teddy heard the air whoosh out of the tough guy.

Mike was sucking for oxygen as he staggered around and tried to grab Teddy; he only caught the left arm, enough to spin Teddy and land a punch to his cheek. It threw him slightly off balance. Teddy was stung, but he recovered quickly, pulled free and circled back with a hard right that landed solidly on Mike's exposed left jaw. Teddy changed his stance quickly and followed with several cutting left hooks to the right eye, chopping deeper into the gaping wound.

Mike was bleeding seriously into his eye; he could no longer see. He kept flailing, unable to see or breathe, throwing wild punches, totally out of control. Someone rang the bell to end the round. Mike kept throwing weak punches; they either missed or glanced harmlessly now off Teddy's sweaty body. Teddy retreated to his corner. Mike followed swinging punches into his back. Teddy turned to face him. "The bell rang, Mike. Didn't you hear the bell?"

"Screw the bell! Come on you (expletive)! We're gonna fight until one of us is dead! C'mon!"

"Okay, your choice," Teddy said. Mike tried to close Teddy in a clinch, but Teddy side-stepped, pushed him back. Teddy regained his closed crouching stance as Mike lunged for him again. Mike met Teddy's waiting straight right to the jaw. It hit Mike with the force of a cinder block thrown at point-blank range. Mike was stopped - he dropped both arms, rocked a few seconds on unsteady feet. His unfocused eyes (what you could see of them) rolled back in his head as his knees started to give out. Teddy rocked him once more to the face with a full-on insurance right.

Mike sagged to the canvas in slow motion. He lay there a few seconds, tried to raise himself, knelt on hands and knees in a crouch, his bleeding face staining the canvas, fighting for breath as it whistled and gurgled through his smashed nose.

"Attention on deck!" a sailor shouted. All the Coast Guardsmen stood frozen at attention. Teddy looked up, stinging sweat poured into his eyes. His eyes focused; he saw a man in khaki uniform walking rapidly, stiffly toward the ring. The man's face was stern and hard as granite. Teddy saw the bronze oak cluster on the officer's collar. Out of old habit, Teddy almost stood at attention himself.

"Just a friendly little game of round ball, you said. I could've been killed by that gangster!" Teddy shouted, as he and Wessman neared the Carlings' home.

Wessman just laughed. "Hey, you were the one with the bright idea to fight him. How dumb can you get? You didn't get hurt because I told you to follow my instructions. And you did! Just what a good junior companion is supposed to do – follow what his senior says!" He laughed again. "We better get cleaned up and in our suits fast. P-day is officially over. Can't be late for the Lord's work."

Teddy grabbed Wessman's arm, stopped him. "But Elder, we *were* doing missionary work just now… we got an appointment to teach Brother Michael Glass the gospel!"

"Yeah… when he heals up from the damage! Where'd you learn to fight like that, elder?"

"I was over a company of MPs in the Marines. We learned something about crowd control … and self-defense."

"That guy was a crowd of one!" Wessman laughed. "I guess there's a lot I don't know about you. We sure were lucky that kid from Salt Lake, Barry whats-his-name, stepped in and saved your fanny from that Navy officer."

"*My* fanny? And it's not Navy… it's Coast Guard, Elder, Coast Guard."

"Whatever." Wessman chuckled as they entered the Carlings' home.

"What's so funny?" Maggie asked.

"Oh, nothing," Wessman lied. "Just a little secret joke between me'n ole Leatherneck, here." He bounced upstairs giggling.

Maggie looked at Teddy. He just shrugged. "A guy thing. Some day maybe we'll tell you."

CHAPTER EIGHT

BROTHER BROWN

"Concentrate, Elder. The discussions aren't that hard to memorize if you just concentrate. Let's try it again. We'll work on it one line at a time. This time I'll be the missionary and you can be Brother Brown, okay?"

"Sure." Teddy was standing in his pajamas, looking out their grimy window. A line from Robert Frost came into his head. "I can't understand it, Elder. In prep school I memorized a poem by Robert Frost about some road in the woods. I can still remember that – all of it. Why can't I memorize scriptures and discussions?"

"Okay, say it for me."

"I can't remember exactly how it starts, it's been so long. But it ends sort of like this:

'Two roads diverged in a wood, and I -

I took the one less traveled by,

And that has made all the difference.' See, it's still in my head. I just can't understand…"

"That was pretty good. Now, tell me what it means. Look outside. What do you see?" Wessman moved to the window.

166

"Rain. A path disappearing in the woods. And trees, lots of trees, big, wet ones."

"No, I mean use your imagination. Let's take your poem, for example. Tell me what it means, in your own words."

Teddy began, "It talks about a guy, a traveler; he comes to a fork in the road. He stops and looks down the road that forks off, wondering where it goes. He stands there a long time, thinking: the paths, all the other forks he's taken. Finally he promises himself someday he's going to return and travel down the other road. The road he didn't take is the better road, the easier, well-traveled one. But he senses that it's not the way for him, that he has to make his own way."

"That's cool. I didn't know you liked poems."

Teddy blushed slightly. "I used to read a lot when I had spare time in Jackson, when I wasn't guiding or fishing, I mean. Novels mostly, Steinbeck, Jim Harrison, Hemingway, Robert Ruark, Tom McGuane. The poetry is from a little book of Robert Frost my mom gave me for graduation from prep school. I still have it."

Wessman spoke. Okay Mr. Poet, tell me more about what *you* see out that window."

"Well…" Teddy began, "Obviously, I see trees. But the trees' branches are hanging down, almost touching the ground. They sweep the ground clean with the wind's motion and the rain that drips from them. The earth gives thanks to the trees for their shade. The small plants, the ground cover and their little flowers, the wild berries, the shrubs, the smaller trees, all are protected and nourished by the giant cedars and firs and spruces. The clouds that sit above everything give their rain as a blessing to the trees and the earth and the things beneath that the trees protect and nourish."

Wessman was silent for a few minutes. He spoke: "That's good. I have an idea. Close your eyes and think back to when you first heard about the church. Can you remember how new and sort of strange it was?" Teddy felt self-conscious, but he closed his eyes and nodded.

"Well, now you're Brother Brown. What's he thinking? This stuff is all new and strange to him. But we bombard him with doctrines that are pretty familiar stuff to us. You can open your eyes."

"Okay, it's all new and strange, and…?"

"We teach basic concepts, principles that Jesus and modern prophets taught. The gospel really is simple, if you think about it. Didn't they tell you in the MTC that each discussion is built on a few basic concepts, basic principles?"

"I think so. I was so tired and culture shocked. I was also darn excited to be going, I just wanted to get here. I don't know what I expected I was supposed to do. All those other guys in the MTC, all younger, shiny faces, eager, Mormon doo-bees. They knew all this stuff cold from growing up in the church, going to Sunday School and seminary and such. I guess I'm feeling a little intimidated by all this."

"I understand; I felt that way, too. I'll tell you a secret: I'm not very good at memorizing things. But I just kept working on the discussions and scriptures over and over and over until I got it. Boy, I tell you, I was so sick of memorizing. I was sick of Brother Brown this, Brother Brown that. Look, you're really good at some things - everyone is. You're an expert at this fly-fishing and river guiding stuff, right?"

"I think I am."

"Did you get it right, all of it, the first time you tried?"

"No." Teddy remembered the first awkward attempts to cast a fly rod, the snarled line, the frustration.

"You had to keep learning and trying, didn't you?" Teddy remembered how he kept at it with the help of a patient teacher.

"Yeah…"

"Missionary work is like that, learning discussions is like that. The more you work at it the easier it gets, I promise." Teddy remembered when he first got it right, the smooth back-cast blending into the forward cast as one fluid motion, the soft landing of the dry fly on water, the first trout that took his nicely-cast presentation…

And another thing…?"

"Yeah?" Teddy said.

"I had to really humble myself and ask for the help of the spirit. Have you done that yet, Elder? Have you asked for the spirit's help?"

Teddy pointed out the window at the incessant rain. Then he pointed to their suits, shirts and shoes drying out in various parts of their cabin. "Elder, tell me honestly, how much more humility do you think we need? We go out in the morning in half-dry suits and shirts. At lunch we come back soaked to the skin. We change out of our wet clothes and put on a second half-dry suit. We change again to go out at night. My shoes never get dry. I've never had athlete's foot until now and my shoes and suits are all falling apart because of all this dang rain!" Wessman just waited patiently, smiling. "Quit grinning! I'm serious, here!" Wessman feigned seriousness.

"And the food," Teddy continued, "Whoever thought you'd be paying $3 for a gallon of milk and a dollar apiece for a banana? Or a tomato? And three bucks for a small head of lettuce that's half brown? Highway robbery! I know, I know: it's the transportation costs."

"That's all?" Wessman asked.

"No, I'm not done yet! I never thought I'd get sick of eating fish. Every day we eat fish at least twice - salmon, halibut, snapper, crab, shrimps."

"At least it's *fresh*," Wessman offered. "And what're you complaining about… the high cost of everything! You're rich…"

"I told you to quit talking about my being rich or not!"

"Sorry. Anyway, Elder, do you know how many of us in this mission have moms or dads or brothers – in my case, my sister - working two or three jobs to keep us here? Lots of guys are being totally supported by their priesthood quorums back home. That doesn't stop them from doing their best, trying their hardest. They're humble, they work hard, and by dang, they keep at it until they learn those discussions."

Teddy thought about this. "Sorry. I didn't realize…" Then Teddy grinned slyly at Wessman. Two could play this game. "And another thing," Teddy picked up his rant where he left off, "I hate doing dishes. I don't mind cooking; in fact I like to cook. I just hate getting my hands in that yucky, greasy dish water."

"Okay, make you a deal: you cook and I'll wash dishes; I don't mind dish water. Anything else?"

"No, that's all. I'm done with my tantrum now." He grinned.

Wessman got into the flow of things. "Well, Brother Brown, I'm sure that after you're baptized and receive the gift of the Holy Ghost as your constant companion, all these things will work out just fine." He was grinning like a leprechaun.

"I hate it when you do that!" Teddy grabbed Wessman in a headlock and wrestled him to the floor. Tad, the college varsity wrestler, quickly escaped and had Teddy in a vise grip that pinned one arm back and forced his head down to the floor. Teddy was helpless. "Okay, I give! You can be Brother Brown now, if that's what's bothering you."

"Just remember, Marine, I know some self-defense moves of my own."

"Is study time over now?"

"Sure. Let's get some nice dry clothes on and do some work for the Lord."

Their first appointment that morning was with Michael Glass. "You okay?" Wessman asked Teddy as they walked through the rain toward the docks and the water taxi that would take them across the channel to the hangar. Mike had asked Barry Bluth to sit in with him for his first discussion.

"I'm fine," Teddy fibbed. Inside his emotions were churning. He wasn't sure how you approached a tough street fighter, especially one you'd whipped soundly a few days before.

"Remember, Elder, Mike is a son of our Heavenly Father, just like you are. Who could use the blessings of the gospel more than a guy like Mike? Three months ago we baptized this tough lumberjack in Kodiak. Before he had the gospel, every Saturday night was totally his for drinking and whoring in town. He smoked like a chimney and in between smokes he chewed. *Real* chewing tobacco, not that sissy, snuff- kind, either. From the minute he heard about Joseph Smith's vision, his life changed. By the time we got to the third discussion, you know that one: the Word of Wisdom…?"

"Yeah, I think I have it almost down now."

"Good for you. Well, anyway, Brother Borger, Jed Borger is his name, when we gave him the third discussion, he got up from the sofa, walked into the kitchen, took all his bottles out of the cupboard, and all his coffee, and all his cigarettes and chewing tobacco, and handed them to us. 'Here, you guys know what to do with this stuff. I guess I won't be needing it any more, will I?' Three months later Jed's the Sunday School Superintendent in their branch in Kodiak now. That's what the Spirit can do if you rely on it"

"I sure hope Mike feels the spirit."

"He will, Elder, he will. You just listen for the spirit and when the time's right, you bear him your testimony. I know you have one inside there." He placed his hand over Teddy's heart. "Be bold, let it out… with power, and let the Spirit testify."

Wessman asked Teddy to bear his testimony at the end of the first discussion. Teddy bore a short and simple testimony directly to Mike. He told Mike how he had recently been a Marine when something special happened to him, too – a friend in the military had had the courage to share the gospel with Teddy. His life had been changed because of that. Because of the gospel, Teddy had a mighty change of heart. He no longer wanted to do bad things (not that he had been all that bad before); he now wanted to do good the rest of his life. He then apologized to Mike if he had hurt him in any way; if he had hurt Mike's spirit by their fighting. He truly wanted to be a friend to Mike. He sensed that Mike was lonely and needed help but was too tough to ask for help.

Mike just shook his head and grinned painfully; the cuts on his lips hadn't yet healed. Teddy could tell it hurt Mike to smile. This was one tough boy. What kind of life had he lived that made him so hard?

Inspired by the spirit, Barry Bluth jumped in and bore his testimony also. He told Mike what a great friend he was, what a great spirit he felt Mike had, and how happy Barry would be if he could have the privilege to be the one who baptized him. He explained that he, Barry, had the priesthood authority to baptize, just like they had talked about in the discussion – the priesthood had been restored - he knew that, he had a testimony of that fact. Mike said he never knew that. Barry said it was because he had been too timid to tell him; he was sorry he had never shared the gospel with Mike.

Then Elder Wessman asked Mike to offer a prayer at the end of the discussion. They taught him the four simple steps to prayer. It was an awkward five minutes as they all knelt – the two elders, Mike, and his shipmate, waiting.

Mike looked up. "I said I'd listen to your lessons. I never agreed to pray."

Teddy spoke. "That's true. You don't have to if you feel uncomfortable. Another time, maybe…?"

"I ain't ever said a prayer out loud."

"I know you can do it, Mike," Wessman urged. "I'm a convert, too. I didn't grow up in the church; I didn't learn any of this stuff until I joined when I was a teen. Before then I never prayed out loud, either. Just take your time. Say what you feel in your heart. The Lord knows you by name, Mike, and he understands what's in your heart."

Mike stood up and paced back and forth; his brow was creased, his countenance dark, troubled. The other three remained kneeling. Teddy could feel the blood going out of his own knees, felt the tingling and then numbness. They waited. Mike leaned against the window, looking out at Coast Guard Cutter *USS Ezra Meadows*, his ship, his floating home, the flags drooping from the main mast above the bridge, sodden in the steady rain.

Mike continued looking out the window. "I'll do it another time, maybe.

They made an appointment for the second discussion for two days later.

"Tough guy," Teddy said, as they slogged home for lunch.

"He's hiding something – I can feel it," Wessman said.

"Do you think he'll ever crack through that shell and be humble enough to pray?"

Wessman pulled his soaking homburg hat tighter around his head, down low, so Teddy could barely see his dark brown eyes. "As a companion of mine said recently, 'I've seen worse.'"

"That hat looks really goofy on you, Elder."

Wessman tipped his head and a torrent of icy rain water spouted off the brim of his homburg onto Teddy's shoes.

CHAPTER NINE

A DOSE OF HUMILITY

The two elders had been in Sitka for a month now. In spite of repeated sincere requests to the branch members to give them referrals to teach, Michael Glass was their only investigator so far. And Teddy felt Mike was really "iffy." He put a big question mark beside Michael Glass's name on their *Golden Contacts* chalk board. Wessman erased the question mark and placed a check mark of his own in the "active" column; he stuck out his chin defiantly. "He's golden. You'll see."

The morning following their first discussion with Mike, after study time - as they planned their activities for the day - Teddy was in their small kitchen, rustling up breakfast. Elder Wessman was trying unsuccessfully to shine his damp shoes. Teddy noticed the heels were almost worn down to nothing. He knew Wessman stuffed pieces of cardboard inside to buffer his feet from the holes in the soles. Teddy would offer to pay for the repairs, but he knew Wessman was too proud for that. Wessman told Teddy what he thought the problem was. "I don't think we're humble enough."

"Not the humility thing again."

"I'm serious, elder. I feel strongly that we need to fast for the Lord to open doors for us. Face it Elder, we've been living pretty high on the hog, eating out almost every night for dinner. Oh, yeah, the members are really glad to have missionaries here. They love to feed us, but they're not giving us what we need most – *referrals* to teach. Don't cook any breakfast for me. I'm starting my fast right now and I'm going to fast until the spirit leads us to someone who really wants the gospel. You with me?"

Teddy ducked his head and guiltily put the breakfast fixings back in their dilapidated fridge. "Guess I'll join you, then. What else do you think we should do?"

"Pray and ask the Lord where we should go knock on doors."

Sitka is a somewhat hilly town nestled against the sea. A narrow strip of forest-covered land sloped from the water's edge, rising steadily for perhaps no more than one hundred yards in some places, a half-mile in others, until suddenly you were climbing the densely covered slopes of the steep craggy mountains that rose thousands of feet skyward. Most of the crags are snow-covered year round. Sitka was a rambling little town; no real city planning or limited development ever crossed the city fathers' minds. On Main Street, bars sat cheek-to-cheek with churches. It was hard work to clear the forests and create open spaces for building. The soil, what there was, was volcanic: thin and poor. Some homeowners tried to raise gardens but without much success; there simply were not enough days of sustained sunlight to grow vegetables. Some tried shrubs or flowers. Most gave up and adapted the native plants to semi-cultivation.

Most of the usable land in the town was somewhat level for building; there were no steep hills like, say, San Francisco or Seattle in the Lower Forty-eight. But there is one very steep hillside in Sitka, where a gaggle of wooden shanty houses cling precariously. It's toward the north edge of town, in the direction of Ellis/Alaska Air's seaport, out where the only asphalt road turns into gravel. It sits across the road from some abandoned docks and dilapidated fish cannery.

The cheap houses were built just before WWII by a salmon-canning company for their workers. The company had long since gone out of business. A few shrewd speculators bought the properties out of bankruptcy and offered them as low-rent housing. Once the tenants were settled, the landlords quickly raised the rents and cut back on services and utilities. The tenants could only complain; they were powerless to really do anything. The hillside was mostly thin soil that had eroded down from the surrounding mountains eons ago and settled as an unstable layer of volcanic pumice or grit on top of basalt rock base. Whenever Sitka experienced a prolonged rainy period (which was often), the sand-like soil beneath the cheap wood houses slowly sluffed away, washed down into the gutters (if you could call them gutters), then into drains, and out into the ocean channel, making a coffee-brown semi-circle stain against the dark green salt water.

When the sun infrequently came out, as it did on the day the elders fasted, the exposed soil dried out, the wind whipped it into a fine dust that blew in gusts swirling into shops, bars, offices, homes. It coated freshly-washed clothes hanging on clotheslines between houses with a thin layer of fine grit. The gritty dust also ground its way into the elders' suits, acting like an abrasive. That, combined with the constant moisture, wore them out twice as fast. Mothers of children who lived in Shanty Town (as the cheap housing was called) constantly warned their children not to play in or around the old cannery – rats and who knows what else could hurt them.

On this day of fasting, Elder Wessman said they should tract out Shanty Town. The elders arrived at their destination. Teddy looked up. They reminded him of boonie shacks but without the bright, wild paint jobs the Guamanians favored. These structures were set out like ascending layers of wooden boxes, thrown carelessly up the steep slope; many were leaning off plane and roofs sagged. Access to the homes nearest the street was no problem. You just went up two or three wooden steps and knocked. The higher up the hill you went, the more rickety, steep stairs to climb. They knocked all morning without any success. Not even street dogs, sleeping lazily in the sun, woke to pay them any mind.

They were near the top of the last row of houses, tired, hungry, weak from fasting, when Wessman pointed up and said, "That's the last one." Teddy nodded, using a handkerchief to wipe a pesky microscopic pumice grain from his eye.

As they came to the last door Wessman told Teddy it was his turn to give the approach. They could hear voices and muffled music from a radio coming from somewhere inside. Teddy knocked and waited. They heard the sounds of feet pounding down a flight of stairs. More stairs inside? The door opened; a shy child peeked around to see who their visitor was. She had black hair that fell in strands over her black, shining eyes. She was

Native American, Teddy guessed, but which band? "Hi, is your mother or father home?" Teddy asked.

The girl, about nine years old, pulled back, giggling. The elders waited.

"Tina, who is it?" from inside, upstairs, a woman's voice. The volume of the music fell sharply. "I can't hear you, Tina. Who is it?" Tina giggled again. More feet down the stairs: light steps, a woman. An Indian woman opened the door wider; Tina ducked behind her mother. "Yes?" she asked. She was thin, a rare thing among native women. She was dressed in men's overalls and too-large work shirt with an old, paint-stained apron on. She wore cotton painter's gloves and in one hand wielded a paint brush - the color was a French blue.

Teddy explained they were Mormon missionaries, elders, and that they had a special message of hope for her and her family. He asked her name.

"I'm Rose Gilbert. I'm kind of busy right now painting, as you can see. Could you maybe come back later?"

From upstairs, a man's voice: "Who is it, Rosie?"

"Some Mormon guys, missionaries. You want to talk to them?"

After a thirty-second silence, Rosie's husband answered, "Sure, have them come in." She waved the paint brush at them, beckoning the elders to follow her upstairs. They climbed after Rosie and Tina. Good smells of something frying met them. Potatoes and onions?

Rosie introduced the elders. "This is my husband, Richard. I don't know your names…"

"I'm Elder Wessman."

"And I'm Elder Buckley."

"That's funny," Richard grinned. "Both of you have the same first names. You guys hungry? I was just making lunch. Do you have time to stay and eat? We can talk about what it is you want while we eat, okay?"

"Sure," they both replied.

The Gilberts lived in a four-room walkup flat. Rosie kept it neat and clean. There were a few family photos, a few art prints on the wall. Teddy noticed several articles of native handicraft – baskets, potlatch bowls, etc. – on a side table. Rosie had been painting one wall in the living room; a drop cloth covered the floor where paint cans and rags sat. She was using a kitchen chair as a make-shift ladder. Teddy smelled someone smoking very strong cigarettes. In the far corner, listening to the now-quieter radio, slowly rocking back and forth and smoking what could only be Camels, was a little wrinkled, white-haired man. He wore an authentic Indian-knit wool sweater, worn cords and slippers. His white hair was pulled back in a pony-tail, fastened with a rubber band. His eyes were closed; he had a smile on his face. "That's Chief Russell, my father," Rosie explained. "He's a shaman, a holy man in our culture." She said the word *culture* almost self-consciously in front of these two white men.

The living room opened into a combination kitchen-eating area. On the table sat a washtub surrounded by spills of water. Water dripped onto the wood floor. Richard pointed to the washtub and explained, "I'm shucking fresh clams for our meal. You guys like fried clams? I roll them in cracker crumbs and fry them in butter. Delicious!"

Teddy took off his suit coat, rolled up his sleeves, loosened his necktie. "May I help you? I don't know how to do clams, but I used to shuck oysters when I was a kid. My family had a summer home on…" He started to say *Cape Cod* – his turn to be self-conscious. "We vacationed a few times in New England, on the ocean. We went to some clam bakes. That's where I learned how to open the oysters."

"It's probably the same way. Watch this." Richard showed him how to insert a thin-bladed paring knife between the two tightly-closed shell halves, cut through the hinge muscle, while giving the knife a sharp twist. "See, they just pop open for you."

"Yeah, it's the same as the oysters - exactly." Teddy said.

In about five minutes Richard and Teddy had shucked enough clams for a big meal. "Now we rinse them in sea water, dip them in egg, roll them in cracker crumbs and plop them into the frying pan full of melted butter, and …just let 'em cook a few minutes," Richard said.

While Teddy was helping with the clams, Wessman helped set the table. He chatted with Rosie and learned they had four children: Ricky Jr., thirteen; Natalie, eleven; Cory, a boy, ten; and Tina, the baby, nine. Rosie gathered the other three children from their bedroom where they had been playing or reading. They shyly shook hands with the elders. When the clams were ready, Rosie dished them up on a huge platter, with sizzling-hot fried potatoes and onions on the side.

Chief Russell rubbed out his cigarette and took his place at the head of the table, the honored patriarch. They all joined hands around the table, bowed their heads to pray. Richard looked at Elder Wessman. "Would you honor us by saying grace?"

"That was really good," Elder Wessman said. "That's the first time I ever ate clams."

Dessert was a bowl of canned peach slices. Rosie offered the elders coffee. "You don't drink coffee? Why not?"

"It's part of our religious beliefs, Sister Gilbert." Wessman was totally comfortable calling these strangers brother and sister.

"I hope I didn't offend…" she said. The elders assured her she hadn't.

Richard said, "Tell us about this religion of yours. As you probably guessed, we are a Christian family. So we are, of course, interested in having good exchanges of religious ideas. Please sit down and tell us all about your church."

Two hours later, after giving the Gilbert family the first discussion using pencil and paper in place of their flannel board, the elders floated home on wings of light and joy. "They prayed, Elder, they prayed! Did you ever hear a prayer like that on a first discussion?"

"They're Christians, Elder. They're used to praying. It's second nature."

"It was a really nice prayer," Teddy repeated. "Brother Gilbert told me a neat place close by where we can catch some dolly vardens on P-day," Teddy said.

"Dolly whats?"

"It's a fish like a trout. We can catch some. You said I could teach you about fly-fishing."

"That's true, I did, Elder. Where is this place? Do we have to go in a boat? You know it's against mission rules to go in small boats."

"No boat needed. We can walk there in about a half-hour. It's out of town on the logging road, about a mile past the seaport. He says we can't miss it – it's a small stream that goes in a culvert under the road and dumps into the ocean. He says there's a nice sandy beach there, too."

"Guess we have to buy fishing licenses."

"Nope. Dollies are an ocean fish. If we catch them at the mouth of the stream, where it flows into the ocean, we don't need licenses. I just need to find some equipment now…"

"Uh… I should tell you…"

"Yeah…?"

"I promised Brother Gilbert we'd help him repair the crankshaft on his fishing boat. He could use the two of us because he can't afford a real mechanic."

"Well… okay. But if we finish soon enough maybe we can still have time to fish?"

"I'm okay with that plan."

"What do you know about fixing crankshafts on boats, anyway?"

"It's the same as a car or truck – these fishing boats use Ford or Chevy engines. I helped some part-member family on Kodiak once. The wife was a member, the husband not. He was a commercial fisherman, too, just like Richard. We helped him fix his boat a few times."

"Did he ever join?"

"Not yet… but I have faith he will. Some day."

That night, Teddy put a big check mark in chalk in the "golden contact" column, next to the Gilberts' names.

CHAPTER TEN

WEDDING BELLS

P-Day was overcast; the clouds hung low, fat, threatening rain. As they left the cabin to walk the half-mile into town, Wessman said, "Are you sure this fishing trip is a good idea? Look at those clouds; it's gonna rain for sure."

"Elder, it always rains here, except..."

"...when it doesn't. I know, I've lived here longer than you have."

"How long have you been here so far, in Alaska?" Teddy asked.

"I was three months in Fairbanks, then three months in Kodiak. That's six months, which is supposed to be the limit for elders in Alaska. I've been here over three weeks now. I don't really know why President Moffatt sent me here. Must be something the Lord wants me to do... Like maybe break in a greenie like you."

They reached the laundromat in town and left their clothes to wash while they toured the old Russian cemetery a couple blocks away. The cemetery was atop a small hill with an aspect that viewed the harbor and surrounding vistas beyond with a view of nearly two-hundred fifty degrees. In the near distance they could see the base of Mt. Edgecumbe, an inactive volcano; the snowy peak was shrouded with clouds. They strolled through the small cemetery, reading the foreign names on the markers. Some of the markers were made of stone; many were carved from wood that was decaying in the harsh weather; many of the graves bore dates as early as 1844. Teddy realized that was the same year the Prophet was martyred.

"Elder, how do you say these Russian names?" Wessman asked. Teddy ticked off the ones that were not obliterated, the ones he could make out: Baranof, Chichigof, Romanof, Rezanof, Shelikof, Plotnikof, and so on.

"When I was younger I watched an old Gregory Peck movie about the Russian fur trade in Alaska," Teddy said. "It was in a time before America bought Alaska from the Russians. I can't remember much about it or the title, except I remember it was set right here in Sitka. This was the Russian capital; Sitka is an Indian name, Tlingit Indian. The Russians named the place New Archangel. Sitka - New Archangel - was the center of their fur trade. The Russians were big on seal skins, beavers, otters. They really loved the otter furs. The Russians also shipped salmon, lumber and ice from here to markets in Europe, Asia, Hawaii and California. Otters are almost wiped out now from so much hunting of them. Did you know that?"

"I didn't know that. How do you know so much about furs? Oh, yeah, I forgot… you're a mountain man. How much did we pay for Alaska?"

"I should remember… a few million, I think. The Russians didn't get very darn much for it. We got the best part of that deal!" Teddy checked his watch. Time's moving fast. I've seen enough for today."

"Me, too. Well, mountain man, you going to show me how to catch those dolly whatcha-callits?"

They hitched a ride on the edge of town with a Forest Service worker who was going their way. "You fellas goin' fishin'?" They nodded and jumped in the cab.

"We heard there was a little stream about two miles out that dumps into a white sandy beach. Know it?" Teddy said.

The Forest Service agent said he did and could drop them there. "That looks like a salmon rod you got there. It's too early for salmon."

"We know; we're trying for dollies. Heard they come up the streams this time of year to gorge on salmon fry."

"That's for sure. You can throw anything at them that looks like a baby salmon and you got a good mess of dollies for dinner! Here we are."

The agent helped them find the stream Brother Gilbert had described, but not before the Elders had asked him the Golden Questions, and he had politely declined. The stream wasn't large, maybe ten feet across. It was clear, cold and fast-running. The stream was unnamed, as many streams in Alaska are. It tumbled a relatively short distance from an ancient, unseen glacier, thousands of feet above them. Above the girdle of dense forest they could barely make out a thin white vertical line dropping from a cleft in the black volcanic rocks far above, a waterfall. The small part of the stream they could see on the other side of the logging road, where it appeared out of the thick evergreens, tumbled rapidly over and through a jumble of boulders the size of Volkswagens before it sluiced through the culvert, under the logging road, and merged into the ocean.

Below the road was another dense line of low-hanging Sitka spruce, red cedar, and fir trees they had to pass through to access the estuary of the stream and the beach. The stream was well-known to the local sportsmen and picnickers – there was a worn footpath leading through the fireweed and salmon berry undergrowth bordering the stream down through the trees. Along the path were scattered cans, bottles and assorted trash, including baby diapers.

They started down the path with Teddy eagerly in the lead. "Wait," Teddy whispered. He motioned to Wessman who was following.

"What…?" Wessman said

"Look, over there, through the trees." Wessman pushed close behind Teddy to see. To their right, through the trees, they saw part of the white sandy beach and the hulking dead carcass of a sea lion left by the last high tide. Perched on the sea lion was a huge bald eagle. A smaller eagle was at the dead animal's side, pulling at its entrails. A gathering of assorted other smaller scavenger birds waited their turn: ravens and seagulls, mostly. "I want to get some pictures of this," Teddy whispered. "Let's get closer." Teddy had a daypack with their fishing gear, some lunch and the one luxury he had bought on his Japan trip, a Nikon camera with extra lenses. He took out the camera and adjusted the setting, the focus. "Okay, ready. Let's move slowly so as not to spook them."

Teddy led the way down the path again, pushing wet tree branches out of his way. One branch swept back and slapped Wessman in the face, soaking his head. "Thanks!"

"Shhh!" Teddy turned and warned his companion.

"Elder, look out…!" Wessman yelled.

Teddy turned in time to be swatted by the pinion of a bald eagle, flying at eye level, knocking off his MSU ball cap. The bird had been sitting in the last tree at the edge of the sandy beach, keeping sentinel watch for the others. Teddy instinctively raised his arm to protect his face. The huge bird screamed as it attacked; its talons grazed Teddy's scalp, causing a scratch. Out of instinct, Wessman dropped to the ground.

During the few seconds of the attack, Teddy's Nikon went flying, tumbling into the stream. "Elder, you okay?" Wessman asked. Teddy nodded. "Elder, you're bleeding!"

Teddy ran his hand through his hair - he looked at the wet crimson stain on his hand. He felt around and located the scratch. "It must have grazed me with its talon. It's not too deep, really small. Should stop bleeding soon." He found his cap, put it back on. "My camera… Where's my camera?" Teddy got on his knees and scrabbled around in the grass and fireweed searching frantically. Wessman joined the search; they looked for ten minutes finding nothing. They were muddy, their hands were scratched, their clothes wet. "I think it must be in the stream," Teddy concluded sadly. Teddy waded across a shallow riffle to search from the far bank; they spent several minutes walking the stream banks back and forth in the area of the attack, looking, finding nothing.

"Was it expensive?" Wessman shouted over the rushing waters

"It was a Nikon, got it in Japan. Cost quite a bit, but it wasn't like it's a Leica or a Zeiss," Teddy shouted back. Wessman shrugged; he didn't have a clue what Teddy was talking about. Teddy motioned to Wessman to tramp on down to the stream's mouth. Out in the clearing on the beach, Teddy said, "We can look some more on the way back. Let's do some fishing. I saw some dollies holding against the banks up there while we were looking for the camera."

Frank Carling had loaned Teddy his lightest fiberglass spinning rod and reel. It was eight feet long and supple; Frank said he used it for trout fishing. He had several heavier salmon and salt water fishing rods. Teddy waggled the trout rod. "This will work." Teddy bought a package of number six hooks from the hardware store that also served as a sporting goods emporium. At the drug store he'd bought pipe cleaners, a small bottle of clear finger nail polish and several permanent markers – red, blue, green and black. He borrowed some sewing thread from Maggie. In the thrift store he found a woman's old hat plumed with pheasant tail feathers; he got that item for twenty-five cents. Wessman couldn't figure out what his companion was doing so he just went along to humor his passion for fly-fishing. After all, Teddy had agreed to the friendly game of round ball.

The night before P-day Teddy had stayed up an extra hour tying up a dozen *flies*. He colored several pipe cleaners mixing black and green for a dark olive effect, let them dry and wound them tightly around the hook for a wormlike body. He added a tuft of pheasant tail for wings, tied it off with Maggie's thread and sealed the thread with a judicious dab of clear polish. He held each one up to their one bare light that dangled on a wire from the living room ceiling. Teddy pronounced them acceptable.

"What's the limit on these things?" Wessman asked after they had caught their seventh dolly.

"I don't think there is a limit. Alaskans consider these as trash fish. They probably think we're crazy for even bothering with them. Did you see the look on that Forest Service guy's face when I said we were after dollies?"

"No. Guess I was looking down the road. Boy, this is fun. I could really get into this fly-fishing stuff. How big you think they are?"

"These are small – about two pounds apiece. I think they get bigger. And this isn't really fly-fishing. If I had my own fly rods and other gear here it would be a lot more fun. You haven't lived until you catch a big brown or rainbow on a light bamboo rod."

"Well I had plenty of fun. Sorry about your camera. Bamboo…they still make those things? I thought they went out with the dinosaurs. What time is it? We probably ought to be getting back. I'd like to check the mail before the post office closes."

"Okay, I'm ready; seven fish is enough for a decent fish fry." Teddy hoisted the forked willow stick with the silvery dollies, their red flesh exposed in the stomach cavity after gutting. Wessman took the rod.

"Elder…you won't believe this!" Wessman waved a square cream-colored card with formal printed script.

"What is it?"

"My wedding announcement!" Wessman had tears in his eyes. This guy cries easily, Teddy thought. He'd probably cry at a super market grand opening.

"Let's see." Teddy looked at the large card. It read that Mr. and Mrs. Charles Cox of Demming, New Mexico, were pleased to announce the engagement of their daughter Carla to Mr. Tad Wessman, son of Laura Wessman, of Thatcher, Arizona. Wedding reception…etc. Marriage solemnized in the Mesa L.D.S. Temple... etc. The date was only three months away. "Elder, it's only three months from now. Did you know this was coming? And when did you get engaged, anyway?"

"I *sort of* knew it was coming. Carla and me, we got engaged before I left on my mission. Actually the night before. We just kept it secret from everyone. We been kind of engaged since eighth grade. She's the real reason I joined the church. She said she would only marry a returned missionary. In the temple. I didn't have a clue what she meant. I had to find out 'cause I was so crazy in love with her… even clear back in the sixth grade when we first met in middle school in Miss Stevenson's home room."

"You can't be engaged in the eighth grade, for heaven' sake!"

"We were," Wessman said defensively, his face starting to redden.

"I'm sorry. Okay, I guess you two are the exception. Well congratulations, you sly dog. Three months, huh?" Teddy hugged his companion.

And he really meant it.

CHAPTER ELEVEN

TOTEMS

Chief Russell sat in his corner by the window smoking and listening to his gospel station on the old, crackling radio. He slowly rocked back and forth with his eyes closed. Sometimes his lips moved in a whisper; sometimes he made a slight smile.

At the conclusion of the second discussion with the Gilberts, the elders bore strong testimonies of the Book of Mormon, its truthfulness and the miracle of a young boy with scant formal education possessing the power from heaven to translate the gold plates. The Gilberts committed to read and pray about the Book of Mormon.

The next morning as the elders were out trying to locate members of the church from a list of possibilities the branch clerk in Juneau had sent them, they stopped by the boat basin. Brother Gilbert was just finishing up some work on his boat engine. The big motor thrummed smoothly, the exhaust burbling out the stern, making oil slicks and little rainbows on the green water. The tide was out; the pier pilings were wet and dark partway up, then silvery gray above the high water line. Exposed starfish of varied colors were stacked on top of each other, clinging to the pilings. A tawny, young spotted harbor seal swam back and forth close by, making a small vee in the calm water and hoping for a free meal of unused bait herring to be tossed overboard. A lone gull stood on a single leg atop a weathered guano-streaked piling.

The air was calm; you could hear the screeching of sea birds and cackling of ravens. Smoke columns rose straight up from the Japanese pulp mill a few miles south nestled along Sitka Sound. Out on the sound a lone tug boat pulled a mile-long flotilla of logs relentlessly toward the mill. Richard wiped his hands with a greasy rag and shook their hands more vigorously than he ever had. "Elders, I'm happy this morning." A big smile spread across his handsome face, his dark eyes shone. "Do you know why I'm happy?"

"Because you got your motor running?" Teddy ventured.

"No, it's something else. Something you can't wait to tell us, isn't it?" Wessman said.

"Rosie and I sat up almost all night taking turns reading the book to each other. We couldn't put it down."

"It has that effect on a lot of people who read it for the first time," Wessman said.

Richard continued eagerly. "We came to the part where Alma is secretly preaching to the people about baptism and bearing one another's burdens and being witnesses at all times and so on, you probably know it. We'd just read where it says 'they clapped their hands for joy' when we both heard this clapping sound coming from our kids' bedroom. We looked in and Tina was clapping her hands in her sleep. I swear to you she was sound asleep. She looked like a beautiful little angel with a smile on her face. I took it as a sign from heaven. We both felt a strong feeling in our hearts, like we were expanding almost to exploding with, with... with total *happiness*! We decided to do as you said when you promised we'd know if we prayed in faith. We kneeled down and prayed to know if this book and this church is true. We both received an even stronger impression of total peace and comfort. We know that it's true. We want to be baptized... as soon as we can. Our kids, too. When can we do it? What do we have to do now?"

"The first thing we have to do is give you and your family the rest of the discussions. There are four more. Then we have to find a font in some church that baptizes by total immersion. We don't even have our own building, let alone a font. Unless you want to be baptized in the ocean," Wessman said.

"I've been dunked in the ocean before; it's too cold," Richard laughed.

"We'll ask one of the ministers in town if maybe we can use their font," Wessman said. Somehow Teddy doubted that any minister would ever let them use his font to baptize one of his flock into the Mormon church. His doubts were based on some recent anti-Mormon articles in the semi-weekly local newspaper.

As the elders walked to their next appointment with Michael Glass and Barry Bluth, they met Chief Russell out for a morning walk. He motioned for them to stop. He was trying to tell them something. They saw he didn't have any teeth. He was difficult to understand. They listened carefully.

"Last night you talk to Rosie and Richard about a book," he began. "You say it is about our people, where they come from. You say this book talk about son of Great Spirit. He come down from sky to visit our people. Many years, long time. Dressed in white robes?" The elders said yes, that was right. "Then he go back up in sky but he promise to come back some day?" The elders affirmed that was right, too.

"I Tlingit chief, shaman. You whites call us medicine man. Not right. Shaman more than medicine. I see things. I hear things. I keep old religion in here," he pointed to his head. "And here," he placed a hand over his heart. "You see totems in park?" He pointed across town. They said they had.

"Tlingit put big black bird on top of totem. Big wings. All spread out like this." He stretched his arms out. The elders nodded. This was getting interesting. Teddy felt a tingle and his neck hairs stood on end. Chief Russell continued. "Big black bird is raven. Raven mean same as son of Great Spirit. Son come down like raven. Son fly back to Great Spirit like raven. Son will fly back to visit our people like raven some day. When white missionaries come long time ago, Chief was little boy. I become Christian. I was saved. I know Jesus now. Jesus same Son of Great Spirit."

The elders stood quietly. The old man motioned for them to bow their heads. They did. He came close and placed a hand on each of their heads and whispered something, a chant, in his native tongue. Then he removed his hands.

"What did you say to us just now, Chief Russell?" Teddy asked.

"I know I know I know salvation free," he chanted.

He smiled at them, pulled out his pack of Camels, lit one and walked slowly away, coughing.

CHAPTER TWELVE

A PORTABLE FONT

Something had changed in Michael's attitude between his first and second discussions, something palpable. He seemed less hostile, more friendly, more focused, truly more interested in what the elders were trying to teach him. He told the elders that he'd read the two pamphlets they left from the first discussion; he was especially impressed by the pamphlet *The First Vision*. He didn't know this had all started a mere hundred miles from his own home in upstate New York. Mike said he and Barry had been having many private talks about how he met the elders, his first discussion, what he had been reading, his feelings about religion in general. They discussed what he thought God was like. He wondered if God really heard prayers. How could God know each and every soul that had ever been born on earth? Mike's buddy Barry had prayed with him in a private place they found. With Barry's help and urging, Mike had finally said a simple prayer on his own. He prayed at the end of the second and third discussions.

The third discussion on *The Word of Wisdom* was a tough one for Mike. He promised to try and give up his tobacco and other habits that were contrary to these new teachings. He never thought of coffee, smoking, or having a little wine, was any way connected with religious practices.

Now he understood somewhat more about "you weird Mormons." He also promised he would pray for strength to give up his habits.

The elders had just finished the fourth discussion on the Atonement. Mike seemed disturbed by something. His countenance had clouded over. Mike got up and paced the room. Barry looked at the elders and shrugged his shoulders. "Anything you want to talk about? Something you want to get off your chest, Mike? We're licensed ministers of the gospel; we can keep confidences, if you want to tell us something," Wessman said.

What's he doing? Teddy wondered. We're not Catholic priests! We don't do confessionals. This is getting murky. I don't have a good feeling about where this might be going.

"Should Barry leave the room so we can talk in private?" Wessman asked. Mike nodded his head. Barry quietly left, closing the door behind.

The discussion on Christ's infinite sacrifice triggered something weighing on Mike's conscience. Mike told the elders he knew in his heart what they were teaching was true. He believed all of it, their testimonies, Barry's testimony. He needed to know if he was eligible for Christ's atoning sacrifice. The elders said of course he was: every soul was eligible for forgiveness and the cleansing blood of Christ through baptism. It's right there in the scriptures; it was especially very clear in *The Book of Mormon*. Wessman helped him turn to the probative verses and they read together. Mike said he wasn't so sure it applied to him. Wessman asked what he meant by that.

Mike asked if everything he told them was in confidence, like someone confessing to his priest or minister or rabbi. Was it legally binding? Wessman assured Mike it was. Mike then confessed to them a dark secret from his past, something so troubling they quickly understood the heavy burden of sin and guilt this man was carrying. What a heavy load!

Michael Glass was not his real name; he couldn't tell them his real name; he was in the federal Witness Protection Program. He had grown up in a traditional Sicilian-Italian family in Buffalo, New York. At a very early age he learned that his father, his uncles, and his older male cousins were all *Cosa Nostra*. There was no pressure on him to become part of the Mob. It was just a thing he was naturally expected to do when the time came. And the time finally did come. His first assignment was as driver for a major heist. They hijacked a truckload of television sets parked at a truck stop on the interstate highway west of Buffalo. Everything went as planned. Mike enjoyed the adrenaline high from the experience; he also enjoyed his cut of the payout. He liked the money, the things it could buy. He had money to take girls out and show them a good time in swank restaurants. He bought a nice car, nice clothes, an expensive wristwatch. Succeeding jobs went pretty much the same for a year.

When Mike was eighteen, he was assigned to be the driver for a hit job over in Rochester. He didn't know it was a hit job; it was all planned with absolute secrecy. The less anyone knew, the less they would have to say if they got caught by the police. The Rochester hit job changed Mike's feelings about the Mob he was becoming part of. Mike had a conscience, or at least he thought he did. No, he wasn't the trigger, just the driver, he reasoned, so it was okay, wasn't it? There was no adrenaline rush this time - just terror and fear. His heart became sickened by the thought that he had part in a murder. He lay awake at nights. His grades in high school suffered; he dropped out. He was driving himself mad with worry that maybe there was a witness or maybe someone ratted to the cops. He quit eating; he lost weight, his mother worried. He started drinking to forget; he became a chain-smoker to "calm my nerves", he told his family. Mike went to his parish priest and tried to confess, but at the last second lied and said he'd done "some sexual things with a girl." He was told to say so many prayers and Hail Marys. It didn't resolve the guilt; he felt even worse for lying to his priest. With time things didn't get any better for Mike; they got worse.

He was assigned to drive for another hit job, this time in Montreal, Canada. Mike worried even more about the consequences if they got stopped at the border crossing the St. Lawrence at Thousand Islands. What if the Canadian immigration guys found the gun? He'd be charged as an accomplice. Canada was really hard on concealed weapons charges, Mike had heard. He had also heard the Mounties were really tough, good at breaking guys down, getting confessions. If he ended up in jail - even a Canadian penitentiary, it didn't matter where – the Mob had long arms and even longer memories. They could get you anywhere. They could get you really easy in jail. They hated snitches, even a guy that snitches under pressure. It made no difference if you cracked under police questioning bordering on near torture. There was no allowance for weakness.

The Montreal job went badly. The shooter was young and not very efficient. The target was not cleanly killed; he lingered in agony for several days before dying while the police searched for the killer or killers. There was a lot of bad publicity; the story was all over the news in Montreal, Toronto, and Buffalo. The *New York Times* ran the gang-style killing as their lead cover story for several days. The Montreal police brought in the Mounties because they thought they had a witness. The witness allegedly stated the getaway car had New York license plates.

Right after the job went badly, the shooter decided they had to split up. He knew a safe house in Hamilton, Ontario, near Toronto where he could lie low until the coast was clear. He gave Mike an address and told him it was another safe house in St-Laurent, a suburb close by in the southwest part of Montreal. He told Mike to ditch the car or at least steal some Quebec plates and throw the "hot" New York ones in a river. They split up. Mike was scared, too scared to phone Buffalo for instructions on what to do next. He was totally on his own. He couldn't speak French, especially the funny French they speak in Quebec. He didn't dare ask for directions to the safe house. He got a map and figured his best plan was to try and drive there at rush hour. He stole some Quebec license plates, threw the New York plates in the St. Lawrence, and finally made his way to the safe house.

Mike laid low for a week in the safe house; he was not allowed to go out for anything. His handler got him onto a big diesel rig that was going south to New York. They hid Mike in the cargo; somehow he got through U.S. Customs without being detected. At Albany, he was transferred into another interstate rig that was headed west, through Utica, Syracuse, Rochester and home to Buffalo.

A decision was made by the bosses: it wasn't safe for Mike to hang around Buffalo any longer. The witness had apparently seen just enough of the hot New York plates, had remembered just enough numbers and letters that the getaway car had been initially traced to the upstate New York region. It was only a matter of time until the FBI zeroed in on the Buffalo mob. Mike had to get out of town for the good of everyone.

Mike explained to the two elders that decisions like this were not made in consultation with the person being sent away. He had no say in the matter. False identity documents were provided; he started growing his beard and hair out. He bleached his hair; he also tried bleaching his beard, but it didn't work, so he left it his natural dark color. At a truck stop in the country along Lake Erie, near the Pennsylvania state line, very late one night, Mike was bundled aboard yet another interstate truck, a reefer, heading west to Los Angeles with a load of apples. Mike hid in the sleeping compartment of the truck, getting out only for bathroom breaks behind bushes along lonely roads in the countryside at night. The two drivers, his handlers, got food and drinks for him. After what seemed like days, they stopped at another truck stop on the edge of North Las Vegas.

His handlers told Mike he was to go to the men's rest room and wait. In a half an hour someone would meet him and transfer him to another truck. They didn't tell him where it would be headed. They handed him a hundred dollars in cash and left; he never knew their names. Five minutes later two men in jeans, denim jackets, heavy boots, and wearing wool watch caps approached him in the rest room.

"You (he used Mike's real name)?" one of them asked him. He said he was, thinking it was strange they got there so soon and that someone could know his name if he was supposed to be under deep cover. The second man grabbed him, pinned him to the wall while the first one put cuffs on him. The first one said they were FBI agents and he was under arrest. He was booked into the Clark County Jail and put in a small solitary cell. No one visited or talked to him except the guards who brought his meals and took away the empty tray. They didn't say much. Days went by before he learned his fate.

Mike was hustled out of his cell, cuffed hand and foot, and transported for about fifteen minutes somewhere in a windowless van. When he got out of the van they were apparently in the basement parking lot of a big building. Mike was escorted upstairs in a private elevator by four large, armed Federal Marshals. He was taken to a small conference room without windows; the marshals waited outside. Two different FBI agents questioned him for what seemed like hours. Mike demanded he have a lawyer present; that request was denied. He was finally offered a deal.

Because of his age, if he would cooperate with the FBI and name the shooter, Mike would be put into the federal Witness Protection Program. He would only have to give a written statement under oath, just enough testimony to warrant an indictment of the shooter. He was promised he would not ever have to appear in court to testify. He would be given a new name and identity. He would be relocated to a different part of the country, provided with a living allowance and FBI protection for two or three years, maybe longer, until the whole thing blew over. "You're asking me to sign my own death warrant," Mike had said.

"Of course, if you refuse our offer, we indict, you get convicted and spend a long time in a federal pen. We're not talking a couple years in a camp, one of those posh country club facilities." The second agent took over and assured Mike that after he did get out of the federal pen, Canada would extradite him, and he'd be prosecuted, convicted, sentenced to a very long term and imprisoned all over again. The agent said he had heard Canadian penitentiaries were even nastier than our good old American ones were.

"Either way, I'm a dead man."

The first agent took over the interview again. "Not if you were to enlist in say, the Navy or Coast Guard. You get assigned to a ship for four years. Ships move around a lot. We can arrange that. We've done that for other guys before, and it's worked out just fine for them. They eventually marry, get nice jobs, go to college, settle down as ordinary citizens. You can be the same as them. Think about it for awhile. You let us know when you want to talk some more." He called the marshals in, and Mike went back to the county jail. He spent another month in solitary. He knew the way they held him was totally illegal. That wasn't the issue. His life was the big issue.

Mike finally took the deal they offered. And here he was now, asking for baptism.

Wessman was silent for a long time. Teddy didn't know what to say; he had no experience in these sticky situations. Finally Wessman spoke. "I think we need to talk to our mission president about this. He would know a clear answer. He's supposed to be here in ten days for a conference with our branch. Can you wait?"

"I've waited several years now. I guess ten more days won't hurt," Mike said.

Wessman asked Teddy to say their closing prayer. Like a good soldier, he complied, but his heart just wasn't in it this time.

The elders were downcast and silent on the way back to their cabin.

Wessman suggested they stop by the docks and see if Richard Gilbert was working on his boat.

"Elders, climb aboard and see what I'm working on." He proudly showed them a plywood box measuring four feet by eight feet. It was held together by hinges that locked to set it up and unlocked to take it down.

"All we have to do is line it with plastic sheeting, fill it with water and presto! Our baptismal font. You said you had asked several ministers to use their baptism fonts and they turned you down. This solves our problem. And you can use it over and over again every time you need to baptize someone! We just need a place to put it that has a drain to empty the water."

"That must have cost you a lot of money," Teddy said.

"I'm Indian, remember. We trade things. I got it for only a few clams!"

CHAPTER THIRTEEN

BRANCH CONFERENCE

The elders located several more members from the list of LDS believed to be living in Sitka. Until the anti-Mormon articles ran in the paper, these members had no idea there was a branch, let alone other Mormons in the town. Teddy suggested they should write an article of their own about the positive things Mormons represented. They paid a visit to the newspaper's editor and he agreed to run the article if they would write it. He asked if they had pictures of themselves he could include. He also wanted a brief biography on each of them. He warned he might have to do some editing, depending on the length and their writing abilities. He politely declined Teddy's invitation to attend their Sunday worship service to meet the local Mormons and learn what they were like firsthand.

A somewhat edited version of their article ran in the next issue. A couple more members came out of the woodwork and made their membership known. Sacrament meeting attendance swelled to nearly two dozen, counting the core they had started with two months before: the two elders, newly-found members, Barry Bluth and his shipmate Marvin Shumway, and the investigators, the Gilbert family and Michael Glass.

Preparations were being made for their branch conference, now only four days away, with President and Sister Moffatt. The elders helped Richard haul his collapsible font across the channel (he preferred to use his own boat) and lug it piece-by-piece into the Carlings' basement. The basement had both a cold water valve they could connect a garden hose to fill the font and a drain hole in the concrete floor. They set up the font in one corner so there was at least support from two sides against the pressure a couple hundred gallons of water could exert. The two witnesses would lean their bodies against the other two sides, pushing back against the bulging sides. The elders reckoned they could fill half the font with the garden hose and haul five-gallon buckets of hot water from the nearby laundry room to top it off. To test Richard's invention, they filled it to where they thought the level would be high enough to completely cover a full-grown man, but not overflow when his submersion displaced the water. They measured Richard's height: five feet eleven inches. "How much do you weigh?" Wessman asked.

"Before I gave up beer, smoking and black coffee, I used to weigh about one hundred seventy. Since you guys taught us about the Word of Wisdom, we've all put on weight," he laughed, patting his stomach. "I'd say I've gained ten pounds in about two weeks. Food has never been so good, now that I can taste it!"

Wessman volunteered to be the test dummy since he was the closest to Richard's weight. They figured the eight-foot sides of the font allowed plenty of room for Richard's horizontal length if the elder performing the ordinance carefully took a spot they'd mark with an X in permanent magic marker on the font bottom. Richard was very scientific in pointing all of these factors out to the elders. They had the font filled and Wessman was ready in his tee shirt and gym shorts. "Phew! Don't you ever wash your gym clothes, Elder? You smell like a moldy locker!" Teddy teased.

Teddy, also dressed in his gym clothes, was chosen to act the role of the baptizing elder for this dress rehearsal. Wessman joined Teddy in the font. Teddy, all seriousness, said "Are you ready, Brother Brown?" The elders moved around a bit until they thought they were standing in the right places to make it work.

Maggie Carling was due to have her baby any day now. Her belly was so swollen Teddy wondered how she could keep her balance. When she walked he saw how she waddled from side to side. It was still a great mystery to Teddy how women could go through pregnancy and childbirth. Someday, he thought, I guess I'll understand it. "I look like a big fat pigeon," Maggie said.

"You walk like one, too, mama," Amy laughed

Maggie agreed to lean against one side of the filled font for this dress rehearsal. Amy and David were eager to lean their light weight against the other side; they giggled when Teddy called Wessman "Brother Brown".

"This is your first time performing a baptism, so I'll walk you through it again, Elder, okay?" Teddy nodded; Wessman walked him through the brief ordinance. He was ready.

Teddy recited the words and then helped Wessman down below the water. For fun, he held his companion under for several seconds. Wessman's eyes opened widely. He tried to struggle free, but Teddy held him down a few seconds longer. Wessman found bottom with his feet, pushed hard and shot up, spraying water over everyone. "You hoser!" he sputtered. "You tried to drown me!"

"Aw, I was just kidding around," Teddy said.

Amy and David laughed hysterically; they were also soaked.

"I hope you don't try that with me on Saturday night," Richard said. "Elder Buckley, would you please baptize me?" He turned to Wessman. "Rosie would like you to baptize her, Elder."

Maggie welcomed the house-cleaning party Betty Tedrow organized among the Relief Society sisters. Larry London's wife was in charge of the food. They had secretly planned a nice reception party to welcome the Gilbert family into their little branch following the conference and baptism Saturday evening.

"Elder, I have this feeling I'm going to be transferred," Wessman told Teddy.

"Why?"

"I've already been in Alaska two months longer than the usual six months. Remember, I've been here eight months now?"

"But you have less than a couple of months left on your mission. Doesn't it make more sense that President would leave you here to finish it out?"

"Elder, don't go by what makes sense. I think the spirit is telling me my days are short here. At least I'm happy I get to see the Gilberts baptized before I go," Wessman said.

"President promised us he'd have an answer about allowing Mike to be baptized. I sure hope he says yes," Teddy said.

"I don't mean to be negative, Elder, but don't count on it…"

"Well, at least I hope Mike will come to the conference Saturday night," Teddy said.

President and Sister Moffatt were greeted at the seaport by a delegation of Mormons consisting of Frank Carling (Maggie thought she was starting labor and stayed home), Larry London, the two elders, and Betty Tedrow. Sparky had agreed to haul the Moffatts' luggage in his pickup and, under duress from Betty, he also agreed to come hear President Moffatt speak. "But no damn necktie!" Sparky insisted.

"Well at least wear your one good sports coat," Betty demanded.

Frank arranged for two taxis, one to carry Frank and the Moffatts, the second one for Larry and the elders. The Moffatts seemed fresh and enthusiastic. This was their first trip to Sitka since they had arrived in Vancouver the first of July the year before. They had been several times already to Anchorage and Fairbanks, and also to Juneau and Ketchikan. This was a first meeting for Frank and President Moffatt, since Frank had received his calling as branch president from the district president three months before over the phone. Because of distances and travel restrictions, that's just the way they did things in Alaska.

The Moffatts commented on what a pretty town Sitka was. Sister Moffatt had obviously done some homework; she knew more of the history of the town than Frank or the taxi driver. She was also delighted to learn they would travel by water taxi a short distance over to the conference. "And how is Sister Carling?" she asked.

"Right now she may be in labor, I'm not really sure."

"Oh, then she's expecting?" President Moffatt asked. He had been eagerly trying to commit the taxi driver to have the elders visit and teach him the gospel.

"Yes, dear,"Sister Moffatt said, shaking her head. "Honestly…"

"Here we are, folks," the taxi driver said. "Have a nice stay."

President Moffatt wrote down the driver's address and the cab company's phone number. "You'll be very glad you listened to our message," he assured the driver.

Larry London had pulled a few strings and borrowed a brand-new electronic keyboard from the Indian high school for their meeting. They would have live music. A nurse at the hospital, Maggie's friend, said she played piano. Maggie invited her to play for their conference. "I used to be the organist for three different churches in Madison, Wisconsin, when I was working my way through nursing school. They paid really well. But I won't charge you," the nurse said, and smiled brilliantly, showing perfect teeth.

Frank conducted the meeting that was set up with folding chairs in the Carlings' basement. He welcomed everyone. Maggie sat close to the door just in case. The Gilbert family, all six of them dressed in baptismal whites, sat on the front row. The elders sat on either side, like bookends, also dressed in white clothes. They all sang loudly and prayed reverently. Betty Tedrow led the singing; the nurse was a better organist than she admitted to Maggie. Sparky insisted that he and Betty could sit on the back row. He fidgeted. He fidgeted through the elders' short talks; through Sister Moffatt's short talk that was directed to the young children. Sparky fidgeted, that is, until President Moffatt rose to speak.

Teddy had been sort of fidgeting too. He looked at the door several times throughout the meeting to see if perhaps Barry and Mike, and the other LDS sailor were hanging outside the door. They didn't show.

The president was a master orator with a booming voice. He admitted that his wife lovingly referred to her husband privately as "Big Thunder." Everyone laughed. He acknowledged he had a booming voice and apologized if he was too loud for the crowded room. He didn't want to frighten the children. The children giggled. He suggested they all get up and stretch. When they were settled he began:

"We just visited the Wrangell Branch yesterday, held a conference last night. We had an amazing feast, a spiritual feast, just like we are having tonight. And that's the reason we're here, isn't it? And we will baptize a family into the gospel here tonight. That's just the first step on the road to eternity for the Gilbert family. Not only are you courageous to be some of the first of your people to accept the gospel, you're exceptionally courageous for stepping into that portable font!" More laughter.

"I'm impressed that Brother Gilbert here made that contraption with his own hands out of materials he paid for out of his own pocket. I'm sure, now that I know your humble circumstances and how you struggle to make a living, that those funds you donated were very dear. God bless you."

"Back to the subject of branch conference in Wrangell. I don't suppose any of you know Sister Rachel Chapman. She's a member of the church, the only one for many, many miles around. That's usually the case here in Alaska, isn't it? Rachel Chapman lives in a tiny community of about a hundred or so people, a place called Kaufman's Cove, over on Prince of Wales Island. The nearest members are at least seventy miles away by boat in Wrangell. She's a tough lady; she owns and operates her own commercial fishing boat. That's a hard and dangerous occupation, as Brother Gilbert here can tell you because he does the same thing."

"Well, when I was introduced to Sister Chapman and I found out where she lives and that she piloted her own commercial fishing boat all the way from Kaufman's Cove to Wrangell through storms and rough seas just to be at that conference, I asked her 'Sister Chapman, why did you come so far all by yourself?'"

"She leaned back and looked me in the eye and said, 'President, I get blessings when I come to this meeting. The Lord's blessing me for coming. And dang it, as big a sinner as I am, I need all the blessings I can get and no storm or rough seas or you or nobody else is going to deny me my blessings!'" The congregation laughed again. Some had tears in their eyes, Teddy noticed.

"I couldn't reply. For once in my life, I was speechless!" More laughter. "I want to quote you a scripture from the Old Testament. I love the Old Testament, I especially love to read Isaiah. We should all read more in the Old Testament." He then read a quote that we are commanded to love the Lord with all of our heart, might, mind, and strength. The president went on to tell the people that when they live the gospel with all their might, when they love the Lord with all their heart and show that love by living the gospel, they were being blessed for that and for all the good they do each day, in their homes, in their jobs, at school, wherever they go and whatever they do. "If we do everything seeking first for the Lord's help, showing we love Him by our actions, he *will* bless us with more blessings than we can ever contain." He looked into Richard's, then Rosie's eyes as he said this.

He left his blessings on the people and then said he learned on the way in from the seaport there was to be a baptism tonight. He ended with his testimony then suggested they proceed with the baptism.

As the baptism part of the service began, Maggie let out a loud cry, a "whoosh!" All the women rushed to her; they knew what was happening. "I think my water's broke," Maggie said. Frank helped her out of the room and up the stairs.

Amy danced around yelling in a sing-song voice, "Mama's havin' a baby! Mama's havin' a baby!" David cried because he couldn't go with his mother.

Before that night, Teddy had never exercised his priesthood to perform an ordinance. "Brother Richard Elliott Quiet Raven Gilbert, having been commissioned of Jesus Christ I baptize you…" He and Richard hugged and cried with each other as they stood in the portable font, dripping wet. "I love you, Brother Quiet Raven," he whispered in Richard's ear.

Around midnight, Maggie gave birth to a fat baby boy. They decided to name him Frank Edward Tad Carling.

The next morning the president wanted to spend some time interviewing the elders. Wessman was first. In ten minutes he came out grinning and crying at the same time. "What's up?" Teddy asked.

"I'm being transferred to Vancouver. I gotta pack, I leave tomorrow. He asked me to be one of his assistants. I'm replacing Elder Hill."

"Congratulations, Elder. But why the tears…?"

"It's just darn hard to leave a place, even if you've only been there a short time. You grow to love the people so fast… someday you'll know what I mean. Whatever you do, be sure and…Mike…" He couldn't finish for his tears.

The president also had a very short interview with Teddy. "Elder, I'm giving you the new assignment of senior companion in this area. You will have a new companion here in a day or two. He's also a new elder, a greenie. His name is J.T. Moon. I know I can count on you to do the right things with him. You're mature. I was impressed with you the first day you arrived as a greenie in the mission home in Vancouver. Remember that? It was only a couple of months ago." Teddy chuckled and nodded, remembering. It all seemed so long ago now. Only two months? "Would you like me to give you a blessing?" the president asked. Teddy nodded.

In the blessing the president said he didn't exactly know why he had felt impressed to give Teddy a blessing. He cautioned Teddy to keep the mission rules. He knew it would be hard now that summer was approaching with the long daylight hours. He counseled Teddy to be with his companion at all times, to set an example of a model missionary. He paused for what seemed like a long time. Teddy could hear Maggie's antique grandfather clock ticking ponderously outside in the hallway.

President Moffatt continued. He said he didn't know exactly why, but he felt impressed to bless Teddy with a special blessing of guardian angels to attend him, to help him through the tests he would soon be facing in his life. When he finished, Teddy sat pondering. The president embraced him and said, "God bless you." As Teddy left the room the president said, "By the way, Elder Moon is part Indian. I think half. You two will get along just great!"

As Teddy came down the stairs to the living room he saw Frank quietly talking with Wessman. His companion's face was ashen; he appeared shaken. When he saw Teddy he said, "Sit down, Elder. Terrible news. The reason Mike and Barry and the other guy didn't come last night to our meeting? Their ship got called out about an hour before we started. A distress call somewhere out in the Sitka Sound south of here. Some Japanese fishing boat in big trouble, a fire onboard or something. Brother Carling just learned that Mike had an accident. He was helping get the Japanese fishermen off the burning boat and he was the last one to get back off. He didn't make it. There was a big explosion. The Coast Guard searched the area for hours and never found his body. They're listing Mike Glass as dead."

———————

CHAPTER FOURTEEN

THE GREENIE

"Elder Buckley, how do you spell *bonsai*?"

"Huh?"

"How do you spell…"

"I heard you. What are you doing?" Teddy asked J.T. Moon, his new companion. It had been a long day; Teddy was stretched out on his cot trying to stay awake for prayers. He looked over and saw J.T. reclined on his bed with a pad of paper, pen poised, waiting.

"Writing a letter home to my mom. I told her I saw Mt. Fuji today and it was all snowy on top just like the Sangre de Christo Mountains back home in New Mexico."

"Why *bonsai*?"

"You forgot what you told me today that you could hear the Japanese yelling *bonsai*! whenever the wind was calm, didn't you…?" Teddy burst out laughing. He laughed so hard his face was purple and he was choking for breath. "Were you joking with me? It really *isn't* Mt. Fuji, is it?" Teddy shook his head and the uncontrolled laughter started again. He had tears running down both cheeks. "That's pretty rotten, Elder. Good night." J.T. Moon turned off his reading lamp, pulled up his covers and rolled over with his back towards Teddy.

"We need to say prayers," Teddy said to J.T.'s rigid back.

"You go ahead without me. I don't feel the spirit. That was a mean thing to do."

"I know and I'm sorry. Forgive me?" No answer. Long silence. "C'mon, Elder, it was just a little fun… Elder…?"

J.T. never heard the apology; he was already sleeping like a spanked baby.

Teddy wanted to visit Maggie and her new baby boy in the hospital on their way to an appointment. She was happy to see him and meet Elder Moon. "This is your new companion? Elder Wessman stopped by to say good-bye on his way to the plane. I was sorry to see him go. I guess I ruined the baptism. Me and little Frankie here." She held up her new baby. "Frank told you we also named him after you and Tad, I mean Elder Wessman." Maggie reached a friendly hand to J.T. "Hi, Elder, I'm Maggie Carling, and this is Frank Junior."

"J.T. Moon."

"Where are you from, how long have you been out?"

"I come from New Mexico. I just arrived here yesterday and I'm new, only two weeks out, if you count my time in the MTC."

"New Mexico - what part of New Mexico? I have cousins in Blue Water. Ever hear of it? They're Mormons, too." And without thinking, Maggie said, "You look Indian. Are you?"

"I come from Shiprock. And, yes, I'm half Navajo."

The baby started crying; Maggie made moves to nurse him, loosening her hospital gown. Teddy took that as their cue to leave.

They stopped by the newspaper office to ask the editor to run another article, one about their recent branch conference, and to add a short piece and picture about Elder Moon. The editor, who had been at least polite, if not friendly in the past, seemed cold to Teddy. "Sorry, boys, but my schedule is all filled up for the next few weeks. No more space to print this kind of article. Now, if you wanted to buy some advertising…"

Teddy got the picture. Some one had gotten to this guy. Teddy thought he wouldn't be at all surprised to see some more bad press in the next issue, more anti-Mormon attacks. He had heard from several sources that a few local ministers had gotten together to plan another anti-Mormon campaign. There was no proof, of course; they could easily deny any involvement. But he knew a storm was coming soon.

They didn't have long to wait. Rosie Gilbert said that she thought her sister, Angela Gomez, was interested in hearing the discussions. They had an appointment to teach her the first discussion at ten o'clock that morning in the Gilberts' home. When they arrived, Rosie met them at the door. She had been crying. "Rosie, what's wrong?" Teddy asked.

"Roland, Angela's husband, came home drunk late last night. He found out she had an appointment with you and he beat her up. She's really bad - she's in the hospital. Roland's in jail. My younger brother Sammy is with her kids right now, but he works swing at the pulp mill. He has to leave real soon for work; he can't afford to lose his job – he needs the work."

"Can you help out…?" Teddy suggested.

"Richard's out fishing. The kids are all in school, but I can't leave my dad right now 'cause he's really sick with the flu. That's why I didn't invite you in. And I don't dare go over there to take care of her kids 'cause I'm afraid I'm contagious. I don't know what to do."

"We'll go over there and spell Sammy off. Don't worry. What's their address?"

The Gomez house was a shambles; the front door was open. Worse, it was a pigsty. The smell nearly knocked Teddy over when they entered. They could hear kids crying and screaming. Sammy was holding one crying child; another, also wailing, was clinging to his leg. The young man was at his wits end.

"We're here to help," Teddy said. He took off his jacket and necktie, rolled up his sleeves and sized up the situation. There was another child, probably five or six, a girl, thin and malnourished, peeking around the corner, scared of these white strangers. She coughed and sniffed at a string of green mucous hanging from her nostrils; her eyes were red and sunken. Teddy smiled at her, which made her start sobbing, too. "Look, Sammy, you go ahead and get to work or you'll be late. We'll take care of things." The young man's eyes were ready to tear up, but he held it back.

"Thanks," was all he could manage.

"Now what?" J.T. asked.

"First thing let's get these kids cleaned up, fed, and in some warm clothes. This place is freezing. See if you can find some dry wood to make a fire. We need lots of hot water to clean them up – and this mess! We need to get them some food, too. They look pretty hungry to me. I wish Maggie was here to help; she'd know what to do. What's that awful smell...? Whew!"

"You're holding it, Elder."

Teddy looked down and saw a dark stain on his shirt; it came from the baby's full diaper. "Oh flip! Where are some clean diapers? Do you know how to change a diaper?"

"Yeah, I changed my little brothers and sisters. Give her to me."

It took the elders three hours to clean up the house and the kids, get them in dry clothes and fed. J.T. got fires going in the pot-bellied and kitchen stoves. Then he made an emergency dash to the grocery to buy diapers, formula, milk, Cheerios and some other basic food. While J.T. fed the kids, Teddy set to work cleaning the filthy house. He first tackled the sink that was overflowing with dirty, food-encrusted dishes, pots, and pans. The stench was overpowering; twice he had to race out the back door to keep from hurling his breakfast. What was that awful smell in there, anyway? Teddy finally got to the bottom of the sink and found a pan of rotting salmon roe. Why it was there and for how long, he had no clue. He held his nose with one hand and the offending pan with the other. He raced out the back and threw the mess - roe, pan and all - as far out in the back yard as he could. He nearly retched again when he let go of his pinched nose.

The elders must have been a sight as they walked through the town carrying two children with the third struggling to keep up, all wrapped in blankets. They decided to take them to Betty Tedrow's place for a while until they could figure out what to do next. They stopped in town and used a pay phone to call ahead and warn her about their situation. Thankfully, she answered.

Betty quickly sized up the situation. "You bring them here, my dear. Don't worry about anything. You did the right thing calling me. Where are you? You stay right there. I'll have Sparky there in five minutes to pick you up and bring you all."

Two of the children were asleep in the elders' arms before they got to the Tedrows'. The older one was still sobbing. Teddy was worried for her; she now seemed to be gasping for every breath. Mucous was running freely from her nose and tears from her red eyes. J.T. tried to use his hankie but only made her sob louder. She was becoming wilder each passing minute. Betty took one look at the sobbing child and said, "You get that child to a doctor. Something's wrong! Here, give me the two sleeping ones. Get going, Sparky!"

Sparky Tedrow helped the elders get the sick child checked into emergency at the hospital. The registering nurse asked for the child's name. She was all business: crisply starched uniform, comfortable, sensible white shoes with thick soles, reading glasses hanging on her ample bosom tethered by a heavy gilt chain. "We don't know, just her last name is Gomez. She's Angela's child," Teddy said.

The nurse's reaction was immediate. "Her mother was admitted last night. What do you three have to do with this child?" She looked at them suspiciously. Teddy wondered if she thought they were pedophiles. Teddy explained who he and J.T. were; Sparky needed no introduction. "Well, whoever you are and whatever you two're doing here, I'm glad you brought her in when you did. It looks like she has T.B. - a serious case. I've seen a lot of it before, especially in these Indian kids. They don't get the proper care. You should know, young man." She looked evenly at J.T. over her half-moon reading glasses.

Teddy watched J.T. out of the corner of his eye. J.T.'s face reddened even deeper, but he didn't react. Teddy could not tell from his face what J.T. was thinking - the stoic Indian. J.T. had heard these slurs from whites many times before. He was only half-blood. But he *was* a Christian; Christians turn the other cheek. He was also a representative of the Lord's true church. WWJD? Teddy gained a new level of respect for his young companion that day. He would no longer think of or call J.T. a greenie.

During their weary trudge home, Teddy asked J.T. a question. "Say, Elder, what do the initials "J.T."stand for? Do you actually have a real name?"

"The first name is Joseph. The "T" is just an initial, that's all." Teddy didn't pursue it further.

It was dark when the elders returned to their little cabin in the woods. They changed out of their smelly, sweaty clothes into p.j.s, slippers and tee shirts. "Phew! We probably should burn these!" Teddy said.

"What's for dinner, Chef Buckley?"

"How about some nice, tasty pickled salmon roe?" They both laughed until they could no longer breathe and they collapsed from exhaustion. They were so tired they skipped dinner and fell into their beds without saying prayers. Teddy hoped the Lord would excuse them for that minor transgression.

CHAPTER FIFTEEN

THE POTLATCH

Teddy and J.T. gladly changed out of their suits into their P-day clothes. This was the evening the Gilberts had invited the elders to be their guests at a potlatch. The elders borrowed Sparky's pickup to drive themselves and the whole Gilbert family to the event. It was planned for a private sandy beach close to the one Teddy had been attacked by the eagle. As they walked to Tedrows' place to get the truck, J.T. tried to explain *potlatch* to Teddy. "Most of the native tribes in America, including Navajos, have big gatherings where we dance, play native games, sing the old songs in the ancient language; the old men and women tell stories while the boys and girls sneak off to make out. Stuff like that. In the old times the different clans would trade things like ponies, furs, flint for arrow and spear points, slaves, even wives. They still do some trading. A lot of drinking and betting goes on, too. We call it *pow wow*. The part I like best is the food. Potlatch is mainly the Northwest natives, British Columbia and the Alaska natives. It's a lot like our pow wow get-togethers. Only here it's more of a time for the host family or clan to invite families or clans that don't have as much riches and make gifts of things to the ones invited.

"Sort of spread the wealth around so everyone has more and nobody goes without?" Teddy asked.

"Yeah. And the host family also provides most of the food, but the ones invited also bring gifts or food, too. It's kind of a religious ceremony, too. They take time to remember and honor ancestors or even family members who maybe died recently.

"Here's the Tedrows'. Hope his old truck starts. I used to have a truck almost like this when I was a guide in Jackson. Seems like years ago. By the way, Elder, I really like your cowboy boots."

Richard and Rosie and Chief Russell crammed into the front with Teddy; the kids and J.T. piled into the back. "I'm used to it," J.T. said. "That's how we Indians ride on the rez." The Gilberts laughed at his understated, ironic native humor. Chief Russell started to light up a Camel and Rosie said something to him softly in Tlingit. He grinned, shrugged and put the pack away in his jacket. Beneath Chief's jacket Teddy could see a beautiful native ceremonial tunic with exquisite bead work. Chief wore ceremonial bracelets on each wrist.

On the way out to the potlatch, Richard explained that his and Rosie's families were part of a large clan, really an extended family. In case Teddy was worried about J.T. fitting in because he was half-blood, Richard assured him many of the clan had married whites or other half-bloods. Rosie's concern was that J.T. was a very good-looking young man. He was tall, well-built and had fairer skin than most Tlingit boys his age. "You better watch him close, Elder. The girls will be trying to get him alone into the bushes tonight." Chief chuckled and nodded his head in agreement; his dark eyes crinkled as he laughed.

The potlatch was in fact set up on the same beach Teddy and Wessman had been attacked by the eagle. Teddy related the experience to Richard as they walked down the trail to the beach. Just in case he might be lucky and find his Nikon, Teddy made a deal with the Gilbert kids: whoever finds my camera gets a $10 reward. They nearly knocked each other over scrambling to scan the stream's depths.

Once down on the beach, Teddy talked privately with J.T. "Elder, I want you to stick really close to me tonight. I think you know why."

"Really, Elder, you don't have to worry about me. I can take care of myself."

"It's all the cute native girls that want you. That's what I'm worried about."

"Not a problem," J.T. said and grinned. After J.T.'s remark about the boys and girls sneaking off to make out, Teddy wasn't so sure.

On the beach Teddy wanted to look around and get a new perspective. The potlatch was already in full swing when they arrived. He looked up the beach where the dead sea lion had been. The picked over carcass – what was left of it - was still there, its bare ribs pointing to the sky. Teddy walked over for a closer look. The magnificent tusks had been neatly sawed off by someone. They must have been at least a yard long. He was suddenly sad. That little ivory Billykin necklace he'd bought for his sister recently in the native crafts shop in town - had it been only recently carved from this dead animal's tusks? He knew that there was a new law on the books making it illegal to harvest ivory. Ivory already harvested before the law went into effect was exempt. There had been a frenzy of killing to beat the deadline and stock up on valuable ivory.

Teddy walked back to find J.T. When he'd left him, his companion was with Richard and Rosie. He spotted him near a big oil drum set above a bed of burning coals. Teddy went to him.

"Elder, look at this."

"What is this?" Teddy asked.

"It's a pot of boiling sea water; they're cooking herring eggs."

"Oh, goody," Teddy said somewhat sarcastically.

"No, really, you gotta try some, they're pretty tasty." J.T. handed Teddy a big cluster of something resembling a gray mass of gelatin. "They catch the eggs by tying weights to hemlock branches and lower them down in a small cove. They keep track of them with glass balls, floats, like big bobbers. The herring come in and lay their eggs in the hemlock branches. These guys get this water boiling and drop a big gob of seal blubber in. It makes a film of seal oil on top and they dip the branches in the boiling pot and lift it slowly back through the hot oil. Watch."

J.T. demonstrated with a fresh branch of hemlock coated and sagging with millions of whitish herring eggs. He pulled it free of the boiling stew and offered it to Teddy. "Uh… no thanks. I like fish but I never been too big on eggs. Thanks." He stepped away from the offering.

J.T. pulled Teddy aside. "Elder, you have to eat whatever is offered to you at the potlatch. It's a sign of disrespect if you refuse."

"Everything?"

"Everything…"

"I'll do it… but only to bring peace between your people and my people." J.T. actually laughed. Teddy was relieved; his companion surely felt comfortable among these gentle people. He decided to relax, go with the flow and be an ambassador of the gospel. What could eating a little native food hurt? It all looked fairly clean.

Teddy was happy they had come. He felt closer this night to his first converts, his new friends, the Gilberts. He kept his eyes, his ears, his mind and his heart open to learning more about these friendly people. Not all the clan gathered that night were friendly to the elders. Rosie introduced Teddy to her sister, Angela Gomez. Angela would not look in Teddy's eyes. Teddy tried to make small talk; Angela was silent. Teddy looked up to see a man approaching carrying a longneck beer bottle. "What you doin' talkin' to this white guy?" he asked in a nasty tone. He took Angela roughly by the arm and pulled her away somewhere else.

"What was that?" Teddy asked an embarrassed Rosie.

"Now you've met Roland."

"Does she know what we did, my companion and me? The other day when her kids were left alone?" Teddy asked as tactfully as he could. "She didn't say thanks." Rosie said that was the native way. They show their thanks; they don't talk much about gratitude.

The sun was down now and shadows lengthened. More driftwood was tossed on the bonfires; flames leaped and sparks ascended into the inky sky. A few stars were showing themselves. Circled around one bonfire were old men and women, among them Chief Russell. They were singing or chanting, Teddy wasn't sure. He looked to Rosie for interpretation. "They're telling the old stories and paying tribute to our ancestors. This is happy singing. Later they will remember the ones who recently went to the other side. Then the song will be very sad. It will make you feel all alone in the world. But now that we found the truth I don't feel alone any more." She smiled. Teddy gave her a warm hug; he knew Richard would not be jealous or misunderstand his actions.

As Teddy looked over the large family celebrating in the night warmed and illuminated by the bonfires, the thought struck him that they were really the same as anyone else. He saw the similarity between the potlatch and the fiestas he'd been invited to on Guam: family, eating, dancing, rites of passage into adulthood, honoring ancestors, remembering the departed - rituals. We all need the security of family. All peoples somehow require the continuity and meaning of rituals, he concluded. "Speaking of rites of passage, where is Elder Moon and what is he *doing*?" he asked, mostly to himself.

Teddy found J.T. nearly in the shadows on the edge where the strip of trees meets the sand. He was surrounded by half a dozen admiring teen girls; they were openly flirting and giggling. He wasn't sure anything his companion might say could be all that funny. Apparently his female admirers thought it was. J.T. was enjoying the admiration. This wasn't good. A few yards off, out of the light cast by the big open bonfires, back in the shadows, Teddy saw more trouble in the form of a half a dozen young native teen boys. They didn't look any too pleased that this half-blood Navajo was making time with their women. Teddy considered how he could break up this little fan club gathering. He called to J.T. from where he stood. "Hey, Elder Moon. I need you for a few minutes. Sorry, ladies." J.T. scowled; the girls whined and pouted. Over his shoulder Teddy could see the young native guys looking more angry than before.

When they were out of the girls' earshot, J.T. asked "What do you need? I was just trying to get some referrals for discussions," he said innocently.

"Yeah, I'm sure you were." Teddy looked at his watch. "Listen, it's getting late and we have curfew in a half hour. We better be getting back to our place. Mission rules…? Also, I'm not feeling so good. Must be something I ate."

"My old man always says it's not what you eat, but what's eating you, that's the problem," J.T. said with a tinge of anger in his voice. "Whatever… Let's just go." He started walking toward the trail to the car park, not bothering to wait for Teddy.

"Elder Buckley! You owe me ten dollars!" Teddy looked up to see a grinning Cory Gilbert running toward him waving the Nikon above his head. The poor kid was soaking wet. Had he spent the last three hours wading the stream looking?

Teddy pulled out his wallet and fished out a bill. "Good work. Thanks.

Now I have to figure out if it still works. Thanks, Cory. You're my hero."
Cory grinned widely.

Before they were halfway back to Tedrows' place the pain in Teddy's stomach increased so quickly it scared him. He was sure he was poisoned. "You take over and drive," he said to J.T. "I'm too sick. Just drive me straight to emergency!" As Teddy went around the truck the need to purge hit him hard. He vomited so violently he threw up blood. Two more waves rapidly gripped him. He retched until he was dry heaving. "Let's go!" he gasped as he fell onto the passenger seat.

Teddy was rushed on a gurney into a side room where the young intern on duty took over. Needles were shoved into his veins. Fluids were pumped into him. Someone must have shot him up with painkillers, for he quickly went out.

When Teddy came to a couple hours later he was in a flowered hospital gown lying between clean sheets. He was shaking uncontrollably; he felt as if he were freezing. "I need a blanket," he said weakly. His teeth were clacking so hard he was afraid his tongue would be bitten off if he tried to talk. He had a lot of questions. Someone fetched a blanket; his shaking calmed down, his teeth stopped rattling in his head.

"What happened?" he asked the nurse who brought the blanket. "Thanks for this."

"Are you feeling better?" the nurse asked, smiling. She had clear brown eyes beneath her halo of strong red hair. Her freckled face gave her a healthy, outdoorsy look. She reminded him of a girl he dated at MSU, a lacrosse player. He nodded, licking his dry, cracked lips. She helped Teddy sit up and take a drink of water. Her arms were strong around his shoulders.

"Hey, I know you," he said. "You played the piano for our branch conference, didn't you? I never did ask your name, I'm sorry."

"I'm Andrea Norton. Yes, I'm the same horrible piano player. I'm glad to see you're on the mend. We can probably let you go home pretty soon."

"Where's my companion, J.T... I mean Elder Moon?"

"After we got you stabilized he called Frank Carling, Maggie's husband? Frank came and Mister Moon left with him. He said to call Frank's when you were ready to be released."

"Okay, so what was wrong with me? It hit me so fast and hard. Never had anything like that. I puked… I mean I vomited so hard I spit up blood.”

“Doctor asked your friend what you had eaten tonight, last night. He told us you’d both been to a potlatch. What *did* you eat exactly… if you can remember?”

Teddy told her while she took some notes in his chart. She kept saying “Mmm- Hmmm.”

“Well…?” Teddy queried.

“All I know is that some of the sea animals or plants they eat at those potlatches can be dangerous. Some of the ones you described have been known to carry highly toxic bacteria. I’m not the doctor, so you’ll have to confirm with him. If you hadn’t thrown up all your stomach contents we could have done a lab analysis. But…”

“Sorry I hurled it all away,” Teddy laughed. She laughed too, showing again the perfect white teeth he remembered from the branch conference. Her eyes crinkled nicely around the corners when she laughed. Her laugh had a musical sound that Teddy liked.

Andrea Norton looked at her watch. “I’d love to stay and talk, but I’m off shift soon. I have to get changed and get to your church services. Maggie’s baby is being christened today and she invited me to attend. “

Omigosh, thought Teddy. It’s Fast Sunday. I’ve got to get out of here. The Gilberts asked us to give their kids names and blessings, too. “Any chance you can sign me out? I really need to be there, too,” Teddy asked hopefully. Andrea smiled and winked. She has a wickedly cute wink, Teddy realized. Cut it out, Elder! Remember who you are!

Teddy used a hospital phone to tell Frank he was in the clear and planned on coming to sacrament meeting. He had to go change clothes and would get there as soon as he could. Teddy didn’t mention Andrea Norton was planning to come, too.

Andrea said Teddy still looked a little peaked, so she drove him to the cabin in her car and primly waited outside while he quickly washed up, changed into his suit, white shirt and tie. Teddy splashed on after shave to cover the fact he hadn’t bathed. He was suddenly starving; he grabbed a couple of slices of white bread and one expensively precious banana to eat on the way. “You look nice. Smell nice, too,” she said as she drove them to the water taxi. Her car was redolent with her own fragrance; Teddy struggled to get the scent out of his head. Whatever it was called, Marley wore it too, he remembered. Andrea glanced sideways and saw a sudden sadness had come over Teddy.

On the water taxi ride across the channel Teddy thrust his face over the side to catch the salt spray. It helped restore his spirits and braced him physically. By the time they got off and began the short hike to the Carlings' Teddy felt better - not one hundred percent, but much better.

As they approached the door the opening hymn was just beginning inside. Teddy had two thoughts. The first was: will it seem odd to the members to see four grown children given names and blessings today? Second: more to the point, what are they going to think when I walk in with an attractive, single woman?

The first person Teddy spotted when the door opened for them was Sparky Tedrow heartily singing *We Thank Thee O God for a Prophet*. He was even wearing a loud, hand-painted orange necktie – with a semi-nude hula dancer. Sparky looked up at Teddy, saw Andrea, and lifted his eyebrows in feigned shock.

After their sacrament meeting and the munch-and-mingle, Andrea approached the elders. "Would it be all right if you could give me your six discussions? Maggie has told me so much about your church, but I've been more impressed with how nice and friendly you all are. You have something I want."

"Sure thing," J.T. said, whipping out his appointment book. "When would be a good time for you?"

Teddy hoped, for the sake of setting the right example for J.T. that the thing she was most interested in was not Elder Buckley.

CHAPTER SIXTEEN

APPLE

When the gathering wound down, the elders reluctantly took their leave. Walking toward the water taxi, they heard sirens across the channel, and a tall column of gray smoke arose east of town. The evening before had been clear for the potlatch. Now rain was threatening. Potluck dinner at the munch-and-mingle restored needed strength; Teddy still felt inclined to lean over the side to catch the salt spray again. By the time they reached the Sitka side of the channel the sirens had died down; the smoke column had vanished. Whatever had burned, Teddy hoped the loss would be minimal.

They walked a few minutes, then came up the last rise in the gravel road before it turned into the forest and bent south toward the pulp mill. Down the left fork they heard the chaos before they saw the two red trucks blocking their view. Surely it wasn't their cabin. Teddy had changed and left in a hurry that morning, but he was sure he had checked the stove before locking up. They hurried down the dirt trail and saw the grisly scene. Their cabin was now a smoldering pile of coals and blackened junk. The firemen had been too late to save anything. They had nothing more to do but secure the place and wait for a fire marshal from Juneau to come and investigate. Teddy and J.T. stood there speechless, stunned.

"This your place?" the fire chief asked Teddy.

"Was, yeah. We rented it from that realtor in town, I've forgotten his name. I guess someone needs to tell him."

"I hope he was insured," the chief said. "That's it boys - let's go," he ordered his company. All but two men loaded up and the trucks slowly backed down the dirt path. The two remaining men raked and poked around the edge of the site, making sure there was no flare up. It was softly raining now and there was no danger of the forest catching fire.

J.T. was the first to react. "Dammit-all-to-hell!" he yelled. I lost everything - my clothes, my journal, my pictures, everything!"

"Easy, Elder, it's just stuff. It can be replaced. We were blessed to be gone. Nobody was hurt or killed."

"Yeah, easy for you to say. You're rich, you can buy more stuff. Well I'm not rich! I don't have any money to buy more clothes or anything. My mom will have to go to our bishop and ask for help now. That will kill her."

Teddy didn't respond to the remark about his supposedly being rich; he let it pass for now. He kept his counsel and waited for J.T. to wind down. "I think we need to sit down and focus on what we need to do next to survive. I'm sure the members will help us out until we can make other… financial arrangements."

"Oh, buzz off!" J.T. stomped away. Teddy let him go. In a few minutes he returned crying. Teddy put his arm around the boy's shoulder and held him. "I'm sorry I yelled at you," J.T. said.

"I've had worse… by real professionals," Teddy joked. J.T. laughed.

"It's *Turtle*," J.T. said.

"What's turtle?" Teddy responded, puzzled.

"My middle initial. The Tee stands for turtle, my native name. My mom's Anglo, she gave me the Christian name. My dad's the Navajo, full-blood; he gave me the names of Turtle and Moon. She's a good mother. She's the member; my dad's not. He's a good man too. He's a cop, Tribal Police. One tough guy. He expects the best from us kids. I'm the oldest, first to go on a mission. He said he wouldn't send me money because he wanted to teach me how to be independent. I earned just enough to make it without having to buy any clothes while I'm here. I thought the money would all work out without any outside help. I guessed wrong. Elder…?"

"Yeah, Turtle Moon?"

"Promise me two things?"

"Sure, Turtle Moon."

"One, you're the only one in this mission to ever know my true name. Two, don't ever tell anyone I cried. Braves don't cry."

"Okay Turtle Moon. Your secrets are safe with me. Torture, even threats of death won't pry my lips loose." Turtle Moon smiled and nodded his satisfaction.

"Turtle Moon…?"

"Yeah, Old Man?"

"You have to promise me to quit coming on to the girls. Okay?"

"Yeah, Old Man. I promise."

Fifteen minutes later Sparky and Betty Tedrow pulled up in his truck. "We heard what happened," Betty said. "You boys hop in; you're coming to stay with us until we work this out. We have a spare bedroom with two beds and a private bath. No arguments. Get in!"

Routines and discipline, the everyday certainty of doing things, even the smallest things of no consequence, done the same way repeatedly made Teddy happy. Without his routine he was not happy. Driving to the Tedrows' he knew he had to get himself and Turtle back into the flow as quickly as possible. Teddy made a mental inventory. LOST: clothes, toiletries, Frank's light-weight salmon rod and the scruffy-looking trout flies he'd tied (need to replace Frank's rod); the Nikon (heck with it – probably ruined from two weeks in the stream); a few groceries, scriptures, and flannel board stuff. SAVED: themselves, their health and safety, their wits, their testimonies, and discussions and scriptures memorized. He was thankful now that Wessman had pushed him so hard to get those discussions committed to memory. Bless you, Tad, he thought.

Teddy borrowed an alarm clock from Betty and set it for the usual wake-up time. He also borrowed her personal set of scriptures so they had some study materials. They could work on the discussions from memory. As soon as they got settled at Tedrows' place, Teddy called the mission home in Vancouver to report what had happened and that they were safe. He asked the mission secretary to please send them a new supply of study materials, scriptures, pamphlets, report forms, Books of Mormon, etc. He was a little put off by the secretary's accusing tone, as if the elders had started the fire on purpose. "Please, just send us the stuff I asked for. And Elder Moon could use some clothes to replace the ones he lost. What do you mean you're not a clothing store? Look, I've been on the third floor; I've slept in the dormitory room up there and I've used the big walk-in clothes closet. I know that you have racks of clothes in there left by missionaries over the last five years at least! *I'm* getting hot? Okay, maybe a little. How would you like to have all your stuff burned up? What's that…? No, I'm not threatening you…"

The line went dead. The secretary had hung up on Teddy. His next call was to track down President Moffatt, who the secretary had told him was traveling over on Vancouver Island for a week of conferences. After Teddy got off the call with the president, he felt much better. The president assured him he would take care of everything. His major concern was always the health and safety of his missionaries. Teddy congratulated himself for not ratting out that idiot mission secretary. The pompous little snot!

"Oh, no, not any more for me. Thank you sister," J.T. said, patting his swollen stomach.

"I just don't want you to leave my table hungry. You boys do a lot of walking in a day and you burn up a lot of calories."

"No problem there, sister," Teddy said. "Thanks so much for taking us in. We thought of the Carlings, but with Maggie's new baby and all…"

"You lads stay as long as you like," Sparky said. "Just don't go preachin' at me and we'll all get along jes' fine. Well, Mama, I got to get to work. Costs a lot to keep these boys in groceries." He bent down and kissed Betty on the cheek. She smiled up at Sparky and patted his cheek too. She blew him a kiss as he went out the door.

In the privacy of their new bedroom the elders knelt to ask the Lord what they should put their labors into that day. When they stood up, Teddy said," I'm going to follow your inspiration today. Someday I'll be transferred and you'll be the senior. Time you started learning responsibility and leadership."

"I think I know a little about that. I'm the oldest of six kids, remember?"

As they left, J.T. turned and stopped Teddy. "I think we ought to go back to that newspaper guy and ask him again to run an article. We could talk about how we lost all of our earthly possessions in that fire but that won't stop us from doing the Lord's work, kind of that angle. What do you think?"

"Hmmm. I'll ponder that while we stroll in that general direction. I have an idea along those lines."

"What?"

"We could tell how you cried when you realized your cowboy boots burned up."

"Elder, some things you say are funny and some things you say are just plain mean. Why do you tease me about things that hurt? You don't know anything about those boots. They were very special to me, at least."

"I'm sorry. I can overdo it sometimes. Okay, tell me about the cowboy boots."

J.T. told Teddy how growing up he wanted so much to be a rodeo rider. But he knew an Indian kid didn't have a chance. Too much prejudice. He hung around a friend's stables learning all he could about horses, how to ride them, care for them. He was especially interested in how you break a horse to the halter and saddle. He became an expert at breaking horses. In the process he learned how to stay on a wildly bucking bronc. The Indian high school he attended had its own rodeo club. He joined up, even though he didn't have a horse or any gear. He worked odd jobs until he saved enough to buy some used stuff so he could compete. J.T. specialized in bareback bronc riding; he was soon winning rodeo meets with other Indian schools around the state. He moved up steadily in the rankings. He won prizes along the way.

Finally came his big chance. He found himself in the state high school championship finals. He kept his mouth shut and ignored the racial slurs from the white kids. He also had to endure the taunts from full-blood natives because they knew he was half. "They called me *apple,*" he told Teddy. "That means you're red on the outside and white on the inside. That one hurts the most." J.T. was only a junior that year, but he beat out a white kid, a senior, who'd been state champ for three years straight and was going for a sweep. J.T. won by just a couple hundredths of a second for first place. The prize: a big silver belt buckle and a pair of hand-made Tony Lama cowboy boots.

"Those boots," Teddy said reverently.

“Those boots,” J.T. echoed.

“I’m really sorry, Turtle,” Teddy said as he put his arm around the kid’s shoulder and drew him close. “Apple, huh? I’ve heard a lot of racial slurs in my time, but never that one. Apple…”

CHAPTER SEVENTEEN

THE REVEREND BODIE BRIGGS

Maggie Carling invited the elders to join them for lunch. They planned to stay after lunch to teach a first discussion to Andrea Norton at 1:30 when she got off work. In keeping with mission rules, she was meeting them at the Carlings'. Lunch, as usual, was great and the discussion went well. J.T. gave the discussion and they set up a second for three days later. Teddy was glad they had Maggie as a chaperone. Whenever Andrea would answer a question, she'd look directly at him with those honest brown eyes.

The elders hung around the Carlings' for a while playing with the kids; the new baby was growing, a happy child in a happy home. They left at four o'clock for a meeting with the Mt. Edgecumbe building administrator. They were interested in possibly using the government's multi-purpose social center for church services. The building was adequate with one large meeting room and many smaller side rooms that could serve as classrooms. The branch was swelling each Sunday as more lost members made themselves known and more investigators attended.

It was after five thirty and the water taxi was late, which was unusual. Some engine trouble kept it on the Sitka side for an hour. J.T. fretted, "We'll be late for dinner. Sister Tedrow said six thirty." They finally got over to the Sitka side a little after seven. The elders were the only passengers.

They were waiting for the elders in the shadows near the boat landing, six of them. Teddy was first to climb the gyrating gangplank and spotted them hanging back in the shadows beyond the chain link fence barrier out of the dim circle thrown by the lone street light. They were huddled up like a pack of young wolves ready to hunt. Teddy sensed something was wrong; kids from the Indian high school never went to Sitka on a school night, especially at this hour. It wasn't a holiday that he knew of. Why were they here? They were all wearing parkas with fur-lined hoods drawn over their eyes. Teddy waited until J.T. caught up and said, "Elder, stick close to me."

"What's up?" Then he saw them, too. He closed ranks with Teddy. "Best to ignore them and act natural." They picked up their pace and struck up a conversation. Teddy nodded to the boys as they passed. The boys averted their eyes.

"What do you think Sister Tedrow has cooked for dinner?" J.T. asked a bit too loudly. Teddy could hear the strain in his voice.

"I don't know," Teddy said. "I sure am hungry though."

The gang followed several yards behind them, keeping pace. Both groups were in between pools of light. Behind them was the dimly-lit car park. Ahead a half a block or so was the boardwalk leading along Main Street and its bars and churches and stores. The first street lamp was in the middle of the first block. From behind the elders someone yelled, "How 'bout an apple for dinner?" The others laughed, nasty, malicious.

The green fruit caught J.T. hard in the back of his head and exploded into flying chunks. Teddy heard the loud smack of the impact and the whoosh of air forced from J.T. His companion, stunned and hurt badly, fell to his knees. "Kill them!" someone in the gang yelled. There were now no doubts about their intent.

Teddy turned as the attackers were on them. He picked out the biggest kid to divert. Teddy lowered his shoulder into the kid's chest; he hit Teddy running and bounced to his right, taking out two more. They landed on the pea gravel in a tangle of limbs and banged skulls.

J.T. was staggering to his feet. "I'll get the apple!" someone else yelled. His mate also went for J.T. Teddy tried to jump between his companion and the two attackers, but was too late. J.T. took a hard smash to the side of his skull as a bicycle chain wrapped with black electrical tape took him out. Teddy heard the sickening crunch of the blow and saw blood spurt from J.T.'s cheek; it was laid open to the white bone. "I got that chicken (expletive) apple!" his attacker exulted as J.T. went down.

The one with the chain was quickly joined by two more. Teddy faced them, crouching. The chain swung and Teddy jumped back. One of the gang caught the chain in his mouth from the momentum of the swing; Teddy heard teeth shattering. The kid went down screaming. The big kid had rallied. Now Teddy had five to deal with again. He quickly moved with his back against the side of a parked car. The big kid came at him again swinging. Teddy brought his knee up sharply and the big guy crashed down gripping his crotch, groaning.

Three still standing. They all came at him; Teddy caught the first kid by his parka hood with both hands and heaved him; the momentum carried him over the front of the parked car. He hit the ground face first with a solid crunch and slid ten feet to a stop.

The others slowed in mid-rush then sprinted around the car to their downed friend. He was lying still and quiet. Teddy could hear his own labored breathing. "He's bleeding bad!" someone said, kneeling over him. "Don't move him!" someone else shouted. The big kid was on his feet moving toward his friends. The four of them clustered around their fallen companion, helpless and panicked.

Teddy heard a police siren wailing, closing fast, coming at them. Later Teddy would wonder that no passing car stopped. But was there a passing car? If so, had someone in a car made the call to the cops? And with all the noise of the fight, why had no one come out of one of the nearby bars?

The mud-splattered Jeep slid to a stop, siren dying, red lights flashing. Teddy slumped down on the parked car's hood. He sat there for a minute looking at J.T. who was still prone but groaning. He was alive. Teddy looked up to find only two policemen working over the other prone body. Where were the attackers?

At the first siren sound the gang had fled, dragging the kid with the busted teeth and the big kid along with them. They were sure their fallen friend was dead; they left him for the cops to deal with. Teddy thought he was dead, too; he truly hoped not.

"Bodie Briggs, D.A. for the state, your honor."

Teddy had hung around to answer the inevitable questions the police had. They called an ambulance and the unconscious kid was taken to hospital. It didn't look good for Teddy. Two white guys against one injured native kid. It didn't matter that one of the two white guys had been knocked senseless with a potentially lethal weapon; there was a seriously injured Indian kid who might not live. The town of Sitka depended in part on the income generated by the Indian school.

The police asked Teddy about the taped bicycle chain they found. Teddy told them all he knew and could remember. They let him go home to the Tedrows', but he spent a sleepless night worrying about J.T. and the kid he had tossed over the car; he really didn't mean to hurt him, just take him out of the fight for a while. He wanted to go to the hospital to find out about both J.T. and the native kid, but the police said he should stay away until further notice. Teddy thought that was very strange.

The next morning at about nine o'clock two policemen appeared at the Tedrows' door with a warrant for Teddy's arrest on suspicion of attempted homicide. He was stunned. Did that mean the poor kid had died during the night? They couldn't answer that; they weren't authorized to say anything. Teddy pulled on his trench coat and went with them.

As he was booked into jail, Teddy asked the desk sergeant if he knew anything about the injured kid's condition. He didn't answer. Teddy went back over the incident in his mind, over and over, trying to piece together what had happened. He thought he recognized some of the attackers; he wasn't sure, but he thought maybe they were the same ones at the potlatch, the jealous ones. Again, he just wasn't sure. The lighting was poor and there had been no moon out. Two faces were distinctly etched into his memory, he would never forget them: the big kid and the one clinging to life in the hospital - he hoped.

"Bodie Briggs, for the state, your honor…"

Teddy's head jerked up. He had been in a sleep-deprived trance. He was confused. He looked around. Where am I? The cut on his head burned and itched. When did he get a cut on his head and how? He tried to scratch it but the hand cuffs prevented him. When did he get those on his hands?

He tried to focus; he needed to be alert. The judge was looking down at Teddy, waiting. The bailiff lifted Teddy's arm, pulling him to his feet. "I'm sorry your honor, but I didn't get much sleep…"

"I said, could you please state your name for the record?"

Where was the lawyer? Teddy was supposed to have a lawyer. He asked for one when they booked him in… or did he? Teddy looked around the spruce-paneled room. He saw Frank sitting a couple rows behind him, behind the bar. Frank looked concerned. Teddy tried to wave, but nodded instead. The prosecutor was making a speech, addressing the judge. Teddy recognized him, but how? Where?

"And so, your honor, we submit that there is probable cause sufficient to bind the accused over for trial. The criminal complaint will show that this man…" he paused dramatically and pointed an accusing finger at Teddy, "did, with malice aforethought and criminal intent to commit homicide on the victim…"

Homicide? Did he just say homicide? Criminal intent? Teddy's knees got weak.

"…so if your honor pleases, the state moves that the defendant be denied bail due to the fact he is a flight risk."

"Anything you'd like to say at this time, Mr. Buckley" the judge asked.

"I don't understand what's going on here…"

"You're being charged with attempted homicide. The state is demanding that bail be denied to you. Care to respond…?"

"First of all I'd like to know if the kid is okay; is he alive?"

"Irrelevant!" thundered Bodie Briggs.

"Sustained!" gaveled the judge.

"I demand a lawyer and I demand that I be given the chance to post bail."

"Can you… pay bail?" the judge asked.

"Well, I can pay in a few days if I can have access to my lawyer to help make arrangements." Teddy said. "How much is it, anyway?"

"Does the sum of two hundred fifty thousand dollars put a strain on your checkbook?" the judge asked. Bodie snickered.

"I don't have it right now, but I can have it here within a week. I can have it wired to my bank account here in Sitka."

"The court will take that into consideration. What about the allegation that you're a flight risk?

"What…?"

"You do have a two-year Canadian visitor's visa and a U.S. passport, do you not?"

"Yes, but what does that…?"

"Bail denied. Court is in recess!" the judge pounded his gavel.

"All rise," the bailiff shouted. Then he led the shackled Teddy down to the dank basement jail cell. Teddy looked over his shoulder at Frank. Frank shook his head, bewildered.

Teddy refused to eat the food the jailer brought him for lunch. "You gonna eat that?" a cell mate asked. There was green soupy gelatin, macaroni and cheese and some kind of lunch meat with a rainbow sheen to it; it looked horrible, inedible. Teddy shook his head. His three cell mates divided it between themselves.

Teddy nearly came close to going insane the first forty-eight hours in jail. He was a mental and emotional wreck. He couldn't sleep and he refused the food, if you could call it food. "Son, you gotta eat or I have to report you and they'll get a court order to feed you through a tube. You want that?" Teddy didn't answer. He motioned for Teddy to approach the barred door. He whispered low, "If you'll eat something I'll check on that Injun kid in the hospital. That what you want?" Teddy said yes and took the ham sandwich that was offered.

The jail had no windows, so Teddy couldn't tell the time of day or the weather or the seasons. Lying on the top bunk, staring at the damp concrete ceiling inches above his nose, Teddy remembered – the D.A. was one of those ministers that got so hostile when they asked to use his font to baptize the Gilberts.

CHAPTER EIGHTEEN

FOR THY GOOD

"**G**ood morning Sitka! This is YOUR hometown radio comin' at ya . That was a Canadian kid, Neil Young, with his latest hit *Heart of Gold,* and just before that we heard George Harrison and *My Sweet Lord.* Right back at'cha with some more goodies, but first some commercials… gotta pay the rent, ha ha!…

"Right, and we're baaack! Now we're gonna hear another set, first from that cute little Linda Ronstadt and her group The Stone Ponies…and that will be followed by The Bee Gees with *How Do You Mend a Broken Heart* and then Roberta Flack and her new hit *The First Time Ever I saw Your Face.*"

"You and I travel to the beat of a different drum, Oh can't you tell by the way I run, Ever'y time you make eyes at me…?

The guard's blaring radio woke Teddy. He opened his eyes facing a cold, damp concrete wall. The smell of rancid coffee and stale bacon made his stomach revolt. For a second he was confused and he remembered the nightmare. He was now living the nightmare: this was real. To request a court-appointed lawyer Teddy had to fill out a stack of forms for submission to the judge for his approval. This is ridiculous, he thought. Nor could he understand why the letters he had written to his father and President Moffatt had not been answered. Teddy also wondered why President Moffatt had not even called to talk to him, hadn't arranged a visit. He was beginning to feel frustrated and discouraged. He fought constantly to keep a sense of balance and spirituality about himself; that was a difficult thing to do in jail with the constant banging of bars, shouting and cursing all around him, the lights on at all hours.

It had been two weeks since Teddy's arrest and incarceration; it was now early May and he was not aware of the subtle changes in the weather outside. Sitka was enjoying several days of sustained sunshine and dryness. Teddy told himself this was a lot like Marine boot camp; he needed a routine, a system. He filled his time with a daily routine: make his bed when he awoke, shower, breakfast (he had to force himself to eat), then a half-hour of exercise. Finding room to exercise was problematic. The cell housed four men. It measured maybe twelve feet square. There were floor-to-ceiling iron bars on two sides and solid concrete walls on the other two. Part of their floor space was taken up by a shower and toilet, both open to public view.

He did numerous sets of chin-ups, push-ups, squats, jogging in place and stomach-crunching sit-ups. Then he started the exercises all over again. He quickly built up the number of repeats to over one hundred a day of each exercise. The rest of the morning Teddy devoted to reading – anything he could get his hands on to fill the hours. He longed to have his scriptures. He asked Frank to bring them to him after his first visit; his request was denied by the jailers. He located an old tattered Gideon Bible in the jail's library (a broom closet with cardboard boxes containing a bunch of books a local women's service organization had collected and donated). The old Bible soon became his fountain of peace, his Balm of Gilead.

He found the Psalms soothing. And surprisingly, Teddy discovered a richness in the references to Christ throughout Isaiah. His favorite passage that comforted him the most reminded him that Christ would not forget him. *I have graven thee in the palms of my hands.* Teddy was amazed that the Old Testament contained such compassion.

Teddy also allowed some time in the afternoons to retreat into what he called his zone. He would sit on the floor next to a wall and allow his muscles to relax. When he felt the tension drain away he would close his eyes and try to remember a favorite scene or place on a stream or river where he used to fly fish. He would focus on the picture in his mind; he would call up a memory of smells, the sounds, the colors, the feel of the rod as he cast the line, the tug of a trout when it took the fly. Then he would silently pray.

After a session in the zone Teddy would be ready to work on his case. Teddy started keeping a diary, his recollections of the facts as best he could remember. He kept his diary and other writings tucked under his pillow, the only storage place he had. Teddy knew it would be important to know the facts cold when he told his story to the jury. He made a list of the critical evidence as best he could determine. He made a list of potential witnesses he would have his lawyer call – if he ever got a lawyer for his defense.

Every afternoon about three o'clock, an orderly would come around with a cooler full of weak Kool Aid and a pot of foul-smelling black coffee on a wheeled cart. The inmates would line up against the bars and hold out their tin cups for a drink. Teddy used this time to stand next to his cell mates and try to harvest some gossip. Teddy was not close to his cell mates; at first he kept himself distanced. Early on they had nicknamed him "The Preacher." He figured they didn't trust him, but he didn't care. If he had learned anything from his days in the military police it was this: jail inmates don't form friendships quickly; you don't know who around you is a snitch. Not that Teddy had anything to conceal; he just felt safer keeping to himself.

Teddy's request for a lawyer was finally granted. On Monday morning of his third week behind bars he and his newly-appointed attorney met the first time for thirty minutes. Max Silverman did not leave a favorable impression. He was one of three lawyers the small town supported. Critter, one of Teddy's cell mates, was also one of Max's clients. Critter spoke in glowing terms of Max's courtroom prowess. "He's a gut fighter, know what I mean?"

Teddy quickly formed his own opinion of Max Silverman after he first set eyes on the man. Max was stocky and wore ill-fitting clothes that were terribly threadbare, his shoulders flecked with a terminal case of dandruff. Perhaps thinking he was courting favor with the native population, Max sported a turquoise and silver bolo tie. He nervously fingered the silver tips of the leather thongs, clicking them together constantly. Was that designed to distract or annoy opposing counsel? Or was it just a nervous tic that would surely irritate a jury? Max had a halo of wild hair that rimmed a huge bald spot; the hair constantly snowed dandruff. His mop gave the impression of a man who'd just wet his finger and stuck it in a bare light socket on a drunken dare. He also had a nervous high-pitched whinny of a laugh that grated. He seemed to laugh at everything Teddy said, giving the impression that life was a big joke to Max, that nothing was serious to him, not even a felony charge.

At the end of their interview Max said, "If I was you, and, of course, I ain't, but if I was… I'd think seriously about taking a plea to a lesser charge."

"Such as…?"

"Criminal assault. That's only two years. Jails are crowded and you'd be out in no time, say less than thirteen months, max."

Teddy was stunned at this man's callousness. "No deal! I'm not pleading to anything. I was defending myself and my companion and we were unarmed. We were attacked and it was unprovoked; we tried to avoid a confrontation. Look at the facts, man!"

"Shh. Keep yer voice down. I was just tossing out an idea to get your reaction and I got it. Keep it cool."

"I'm not finished," Teddy said. "We were attacked by six of them. Someone used a weapon. My companion got fracture of the cheekbone, skull and a serious concussion…"

Max cut in, "But the kid you did a number on is still in a coma. They're saying his spine is severed and he'll be paralyzed from the waist down. To say nothing of possible permanent brain damage. They're saying if he pulls through…"

"Who's giving you this information?" Teddy cut him off.

"The DA's secretary and my secretary, they play bingo together." Max got up to leave. "Well, my friend, you think about it. When you're ready to talk reasonable to Max, have the jailer call me." He stuffed his papers into his old leather briefcase and snapped it shut.

On Frank's next visit Teddy learned that President Moffatt had transferred J.T. Moon as soon as he was released from the hospital, which had been just a couple of days ago. President Moffatt had called Frank to tell him of the transfer. He also told Frank that church headquarters was aware of the situation in Sitka and was having its outside lawyers, a law firm in Salt Lake City, look into the legal issues involved. He would try to visit Elder Buckley on his next trip to Alaska, scheduled in a few days. He and Sister Moffatt were praying for his quick release from jail. He said he would write a letter to help build Elder Buckley's courage. Frank said there was an increase of bad press in the local paper, anti-Mormon stuff. It was having a negative effect on the members; they were having a hard time dealing with the situation. Friends and co-workers were starting to be influenced by the newspaper articles. The members just couldn't believe that Teddy was capable of doing the kind of thing he was being accused of. They always remembered Teddy in the prayers in their meetings.

Sparky Tedrow visited Teddy the day after Frank. He apologized that Betty hadn't been able to bring herself to come down to "that awful place," as much as she loved Elder Buckley. Teddy asked why Barry Bluth hadn't been to visit. Teddy had put Barry on his authorized visitors' list. Sparky told him he heard Barry was going to be called as a prosecution witness, so he wouldn't be allowed to visit. Sparky took off his jacket and rolled up his shirt sleeves. "It's getting' warm outside; spring's here," he announced. Teddy noticed he wore a tattoo on each of his forearms; one was a professional job, a furled flag with the words *Semper Fi*. The other one was a very poor job; the irregular, faded letters said *Hard Luck*.

"What are you hearing - what's the word on the street about all this?" Teddy asked across their small table in the closet-sized visitor's room.

Sparky lowered his voice a bit and said, "This guy Bodie Briggs, the DA? He's a politician, got his eyes set on bigger things. He needs the native vote to help him. He figures he's got the born-againers' votes all locked up 'cause you're a Mormon. I hear from a good source that he gave an I-told-you-so kind of sermon just this last Sunday. He was too smart to mention your name, but he said it was pretty clear to him that this was a typical example of what good Christian folk could expect from Mormons. He said the Missourians was right in driving the Mormons out way back then. If it was legal he'd help his flock do the same thing here in Sitka. Don't sound very Christian, does it?"

Teddy sadly shook his head. Sparky continued," Shoot, almost makes me want to become a Mormon myself if I thought it could help your case." Teddy laughed. "Son, I'm so sorry for what's happened to you. You're too nice a kid to deserve this. If you don't beat this rap I'm afraid it'll ruin you for life. These things have a nasty habit of following guys around... I should know, I..." He stopped.

Teddy reflected then said, "Sparky, I believe I'm going to beat this thing. It's a set-up all right. It's rotten, it stinks, it's not fair. But the president gave me a blessing when he was here that I'd have guardian angels to help carry me through this test." He looked in Sparky's eyes and put his hand on his friend's arm and said, "I think you're going to be one of those guardian angels."

"I'll do anything to help, kid. Just you tell me what to do."

"Time's up," the jailer said.

"I'll come back in a couple days, I promise. Don't give up."

"I won't," said Teddy. And please be sure and tell Betty thanks for the cookies. I use them to get favors." Teddy winked and inclined his head toward his jailer.

As Sparky got up to leave he shook Teddy's hand and said, "Semper fi, kid." Teddy grinned and returned the greeting all Marines know. Sparky started for the door and stopped. "Oh, I almost forgot – Miss Norton the nurse wants to know if it's okay for her to come visit you."

Teddy grinned. "Andrea... Sister Norton? Visit me...? Tell her I'll think about it." For the first time in several weeks his spirits lifted a little.

The days ticked off the calendar. Teddy couldn't understand why his many letters to his parents asking for help and assuring them he was okay went unanswered. So did his letters to President Moffatt, and likewise his letters to Zack.

"Hey Preacher, you think it's okay with God if you play cards with me?"

"Sure, Critter, I think he'd approve," Teddy said, pulling up a straight-backed chair. "What's the ante?"

"The usual, Preacher." The afternoon cribbage game had become a ritual. Teddy had quietly watched a few times to learn the game and its rules. Critter and his sidekick Marty, another rummy, played cribbage games that went on for hours while they smoked foul-smelling cigarettes and coughed so hard that sometimes one or the other nearly passed out from dizziness. "Gotta quit this damn habit," one would say and the other would nod or wag an accusing finger. Vast sums of money were wagered, won and lost. The longer the games went on, the bigger the "pot", the more violent the game. Teddy could tell who was winning by the loud slapping of cards on the table when an exceptionally good hand produced a long run. Marty slapped faster and louder; Critter made more of a show, slapping the cards down agonizingly slow just to annoy his partner. "Okay, okay, you got a big hand, now you gonna lay 'em down so's we kin git on with this sorry game or you gonna take all day, you ole coot?" Marty would say. Critter would just grin a toothless grin and gloat. Just as often the cards would go Marty's way and he'd pay back the insults.

Sometimes the quiet would be shattered by a loud "I shoulda known you'd try to cheat!" Critter would yell. "Man if I just had my old .44…!"

"You'd what…?" Marty would yell back. "What would you do, shoot me with it? Ha! You old rummy, you're so damn drunk you couldn't hit the broad side of a polar bear's butt at six feet! Ha!"

"I otter know better than to trust a rummy at cards. My momma taught me better!"

"Whydn'tcha listen to her then, you old lush?"

The arguing would go on for minutes until the jailer would tell them to shut up and play or he'd take their cards away. Teddy soon learned that one or the other of this pathetic pair would occasionally be released back on the street when he got sober enough. Within two or three days the offender would have spent all of his disability or pension check on alcohol and be back inside, busted for "D&D – that's drunk and disorderly, in case you didn't know, Preacher," Teddy would be told.

Their third cell mate, Arthur, a gaunt, tall, pale young white man slept around the clock with his rough wool blanket pulled up over his head. He never showered; he came alive for meals and the weekly change of sheets, underwear, socks and the orange jump suits they all wore that bore the stenciled lettering *JAIL INMATE* that were exchanged for freshly laundered ones.

One day when Teddy and Arthur were standing naked at the bars awaiting their clean laundry, Arthur quietly said, "They're holding up your mail, outgoing and incoming."

Teddy was surprised. "How do you know?"

"Everybody thinks I sleep all the time, right? When you guys are all asleep at night I'm awake. I heard the hacks (guards) talking the other night. But you didn't hear it from me, okay?" Teddy nodded.

Teddy was shaken awake during the night by Critter. Teddy was in the middle of an especially nice dream having something vaguely to do with Andrea Norton. He thought he remembered he was standing behind her very close. He had his arms around her and was teaching her how to cast a fly rod. The soft breeze blew her red hair into his face; it tickled. It smelled like fresh cut hay in the meadows around Jackson Hole in late June. "What?" Teddy mumbled.

"Shhh. Shush," Critter said.

"What...?"

"It's Marty. He's got a really bad case of the tremors. I need your help."

"What can I do?" Teddy asked as he climbed down. His feet hit the cold dank concrete and he was jolted fully awake.

"You're a preacher, right?" Teddy nodded. "You can pray for him, you know, with the layin' on of hands kind of prayin'?" Teddy nodded.

Teddy knelt down next to Marty's cot. "What's his name?"

"Uh, I dunno, just Marty's all I ever knowed."

"That will have to do," Teddy said. He placed his hands on Marty's wet head, his scalp was scalding to the touch. "Marty," Teddy began, "by the power of the holy priesthood which I bear, I place my hands on your head and give you a blessing. I give you the same blessing that Jesus himself would give, in deepest love, if he were here himself..."

Teddy summoned the night guard and they got Marty to the hospital in time to save his life. "That was the prettiest prayer I ever heard, Preacher."

"Thanks."

"If I needed one would you give it to me, too sometime...?"

"Sure, Critter, but I'd have to know your real name."

"Everyone has always called me Critter."

"I'm sure the Lord knows your name by now..."

"You really think so? I'm such a no-good sinner. How could he even care about me?"

"Let's get some sleep. Tomorrow, if you really want to know, I think I have some answers to your question."

"G'night, Preacher."
"G'night, Critter."

President Moffatt waited in the outer room of the jail while a bailiff shuffled papers. President Moffatt had traveled hundreds of miles and many hours and was exhausted. He checked his watch. He had been waiting to see Elder Buckley for two hours. What was the delay? He got up and confronted the bailiff, "See here, I've been waiting to see the prisoner, er, Elder Buckley, for over two hours. I've traveled all the way from Vancouver just to see this young man. Can't you speed things up?"

The bailiff shrugged, "Not my call, sir. It's up to the judge and he's in a trial settlement conference."

"Well, could you tell him I'm here and I want to see my missionary?"

The bailiff went back to shuffling papers. The big wall clock clicked off the seconds, the minutes, another hour. It was closing time, and clerks and secretaries were gathering their personal stuff and closing down their files for the day.

President Moffatt had finally had enough. He rose and headed down the hallway where he was sure the judge's chambers were. The bailiff clipped around the counter to head him off. "I wouldn't do that, sir."

"Why not? I've had it with this waiting!" the president snapped.

"Sir, sit down and I'll see if I can interrupt the judge."

President Moffatt sat back down, "You do just that!"

The bailiff slowly shuffled down the hall and disappeared. In fifteen agonizing minutes he came back, shamefaced.

"Well...?"

"His Honor says you can't visit the prisoner 'cause you ain't on the official visitors approved list. Sorry."

"What...?!" the president roared. "Where's a phone? I'm calling Max!"

CHAPTER NINETEEN

AND YE VISITED ME

Right after Teddy's first meeting with Max, his lawyer suggested Teddy grow a beard. "Why?" Teddy asked.

"The jury will be made up mostly of men, we hope. Almost all of the men in this town wear beards, in case you haven't noticed. At least all the white guys do…" Teddy noted that Max did not wear one. "That's different. I have to look professional."

Teddy was skeptical, but he grew a beard anyway, even though it was against mission rules and he was technically still a missionary. At least he had not received any communication saying he had been released. Teddy was still bummed out about President Moffatt's abortive attempt to visit him. But at least he took some comfort knowing his president had tried.

The fourth week after his incarceration Teddy had a pre-trial hearing set. Its purpose was to determine if Teddy had changed his mind about proceeding to trial and instead wanted to enter any kind of a plea.

"Your honor," Max began, "my client is not interested in any pleading to any kind of offense, lesser or otherwise. Consequently, I have not had any discussions with Mr. Briggs in this matter."

"I think you should take some more time and have some serious talks with your client," the judge said. Bodie didn't say anything. He didn't have to; Judge Bumpus was doing his dirty work for him. Bodie just smirked. "The court will tentatively set trial for the first week in October. In the interim, the court will postpone this hearing for one month, at which time I trust you will have talked some sense into your client, Mr. Silverman?"

During the brief hearing Teddy had been surprised to see sunlight streaming through the tall courtroom windows. Outside the courtroom Teddy and Max held a brief conference. "I told you I'm not pleading," Teddy said emphatically.

"I wish you'd really think about it instead of being so dang stubborn," Max pleaded, whining.

"And another thing," Teddy said, "what about my Constitutional right to a speedy trial? What's this early October date, anyway? Is that so Bodie can get the most political mileage out of a victory just before the elections?" Max shrugged. "Well I think you should file an interlocutory appeal to the state supreme court demanding they speed up this thing. My rights are being violated here."

"Whoa, slow down, who's the lawyer here? And how come you know so much about interlocutory appeals?" Teddy explained that he had been a commander over a company of Marine MPs. He had spent a lot of classroom time learning the UCMJ and a lot of that manual had parallel applications to what was happening here. Max raised his eyebrows; he was suddenly more impressed with his client. "Look, kid, I get paid by the court to defend you. The judge has a lot of say when I submit my bill… as to how much I get paid and so on. And believe me, the old coot really goes over our public defender legal billings with the old fine tooth, if you get my drift? I know he won't go for paying lawyer fees for any interlocutory appeal, especially if the whole issue brings his handling of your case into question even before it comes to trial. Get me? Think about a plea bargain deal."

Teddy got his meaning loud and clear. He considered filing his own appeal on two issues: lack of speedy trial *and* lack of adequate representation by legal counsel. He'd go back to his cell and give it a lot of thought and prayer.

Teddy's first visit from Andrea was awkward at first. They hadn't seen each other for nearly two months. It was further complicated by the fact that Teddy still considered himself every inch a missionary, 24/7. He truly did not want her to get any false impressions as to his motives. They shook hands across the table. *Keep this on a business-like level*, Teddy reminded himself. "You've grown a beard," Andrea said after they had settled themselves. Teddy smiled. "I like it. Do you know you have some gray whiskers?" she asked. Teddy shook his head. "You also have a few gray hairs along the sides." She reached up and softly touched his lush sideburns.

Teddy felt awkward; he needed to shift the focus away from personal subjects. "How is the kid... the one that got hurt in the, uh, *accident*?" Teddy asked, obviously meaning the native kid he had hurt in the fight.

"He's recovering nicely. Doctors think there may be some permanent brain damage, some possible paralysis of the lower limbs, but he's starting to respond nicely to physical therapy. "You know Larry London, who teaches at the Indian high school on the island?" Teddy nodded, Andrea leaned close and he became momentarily dizzy from her fragrance. "Larry says he hears lots of scuttlebutt around the hallways at school. All the kids talked about the fight before school got out for summer vacation...?"

"It's summer vacation...?" Teddy was temporarily disoriented.

Andrea nodded, continued. "Larry knows the names of at least three of the kids involved, besides the kid in hospital. If your lawyer needs the names, let me know and I can get the info to him." Teddy nodded. "The other thing I wanted to ask you...?" Teddy waited. "We never had any more discussions - only the first one, the day you guys got into that fight."

"That's right, it was that same day, wasn't it? Seems so long ago. What are you saying, that I you want the rest of the discussions?"

Andrea nodded. "Would you mind? I really want to finish it up. It would mean so much to me if you could."

"Time's up," the guard said.

She reached across and squeezed Teddy's hand. "I'll be back soon, I promise."

The next few days Teddy devoted a lot of zone time to her request. He decided it would be all right if Frank or some other priesthood holder could also be present. He could also give a summarized version of each discussion. It would be hard to cram all those gospel principles and concepts into thirty-minute visits, but it could be done. He began practicing his discussions on Critter, one a day, for six straight days. It was a little awkward giving the second discussion on The Book of Mormon with no book for Critter to read, but Teddy found enough scriptures in his tattered Gideon's Bible to supplement. Critter made a good Brother Brown and Teddy told him so. Critter grinned his toothless smile. "You're practicing on me so's you can give these sermons to yer girlfriend, ain't ya?" Critter said.

"She's *not* my girlfriend," Teddy protested. "I told you, Mormon missionaries do not have girlfriends."

"That wasn't the case where I grew up. I knowed lots of fellers had girlfriends on their missions. They'd bring 'em back home from England or Brazil or Finland or wherever. Oh man, those Finns, blondes and pale blue eyes. Wow, they was pretty!"

"How do you know so much about Mormon missionaries?"

"I growed up in a small town in Idaho, place called Franklin. We wasn't Mormons, my family. In fact we was the only non-Mormons in the place. My old man owned a bar. All the good elders and high priests used to sneak in and tip a few now and then. All my pals in school growin' up was Mormons. I probly shoulda been a Mormon, 'cept nobody ever ast me to join."

Teddy was speechless. It just proved you never really knew a person until you got to know more about them. "Critter, let me ask you something…"

"Yeah…?"

"What do you think about all this stuff we've been talking about these past few days, these discussions? Could you believe it's true, I mean about Joseph Smith seeing the Father and the Son?"

"Dang right it's true. I've always knowd it was true ever since I first heerd it told me as a kid. Like I says, nobody ever ast me what I thought. Same's you. You wouldn't be here in Sitka on a mission if you didn't know it was true, now would you?"

Teddy bore Critter a simple, pure testimony. He gave the details of his own conversion, how he had been touched by the Spirit at the LDS Servicemen's conference at Mt. Fuji, how he had struggled as he read through The Book of Mormon and fasted and prayed and finally got a testimony from the spirit. "You can get that same testimony, Critter. All you have to do is ask and the spirit will tell you just like he did for me."

"Oh I did… I ast. Long time ago. I know it's true. But like I said, nobody ever ast me to join up."

"I'm asking you now. Critter, would you like to be baptized? You know of course what that means? That you'd have to give up your habits, your coffee and cigarettes and the drink…? Can you do that, make that commitment to the Lord and keep it?" Critter had tears in his already watery eyes as he nodded.

Under his blankets Arthur, too, had tears.

CHAPTER TWENTY

BIG MEDICINE

Teddy lay awake going over Andrea's question from their last abbreviated discussion. Teddy was not satisfied with giving her the *Small Plates* version as he jokingly referred to the shortened lessons. Her question was: Who do I have to confess my sins to before I can be baptized? It caught him by surprise. He gave her the first thing that had popped into his mind: Only to the Lord. But was that right? Why should she have to confess anything to Frank Carling, the branch president, who would conduct the interview when the time came? And, judging by Andrea's sincerity and the spirit telling Teddy she was indeed converted, the time would be close for her. Andrea said she wanted to wait until Teddy could be the one to perform the ordinance. He cautioned her that could be a long while because of the uncertainty of his situation. She said she had faith that the Lord would soon have him out and his name cleared. His honor would be vindicated; she knew it would.

As he lay staring at the pair of cockroaches chasing each other across the concrete ceiling inches from his nose, Teddy wished he could have the same degree of faith she had. Teddy couldn't sleep. He turned his thoughts to his case, going over the facts again until he couldn't stand to think about it any longer. He got up as quietly as possible to use the commode. "Preacher?" Arthur whispered.

"Yeah?"

"Could we talk?"

"Now?"

"You mind?"

"No, Arthur, I don't mind. Your office or mine?"

They sat against a wall, side by side, like guys do when they talk. Arthur disclosed to Teddy that he had been listening to the discussions when he practiced them on Critter. Something had told Arthur what Teddy said was the truth. Arthur had been a philosophy student at the University of British Columbia, in Vancouver. Two years ago he had been arrested when he got off a fishing boat he'd been working on during summer vacation. Arthur made the mistake of buying a stash of pot in Sitka, not very much, just fifty dollars worth. It turned out his seller was an undercover informant. He was busted and jailed. He drafted and filed his own appeal to be extradited back to B.C., but his appeal was still pending. He had been in jail waiting all this time. He wasn't sure he could take it any longer; he was about ready to crack and make a deal with Bodie.

"That voice you heard telling you it was true…? That's the Holy Ghost bearing witness to your spirit," Teddy said.

"I know. I heard you teaching that to Critter. When I get out I plan to look up your Mormon missionaries in Vancouver, or maybe Victoria, where my folks live, where I'm from."

"That would be a good thing. If I get out before you do, I promise to send you a letter with their contact info, okay?"

"Sure, thanks. Uh, I don't know how to ask, but do you think you could say a prayer for me, like you did for Marty that night he was really bad? I felt something then, too. It was, I don't know, really soothing to hear you say those words. It's funny… I never believed in God before. They beat that out of you pretty fast when you're a philosophy major, the profs and the other students…"

Teddy gave Arthur Hamilton Treadwell III a simple blessing of comfort and strength to endure his trials. As Teddy lay on his bunk looking at the ceiling again, he remembered something he learned in MP school at Treasure Island: many an inmate becomes a believer in God when they rot in jail long enough.

In the early morning hours Teddy got up and asked the night warder what the date was. "It's August sixteenth." Teddy went back to his bunk and quickly fell asleep.

On her next visit Andrea offered the usual handshake; she was somewhat puzzled when Teddy gripped her with both his hands, not releasing hers until she felt the small scrap of paper. She enclosed it in her fist and withdrew her hand. "And how are you today, Elder Buckley?" she asked, tossing her hair in that maddening way she had. She smiled at his discomfort. "Oh, come on, we're very tightly chaperoned here. I'm not going to attack you," she flirted. "In fact, I should be worried about you, being locked up here with all these men... " She sniffed for effect. "I can almost smell the testosterone." She laughed.

Teddy leaned close. "Seriously, I need your help. Can you follow through on something for me?"

"My, we *are* serious today..." Teddy nodded, his face firmly set. "What is it, something wrong?"

"Remember when you said you had the faith I would get this ordeal over with really soon?"

"Yes, and....?"

"I have a plan. You can help me."

"You're planning an escape! You want me to bake a cake...?" Andrea teased.

Teddy shook his head. "Are you good at listening and memorizing stuff?"

She nodded. "I graduated from nursing school, remember?"

"Listen very carefully..." Teddy proceeded to give her some detailed information, a name, another name, a telephone number. "That second name I just gave you...?" he said. "Just tell him you're a friend of the guide who pulled him out of the Madison three summers ago when his boat capsized. The kid now needs his help and the kid can pay. Then you tell him the details of me, my case, where I am, and so on. Can you remember all that?"

"Of course I can. As I said, I went to nursing school. That was all about memorizing." Andrea repeated word-for-word the information Teddy had just given her.

"Good. Thanks a lot. I can explain it all later." They chatted some more until her visit time was up. Teddy had the strong impulse to take her in his arms and hug until he squeezed her breathless. That would have to wait for another time. He went back to his cell humming *You and I travel to the beat of a different drum....*

Back in his cell Teddy fashioned a calendar out of scrap paper. He crossed off all the days up to that day, August the sixteenth. He circled August twenty-fifth, his birthday. That would be the day things would turn around for Teddy Buckley.

Andrea visited two days later; Teddy waited impatiently for her visit. "Well, any news to report?"

Andrea beamed. "I not only contacted him, he said yes, he "vividly remembered the kid who rescued him." He even remembered your name, Teddy! He's already on the job. He checked with the other names and numbers you gave me and it all checked out, he said when he called me back. He said for you to be patient, that things were already rolling in your favor and he'd get it all worked out and be here soon."

Teddy broke down and wept with relief and joy. "I'm sorry, I'm not usually a boob," he explained. "It's just…"

She put her arm around his shoulder as he wept again with his head cradled in his arms on the table. For once, the guard looked the other way. "It's okay. Let it out. You've been under a lot of strain. It's a lot like being in battle," she soothed. Teddy realized that what he'd been going through was indeed a battle.

"Max, I'm replacing you as my lawyer," Teddy said.

"I don't think that's wise. I know you said you knew all about law and stuff, but…" Teddy raised his hand, cutting him off.

"The court didn't believe me when I said I could post bail. The judge didn't give me a chance to prove it. I turn twenty-five today…"

"Happy birthday. Mazeltov!" Max said, his voice edged with sarcasm. He raised an imaginary glass in an imaginary toast.

"Thanks. I won't explain all the legal and financial ramifications, but don't submit a bill to the court. I can take care of it now. Thanks, Max, for all your help. But I'm confident I won't be needing you any longer."

"If I may ask, who do you get to replace me, who's going to represent you now…?" Teddy borrowed Max's Bic pen, took a page of Max's long legal pad of lined yellow paper and wrote out a name. He rotated the sheet so Max could see. Max let out a long whistle through his teeth. "I see… Boy, I'd sure like a ringside seat when that man comes in and kicks Bodie's butt clear back to Arkansas! Whooeee!"

"Oh, you'll be there, Max. You'll be there as co-counsel, I promise."

Teddy's motion to dismiss the case in its entirety was duly filed on his behalf by Max and his new associate counsel. Because of the Labor Day weekend, the hearing was set for the Tuesday following the holiday. Max got the court's permission for Teddy to be dressed in a dark suit, white shirt and tie for his hearing. And no handcuffs! Teddy also shaved off his beard. In an extended long-distance conference call, Max's new associate counsel had made it perfectly clear to Bodie Briggs that the publicity Bodie had been so eagerly seeking would be assured. New counsel had arranged for a reporter from the Anchorage daily news and another representing two Seattle papers to be in attendance… with photographers. The message was clear: the world would be watching how the court system in far-off Sitka dispensed justice.

Further, Bodie was informed as to Teddy's family name and background; Teddy did indeed have the resources to post bail, as he had represented to the honorable judge. And his client certainly had the financial resources to engage the services of the lawyer now speaking to Bodie.

Bodie slammed down the receiver and swore a string of obscenities. His secretary hurried in to his office. "Out!" He kicked his secretary out, yelling at her when she asked if he wanted coffee. "No, I don't want any of that damn swill you call coffee! And leave me alone, no calls, is that clear?"

"Yes, sir," she said meekly. What had pushed his hot buttons?

Five minutes later she buzzed Bodie on the intercom. "I said no disturbances, dammitall!" Again he slammed down the receiver, knocking off stacks of cases and legal papers from his desk. She stuck her head in a small opening of the door and said meekly, "I think you better take this call. It's Judge Bumpus…"

Bodie knew this call would be coming, and he dreaded it even more than he … he started to say his wife's calls, but bit his tongue. "Your Honor, how nice to hear from you…what may I do for…?"Bodie said in his pleasantest voice.

His Honor cut Bodie off before he could say another word. "We're in a (expletive) fix! I think we better meet in my chambers and get this mess all worked out before that three hundred dollar-an-hour lawyer gets here, don't you agree? Now!" His Honor slammed down the phone, not waiting for his craven colleague's reply.

"Almost ready, judge," Ralph the bailiff stuck his head in the judge's private door. A moment before coming onstage, the Honorable Albert W. Bumpus was bracing himself with a double shot of vodka. This public hanging of Bodie was not going to be pretty. He sure as hell was *not* going to lose control of this dismissal hearing if he had anything to say about it. He was not going to let his career - his possible appointment to the state supreme court - get sidetracked by this nothing of a hearing turning into a circus. He had privately warned Bodie to work out a plea deal for a misdemeanor, and, if he couldn't get that one simple thing in the bag, to please find a fig leaf – any fig leaf would do - and let the whole damn mess just go away.

The Honorable Bert Bumpus had had some misgivings about the case, the way Bodie was pushing it to stir up publicity for his re-election campaign. Hell, the Injun kid was mostly better now and the police report had shown that the Mormon guys were attacked by more than one person. Surely that little Injun kid in the hospital couldn't have stirred up the crime scene and made such a mess all by himself. And how could he have disabled the other half-breed kid and still taken on the ex-Marine all alone…? Just didn't wash.

Let's start the show and get this over with. Bert peeked out the door. Good grief, who are all those people in my courtroom? It's standing room only!

Teddy turned around to see the crowd filing in. He looked for his parents, who had arrived by air just that morning. They came in and he waved; his mom burst into tears. Frank and Maggie entered; he waved. Andrea came with Sparky and Betty. He waved. Andrea rubbed her hand over her chin signing that she noticed he had shaved. She pulled a pouty face that was too cute for words. You're still a missionary, Teddy reminded himself. A lot of people Teddy didn't know or recognize filed in and squeezed into the hard benches. The Gilberts and Chief Russell were among the last before the doors closed.

Teddy leaned over to his two attorneys. "I don't know who's the main attraction here, you or I," pointing to his new attorney. Max let out one of his shrill, nerve-rattling laughs.

The crowd suddenly hushed and Teddy turned to face the front; he could feel Andrea's eyes aimed at the back of his head.

"All rise. Hear ye, hear ye. The district court for the state of Alaska is now in session, the Honorable Judge Albert W. Bumpus presiding. All ye who have business before the court draw ye near and be ye heard," Ralph dutifully droned.

The Honorable Bert Bumpus took his seat on the bench with a flourish of black robes and stern countenance. "In the matter of State v. Buckley, Mr. Silverman I believe you have a motion you'd like to present to the court?" Bert smiled benignly at Max.

This was Max's cue. "Your honor, may it please the court, I would first like to introduce my esteemed associate, my co-counsel, Mr...."

Bert cut him off. "Mr. Silverman, your esteemed co-counsel needs no formal introduction. May the court also presume you wish to move he be admitted to practice before this court for the sole purpose of assisting you with the case at hand?"

"That's correct, your honor, thank you. Now we would like to move..."

Again Bert cut him off with: "The court has read the file, the pleadings, the affidavits and sworn statements of the various witnesses. The court has also carefully read and considered the learned and very well-written brief filed by you and your eminent co-counsel. The court has also read the precedent cases cited therein. Therefore, in the interest of justice, and for good cause shown, if there are no objections from the state's attorney..."

That was Bodie's cue to simply stand up and say the state had no objections, your honor, thank you, and the court may proceed to grant the defendant's motion to dismiss, etc. Bingo! Done and over with. Now for that nice soothing glass of Smirnoff's... But no... the big fat idiot! What was Bodie doing? Bert could not believe his ears.

"Your honor, Bodie Briggs for the state. Yes, your honor, we do have a few matters we wish to bring to the court's attention before we too hastily rush to a decision in this grave matter... As the attorney for the good people of this great state, I feel it is my duty to see that justice is done, that every crime is punished, and I am inclined to resist this motion on the grounds that…"

"Bodie!" Bert cut him off in mid-sentence. "Chambers! Now!" Bodie's head snapped back like he'd been slapped. Bert was off the bench, robes flapping, storming into his chambers before Bodie could find his tongue. "Mildred, Ralph! Chambers!" Bert shot over his retreating shoulder. This was a crisis: his clerk and bailiff were needed immediately.

"All rise!" Ralph shouted as he hurried after Mildred and the judge. Bodie moved like a zombie slowly toward the good old-fashioned, country-style butt-whipping that awaited him in Bert's chambers.

Teddy's new lawyer took the opportunity to stand, stretch and yawn and grin as if to say "Aw, shucks, folks, this is all in a day's routine for this po' boy country hick lawyer." He stood almost as tall as Teddy. Under heavy brows he had black, piercing eyes that could have come from native genes; you weren't sure. His face was deeply tanned, lined, chiseled high cheekbones and a prominent Romanesque nose. He wore his graying hair long, brushing the shoulders of his tailored buckskin jacket with fringes down the sleeves. That jacket, plus the cowboy boots and the big silver belt buckle, all added to the mystery – native or not? His hair was taking on streaks of silver. His pearl grey Stetson hat with the braided leather and silver concho band lay on counsel's table in front of him.

The only other prop needed for this show was the slim legal brief sheathed in pale blue parchment – Teddy's motion to dismiss – lying on counsel's table. It spoke for itself - Justice personified. He never touched it and never even glanced at it. The brief lay there in repose, its thinness devastatingly dangerous.

This man was beyond formidable as a courtroom lawyer; only a small handful of trial lawyers dared play in his league. The monetary damage awards he won for his clients were the stuff of legends. His deserved reputation stretched from coast to coast in the lower Forty-Eight, in fact, around the world. He was in demand as a featured speaker or panelist or lecturer at any number of bar conventions or law schools or legal symposia. His most lethal weapon, however, was his aw-shucks demeanor. He fit right in with common folks, the ones who made up most of the juries in America's legal system. If you were in trouble and needed Big Medicine, he was it.

In short, Bodie and this bush-league judge were toast before the fight even started that day. Bert Bumpus sure as heck knew the score even if thick-skulled Bodie didn't.

The press took advantage of the recess to cluster around, flash bulbs popping. From somewhere inside the judge's chambers they could hear muffled shouting. No one out in the court room paid any mind; the *real* show was right here.

"Dammit to hell, Bodie! What are you trying to pull? I told you to keep your freakin' big mouth shut except to say yessir, nossir, now did I not?"

"Bert… Judge, I was only trying to…"

"To do what? And I warn you you're on the verge of contempt right now."

"I was just doing my duty as the servant of the people of the state of…"

"By God, that does it! You're in contempt. Three days in jail and five hundred bucks fine! Mildred, write that down." Mildred scribbled on her steno pad. Ralph the bailiff started to take Bodie's arm.

"Now just a minute, Bert…" Bodie pled.

"Damn you, Bodie! You don't get it, do you? Five days and a thousand!"

"Aw judge, Bert, c'mon be reasonable…"

"You want reasonable? Make it ten days and five thousand! Ralph, get that damn idiot whiner down to the lockup."

"Yes, sir. General population, judge?"

"Judge…" Bodie yelped.

"Yessir, that's the ticket! Throw him in with all those damn rummies he keeps prosecuting!" Ralph dragged Bodie off to jail; Mildred marched stiffly back out to her assigned seat in the shadow of the bench. Bert helped himself to the last of the Smirnoff's straight from the bottle, draining it dry. The slug of alcohol hit his stomach ulcer with a jolt. He fumbled through his medicine cabinet until he found the Pepto, downing a huge glob of the pink goo. His lips were bright pink as he re-entered his court room, determined to restore judicial decorum to the proceedings.

Bert looked around the courtroom until he spotted the man he wanted. "Mr. Daynes, approach."

Harrison Daynes, one of the other three private attorneys in town approached with feelings bordering on trepidation. "Your honor…?" he spoke hesitantly.

"Mr. Daynes, it seems Mr. Briggs has been taken suddenly ill… very suddenly, you might say. Would you be willing to step in as deputy?" Daynes nodded, unsure of what was happening. Bert continued, "Raise your hand. By the authority vested in me I appoint you as interim deputy district attorney. Do you swear to faithfully execute the duties of your office? Good." Harrison Daynes stood there dumbstruck.

"Mr. Buckley, will you please stand?" Bert asked with utmost politeness. Teddy stood. "Mr. Buckley, based on the motion of your attorneys and for good cause shown, the court hereby dismisses the case of State v. Buckley."

Cheers went up and Teddy grinned. Bert pounded his gavel for order.

"However, I am charging you with a violation of city ordinance one-oh-three dash three, disturbing the peace. You are fined one hundred dollars, court costs of one thousand dollars and thirty days in jail." Teddy looked shocked. What had suddenly gone wrong? "However, jail time is reduced to time already served. Mr. Buckley, please keep out of trouble in future, no matter how much longer you choose to stay in our fair city. Court is adjourned."

"All rise," Ralph bellowed. He was the first to rush Teddy to shake his hand. Mildred demurely blew her chronic runny nose and tucked her steno pad away in her big purse. She exited through the judge's private door to avoid the crush of the crowd that was now pressing Teddy.

The next person to greet Teddy was Andrea who threw her arms around him with a wildness and a flood of tears that scared him. But only a little.

CHAPTER TWENTY ONE

A TIME TO HEAL

Teddy pried himself loose from Andrea long enough to shake hands with the country lawyer from Jackson Hole that he'd rescued from the Madison River several summers before. The great lawyer shook his hand, settled the Stetson on his head and gathered his papers into an expensive, slim, genuine alligator valise. "You'll be sure and send your bill to the trustees, won't you? And thanks again." Teddy said.

The lawyer nodded, put two fingers to his hat brim and started off. He turned and said, "Semper fi." He held up his ring with the Marine crest on it. I should have known, Teddy thought. The press corps followed the great man outside like the wake of a great ship.

Teddy had already given a brief statement to the press about how he knew he would get justice, it felt good to be free, didn't know for certain what his future plans were, probably finish his mission, etc.

Next he needed to stop by the clerk's office to sign some papers, pay the fines and court costs and collect his few personal possessions. The jailers gathered around and wished him luck, no hard feelings, etc. Teddy grinned and waved them off. Suck-ups, he thought. He walked out into the sunlight, paused on the front steps of the courthouse and breathed deeply the air of freedom.

He had more business to tend to, but first they would celebrate.

The branch members had organized a reception for Teddy; he was embarrassed by the fuss. They were treating him like some kind of hero and he felt anything but a hero. The sisters had put together a nice table of potluck foods and a banner in front of the Mt. Edgecumbe multi-purpose center that read WELCOME BACK, ELDER B.

The water taxi was kept busy carrying the Mormon revelers across from Sitka. Teddy's mother said it was the first time she had ridden in such a small ship; Teddy didn't correct her and tell her it was only a boat. Everything Teddy was seeing was as if for the first time; it was all familiar yet new. The calendar said it was September, but already the seasonal change to winter was in the air. Storms were brewing in the Gulf of Alaska that would blow in within a few days. The sea birds were a sure indicator, Richard Gilbert pointed out to Mrs. Buckley. The natives could always predict the weather by watching the behavior of animal life around them, he said. She was impressed.

"Mother, dad, this is my friend Andrea Norton. Andrea, my parents."

"I'm so pleased to meet you, my dear," Mrs. Buckley said, extending a white-gloved hand. Mrs. Buckley presented herself in court that morning wearing a smart Navy suit with white trim and wide-brimmed white hat. It was not her way to stand out in a crowd, but that was just the effect she had in tiny Sitka. That was always the way she had dressed for public functions since Teddy could remember. Mr. Buckley, in a gentleman's country tweed suit and knit plaid tie, with his guards' mustache, cut a figure to match his wife's. That was just the way they were; Teddy saw them for the first time in a new light. He felt a sudden rush of love for his parents that he never had before. Now that he knew the truth, that all his mail in and out of the jail had been held up, he knew the worry they must have experienced. The fact they had traveled all this great distance to be his support in this trying time was a quiet testament of their great love for him.

"Teddy, I mean, Elder Buckley, has never said much about the two of you. I even wondered if he even had parents. I mean, of course, everyone has parents. He just never talked about you. I am so glad to meet you. It was so great of you to come all this way to be with him," Andrea said.

"Oh, my dear, you have no idea. We were worried sick about him, with no news. I just knew something was wrong but didn't know. Well… it's over now, isn't it? Now he can come back home and resume a normal life," Mrs. Buckley said.

"Well, not quite yet, Mom," Teddy cautioned.

"Why ever not, son?" Mr. Buckley asked. "Surely…."

"Officially, I'm still on my mission," Teddy tried to explain. "I haven't been released and I still have about fifteen months to go. That is, if they allow me to finish…"

Their brief discussion was interrupted by Frank Carling welcoming everyone and calling on Richard Gilbert, his new second counselor (Teddy was pleased and surprised to learn), to say a blessing on the food. After the blessing everyone moved to the food tables that were groaning under the load of casseroles, salads, hors d'oeuvres and desserts. Teddy used this as a cue to excuse himself to go talk to a few more people. Mr. and Mrs. Buckley continued to visit with Andrea. "Did you notice how her eyes followed Teddy round the room?" Mrs. Buckley would mention to her husband on their long flight back to Pittsburgh. "I think she's in love with him." "She seems like a nice enough girl to me," Mr. Buckley said from inside his Newsweek magazine. "Look at this, Madeleine, there's an article in here on…"

President Moffatt arrived in Sitka just in time to say hello and goodbye to the branch members as the reception was winding down. Teddy was happy to see his president after so many months. After the president had been fed sufficiently and had greeted the members who still hung around, he indicated that he and Teddy needed to have an interview. "Can you find us a private room, Elder, where we can talk about, er, recent events…?"

Teddy truly did not know what to expect about the future of his mission. Frank had said the authorities usually released missionaries after a public incident like Teddy's that brought the wrong attention to bear on the church. Larry London's opinion was that they would probably let Teddy continue his mission but obviously he would be sent back down to B.C., probably somewhere out in the interior, like Kitimat, or Prince George, someplace really remote where the locals had never heard about Teddy's arrest. Teddy tried hard to keep an open mind and a sense of faith the authorities would make the right decision in his case. He was willing to be obedient to their decision, no matter if it meant being released and sent home. Of course, if they asked his desires, he wanted to finish the job he started…

President Moffatt was brief yet compassionate. As always, he assured Teddy that his first concern was, and always had been, the health, safety and spiritual well-being of his missionaries. He had worried and prayed constantly for Teddy. He had been extremely upset and frustrated when he'd tried to visit Teddy and they wouldn't let him due to some silly technicality. But he was so happy and relieved that things had worked out so favorably for him. Of course, there were many questions he needed answers to. He had interviewed Elder J.T. Moon and knew his version of the story. He asked Teddy to recount what happened, not only that tragic night, but the events leading up to that hour.

Teddy started with the potlatch on the beach, the flirting native girls and the jealous boys. He recounted the burning of their cabin, which the president already knew about. Then he recited the facts - he knew them cold - of that bad night of the fight. He assured the president that he was only trying to defend himself and J.T. He honestly tried to get away from the gang and avoid a fight. Yes, Teddy was trained in the military police. Yes, Teddy knew martial arts and techniques of self-defense. Yes, Teddy used restraint and only as much force as necessary to repel their attackers. And, yes, Teddy was deeply sorry for the hurt he accidentally caused. Most of all, did Teddy have a plan for restitution to the injured boy and did he plan to ask the boy's forgiveness and his family's forgiveness?

"President, I have spent many sleepless nights on my cot in that jail thinking about your question. The answer is yes. I plan to get over to see the boy tomorrow morning. Sister Norton, you just met her? She works there as a nurse. She has a meeting all set up for me. I just hope he isn't so bitter he won't accept my offers of restitution and my pleas of forgiveness."

"I'm sure he will, elder." Then, after a long pause, the president asked Teddy if he would like another blessing. Teddy said he would, but first, he really needed to know what was next for Elder Buckley. "I expect to hear back from the member of the Twelve who has responsibility over the missionary program. As soon as I hear from him, you will know. I will be here through day after tomorrow. Now, that blessing you wanted…?"

Toby Dutcher had lain in a hospital bed in Sitka since that fateful night Teddy threw him over that parked car. He had sustained multiple head fractures, a broken pelvis, several broken ribs, broken wrist and forearm. As for his face, most of his teeth had either been broken out or knocked loose. His nose was shattered, as were his right cheek bones and right jaw bone. At first the diagnosis included a severed spinal cord in the neck region, but that later was changed to partial severing. Either way, the injury would permanently affect his motor skills. He would walk with a serious limp in his right leg, and he would require a great deal of physical therapy to ever use his right arm and right hand. So far, he was still unable to begin physical therapy. He was not a large kid before the accident, but now he was barely one hundred pounds, with a pronounced skeletal look. His cheek bones protruded starkly and his eyes were bulging instead of buried in their sockets, as Teddy expected. The good news was that he was slowly gaining weight, a few ounces at a time.

On the day Teddy visited him in hospital, Toby's jaws were wired shut following recent surgery to repair the broken bones. He couldn't talk and took his food in liquid form through a straw. He communicated by writing brief notes (or rather scribbling them) with his left hand, a skill that wasn't very efficient - you had to study closely to decipher the meaning. "Do you know who I am?" Teddy asked. Toby nodded his head slightly. "Are you doing okay?" Teddy continued. Another nod. "Do you know why I came to see you?" He shook his head slightly, it was more of an effort.

Teddy draped his trench coat over the foot of the bed and knelt down beside Toby. "I came to say how sorry I am and how much I wish you would forgive me for hurting you." Teddy looked into Toby's eyes and waited.

Toby pulled his writing clipboard onto his stomach and slowly scribbled a short note: i sor. Andrea interpreted, "He means he's sorry."

Tears came to Teddy's eyes. "Why are you sorry?"

Toby wrote: u no do fit. "He says you didn't start the fight," Andrea said. "Is that what you said, Toby?" Toby nodded slightly.

"It doesn't matter, Toby. I'm not angry at you or your friends. I'm just sorry I hurt you. Can you forgive me?"

ok. Toby wrote. Teddy didn't need Andrea to interpret.

"Truly?"

yes.

Toby slowly held up his one good hand, Teddy took it in both his and kissed and bathed his hand with tears. "Thank you, Toby. I want you to know I will do whatever is necessary to help pay for your medical bills and your therapy. Don't worry about the costs because I will cover it for you. Would you like your family to come and be with you, too?" Teddy asked. Toby nodded again and his eyes seemed to come alive with a light that had been missing. Teddy saw that tears were brimming in Toby's dark eyes. "Would that make your mom and dad happy to be here with you?"

"Yes."

On his way out Teddy met with the hospital financial administrator and left the names and address of his trustees in Pittsburgh with a letter he had written directing that Toby's medical bills be all paid by the trust. Andrea walked as far as the front doors. "That was a remarkable thing you did for that boy. I don't think I have ever seen anyone do anything like that, and I probably never will ever again. Teddy Buckley, you are the most remarkable man I have ever known." She started to hug him, stopped, offered her hand. "I know, I know. You're still on your mission. But some day, I promise you…" she grinned, squeezed his hand three times. Teddy blushed and squeezed her hand back.

President Moffatt gave Teddy permission to baptize Andrea before he had to return to Vancouver with the president. There he would work while he awaited the decision from 47 East South Temple Street in Salt Lake City as to his fate as a missionary.

The baptism of Andrea Norton was a simple, low-key affair; she wanted it that way, so very few members of the branch were alerted. But good news travels fast in a small branch, and every new member strengthens the ranks. The good sisters scrambled together a reception following the ordinance. Andrea was baptized in the portable font built by Richard Gilbert in the Carlings' basement. They had considered holding it in the Mt. Edgecumbe multi-purpose center, but decided this venue would be more private. Andrea radiated a spiritual glow in her white clothes. Teddy's breath was taken away when he first saw her enter the room; he could not take his eyes off her during the opening hymn, prayer and brief remarks by President Moffatt. Betty leaned over to Maggie and said, "She looks like a new bride, doesn't she?" Maggie nodded and said, "She could be in a year from now." Betty nodded knowingly.

While Andrea was changing from her wet whites into street clothes, Frank interrupted the hymns that were being played on the electric keyboard. "Brothers and sisters, if I could have your attention for just a minute… Thank you. Sister Tedrow, we have a surprise for you…" Frank pointed to the stairs leading from upstairs. Every head turned. Standing at the foot of the stairs dressed in white was Sparky. Betty burst into tears and ran to her husband, hugging him so hard he couldn't breathe. "You stinker!" she cried. "Why didn't you say anything?"

Sparky grinned, shrugged and said, "I wanted to surprise you, honey."

"You sure did that all right, you silly old coot!"

CHAPTER TWENTY TWO

THE TOTEM

It was getting late and most everyone had gone home. Teddy was allowed to be alone with Andrea for five minutes to say his good-byes. When they were finally alone the awkwardness set in and precious seconds ticked off without any words spoken. Teddy broke the ice. "Look, I guess you know by now I have to return to Vancouver." Andrea nodded. "Thanks for the honor of baptizing you." She nodded again, afraid to look in his eyes. "I feel like I need to say something, to tell you…" She put her hand on his lips quieting him. He could see she was crying.

When Andrea could speak she dried her eyes and said, "I know you can't make any promises to me and I don't expect any. I know the future for you is uncertain. I know, at least I think I do, how your emotions are all mixed up right now. You want to finish your mission. That's honorable. I want you to be released so we can be together and maybe part of you does, too. That's selfish of both of us, me especially. Let's leave it like this: When you finally know what's to become of you, you can write or call and tell me. That will be a big relief for both of us, at least *knowing*. Is that okay for now? If you can live with that, so can I. And anyway, you know where to find me."

Teddy nodded and smiled. Then he broke mission rules and hugged her long and tenderly.

President Moffatt accompanied Teddy to the sandy beach outside town where the potlatch had been held months before. A steady wind was blowing from the northwest touched with moisture. Sparky gave Teddy the use of his old pickup to drive himself, the president and the Gilbert family to the appointed place. It was getting late, well past ten o'clock, when they got to the car park near the stream. Teddy recounted the adventure of the eagle attacking Elder Wessman and him that P-day. The president was impressed. Through the trees they could see the huge bonfire sending flames high into the sky, the sparks rising higher in the updraft, ascending into the darkness until they winked out. In front of the fire was a simple small wooden table. A woven native blanket covered an object. Beyond the fire and sand strip the waves lapped closer on an incoming tide. A night owl, disturbed by the human intruders, screeched nearby. Several of Rosie's brothers, sisters and cousins had gathered for the ceremony. A small band played haunting native tunes on flutes, rattles, and softly beaten drums.

When everyone was gathered, Chief Russell raised his arms and the music stopped. The only sound was the lapping of the surf and snapping of silvery driftwood logs. Chief Russell raised his arms and began a sad slow chant in Tlingit. Richard whispered the translation in the president's ear. "He is making first a tribute to our ancestors, to honor them. Then he invites the spirits to join us, good spirits that will bring food and family and happiness and peace. Then he will ask the ancestors for permission to bring this young man into their family, this young man who has brought peace and truth to his daughter and her family."

Chief Russell stopped and beckoned Teddy to approach him. He placed an ornately patterned, hand-woven ceremonial shawl on Teddy's shoulders. He next rested his hands on Teddy's shoulders and gently nudged him to a kneeling position. Chief Russell moved his hands to Teddy's head and closed his eyes and began to chant softly. "Now he gives his new son a blessing in Tlingit," Richard interpreted for the president. "Most interesting…" whispered President Moffatt.

When Chief Russell had completed the prayer he raised Teddy by the hand and embraced him. Chief Russell turned to the little table, lifted the blanket and presented to Teddy a newly-carved potlatch bowl. Teddy held it so everyone could see and admire its beauty and fine workmanship.

"What is it?" the president whispered.

"A potlatch bowl. Teddy will use it to eat from when he attends our family potlatches in the future."

"I can't make out the figures carved on the sides," the president said.

"It has a jumping coho salmon on each side. That is the totem for Teddy's new name."

"What's his new name?" the president asked.

"The Man Fisher," Richard said.

President Moffatt smiled, as proud of this great elder as if he were his own son.

CHAPTER TWENTY THREE

47 EAST SOUTH TEMPLE STREET

Teddy flew back to Vancouver with President Moffatt and spent nearly a week working out of the mission home, a beautiful Tudor mansion on Connaught Drive in the ritzy, Shaughnessy Heights area of the city. Each day Teddy threw himself into the work, putting all thoughts of Andrea or Salt Lake City out of his mind. "It's getting close to General Conference time, so I think the Brethren will postpone any action until after the first part of October," President Moffatt explained. He was wrong. An early morning call came from Salt Lake the next day: Elder Buckley was to come to church headquarters as soon as travel could be arranged to meet with a member of the Twelve, who would make a decision after the elder was interviewed. Teddy was on a plane bound to Salt Lake via Seattle before early afternoon. President Moffatt personally drove Teddy to the airport in Richmond. On the way he said, "Elder, I hope they send you back to me. I had hopes of making you my assistant. But if they don't, I want you to know you are a very special young man. I have learned a great deal from you."

Teddy was not sure what he ever could have taught Big Thunder.

He was ushered into the apostle's marbled office at exactly nine o'clock the next morning. "He will see you now, Elder," the smiling secretary said. Teddy hitched up his courage, buttoned his suit jacket, straightened his dark striped tie and followed her into the inner office. Teddy was not exactly prepared for what he saw. A short little man with big ears came around his desk and threw his arms around Teddy in a vise grip hug. For a second Teddy thought that this must be what it felt like to be embraced by the Savior; he had never felt such a spirit of love coming from another person. He instantly felt a spirit speaking to his own spirit, which calmed him and removed all fear.

"Sit down, please," a gravelly voice whispered. Teddy sat. "Tell me about yourself, Elder, who you are, where you come from, what I can do for you." Teddy was disarmed.

He spent nearly an hour pouring out his story, what had happened, how he had become converted, the bad experience in Sitka, the good experiences – the ones that caused his faith to grow, how badly he wanted to complete his mission, his testimony of the gospel. When he finished the great apostle said, with a twinkle in his eye, "That Junior Hartmann is quite the character, isn't he? You really met him in a Japanese bath and he only had a towel wrapped around his waist?" Then he laughed a deep raspy-throated laugh. His laugh made Teddy feel better somehow.

Then the talk turned serious. "Elder, I feel I need to caution you that we take a sober look at these situations. I feel strongly your spirit and your desire to complete your mission. What I need to do now is pray about your case, take it to the Lord to seek His will. How long will you be in town?"

Teddy thought that was an odd question. "As long as you want me to be here."

"Good. Tell you what. Conference starts in two days and I'd like you to be my special guest. My secretary will fix you up with the passes and you'll sit in a special VIP section in the Tabernacle. How does that sound?"

Teddy was astounded. "Great," was all he could manage to say.

General Conference was the perfect tonic for Teddy's sagging spirits. He enjoyed the unique vantage point of being close to the General Authorities, auxiliary presidencies and the Tabernacle Choir. The music and hymns moved him as much as the prayers and talks. The weather outside was perfect - Indian summer blessed the Saints with a glorious weekend of sun and fall colors.

His appointment to learn his fate was set for Tuesday mid-afternoon. Teddy spent the morning touring Temple Square, this time truly appreciating all the things he had hardly noticed when he toured with Zack many months ago. Shortly before noon Teddy got the quirky idea to try and find Elder Hartmann and pay him a surprise visit. His secretary said he could spare five minutes but then had to leave early for a luncheon meeting at Rotary, where he was giving a speech. She ushered Teddy in. "The face seems familiar and I should know you, but forgive me if I'm a little fuzzy; I meet so many people every week…" He extended his hand. They shook. "Sit down, sit down."

"You probably don't remember me, but we met a few years ago in a Japanese bath at Mt. Fuji, the servicemen's conference where you spoke," Teddy began.

"Tell me more, it's starting to come back to me."

"We were both wearing bath towels. I bumped into you as you were coming in and I was going out. I stopped and asked if you were an apostle… does that ring any bells?" Teddy said.

"Oh, yes, I think I remember. And what did I say to you? Can you recall?"

"Clearly. You said you were not an apostle, but that you had a special calling to travel the world testifying of Christ. I need to tell you something about that experience…" Elder Hartmann waited. "I was not a member of the church then. I was sort of dragged along by a… a friend, you might say. What you said in your talk about your own conversion and that spirit I felt when we met in that steam bath made a profound impact on me. I decided I needed to find out more about these Mormons. I started reading The Book of Mormon, and the rest, as they say, is history."

"Tell me more. What are you doing in the church now? What callings have you had?" His secretary poked her nose in and pointed to her wrist watch. "My trainer is telling me it's time to go," he joked. "Walk outside with me. No, you come with me to my luncheon. They always have an extra plate or two. We can talk on the way; it's only a couple blocks. It's a pretty day, so let's walk."

By the time they had walked two blocks to Lamb's Grill on Main

Street, Elder Hartmann stopped and said, "You mean to tell me you want to finish your mission and you're afraid they're going to release you?" Teddy nodded. "Well, don't worry. I'm on the missionary committee and I have a direct pipeline to The Man."

"God?" Teddy asked.

"No, but close. I mean the apostle you met with already. Let's eat some rubber chicken, you can listen to some of my Navy stories – the Glory Days - and we'll go back and make that phone call for you, okay?"

"Okay," Teddy said.

Teddy waited nervously outside the marbled office on 47 East South Temple for forty-five minutes. The ticking clock in the marble hall echoed ponderously. Finally the secretary came out of the apostle's office and motioned him to come in. This time the apostle sat behind his desk frowning. Teddy stood until he looked up and motioned Teddy down into a comfortably upholstered, brass-studded side chair. "Elder Buckley, seems like you have gone over my head…" Teddy squirmed in his seat; he felt little rivers of sweat run down the inside of his shirt. "I…" His interviewer waved a hand.

"As they say in England, I've been *nobbled*." Teddy was puzzled. A big grin spread across the man's face. "That Junior Hartmann is one of a kind. I wish we had more General Authorities with his sense of humor, but with a little bit of reserve thrown in. He called me, as you might have guessed. He counseled me that the church would be making a big mistake if we lost the services of this fine elder. I believe he meant you. Imagine, he called to counsel me!" He laughed. Teddy began to relax a little. Then the apostle got serious again. "I have to be honest with you, Elder, I have spent a long time pondering and praying about you. You are a special young man. We tend to release elders who find themselves in your situation." Teddy's face began to cloud. "Did you tell me your first converts were Indians? What nation were they?"

"Yes, sir, Tlingits, coastal natives."

"And I hope you grew to love them not simply because they were your first converts?"

Tears formed in Teddy's eyes. "They adopted me into their family as a son. They gave me a totem. My new name is The Man Fisher."

His interviewer smiled and said, "The Man Fisher. Now I know what the spirit was trying to tell me. Elder, I feel inspired that the Lord wants you to continue and complete your mission. I feel inspired that you are foreordained to do a great work among the Lamanites. How would you like to be transferred to the Southwest Indian Mission?"

"Really?"

"Really."

"How soon can I leave?"

CHAPTER TWENTY FOUR

THE FIELD IS WHITE

A mere twenty-four hours later, Teddy reported to his new mission headquarters in Farmington, New Mexico. He was welcomed, interviewed by his new mission president, President Thomas Isaacson, briefed on his new area, and was on his way out to the field the next day. His new companion was an Anglo from East Los Angeles named Randy Pratt. Elder Pratt was a former surfer, also a convert, and spent much time grooming and applying pomade to his ducktail hair cut. Their area was down in Gallup, New Mexico. On the drive down to Gallup in their topless Jeep, Elder Pratt briefed Teddy on their mission. Most of the natives spoke English, so he didn't have to learn a foreign language. Unless he wanted to learn Navvie (as the natives were called). The local word for reservation, used by everyone, red or white, was the *rez*. Their diet would consist mostly of fried mutton, fried bread, rice, beans, cornmeal tortillas, and red chilies.

"And you better get used to fleas. Lots of them here, especially in your mattress."

Teddy also learned that their suits would only come out for church, mission conferences, visits by the president, and baptisms, if were lucky enough to have any. The standard dress was blue jeans, Stetsons, cowboy boots and white shirt with sleeves rolled up, no tie. When they traveled to the far reaches of their area, which was every week, they took a sleeping bag and extra food, water, and gas for the Jeep. They spent a lot of nights sleeping under the stars, no matter the time of year. This was all sweet music to Teddy's ears.

"So, Elder, tell me about the mission you just got transferred from. What did you do that was so bad you got busted?" Just kidding!

"First, let me ask you some questions," Teddy responded. "Okay, what's there to do on P-day? I mean besides the obvious: wash clothes, shop, write letters. Any chance for some fishing?" Teddy was dreaming about the monster rainbows of the San Juan River and the Colorado below Lee's Ferry.

"Sure. We got some members and some contacts that can show us some good places on the res. You like to fish? Dumb question. Of course you do or you wouldn't have asked. Duh!" Pratt pulled to the side of the highway. "Gotta take a leak."

"Here? In public?"

"Where else?" He motioned around at the vast, empty landscape. When he finished he said, "Okay, you drive, I sleep."

"How do I know where to go?"

"Elder, look down that road. See how straight it is. Just keep going until you hit Gallup. Then you can wake me up."

As they neared the town of Shiprock, Teddy had a flash of inspiration. He stopped the Jeep. Pratt woke up. "We home…?"

"No, this is Shiprock."

"I told you to drive until we got to Gallup. Is this Gallup?"

"Woo, testy are we? So happens there's a golden contact lives in this town."

"You just got here. How do you know about any golden *anythings* in Shiprock?"

"Where's the Tribal Police headquarters?"

"What…?"

"Tribal. Police. Headquar…"

"I heard the first time. Why the Tribal Police?" Teddy told Pratt the story of J.T. Moon and how his father was chief of police, a non-member.

"Oh, man, are you naïve. The chief of police on the res is the *last* guy who'd ever join the church. They are hard, mean suckers. Most of them reformed alkies, barely. No way. Just keep driving south."

"I'm at the wheel and this truck is stopping at the Tribal Police. Period."

"I'm senior companion and what I say goes. Now keep driving!" Teddy bowed his head and closed his eyes. "What are you doing?"

"Asking the Lord to forgive you for your lack of faith. And keeping a promise I made to a former companion. I said I would meet his dad and talk to him about the church, and that's all I'm doing."

CUMORAH

Monty Padgett was just as Teddy had imagined he would be. Elder Padgett would be Teddy's last proselyting companion. He met Monty at the Trailways Bus depot in Gallup at eleven thirty at night; it was early May and cicadas thrummed in the myrtle trees across the street. Although the air was still, rain was threatening. The air was heavy with humidity; it draped over you like a sweaty wool saddle blanket just taken off a horse that had ridden hard all day. Moths flocked to the mercury vapor street lights as Teddy waited in his Jeep. The bus from Salt Lake City was late. Elder Padgett rolled off the bus like a bowling ball swathed in wool. He was dressed in a new dark missionary suit from Mr. Mac's in Salt Lake City; it was hopelessly rumpled. His white shirt, soaked in perspiration, stuck to his heaving chest; you could see his black curly chest hairs matted through the soaked fabric. His necktie hung at a crooked angle, it had a slanted crease in the middle where he had fallen asleep on the long ride with his crisp new triple combination pressing across his round tummy. He had a black canvas shoulder bag slung over each shoulder, his scriptures in their black case in one hand and a suitcase half his size that he dragged with the other hand. Teddy moved forward and said, "Here, let me help you with that."

Elder Padgett pushed his fogged glasses up off his nose where the sweat had made them slide. "I can manage, thank you," he replied in a strong British accent and he shouldered his way past Teddy into the drugstore/post office that served triple duty as the bus depot.

Teddy let the poor greenie suffer along until he was almost through the door. "Elder Padgett, it's me, your companion."

Padgett turned around swinging his scriptures and one shoulder bag into a Navajo woman in beautiful velvet carrying a young girl. "Oops, pardon, ma'am." Padgett squinted through his fogged glasses. "Elder Buckley?"

Once outside the town the night air blowing through their open Jeep cooled them. Teddy briefed his companion on their area of labor, what to expect, how they dressed, how they lived, what they ate, pretty much the same briefing he had received many months before from Elder Randy Pratt.

Teddy wondered why the church had sent a seemingly cultured young man like Padgett all the way from England to this mission. The southwest was a very harsh environment, winter or summer. He was obviously the proverbial fish out of water. Padgett was from the town of Banbury Cross in England, near Oxford. He was a scholar, a musician, and had been studying the flute. At the last second, on impulse, he had packed his flute with him, carrying it across the ocean and the vast continent of America. After the first fifteen miles Teddy suggested Padgett take off his jacket and tie, as the poor boy was soaked completely through with his own sweat. He did. "Feel better?" Padgett smiled weakly, it seemed to Teddy he was finding it difficult to speak. Teddy suggested he drink from the canvas water bag that hung from the grille of the Jeep. "Just like your British troops did in North Africa," Teddy said. Padgett gulped down water like a parched camel.

"It's actually cold," Padgett remarked.

When they got underway again he was silent for a long period. He became animated when a coyote crossed the road, briefly silhouetted in their headlights. "Was that a wolf?" he asked.

"No, Elder, that was only a coyote, the wolf's younger cousin."

"Are they dangerous?"

"Only if it's a mother and you mess with her pups."

"Oh… Elder…?"

"Yes?"

"Is there a WC nearby?"

"A *what?*"

"A wash room."

"Sure," Teddy said and he pulled to the side of the road, killed the motor and the lights. "Just step over there and turn your back." Padgett did as instructed, walking slowly to the edge of the verge. "And keep an eye out for rattlers, Elder!" Padgett jumped like he'd been stuck with a cattle prod. Teddy laughed.

"That was not polite," Padgett said as he climbed back in the Jeep.

"Go to sleep, Elder. We still have nearly a hundred miles 'til home and it's all rough road from here," Teddy said as he took a fork to the left. They put the asphalt highway behind them and started angling up the side of a mesa on a primitive dirt trail. Despite the jouncing, Padgett was soon asleep.

They pulled into their home in the desert, a spacious canvas Army surplus tent nestled against a mesa with its own source of cold spring water, just as the sun was making pink streaks in the clouds over the mountains to the east. This stunning scene had become Teddy's favorite time of the day. He was sure he would miss the desert and its unique beauty and solitude. He would miss the lonely cry of the ravens in the early morning and the haunting call of the night owls. He would miss the blossoming of the desert following a surprise thunder storm when wild flowers and cacti came into full bloom out of previously dry, cracked earth. Most of all, he was going to miss the people, the natives, the Hopi and Navajo he had come to love as much as he had loved the Tlingits in Alaska.

Did he really have to leave this country behind and go anywhere else, he wondered. Teddy was not counting the days remaining on his mission; he was anything but trunky, nearly working his last three companions (including Pratt) into the ground. They complained to him, to branch presidents, and to the mission president that "Elder Buckley works us too hard." Teddy took that as the supreme compliment. He had promised the apostle with the raspy voice in Salt Lake City that if he were allowed to complete his mission, he would work as hard as two missionaries. He was doing his best to keep that promise - to the very end.

No, he wasn't counting the days, but he could feel the time was getting short. He also had a feeling that he still had at least one more person to baptize and, as the sun broke free from the last mountain peak and splashed happily over their little valley, he prayed fervently that he and Elder Padgett would soon find that person... or persons.

Florian Lazlo was Hungarian, a refugee who had sought and received political asylum in the United States. Florian was one of a group of disgruntled university students in Budapest in the fall of 1956 who had dared to present a list of very benign requests (not demands) to the puppet communist government for more liberal policies for students and their curricula of study, rights to assemble for meetings, and so on. The factory workers around Budapest, also dissatisfied with their poor pay, lack of benefits, and abominable working conditions, to say nothing of all the broken promises by the government, soon joined the students. Suddenly, the government had an open rebellion on its hands. It quickly spread to the general populace, first in Budapest, then to the outlying cities, towns, villages and farms. The Russian masters mobilized the Hungarian army and ordered them to put down the rebellion; the national army moved in and surrounded the university but did not attack. Their sympathies lay with the students and workers, many of which were their own relatives (Florian's older brother was a tank captain, a commander of the very first tank company that moved in to confront the students, now barricaded inside campus walls).

The situation escalated, growing more tense, made worse by the Russians sending in several regular army tank divisions and paratroopers to back up the reluctant Hungarian reservists. The students, holed up in the university for several weeks, held off constant bombardments from the tanks and machine gun batteries mounted on nearby roof tops by employing the very mandatory guerilla warfare techniques the Russians had been teaching them. Most of the Russian tanks and machine gun batteries were neutralized or taken out of action, torched by Molotov "cocktails" made and thrown by the students. The rebellion became bloodier by the day, with more and more casualties; many workers and students were brutally murdered. Then Russian MiG fighter jets were brought in to bomb and strafe the last desperate hold-out positions on an island in the Danube River. The river ran red with the blood of Hungarian patriots. Within a few days the rebellion was crushed.

Before the final days, Florian could see it was hopeless. With the help of his older brother, Florian, his girlfriend Serena, and several of their friends rode in his brother's Hungarian Army tank on forged papers north and west to the Austrian border, where they arrived at dark. Providence gave them a miracle: a blanket of fog rolled in over the marshy no-man's land between the heavily patrolled Hungarian and Austrian borders. Using the cover of the heavy fog and the dark, starless night, the students dodged the patrols and their vicious dogs, making their way safely across the frontier and into a refugee camp set up just inside Austria. Within a week they were granted political asylum and were headed for America. Florian and Serena had no official papers, and they needed proof they were married, as they claimed when they filled out the many official forms. A priest was located, and, because religion had been forbidden them in Hungary under the communists, they received the first sacramental rites ever in their lives, the sacrament of marriage with the precious certificate to prove it. Their real names before they married were not Florian and Serena Lazlo. For political reasons and their future security, these became their adopted names, by which Teddy and Elder Padgett would know them.

Florian was a poet, a student of literature and poetry. Because of their anti-communist views, Florian's popular poems had been published mostly by student underground newspapers and read in clandestine gatherings in *kaffe hausen*. He managed to smuggle most of his manuscripts out of Hungary. But he soon found that poets in America were not honored as in the old country. America wanted pop music by Elvis and the Everly Brothers and Harry Belafonte. Americans wanted big cars painted poodle pink and black, with lots of chrome and powerful V-8 engines. Americans wanted TV and The Ed Sullivan Show and "Gunsmoke" and the new Disneyland in Anaheim. His poems were only interesting to a few wonks in green eyeshades at the National Security Agency in suburban Washington, D.C. for their possible political content. They actually believed Florian had been sending coded messages to the Hungarian Resistance through his poetry. Florian tried several publishing houses but nobody was interested. He tried getting published by a few Hungarian nationalistic newspapers in New York and Chicago, with more rejection slips. "Too sentimental," were the notes in the margin.

Florian took a job as a long-haul truck driver and Serena accompanied him on his first cross-country trip from Chicago to Los Angeles. The big diesel truck broke down in Gallup, and they holed up in a motel waiting several days for repairs. To fill the time, they hitched rides north to Shiprock and on to Cortez, Colorado. They wandered around on foot, dazzled by the wide open spaces, the clean air they breathed and the utter freedom that washed over them. They were happy in this environment. It didn't matter what they did for work; they could survive. They had already survived death – how many times had they stared down the gun barrels of Russian tanks?

They had a small stash of money they had hoarded, and they talked about what to do with their lives. They wandered into a small café in Cortez and ordered the only things on the menu they could recognize: a liverwurst sandwich and coffee. They were both surprised at how good the wurst tasted; it was fresh and full of pungent spices. Florian asked to talk with the cook who was an Austrian from Salzburg and the owner of the little cafe. His name was Johann Karoly. He was tired, getting older and wanted to quit the business but had a sentimental attachment to his recipes. They learned that every day Johann offered a luncheon special, old country recipes of knockwurst and kohl, rolladen, fresh, hand-made egg noodles, cheese cake, and goulash.

Goulash? They had not tasted real goulash since arriving in America. Would he make some for them tomorrow if they came back at lunch? He would make some for them right now, and they could stay and enjoy it for dinner with a bottle of lovely Reisling he had imported from Salzburg and was saving for a special occasion. And this night was to be that special occasion. They ate until they were stuffed; they drank and sang songs in German. Florian recited many of his poems from memory, and Johann wept with sentimental longings for the old country.

Serena was behind the counter and Florian was in the kitchen the day Teddy and Padgett stopped in for lunch. The elders had been in Dove Creek, Colorado, to track down a referral the day before. They stayed overnight with some members after sacrament meeting. Since the next day was P-day and they were only an hour or so drive from the Anasazi Ruins, they had spent the morning absorbing some local culture. They were on their way back to their tent to change and make their rounds visiting the few scattered members on the rez when they stopped at Florian's and Serena's roadside café for lunch.

As these two young men finished their lunch and were paying, Serena noticed there was something different about them. They were clean-cut, with short hair cuts, and they spoke politely. She was especially curious about the one who spoke with a British accent. What was he doing out here in Cortez, Colorado, the middle of nowhere? Teddy explained they were missionaries from the Church of Jesus Christ of Latter-Day Saints, the Mormons.

"Oh yes, we have Mormons come in here sometimes. They never order coffee, just like you two didn't ." She was tall and pretty and carried herself with pride. She also had red hair and lots of freckles, but her eyes were blue, not brown like Andrea's, Teddy noticed.

Padgett, to Teddy's surprise, asked Serena the Golden Questions: How much do you know about the Mormons, and would you like to know more?

"Let me get my husband out here. He might be interested. We're Catholic, sort of... Florian!" The noon crowd had all left to return to work or to pursue their plans for the afternoon. Florian Lazlo wiped his hands on his stained apron and greeted the elders with a pleasant smile. He was handsome, with long wavy blonde hair and deep brown eyes that reflected a hidden mystery, or maybe it was a deep sadness.

Padgett proceeded to give the Lazlos a modified door approach and they listened respectfully. Florian asked them to sit down and he briefly told the elders their story. He explained that although they had been married by a Catholic priest, they weren't very religious; at least he personally wasn't too inclined toward religion. He was a poet and found his own religion through his expressions of poetry. Cortez was a small town and sadly lacking in culture. He would be happy to listen to their religious philosophies for the intellectual stimulation it might provide to break the boredom, but he was afraid they would be wasting their time otherwise.

Elder Padgett then felt inspired to quote some lines from Wordsworth, "trailing clouds of glory," and asked Florian what he thought the poet was trying to express.

"Maybe he's seeing a vision of heaven?"

"And what do you think heaven is like? Do you think we came from somewhere, that we have a purpose on earth, and that someday we will go somewhere after this life, someplace meaningful and with our families, our loved ones?" Padgett asked.

Florian was pensive and said, "I haven't thought much about his poem in that light, in light of the spiritual. Look, I don't mean to be rude… We have to start getting things ready for the dinner crowd. I wish we could chat more but I have to excuse myself. If you're in the area in the future, please stop by and we will exchange philosophies again. And next time your dinner will be on us with our sincere compliments. It has been pleasant." He shook their hands. Padgett left a pamphlet with Serena and she promised to read it. On the back was a photo of the Hill Cumorah. "That's the location in New York where Joseph Smith found the gold plates that were translated into the Book of Mormon," Teddy explained to her.

The elders were getting into their Jeep when Florian hurried out after them. He was waving the pamphlet, he was excited. "Uh oh," Teddy thought.

"Gentlemen, gentlemen! Don't leave yet. I need to know something. This booklet…" he showed them the picture on the back cover. "It says 'The Hill Cumorah'… Where is this place? I must know more about this, where you got this, where it came from."

"What's so special to you about this place, Mr. Lazlo?" Teddy asked.

"Come back inside so we can talk." When they were settled at a table Florian explained. "This word 'cumorah' in my language…? It means a safe place, a hidden or hiding place. I need to know how that mountain got its name, so, please explain. The food preparation can wait. Take all the time you want. We are very interested, aren't we, Serena?"

The Lazlos were baptized three weeks later. They were Elder Padgett's first converts. The Lazlos asked Monty Padgett to play his flute at their baptismal service. He played two numbers, a Bach unaccompanied sonata and a Navajo lullaby he had learned from an old shaman to play especially for the Lazlos. Teddy thought it was some of the most beautiful music he had ever heard.

A WORN OUT SUIT

Teddy's Journal: "July 19th. New mission president replacing President Isaacson. Only a little more than six more months left for me. Where does the time go? Just called into mission home in Farmington by new mission president, Donald Durrant. I have been asked to be his assistant and I feel very honored. (It also puts me an hour's drive to S.J. river for P-day fly-fishing - can't wait. The fishing holes Pratt talked up turned out to be mud holes. Will be nice to see clear running water.) Asked Pres. D. if any relation to you-know-who? Yes, he's her uncle. Funny how I'm now over that phase of my life. So long ago. He says she and Scott happy and expecting first baby. Good for them. Scott just passed foreign service exam and is waiting for a posting with State Dept., I guess because of his language ability. Sometimes wish I had a foreign language other than pidgin Navvie.

"Guess I should be thinking about what happens in six months. Dangerous to think about because then I get to thinking about Andy and the time starts to drag. Better to keep my head down and work, work, work! Speaking of which, how long before mail catches up to me? Should have a letter any day. Tired, going to bed. I love the Lord and I love his work and these native people."

Teddy's last P-day of his mission found him on the San Juan River giving President Durrant his first-ever fly-casting lesson. He was a determined, quick learner. "I think you're getting the hang of it, president."

Don Durant grinned his appreciation. "You're a good teacher."

"Now the next thing I'll show you is how to fish with nymphs. Here, look at these." Teddy showed him the tiny red and black zebra-striped size-22 chironomid flies they would use that day. Teddy explained the theory of matching the fly pattern to what the fish were accustomed to eating. "It's called matching the hatch."

"How do you know that's what they want to eat?" the president asked.

"Good question. Watch…" Teddy took a small aquarium net out of one of his vest pockets and held it under the water for a few seconds. After he scooped it out and let the water drain, he pointed to some tiny, wiggly worm-like things caught in the fine mesh. "Those are the critters these trout are feeding on. These little things start out as eggs that the adults laid in the mud on the bottom of the river. These guys hatch out in this form and wiggle their way to the surface. The fish lie close to the bottom and wait for the little creatures to hatch, and as they start swimming their way to the surface the current simply carries the food to the trout. They just sit there slurping and pigging out on these protein-rich morsels. That's why, when we catch one of these trout, you'll find it looks more like a football than a fish. They get huge in this river!"

"These worms are so tiny. How can the fish even see them?" Don asked.

"Oh, they can see them okay," Teddy assured him. "The tough part is my seeing the darn tiny hole to tie on the leader." Teddy fumbled several times with the little #22 fly, trying to thread the tippet through the eye.

"Here, use these." Don Durrant handed Teddy his 2x reading glasses. Teddy put them on. "Better?"

"Wow, I can see! Guess I better have my eyes checked. Must have been those months trying to read in poor light." A sudden wave of sadness came over Teddy as he remembered the months in Sitka jail. He was surprised by the memories sometimes. At times the bad things waited in the shadows of his memory and jumped out at him in all the wrong times and places. He shrugged it off. That was in the past, thankfully. He had his future to look to now.

They were in the first hole below Navajo Dam, the Kiddie Hole. "Why is it called the Kiddie Hole?" President Durrant asked.

"You'll see in a minute," Teddy said. He made the first cast, a short one slightly upstream. The strike indicator had drifted barely a foot when it winked ever so gently, and Teddy gave an experienced slight lift of the rod with his casting hand. The fish was stuck and it headed downstream like a runaway bulldozer, stripping line off his reel; he was quickly into his backing. "Whooee! That's what I'm talkin' about!" Teddy yelled. "This is twenty-twenty fishing!" as he splashed clumsily downstream after the big trout. President Durrant looked blank. "That's a twenty-inch trout hooked on a size twenty or smaller fly. Nothin' finer!" Teddy yelled over his shoulder. "Now you do exactly like I just did and you'll be a member of the San Juan 20-20 Club, president," Teddy said after he returned with the shiny, wiggling prize, wet and glistening in the sun. President Durrant took pictures of Teddy and the huge rainbow. Then Teddy gently released it back to the river.

Don Durrant did exactly as he was told. Barely five minutes later he held up his first dripping wet, wiggling trout caught on an artificial fly: a butter-yellow, fat brown. After that day the enlarged picture held a special spot on his office wall in the mission home: his first-ever trout on a fly!

"Well, Elder, I am officially giving you an honorable release as a missionary of the Church of Jesus Christ of Latter-Day Saints. Congratulations for a job well done. I'm going to miss you," he said with tears in his eyes. They stood and embraced like a father and son. He stepped back and looked at Teddy appraisingly. "What will you do now?"

"First, I'm going to buy a used Ford pickup from one of those second-hand car dealers outside of town on the Durango highway. Then I'm going to throw away this worn out suit and fly-fish my way across America until I get to Pittsburgh. I think I'll hang around my folks for a week or so, long enough for my mom to get tired of my bad manners, then… maybe I'll send off to Brooks Brothers for a new suit for my home-coming speech, then… I don't really know what's next. Any ideas?"

"Can I give you some counsel?" Teddy nodded. "You're older than most missionaries are when they get released… by about five or six years. You've already completed college and the military. The next step in life is usually marriage. I know about this girl, the one you told me about. The one you baptized in Alaska. What did you say her name was?" Teddy mumbled her name. "I think Andrea is a very special person to you. I think maybe your feelings for her are more than brother-sister-in-the-gospel spiritual feelings. I think you love her. Do you? Love her…?" Teddy nodded and grinned. "Does she love you, too?" Teddy nodded again.

"Is she the one the Lord wants you to be with as your eternal companion?" Teddy could feel the blush reddening under his tan. He nodded.

"Then what are you waiting for, son? Grab your stuff, get out of here and marry the girl!"

EPILOGUE - THE HOMECOMING

Teddy drove as far east as Taos and stopped for the night. Even though he'd never been there before, he got a strange tingling feeling in his scalp that he *had* been there before. He felt relaxed and at peace, like a great weight had been lifted from his shoulders. This was the place he'd been looking for; he always knew somehow he would have this feeling when he found it. Teddy had come home at last. He spent several days driving around the area, looking for just the right location to settle down and build a home for his family, the family he and Andrea would start... soon, he hoped.

He found a perfect little ranch that wasn't on the market. He talked to the owners, an older couple who wanted to retire from ranching and live the good life while they still had some life left to live. The ranch was nestled in its own little valley between two red rock mesas dusted with fresh snow. A pretty spring creek ran through the meadows, where white-faced Hereford cattle got fat in summers grazing on belly-deep grass. There was a snug, spacious single-level ranch house built of whitewashed adobe with a red-tiled roof and baked clay tiles on the floors, which were covered with an assortment of woven native rugs. The ceilings throughout were open, exposing massive cedar beams logged from the nearby forests.

The great room was built around a huge fireplace tall enough for a man to stand in it upright. With fondness, the owners recalled many a time they would roast whole sides of beef there for parties when family, neighbors and friends came.

Their kids had all moved to the city, Albuquerque and Denver, and elsewhere, rejecting the hard ranching life. Most of their friends and neighbors had moved to warmer climates, were in rest homes, or had died. The woman wanted most of all to visit Florence, Italy, while they still had the health and energy to travel. Her husband's dream trip was to see the Big Apple, ride a carriage down 5th Avenue and through Central Park, dine at 21 Club, see a Yankees' baseball game and eat ball park hot dogs ("even though my tummy couldn't take it"), ride to the top of the Empire State Building, take in a Broadway musical or two, and end the trip with a week of wading the surf on Martha's Vineyard and leaf peeping on up in Vermont. "That would mean a trip in late September or early October," she said. Her husband nodded, his eyes shining.

The barn and outbuildings and all the farming machinery were well taken care of, and their livestock was healthy. The owners of this ranch had built and maintained it with pride. They no longer ran cattle; they still owned two dairy cows, some pigs and a menagerie of chickens, ducks, geese, turkeys, dogs and assorted cats. Pigeons nested peacefully in the barn's rafters.

Teddy asked the owners if he could try some trout fishing in their little creek even though it was still winter. They said of course, give it a try, and bring us a mess for supper if you catch any. Teddy went even one better: he cooked a stringer of fresh brook trout rolled in corn meal and salt and pepper, and fried in sizzling bacon grease. "Never tasted better, have you, Mama?"

They invited Teddy to stay as long as he liked; they began to treat him like their own son and he returned the same feelings toward them. After three days Teddy made an offer to buy the place for cash. He offered generously more than the appraised value, guessing they would quickly accept. They did. He offered to let them stay on in the guest house whenever and as long as they wished.

Teddy borrowed their phone and called Alaska.

The Cessna twin-prop commuter had barely taxied to a stop when Teddy ran onto the tarmac waving his Stetson. The props quit chopping the thin mountain air, the ladder clanked down and the first passenger off was a pretty red-headed girl with lots of freckles. She squealed his name as she ran toward him.

They met each other in a happy crush. They held on hard and kissed slowly, without inhibition, as the other passengers and baggage carts flowed past them like a stream around two granite boulders.

Marley and Scott Mathews now live in Paris where he is the number two man at the American Embassy. They are active in the Paris 2nd Ward that meets at 12 Rue Saint Merri next to the Centre Pompidou in the 4th Arrondissement. Marley is Laurel adviser, adored by her girls. Scott is bishop; he speaks flawless French (his French is better than his now heavily-accented English).

Chris Pennington works for the Library of Congress in Washington, D.C., as a research specialist in the Naval History section.

President Moffatt returned to Utah as an Institute teacher. His colleagues complain that he talks so loudly to his students that the other teachers in nearby class rooms have to close their doors and windows so their own students can hear. He's affectionately called *Big Thunder* by all the LDS students on campus.

Barely a month after his mission Tad Wessman was married in the Mesa Temple. He went back and finished his degree in secondary education at Northern Arizona State. He taught physical education in an Indian high school in southern Arizona for thirty-one years. As Teddy was recently writing his life story, he remembered he *had* watched Wessman play in a basketball game that snowy spring night in 1969. Tad died from a rattlesnake bite while on a weekend camp out with a troop of Boy Scouts. They were just too far away from help.

J.T. Moon became a professional rodeo rider after his mission. His leg was smashed when a frightened bronc went crazy in the chute. He doesn't ride rodeo any more; he walks with a severe limp. He owns an equestrian center in Shiprock; he's married to a beautiful Navajo woman and they have five children. J.T. Moon's father never joined the church, but he always looks out for the safety of the Mormon missionaries. Teddy visits J.T. and his father in Shiprock a couple of times each year; they are close friends.

Randy Pratt set up a small surf board shop in San Juan Capistrano after his mission. He married a beautiful *wahini* he met at a surfing competition in Hawaii. He developed a complete line of outdoor shoes, clothing and accessories (surfing, trail biking, running, rock climbing, kayaking, etc.) that he manufactured and imported from China. He recently sold his business to REI for a fat seven-figure contract and retired to Maui.

The Lazlos operated their little roadside café in Cortez for several years and eventually added a shop that specializes in fresh Hungarian deli meats and home-cured sausages. After the fall of the Berlin Wall, they returned to Hungary as a missionary couple and are serving their third mission there.

Monty Padgett graduated from Cambridge with honors in music. He teaches jazz improvisation and arranging at Winchester University. In his home ward he teaches gospel doctrine. On some weekends when he doesn't have church duties, you can hear Monty play flute and alto sax with his group (The Trout Quintet) at various Paris jazz clubs in Montmartre or the Rue de la Huchette in the Latin Quarter. But get there early because it's always crowded. He has released dozens of jazz albums featuring his own haunting arrangements of Hopi and Navajo chants and lullabies.

Maggie and Frank Carling divorced after fifteen years of marriage. Maggie owns a chain of day-care centers in Idaho Falls. Amy married an Alaska state policeman and lives in Seward where she's a mommy. David and Frank Jr. both served honorable missions for the church in Central America.

Richard Gilbert formed a commercial fishing partnership with Rachel Chapman. Together they own a fleet of ten fishing boats and employ over seventy people. Teddy helped Richard and several other natives form an independent bank in Sitka; Richard is chairman of the board of directors. He served for many years as the first bishop of the Sitka ward and presided over the building of their first chapel. Both of Richard's sons served missions.

Chief Russell died peacefully at home surrounded by his loving family and was welcomed home by the spirits of his ancestors.

Betty and Sparky Tedrow moved back to Ogden, Utah, when Alaska

Airlines offered him a handsome retirement package. They are temple workers in the Ogden Temple.

Elder Junior Hartmann is emeritus general authority; he writes his memoirs, travels some with his still-beautiful wife, and spoils his grandchildren.

Clark Tanner was called as a member of the Seventy (as his wife always knew he would be), essentially replacing Elder Hartmann.

Jerry Hatamiya bought a small ranch outside Telluride, Colorado, where he retired. Shortly after retiring, he lost his wife. A year after her death he was paralyzed on his right side from a stroke. Ki cares for him full-time.

The Hon. Albert W. Bumpus proved the Peter Principle when he was elevated to the Alaska State Supreme Court. He became a full-fledged alcoholic and died from a heart attack just a few years after his appointment.

Bodie Briggs moved back to Arkansas soon after the *State of Alaska v. Buckley* debacle. He quit law practice to become a wealthy televangelist.

The mysterious stranger, the world-class lawyer from Jackson Hole still practices law from his unassuming office in town. Jackson Hole has grown considerably around him. He's still powerful and effective. He and Teddy chat about private legal matters from time to time when Teddy needs his advice. They fly fish together sometimes on the Madison, the Firehole, the Yellowstone, the Gallatin or the South Fork.

Max Silverman now lives in Las Vegas; he became the world's foremost expert in gaming law. When he feels like it, he lectures to groups of lawyers on high-priced luxury cruises. He is on retainer to many of the Coastal Native tribes as consultant to their gaming operations. He no longer has a dandruff problem, as he is totally bald.

Arthur was quietly released from the Sitka jail and deported to Vancouver, B.C., when Teddy's lawyer from Jackson Hole had a discreet discussion with the Hon. Bert Bumpus. Arthur relocated to Toronto, Canada, where he became a booking agent. He has successfully brought many first-run Broadway musicals and stage productions to the good folks of Toronto.

Critter went straight, sobered up, cleaned up, eventually joined the church and became one of the prime contractors building the new international airport in Sitka. He recently retired and is the High Priests

Group Leader in the Sitka ward. He never married. He spends hours every week playing cribbage with inmates in the Sitka jail.

The apostle with the raspy voice became one of the most beloved prophets of modern times.

Zack Zundel got his doctorate from Duke University and is a distinguished professor of economics at an Ivy League college back East. He married his girlfriend from Park City High School, and they have a large, boisterous family. He makes an annual trip out west each summer to fly fish and remember old times with Teddy.

Teddy kept his promises to Toby Dutcher, who is now managing director of a Native Arts center in Wrangell, Alaska, where native artists and crafts persons from all over the northwest come to revive the ancient coastal Indian traditions in art, instrumental music, carvings, songs, story-telling, dance, weaving and other handicrafts. Toby is making a valuable contribution to the fostering and preservation of native culture and traditions. He walks with a very slight limp, has one artificial eye (although you would never notice), and he writes and paints beautifully with his left hand. The trust also made an anonymous gift to the hospital in Sitka to set up a perpetual fund for medical care for natives who could not otherwise pay.

The little branch in Sitka that started out in the Carlings' living room is now a ward, part of the Juneau Stake of Zion, housed in its own beautiful chapel that sits on a hill overlooking Sitka Sound.

The Alaskan-Canadian Mission was divided; there are now two missions: Vancouver, B.C., and Alaska Anchorage. The beautiful Tudor mansion on Connaught Drive in Vancouver was sold by the Church Property Department. The mission office is now located in a strip mall in Richmond, B.C.

Teddy's father is retired; his mother is in an Alzheimer's care facility. Teddy and Andrea visit often, but Madeleine does not recognize them.

And what about Andrea and Teddy?

Two months after Andrea met up with Teddy in Taos, they married in the Salt Lake Temple. Elder Junior Hartmann performed the ordinance for them. They had a small reception in the Lion House with just a few friends and family invited. They slipped out of the reception early by the back door and made a wild dash for an undisclosed honeymoon retreat in

Park City.

Teddy was called as a bishop, then stake president in Taos. He owns a fly shop called The Man Fisher High Country Fly-Fishing & Guide Service. He was asked several times to run for a seat in the state legislature ("a sure bet to be elected"), but he always turned it down. "Cuts into my fly-fishing time," he explained.

Andrea (now called "Andy" by everyone) founded a halfway house for abused women. It's named The Momma Freckles Women's Shelter.

They have a large family; their oldest daughter is named Marley. They have many beautiful, smart, talented grandchildren. It's a wild rumpus when the family gathers on the ranch for holidays. The grandkids never tire of having Grandpa Teddy tell them of the time the eagle attacked him on the beach in Sitka. The potlatch bowl with the two jumping coho salmon painted with authentic native pigments of rust and turquoise and white and black occupies a special place on the rough-cut cedar beam mantel above the huge open fireplace in the great family room.

If you have skied recently in Taos, you might have slept in one of the dozens of comfortable condo units owned by Buckley Properties, Ltd. And if you run into Teddy around town he'll probably be driving his old, mud-splattered Ford pickup with his chocolate lab, Lefty, and sacks of barley or rolls of barbed wire in the back. Teddy is still a trout bum: his hair is mostly gray and longish; Andy talked him into growing a mustache. He wears jeans and tee shirts or sweatshirts with cowboy boots six days a week. He puts on a suit and tie when business trips or church duties require. He fly fishes with his old favorite bamboo Granger and Leonard fly rods on the San Juan River, and other waters close by, as often as he can. His favorite stream is still the little unnamed spring creek on the ranch, teeming with the eager brook trout.

He and Andy slip back to Alaska every summer to fly fish for rainbows and dollies and silver salmon on a secret stream close to town. They always stick around for the family potlatch with the Gilberts on the sandy beach where the eagle attacked, and they bring freshly-caught salmon as their gift for the feast. The Gilberts and their guests still build the same giant bonfires from silvery driftwood. The teenagers flirt and hang out with each other in the shadows. The surf can still be heard lapping against the beach and night owls cry in the darkness away from the great fires that pop and make small explosions and the sparks fly up until they wink out high up in the hot drafts in the velvety black night sky.

Then everyone joins in and they bake big slabs of salmon over white-hot coals on split green alder planks, and they boil herring eggs in seal oil and cook clams and shrimp and crab and many other delicacies the old way.

They welcome friends and family, and together they play their native instruments, flutes and rattles and small drums that they beat ever so softly. And they dance the ancient dances and sing the same ancient songs and chants, and say prayers of tribute to the ancestors. Then they all join in the grand feast and eat and drink until they can't possibly eat another bite, but they still manage to eat and drink some more.

And when the fires have all died down to gray ashes and no more sparks fly up, they leave the sandy beach happy and renewed.

Teddy is more careful now about what he eats at the potlatch.

But he always remembers to bring the special bowl with the leaping salmon.

www.ingramcontent.com/pod-product-compliance
Lightning Source LLC
Chambersburg PA
CBHW061555100726

47898CB00002B/388